The Lucky U

by Kathleen Willett

1

Chapter 1

If it had been rain, it would have been a cold, drenching storm. A bone soaker, as Marge would have said. However, it was snow. Huge flakes. Some single, some hooked on to other flakes. Just like life, Mitch Tanner philosophized, as she steered her battered Yugo into the parking lot of the Lucky U. It was seven p.m. The bar had been open nearly all day, but Mitch was superstitious on this day. She had just left the polling place, having waited in line twenty-two minutes to exercise her right to vote. Now, she would exercise her right to drink. The minute she opened the door, a rush of warm air began to work its magic, easing the ache of cold.

For the one-thousandth time, she murmured quiet thanks that the air was smoke free. Then, she sat at her usual place at the bar. A beer was automatically placed in front of her, and she took a long drink before removing her thin coat.

"Where you been?" rasped Marge, the owner, proprietor, and relic of the Lucky U.
"Voting."
"Oh yeah, I wonder when the returns will be coming in?"
"Turn on the news, Marge."
"So soon?"
"These elections are sometimes called with one percent of the vote."
"And does that tick off California or what."
"I wouldn't know."
"Well, why don't you drink a couple more beers before we switch the channel. You know how these kids get if they don't get their sports recap."

Mitch gathered the two beers that Marge had put in front of her and settled down in a booth to wait out the sports report. By eight, the crowd had swelled to fill every seat in the place. Snowstorms seemed to have this effect on people, they come for a drink and stay in the cozy warmth to avoid the bitter cold of the night. In the space of an hour, Marge had managed to reclaim control of the TV set and talking heads were reporting election results as fast as they flashed on the screen. As the numbers revolved, the crowd either cheered or booed, depending on the candidate or issue. Mitch cast only a cursory glance now and again at the set until one particularly raucous chorus of boos grew louder and louder, until all eyes in the bar were focused on the two people on the screen.

One was the comely reporter from the local TV news station, the other was apparently the newly-elected governor of the state of Colorado. To most observers, it would have been a strange sight indeed to see a roomful of women booing a pending woman governor, but this wasn't your usual group of women. The Lucky U just happened to be a lesbian bar. Probably not the most popular nor fashionable in the city, but it did have its loyal clientèle. As for the governor, opinions were being tossed around like peanuts at the ball park.

"She's so right wing that she makes Sean Hannity look like a flaming liberal."
Another voice lamented, "The first time this state decides to elect a woman governor, she's the most anti-woman woman on the planet."
"But she is kinda cute. Hey Mitch, why don't you get involved in politics and set this new governor on her ear!"
Chants of, "Go Mitch, Go Mitch," filled the room as the TV cut away to other news.

Numbers of a different sort popped up on the screen and Mitch recognized them as the lottery numbers of the week. Oh yeah, it was lottery day as well. The chants of "Go Mitch" were dying off, but she stood anyway to address her supporters.
"My fellow country people, I have only one statement to make."
The bar became oddly quiet.

"I have a better chance of winning the lottery, all $27 million of it, than I do of ever ensuring that this new governor of ours, however cute but hopelessly right wing, would ever see the redeeming qualities of liberalism."

"Did you buy a ticket?" someone asked.

"What?" Mitch asked over the din.

"Did you buy a lottery ticket?"

"I bought ten tickets, as usual."

"I'm keeping my fingers crossed."

Laughter drowned out further comments as Mitch drank the last of her beer and donned her coat for the long trip home. She planned to buzz home, flip on the TV and watch the rest of the election returns in the privacy of her small apartment. Small being the operative word. Tiny was more descriptive. Prison cells were bigger than her bedroom. She was propped up in bed before ten, with a mystery novel to keep her company as she watched more election news out of the corner of her eye.

The black and white images on the screen ebbed and flowed from candidate to candidate, faces happy and sad worked their mouths endlessly. Mitch glanced up from her book in time to watch the newly-elected governor spouting family platitudes coded in such a way to suggest that gay people didn't have them. In the corner of the screen flashed the winning lottery numbers again. Mitch studied the tickets that she used as a bookmark.

"Well, how about that," Mitch said to herself. There was no one else to hear since she lived a solitary existence. She gazed one more time at the flickering image of the attractive she-governor elect, shook her head and shut off the news. Sleep visited in five minutes and spent the night.

Chapter 2

Marge had worked all morning cleaning the floor of the
Lucky U. Forty years she had lived in snow country. Forty
winters of dirty floors hadn't driven her from the place.
One more floor didn't have a chance. She finished up her
chores at ten-thirty and was just lighting up a cigarette
when Mitch came through the back door. The front was
still locked.

"What the hell are you doing here?"

"What the hell are you doing smoking?"

"I asked first."

"I came in for a drink."

"You're only getting cranberry juice until eleven."

"It's ten forty now."

"So? You won't have long to wait, will you."

"I won the lottery last night," Mitch sat at the bar.

"Yeah, sure and I'm the new governor elect."

"You're not that cute."

"She is kinda pretty, for an older woman," Marge mused.
Mitch smirked. This was sixty-two talking about forty-five

"So you won the lottery for real?" Marge asked, proving
that she had been paying attention after all.

"All seven numbers. All $27 million. It took about three
hours for it to sink in this morning."

"You been to lottery headquarters yet?"

"Been there."

"Picked up your first installment, yet?"

"The paperwork is in process. Actually I took the cash
instead of the annuity."

"So it really isn't $27 million, after taxes."

"I'm Uncle Sam's new best friend."

"And, of course, you quit your lousy job."

"Yep."

"And now you think that you can waltz in here before
eleven and get a drink from me."

"It's ten forty-five."

"I still don't believe it."

"I'll be on the news at noon. They taped an interview."

"And then all hell is going to break loose. People will be asking you for money hand over fist."

"Don't worry, I'll invest it wisely."

"And you're going to buy yourself a beer to celebrate?"

"And one for you, too."

"Well in that case, pour one for the both of us. But just this once, mind you. Then no more early-morning drinking."

By the time they toasted good luck and bad government, the clock struck eleven and the lunch crowd began to drift in.

"Mitch, one of my servers called in sick today. Since you're now unemployed, would you give me a hand? Unless, of course, that kind of work is beneath a millionairess."

"Only for you, Marge."

Mitch donned a half apron, just like in the good old days of working her way through school, and began to take orders. She lost track of the time until someone hollered from the bar, "Hey, that new waitress is on TV. And she's a millionaire!"

Three people automatically picked up their tips. Marge referred to them as "cheapskates" under her breath.

"I guess I should be the one leaving tips since they're putting up with my rusty service," Mitch admitted. "This is a lot more work than I remember."

"That's because you're getting older."

When Mitch took her three o'clock break, she fell asleep propped up in a booth. The five o'clock happy-hour crowd roused her for congratulations.

"So, what's it like being rich?" razzed Trish.

"It's exhausting. Marge worked me to death."

Trish, a regular patron of the Lucky U, always arrived cheerful. Her breezy personality helped her real estate career. Which in turn, explained her sizable bank account.

Mitch had always admired Trish not only for being a hard worker but also for her down-to-earth good nature. It didn't matter that Trish had more money, they were still good friends.

"I'm happy for you."

"Thanks, Trish, and I know you mean it."

Trish moved on to chat with several friends, but Mitch didn't have time to notice. She was busy answering half a hundred questions about her spending proclivities.

"You need to buy a boat," asserted a new friend. Several "new" friends had gathered around after the five o'clock news.

"Sorry, I get seasick."

"Buy a huge boat and then that won't happen."

"That's ridiculous," piped up new friend number two. "I was on a luxury liner and threw up all the way to Alaska and back."

"Gee, thanks for sharing," Mitch tried to be polite.

"Buy a ranch with horses instead."

"Don't they eat a lot?"

"And that's not all."

"I'll go home and watch reruns of Mr. Ed to see if I can get enthused."

New friend number two, who looked all of twenty-two, looked puzzled, "Mr. Ed who?"

"It's an old TV show," Mitch explained as she stood to leave.

"Going so soon?" Marge asked.

"I'm worn out. I'll see you later."

"Don't be a stranger."

"I'm always stranger."

Marge nodded agreement, just like always.

Mitch went out into the cold night and sucked in air as if she had been drowning. The Lucky U seemed unusually crowded, but she reminded herself that she had spent the better part of the day there. Fresh air smelled sweet so she drove home with the window part way down. She walked into her small apartment and made a couple of decisions right on the spot.

"I'll start tomorrow," she assured the walls.

The walls didn't answer back. They never did.

Mitch went to bed. Images flashed in her mind as she tried to sleep. The look on her boss's face as she handed in her resignation had been priceless. A mixture of shock and envy had strained his countenance almost beyond recognition. It wasn't like she was leaving him in the lurch. Data entry wasn't exactly rocket science. He'd have a new employee within the week. It had to be the millions that had wiped that sanctimonious smile off his face. Before resigning, Mitch had taken care to assure that she had been the sole winner of the jackpot and had calculated some preliminary interest figures in her head. She could live modestly for years, even if she splurged on a few things. Like, maybe that cruise to Alaska.

Chapter 3

Trish arrived early at the Lucky U. That in itself wasn't too unusual. The Thanksgiving holiday was fast approaching and people didn't do much in the way of house selling this time of year. Summers were the hot market. Winter and holidays were a sort of cooling off time. People still found themselves moving, but holidays put the damper on sales.

So, although Marge said it wasn't an emergency but she wanted to talk, Trish honored her request willingly. She ordered a drink from one of the waitresses and waited for Marge to get free. If holidays were bad for real estate, they were a boon for bar business. It took Marge about ten minutes to settle in for their chat.

"What up, Marge?"
"Where's Mitch?"
"I don't know. Is she supposed to be here?"
"That's my point exactly."
"I'm not following, Marge."
"She hasn't been here since she won the lottery. Been three weeks."
"Well, maybe she took a vacation?"
"Without telling anybody? Have you heard from her?"
"No, but that's not unusual. She doesn't seem the type to check in with anybody."
"We can't call work, she doesn't do that anymore."
"Has anyone thought to just call her at home?"
"I knew you'd have the best idea, Trish. Here's the phone."
Marge handed her the house phone.
Trish knew she had been tricked into this, but Marge had such a worried yet sweet look on her face that the duplicity didn't bother her. Much.
"You set me up."
"It was your idea."
"Okay, I'll call her."
"Tell her that we're doing the usual turkey dinner here on Thursday."

"I'll see if I can remember that." Trish hadn't forgotten about the turkey dinner in three years.

"I'll sit here and remind you."

"You don't need to do that. Go and take care of your customers. I'll take care of the phone call."

"Okay, but don't forget, it was my idea."

Marge reluctantly left Trish alone. She dialed the number she had for Mitch. It rang ten times before Mitch picked up.

"Hello!" Mitch sounded breathless.

"Hi there, Mitch. It's Trish."

"Oh hi, Trish. How are you?"

"I'm fine. I think a better question is, how are you?"

"Me? I'm okay. Why?"

"Well, Marge and I were talking and we realized that we hadn't seen you in a while, so I decided to call you."

Marge was back at the booth, listening intently to one-half of the conversation.

"I have been AWOL, I know."

"Are you okay?"

"Oh sure. It's just that, well the day after I won the lottery, it was intense at the U." The term "U" was their verbal shorthand for the Lucky U. It hadn't exactly taken buckets of creative thinking to come up with that shorthand, but it worked for them.

"Lots of new friends with lots of advice," Trish nodded.

"They practically smothered me."

"Lots of new friends with lots of advice about how to spend your money," Trish spelled it out for the edification of Marge.

"I'm just taking a break."

"And a well-deserved break at that. We just were, you know, worried. A little."

"I'm sorry. I didn't mean to worry anybody."

"So you can make it up to us by coming here for Thanksgiving dinner. Marge has the usual feast all planned."

"It sounds fun…."

"Did you have other plans?"

"Well, no."

"So maybe we'll see you?"

"My car's been acting up."

"I'll come by and pick you up. What time?"

"What time's dinner again?"

"Marge, what time's dinner on Thursday?"

"Anytime after ten-thirty. You know, kickoff!"

"How about I come pick you up about ten? Is that too early?"

"That's okay," Mitch agreed, all out of excuses.

"See you then."

Trish hung up and announced to Marge, "Guess who's coming to dinner!"

"You shouldn't have told her we were worried. It will just go to her head!" was Marge's way of saying "Thanks" to Trish.

Thursday morning rolled around. Mitch put on a fresh pot of coffee. It sounded easier than it was with her new cappuccino machine. It whirred, coughed and fizzed, but it did make a nice, strong brew. Throw in enough cream and sugar and it could qualify as a meal. The doorbell rang, a tinny ding, and Mitch went to the door. It was Trish, on time and glowing. November was agreeing with her.

"Hello," Mitch greeted.

"Well, hello there stranger. How are you?" Trish came inside, happy to be surrounded by warmth after the chill of the great outdoors.

"Have time for a cup of coffee?"

"Love some. Hey, wait a minute. Come back here."

"What?" Mitch said.

"Let me take a look at you. What have you been doing? Going to the spa?"

"What are you talking about?" Mitch asked, but knew full well what she was talking about.

"You're looking buff, lady. You've been working out, haven't you."

"Come, take a look," Mitch beckoned.

She led Trish to the other room of her two room apartment. Crammed into her bedroom was a brand new four-station weight machine. There was no bed anymore.

"Where do you sleep?"

"On the couch."

"You sold your bed?"

"No, it's in storage."

"This is a nice setup."

"I thought my landlady was going to have a stroke when she saw them bring it in."

"I'll bet."

"I had to have some sort of inspection of the flooring before I could even have it assembled. The guys who delivered it were so nice. For a couple hundred more bucks, they assembled it. Those guys can lift a lot of weight."

"I'll bet you're doing good too. Come here and let me see your muscle definition."

"Oh stop it. Now you're teasing me. The first two days I sort of overdid it. Couldn't move around very much. I've learned my lesson and I'm going slow now."

"Can I try it out?"

"Sure. I'll get your coffee."

"Smells great."

"Something butter pecan, I think the label said."

"Easy on the cream and sugar until I taste it."

Mitch poured and doctored two cups before carrying them to the bedroom. Trish was testing the middle weight range, and moving with ease.

"Showoff," Mitch smiled.

"Our company has an employee health center. I visit the weight room about twice a week. Three times if business is slow."

"Well, before you show me up anymore, come out to the other room of my two room apartment."

Trish followed Mitch to her combination living-room kitchen.

"Have a seat on my bed."

The room was sparsely furnished, but it was sparkling clean.

"This is a nice place," Trish lied.

"Would you help me find somewhere else to live?"

"Well, sure, Mitch."

"Since business is slow, I wanted to ask for your professional help."

"I figured you'd be moving soon. You want a house?"

"I don't know."

"But you want something different."

"I want to be able to fit an exercise machine and a bed into the same house."

"That's a beginning."

"I'm serious about buying another place to live."

"Okay, but you need to take your time."

"I'm sick of this apartment."

"Well, you can rent another place for six months until you find something that suits your new lifestyle."

"Will you help me?"

"Let's talk about that later. We are expected for turkey at the U."

"Everybody's going to be there, aren't they?"

"The usual crowd. You're still hesitant?"

"I just want the advice part to be over."

"I have a great financial advisor. His name is Daniel Rojas. If you want, I'll talk to him Monday. He's a genius. You'll like working with him."

"Okay, that sounds good."

"And today, when anybody tries to give you advice, just tell them that you'll have to consult with your financial advisor about it. That usually puts a stop to that quickly."

They drank their coffee, paying little attention to the black and white flickering of the football pre-game show on the TV.

"Did I actually worry you guys?" Mitch asked.

"I wasn't too worried. Marge was concerned. Don't tell her I told you."

"That's nice. I mean, to have someone a little worried is okay, isn't it. I didn't do it on purpose…."

"You needed a break. I figured you were on an Alaskan cruise or maybe just jetted to Las Vegas."

13

"Alone? Hey, when I get up enough nerve to go to Las Vegas, I'm taking somebody with me!"

"And Alaska?"

"Let's not talk about boats before dinner."

Trish drove the usual ten-minute drive in fifteen minutes. She was careful on the icy streets and they pulled into the crowded parking lot a little before noon. The minute they walked in, Mitch was surrounded by the wonderful smell of turkey. Greetings were exchanged, but everyone seemed a little reserved. Mitch and Trish settled into a booth and ordered a pitcher of beer. The football game was still in the second quarter and the Lions were losing. What a shock. Marge came over and sat with them.

"Hello, stranger," Mitch put her arm around Marge and kissed her on the cheek, which embarrassed Marge to death.

"I heard you were worried about me," Mitch asked, forgetting that she wasn't supposed to bring up the subject.

"I called all the hospitals, and you weren't dead."

"I'm sorry to disappoint you."

"Were you sick?"

"Well, I did hurt myself," Mitch remembered the sore muscles from her too ambitious workouts.

"Well, you should've called."

"I will, the next time I pull a muscle. Why is it so quiet in here?"

"I told everybody to be on their best behavior. You were coming!"

"I didn't know this group had a best behavior mode," Trish teased, "especially when they know someone's coming!"

"Do me a favor, Marge?" Mitch asked kindly.

"It depends. You're still on my didn't-bother-to-pick-up-a-phone-and-call list."

"Give everybody a drink and put it on my tab. Just don't tell them it's from me, okay?"

"Well or brand? Tap or bottle?"

"Anything they want."

"Must be nice to be rich," Marge wrestled out of Mitch's embrace and stood up.

14

"Got an announcement, everybody."

Marge still had a hold of Mitch's shoulder, and was squeezing hard enough to make a dent.

"Someone here today, someone who wishes to remain anonymous, wants to buy a round for everyone. Take your time, don't swamp the damn bar!"

With that wonderfully abstract declaration, she went back to work.

"How long do you think she'll stay angry with me?"

"Until the Lions lose the football game."

Mitch checked the score. It wouldn't be too much longer. Trish insisted on waiting on Mitch. She brought back two plates of steaming food from the buffet table. It was the one day of the year that Marge caved in and used a catering service. Years ago, when she was younger, she would fix up nine or ten turkeys all by herself. Now, she let someone else do all the work. The food wasn't as good as her own, but at least she could watch football without going to sleep in the middle of the second game. She settled back in with Mitch and Trish for a moment's rest.

"This isn't as good as your cooking, Marge."

"And it took you two and a half plates to make that decision."

"I had to give it a fair test, didn't I?"

"You tested out the pie to the point where I might need to go and get some more whip cream from the store."

"Hey, I'm a growing girl. If I didn't eat enough, you know damn well you'd be hauling more food over here for me to eat like you did last year."

"Don't feel special. I took more food to everybody last year. Had way too many leftovers looming in the kitchen."

"How's it look this year?"

"Stick around after the crowd goes home and I'll pack you up a doggie bag."

"Arf, arf," was Mitch's reply.

They watched the rest of the football game, and then the crowd began to drift to the door. Many were arm in arm, making plans for the evening. How anyone could have that much energy after a three-course turkey dinner was beyond Marge.

15

"I'm going into the kitchen. Don't leave until I get your food ready."

Trish sat back and laughed, "She's something else, isn't she?"

"She sure is. Hey, listen to that music. Marge must have turned on the sound system."

It was the Motown sound, straining out of speakers that needed either a new tweeter or a better woofer.

"Let's dance. Nobody else is around."

"Okay, but I'm not very good on my feet."

They walked over to the tiny dance floor and moved slowly to lyrics caught here and there, "hey there, lonely girl, my only girl." Motown was a hot thing, even on a cold day.

"Trish?"

"Hum."

"We've been good friends for a long time now."

"Uh huh."

"I don't want that to change."

"Why would it change?"

"Why does anything change?" Mitch was in a vague, philosophical mood.

"Why don't you say what's on your mind."

"You know me too well. That's why we're friends. I don't want that to change."

"You said that already."

"Then I must mean it."

"You must, but you still haven't told me what's bothering you."

"We're friends, but we're not lovers."

"Right."

"And that must be for a good reason."

"Right."

"And as strange as it sounds, I don't want that to change. And no matter how I had planned to say that, it still comes out sounding awkward."

"I understand perfectly what you're saying. Lovers come and go. Friends stick around."

"I want you to stick around. I need you to stick around."

"I'm here, aren't I?"

"You're a good dancer."

"So are you."

Mitch relaxed a little more into the embrace. Up until that point, it must have felt to Trish like she was using her for a life jacket, holding on out of panic.

"Find me a new house."

"We'll begin tomorrow, if that will make you feel better. I can spend the entire day with you, talking about what you want, and then we can finish with dinner."

"Pick me up early."

"How about 8 a.m.?"

"I'll be ready."

Chapter 4

An incessant ding dong stirred Mitch awake, right in the middle of a dream where she was the ringmaster of a nine-ring circus. Bells were ringing everywhere and she bumbled her way to the door. Trish was waiting patiently.

"Good morning. Did I wake you up?"

"Come on in, I overslept."

"Getting used to a life of leisure?"

"I think it was the turkey, or maybe the stuffing? Or maybe the two kinds of pie?"

"Let's go eat breakfast and you can fill me in."

"Give me ten minutes," Mitch wasn't sure if she was going to be hungry after yesterday's feast.

"You got yourself a deal."

Mitch spent nine minutes in the bathroom and emerged feeling like she needed ninety more. They rode in silence to the nearest fashionable coffee bar and chatted about inconsequential trivia until breakfast arrived.

"Will you lose your appetite if we talk about something more serious than the weather?"

"My appetite is the least of my worries," Mitch had ordered light.

"Well, for starters, you should upgrade your transportation."

"I like my Yugo!"

"Get something better. You know, something that actually runs!"

"How about a Yugo deluxe?"

"What's that? A Yugo with cheese!"

Mitch chuckled. Trish's magical humor was up and running.

"It's been a good car."

"Buy yourself a BMW."

"Okay, so I buy a house and a car and before you know it, I'm back in debt."

"Not with the help of Dan."

"He's that good?"

"He made me a millionaire, and that was no small feat."

"So I need to relax."

"You need to start making good choices. A house and a car are good choices. A house for an investment and a car for safety reasons."

"I hope you have a lot of houses to show me."

"Actually, no. That's not how I do it."

"Well, how do you do it?"

"I sit here and feed you breakfast and listen to what you think your dream house would be and then I go back to the office and sort through the listings with my staff until we find a few good prospects to show you."

"So you do all the work and I sit here and eat."

"That's right. In fact, that's how it's supposed to be. I'll search through the information until you're satisfied."

"Will you help me buy a car, too?"

"I'll help you buy a pair of socks if it will put your mind at ease."

"Gosh, what a relief. You don't know how hard it is to get good socks these days."

"Tell me about it," smiled Trish.

They leisurely finished a refill of coffee while Trish talked about the real estate market.

"I don't want anything huge," Mitch emphasized.

"A cozy mansion?"

"I own an exercise machine, a couch, a TV, two chairs, a table, a bed, a chest of drawers, and two lamps and one of those is missing its shade. If I move into a mansion, it'll make the Beverly Hillbillies look like furniture brokers."

"You could buy more furniture after you move in, to go with your socks, of course."

"I can only sit in one chair at a time."

"You could upgrade gradually. Maybe start with a new sofa, or a love seat."

"Do you realize how ridiculous this conversation sounds?"

"What?"

"I could afford to buy rooms full of furniture and I'm breaking into a nervous sweat over a new sofa."

"You have plenty of money, don't sweat it."

"That's right, I do have money, but I don't want to make the mistake of turning into a female version of the Great

19

Gatsby. I don't want to use my money to buy friends or influence people."

"I don't think that buying a new sofa is going to lead to that transformation."

"How will I know when I've crossed over into the lifestyles of the rich and famous?"

"I'll tell you when it happens."

"And in the meantime?"

"Does Lisa know you've won the lottery?"

The question made Mitch's head jerk up like a poorly manipulated marionette.

"I hadn't given that any thought."

"You look as white as a pale ghost."

"It's been a whole year since we split up."

"I remember. Hell, half the town remembers."

"And you think…."

"She might magically reappear and cause trouble."

Mitch toyed with her spoon for a moment before Trish broke the silence.

"She really broke your heart, didn't she."

"I haven't been the same since. Hell, I can't even make a decision about something as minor as furniture. It's been a nightmare."

"What went wrong?"

"I never told anybody, for good reason."

"I know that. We all thought you were so noble and dignified to keep it all inside."

"She swindled me out of all my money. My entire life savings, my inheritance."

"How much did she take you for?"

"Roughly $42,851.32, and a lamp shade that she took a fancy to."

"Why didn't you have her arrested?"

"I couldn't bring myself to do it."

"And that's why you moved into the apartment?"

"I couldn't afford anything else."

"Well, let's go downtown to my office and change all that."

"Beats waiting tables at the Lucky U."

As Trish expertly maneuvered her silver BMW through downtown traffic, Mitch relaxed into the exquisite leather seat and allowed her vision to travel unfocused along the store fronts. Almost everything that could be bought was for sale along this street. Jewelry, antiques, cars, computers, TV sets, and yes, even sofas. By the time they pulled into the parking area, Mitch was on sensory overload. She had never done so much mental shopping in her life.

"My office is on the thirty-third floor," Trish talked as they walked through an expansive lobby toward an elevator. "I had to call security ahead of time. It's a holiday for everyone else, but they're always on duty."

A guard appeared and escorted them thirty-three floors upward. Mitch was hoping the bathroom was close. Trish was psychic. Mitch had suspected this for years, and the proof was now displayed. She unlocked the door.

"Here's the ladies room. My office is just down the hall and to the left. You can't miss it."

"If I get lost, I'll use my trusty girl scout compass."

"Down the hall, left. You won't get lost."

Mitch spent twelve minutes in the restroom. Five minutes were taken up with absolute necessities. The remaining seven were spent exploring the various luxuries of the executive bathroom. There were cushy sofas, chairs, tables with lamps, areas with Broadway style lights to help with makeup and three lounge chairs with heat and massage built in. Mitch was four minutes into one of the best massages she could recall when Trish reappeared.

"So that's what you're doing in here."

"You were out there wondering about me? You must not have a lot to do!"

"The security guard was out here wondering what you were doing in here."

"What, he doesn't have a wife or sisters?"

"So you enjoy the executive treatment. This is the restroom for women who have sold over a million dollars-worth of real estate a month for an entire year."

"I noticed it wasn't crowded."

"Come on, I've got something to show you, and besides," she lowered her voice to a whisper, "I've got a chair just like this one in my office."

"I'm right behind you."

Mitch followed Trish down the hall, to the left as promised, past a desk for a secretary and into Trish's office. It was slightly larger than Mitch's entire apartment and decorated with enough gewgaws to qualify as a museum.

Charmingly, there was a photo of the softball team that the Lucky U had sponsored two years ago, and in the front row, were Trish and Mitch.

"I still have this picture, too!" Mitch said.

"It's my favorite."

"Lisa stole the frame, but I have the picture."

"I found five properties right off the bat, although the possibilities are practically endless," Trish talked while she typed on her keyboard.

"How much would it cost to go to Aspen?"

"You're talking millions, just for property. Then, you'll want to custom build a home."

"That much?"

"That much."

"How much would it cost to look around?"

"In Aspen?"

"Yeah."

"Every time I go up there to look, it costs a bundle."

Mitch chuckled at Trish, who was the shopping maven of her peer group.

"Have you seen a shrink about that shopping disorder."

"No, I spent his fee in a kitchen store instead. So, you want to put off looking at properties until I can line up some prospects in Aspen?"

"Is that hard to do?"

"The company has a condo up there for business just like this. Let me talk to my secretary on Monday to see if he can get us booked in."

"You have a male secretary?"

"Yes, I do."

"Is he cute?"

"You would care?"

"Hey, I'm gay, not blind."

"Come by Monday, see for yourself."

"In the meantime, I don't mind looking at other houses you have found."

"Let's drive around, look at a couple of the properties from the street, and stop somewhere for an early dinner. Then, you can have the weekend all to yourself."

"I have every weekend to myself."

Chapter 5

Judy savored the last of her steaming double mocha cappuccino latte as Lisa polished off her third after-dinner brandy.

"How do you drink three of those without going under the table?" Judy asked.

"Years of practice."

Judy smiled at the remark. Lisa was all of twenty-two. Judy didn't feel like pursuing the conversation mostly because she usually found herself speechless at times like this. Besides, it was difficult to argue for moderation in one respect while so enthusiastically enjoying indulgence in her other activities with Lisa. They had run into each other, quite literally, on the ski slopes in Aspen, Colorado. Their ensuing relationship had evolved so precipitously that neither had opted to stop and question it. Until lately.

At first, Judy had secretly been flattered by the young woman's attention, almost obsequious, in nature. When you're forty and counting, and have several silver streaks sprouting from an otherwise conservative brown hair color, attention wasn't automatic anymore. Not that it ever had been. That kind of attention was usually reserved for twenty-two year old blonds with flowing hair and perfect complexions. Like, for instance, Lisa. Judy countered her subconscious urge to act and feel absolutely ancient by keeping herself in great physical condition. She skied, exercised, monitored the alcohol consumption and indulged only in safe sex and rich coffee. Lately, all these proclivities, particularly the last two, had been leaving her feeling a little tired around the edges. Maybe she should cut back on the coffee....

"What are you thinking about?" Lisa quizzed, her mouth in an impish grin.

"I was thinking that I'm going to cut back on these double caps."

"Oh sure you were."

"Okay, Lisa the mind reader, what was I thinking about."

24

"You were thinking about later this evening," Lisa replied as she ran her finger around the top of her brandy glass. "As usual."

"Are you suggesting that I have a one-track mind?" Judy asked with a smile.

"Not only am I suggesting it, but I'm thanking the goddesses for it and hoping the train is leaving the station soon."

"You're ready to go?"

"Thought you'd never ask!"

They walked arm in arm the three blocks to Judy's condo. The frigid, frosty night air felt good to Judy. Between the walk and the feel of Lisa's arm around her, she felt suddenly rejuvenated. When they arrived home, it took less than five minutes to ignite the gas fireplace, fix another drink, strip naked and wrap up in each other's arms. After a moment, Lisa asked, "Are you okay tonight?"

"Why do you ask?"

"You seem a million miles away."

"Sorry. I was thinking about the problems in the Middle East."

"The what?"

"The Middle East."

"Is that a new college football conference?"

"Not exactly."

"Why are you thinking about college football at a time like this?"

"I wasn't."

"Well, what else is troubling you?"

"Wall Street has been quite volatile lately."

"I know about this," Lisa gave fair warning. "It goes up and down all day and people lose money. Are you worried about your investments? That's why you're so uptight. I'm going to fix you one of my special hot chocolate drinks. It'll relax you."

"You don't need to do that. I'm not losing money."

"I know I don't need to fix you something, but I want to."

"Okay," Judy surrendered to the pampering. "Just no booze."

"I promise, no booze."

They cuddled on the couch while Judy sipped down the warm drink, feeling more relaxed by the minute. She couldn't stop yawning.

"So, now, is there anything else pressing on your mind?"

"Well," Judy yawned again, "how about those Cubs."

"Gee, I didn't know that there were bears in Aspen. I knew there were bears in Yellowstone."

Judy had closed her eyes and fallen asleep during the nature lecture, secure in the knowledge that bears roamed the backwoods of Yellowstone, all narrated by the soothing tones of Lisa.

Chapter 6

"I'm not wearing this dress!" Mary stated firmly.

"But you look lovely in it, dear."

"No I don't. I look like I'm going to the prom. Again."

"What about that other dress?"

"That makes me look like the blue nun."

"The what?"

"Never mind, mother. I'm going to wear my usual blazer and slacks."

"Honey, you need to dress up more than that!"

"No, I don't. I'm not the governor-elect like you. I can still dress to please myself instead of your constituents."

"You need to look like a proper young woman."

"I am going to look like a proper young woman, but I draw the line at dressing like a milkmaid!"

Mary stormed out of the room before her mother could debate the point further. Governor-elect Rebecca Louise Fairbanks had spent the better part of the year debating the greater and lesser points of every issue germane to the state of Colorado. So much so that she had often come home too hoarse to talk to her only daughter, her only child. Only they never seemed to talk much anymore. Arguments were the order of the day and they rarely agreed on anything. Rebecca had won the minds and hearts of the majority of Colorado voters with her family values platform, and yet it all came up short at her own doorstep.

"I guess it's to be expected," she explained to the walls. "She is a young adult. She has her own opinions and besides, she did behave well during the campaign."

The walls chose to remain silent. This was a relief to Rebecca. After a year of non-stop discussions, silence was a blessing. She stretched out on the bed, vowing to close her eyes for just a moment.

"So, she's going to wear a blazer and slacks."

Rebecca bolted awake, fearing that the walls had finally seen fit to engage in chit chat. Instead, it was her husband, Jeff.

"Were you sleeping?"

"I must have dropped off for a few minutes."

"So, Mary's wearing-"

"I know what Mary's wearing! I've already heard about it. Loudly," Rebecca didn't need to raise her voice to sound irritated.

"She is twenty-two years old. Mothers stop dressing their children when they turn two."

"Most mothers don't run for governor, and most mothers don't win this important of an election and most mothers don't have a million campaign promises to keep and an image to uphold."

Jeff studied his wife in silence. He knew after watching her in countless debates that further argument would be useless. After a while, her overriding, all-consuming desire to win the argument overshadowed the concept of communication. He forgave her political knee jerk reaction, again. He just couldn't forgive the damage it caused. His silence was his only weapon, and he used it well.

"You just don't understand," she announced.

"What don't I understand?"

"Appearances are important."

"She looks nice."

"But she doesn't look-"

"Right-wing enough?"

"The conservative people of this state voted me into office."

"You certainly carried the right-wing nut conspiracy group."

"Everyone is welcome in the Republican Party!" Rebecca replied hotly.

"Then that must mean that young women in blazers and slacks are welcome too."

Rebecca, much like Mary, stormed out of the room, slamming the door behind her. Jeff chuckled. He didn't win many, but when he did, it was a grand spectacle indeed. He gave her one minute to clear the hallway and then went to his daughter's room. Mary was standing in the doorway.

"I heard the door slam. What's going on?"

"Girls in blazers and slacks are welcome in the Republican Party."

"They've lowered their standards that far?"

They both laughed, but Jeff admonished, "There'll be hell to pay for this one."

"I have a feeling, Dad, that she won't have much time for either of us now that the duties of state are calling. She hasn't even been sworn in yet and already her appointment book is full."

"People are standing in line to fawn and praise, that's for sure."

"Maybe we'll be a welcome diversion for her."

"Either that, or-"

"Or what?"

"Never mind."

"No, tell me, Dad."

"I'm proud of your mother. Don't get me wrong. It's just that I get the creeps from some of her supporters."

"Some of them scare me to pieces."

"It wasn't always this way with your mom."

"I know, but, now, she doesn't have much of a choice, does she?"

"I just hope she isn't in over her head."

"Dad, can you help me with something else?"

"You mean, the miracle of the blazer and slacks wasn't enough for one day?" Jeff laughed.

"It's about my work at the Center?"

"It kept you sane during the election."

"Well, they're always looking for funding, and I was wondering if you could help me locate the newest winner of the lottery?"

"Didn't they publish her name in the paper?"

"I'm sure they did, but I could use your help in tracking her down."

"You can count on me. I could use some honorable diversion about now."

"Me, too!"

"In the meantime, we're overdue at another banquet from hell."

Chapter 7

Mitch and Trish wandered around the lobby of the
Reindeer Hotel Complex. Trish's heartthrob secretary had
come through with condo reservations for the Christmas
holidays. It was a three-week delay from when they had
first planned to come, but it was worth it. No one in the
company had scheduled business over Christmas, and the
company party had already happened the week prior.
Mitch and Trish were on their own for real estate browsing
and dinner reservations. Mitch was admiring the view from
the lobby window while Trish checked on their room
reservations. The complex was located right at the bottom
of one of the most magnificent ski slopes in North
America, and the skiers had long since come down from
the mountain after the last run of the day. The corporate
condo, not more than a half a block away from the hotel
lobby, was a luxurious eight bedroom affair with four
bathrooms, two kitchens and a lounge complete with a
twenty-five foot oak bar. Real estate sales had been good
this year.

Hotel personnel delivered suitcases to their respective
rooms and after unpacking her modest wardrobe, it still
seemed to Mitch that she had space leftover for an entire
department store's inventory in her closet and bureau.
Well, maybe not quite that much, but her own limited stock
looked puny. The crackling sound of ice and fire mixed
with soft Christmas carols gave away Trish's location.
"This is very cozy."
"It impresses many, uh, people."
"You were going to say 'clients' weren't you?"
"It impresses them, too."
"I know I wouldn't be here unless it was on business."
"There are company rules."
"And I expect you to follow them. Don't worry, I'll buy a
house from you. Do you want to talk about properties
now?"
"Would you like to?"
"Sure, show me what you've found so far."

Trish spread out photos and floor plans on the bar and for the next thirty minutes, they pondered together points good and bad about the top contenders.

"Don't even think about making a decision right now," Trish warned. "In fact, tell me what you like about each property and I'll find five or ten more choices that you can look over later. Then, if you think that Aspen is out of your price range, that's okay, too."

"Can we sit back now and enjoy the fire."

"Of course."

A moment or two passed before Trish asked about Mitch's serious countenance.

"Are you okay?"

"I'm just puzzled."

"About the houses?"

"No, about you."

"What about me?" Trish asked, now suspicious.

"I've often wondered why you don't have a steady girlfriend."

"I prefer to think about it this way, I'm between girlfriends. I don't need any of your smart ass remarks!"

"Who me, have a smart ass remark about being between girlfriends?"

"Yes, you. Besides, my work keeps me busy."

"What if you didn't have work? What if a million was enough?"

"I've enjoyed my work more than I've enjoyed most if not all of my relationships."

"Sounds like you just haven't found Ms. Right yet."

"And neither have you."

"Let's drink a toast to keeping our eyes and options open for all of those Ms. Rights out there."

"Here, here. Time for dinner. Let's go and celebrate your good fortune."

"My good fortune is having a friend like you."

They set off to a pricey yet subtle restaurant, promised from hearsay to be brimming with famous people. It was the newest in a long line of hot spots, and Trish found their reservation at the top of a very long list of names. The table was back in an intimate corner, and they engaged in people watching until their dinner arrived. They ate leisurely, soaking up the ambiance of the atmosphere. Christmas red and green dotted the decor, but it was still a ski town motif that stood out. Over coffee, Mitch suddenly emitted something between a yelp and a swear word.

"Coffee too hot?" Trish asked.
"No," hissed Mitch, trying to hide her face behind her cup.
"You look like you've seen a Republican!"
"Worse than that, I think I've spotted Lisa."
"Your Lisa?"
"Well, I'm not talking about the Mona Lisa! That's her, over at the bar."
Trish craned her neck around to see. Mitch warned her, "Don't let her see you. She might recognize you!"
"She wouldn't know me from Eve."
"Still, I don't want her looking over here. Oh God, here she comes! She's coming over here, isn't she!" Mitch looked around for something else to hide behind.
Suddenly, Lisa made a sharp left.
"Relax, she's going to the restroom."
"Do you see the woman she's with?"
"Yes, I did. She'd be hard to miss!"
"I've got an idea. You grab the check, and meet me out front. I'll pay you back," Mitch promised as she rose from the table and started toward the bar.
"What are you going to do?"
"I'll tell you later."
With that, Mitch hurried over to the woman at the bar. She launched into her speech before the woman could object.
"Hi, my name is Mitch, and I don't have much time, but the woman you're with, her name is Lisa, right?"
"Who the hell are you?" the woman asked, piqued at the obvious pick up efforts of this all-too-obvious amateur.
"I'm Mitch Tanner."
"Oh, aren't you the lesbian who won the lottery?"
"That's not important right now. I know all about Lisa."
"Lisa."
"The woman you're with. Her name is Lisa, right?"

32

"Right. How do you know that?"

"Look, we need to talk later about Lisa. She stole my money, all of it, before I won the lottery, that is. Anyway, I'm worried about you. You need to call me and we must meet as soon as possible. She can't know we've talked. Call me at this hotel phone number later tonight or early tomorrow." Mitch scribbled the phone number on a drink napkin and boldly tucked it into the woman's shirt pocket. "I have to go before she sees me."

Mitch slid out of the bar as Lisa was dancing her way back to Judy through the crowd. Her last vision was of a calm, cool total stranger and a red hot Lisa. This was going to be challenging.

Faithful Trish was waiting outside, dancing from foot to foot herself. Mitch filled her in on the details as they trekked their way back to the condo. They barely had a chance to stomp the snow off their boots before the phone rang.

"I can't talk long. Meet me at O'Brien's Pub tomorrow at noon."

The phone clicked in Mitch's ear before she could utter a simple goodbye.

"I have a lunch date with Lisa's latest mark. Can I stay here another night?"

"Correction. We have a lunch date with Lisa's latest mark, and, yes, I have us booked in here for three nights."

"You are as brilliant as you are smart."

"And I'm good looking, too."

"Didn't I mention that?"

"I'm sure you did, sometime."

By the time Trish changed into her robe, Mitch had fallen asleep on the couch. Trish covered her with a thick cushy comforter and went to bed.

O'Brien's Pub was an exquisite establishment furnished from wall to wall and floor to ceiling in dark wood, leather chairs, and crisply attired wait staff. No red and green in here. It would have been too brash. Two of the wait staff had ushered Mitch and Trish to a table and delivered

33

perfectly chilled wine to them moments later. A third waitperson brought complimentary finger food and menus. Mitch had insisted on being early and tipped the waiter for the privilege of being seated promptly. They set aside the menu and relaxed with wine and small talk for ten minutes. As noon approached, Trish asked, again, "So what are you going to tell her?"

"The truth."

Mitch had already explained the strategy to Trish twice. For some reason, she was distracted.

"The truth?"

"Lisa stole my money and broke my heart."

"There's more to it than that, isn't there?"

"Yes."

"She's not coming. I can just feel it."

"Would you relax. She'll be here. Extracting oneself from Lisa isn't as easy as it sounds."

"There she is!"

The woman was dutifully guided to the table by an efficient host.

"I see you found the place," she said, pleasantly, as if they had gathered for a garden party in the middle of winter.

"It's a nice spot," Mitch nodded.

"I thought you'd be alone," she glanced cursorily in Trish's direction.

"This is my friend, Trish, and your name is…?"

"Judy."

"Would you care for a drink?"

The waiter appeared soundlessly and took Judy's drink order. When he left, she got down to business.

"Why did you want to talk to me about Lisa?"

"Lisa is a con artist. She and I had a relationship a little over a year ago, and she swindled me out of my family fortune, such as it was."

"Fortune is such a relative term. How much was it?"

Mitch took an instant liking to Judy. She didn't beat around the bush, cutting right to the heart of the matter.

"Less than $50,000, but it was a fortune to me, at the time. I ended up in a two room apartment, and driving a Yugo."

34

The expression on Judy's face became more serious instantly.

"You have more to lose, don't you?" Mitch did a little nosing around herself.

"Substantially. But then again, so do you, now. What is it like to win the lottery?"

"My good friend, Trish, is helping me to find a new house." Judy turned her full attention for the first time to Trish.

"In Aspen?"

"Yes and no," Trish replied with a sexy smile that Mitch had never seen before. For a brief second, the two women seemed to be transfixed. Mitch hesitated to break into the silent communication floating across the table, but time was of the essence.

"How long have you been, uh, seeing Lisa?"

"Huh?" Judy asked, dragging her attention unwillingly back to Mitch.

"How long have you been sleeping with Lisa?"

"Not long." If Judy was put off by the directness of the question, she hid it well.

"Does she have access to your money?"

"Well, I guess?"

"Don't guess! How much of your money does she know about?"

"I have bank accounts, money markets, and stock. The usual portfolio, I guess. I've probably mentioned all of those to her, but you seem way more interested in my money than Lisa ever was. Maybe it's you I should be wary of?"

"I'm worth millions, remember. I don't need your money, and neither does Trish. She has bundles as well. Trust me, we're not your problem."

"I'm going to need a little more convincing. Lisa seems harmless. She doesn't have the brains to pull this off. She thinks the Middle East is a sports conference."

"Tell me, how much attention have you been paying to her brains?"

"What's that supposed to mean?"

"I know how Lisa operates. You don't. Have you been feeling a little tired lately?"

"Mitch, don't you think that's, well you know, a personal question?" Trish interjected.

Mitch ignored her and continued, "Does Lisa fix you a nice hot cup of coffee or tea at night?"

"Hot chocolate...."

"And you drift off to sleep soon afterwards. Nice and cozy."

"That happens...."

"More lately?"

"It happens. What's your point? It's normal to be tired."

"She's drugging you. You go off to sleepyland and she goes through your financial papers."

"You cannot be serious."

"I know from firsthand experience. You don't have much time. You must do three things tomorrow. Immediately."

"Tomorrow? It's the holidays!"

"Number one – don't take any more 'special' drinks from Lisa."

"Okay."

"Number two – take steps right after the holidays to liquidate all of your assets and stash the cash in a new safety deposit box in a bank that Lisa doesn't know about."

"That's going to take some time, and will cost me money in penalties," protested Judy.

"Would you rather lose some of it, or all of it?"

"What else?"

The waiter reappeared with a new carafe of wine and refilled all of their glasses. Trish was on drink number three already. He moved out of orbit and Mitch continued, "Third thing, make Lisa think that you've had a sudden windfall."

"Why would I want to do that?" Judy asked.

Trish found her voice, "Why should she do that!"

"Because we're going to set a trap."

"Oh God," muttered Trish.

"A trap?" Judy repeated, as if to check her hearing.

"Sure. We already know that Lisa is at the drugging-your-drink stage. That means she's about ready to pounce."

"So if she thinks there's even more money to be had, she'll back off and try to get more information."

"And that buys us more time!" Trish piped up, suddenly enthused about the chicanery.

"Now, all we need is a plan," pondered Judy.

"I bet Mitch is already working on that, aren't you Mitch," Trish ventured.

"I'm working on it, but I need a little more time."

"It doesn't need to be too complicated. We only need to catch her in the act, right?" Judy asked for clarification.

"We need to catch her, that's true. But I don't want her to end up in jail."

"Why on earth not," Trish registered a protest.

"Because no one is beyond redemption."

Lunch arrived and they ate quickly and in relative silence. Mitch glanced from time to time at Trish, who gazed at Judy whenever she thought it was safe to do so. Judy, meanwhile, was studying her food, as if to practice ferreting out poison.

"You have something else in mind for Lisa besides prison?" Judy asked, just to make sure she had heard correctly.

"I just don't think hard time is warranted in her case."

"You're a very forgiving person."

"Just practical. Besides, if we bring the authorities into this, we'll all be on the six o'clock news. Who at the table wants that?"

When no one objected, Mitch considered the matter closed. Judy left first, obviously shaken, but prepared to take the necessary steps.

"I don't blame her for being nervous. Finding out that your lover is up to no good can be quite unsettling," Mitch said.

"I'm worried about her," Trish replied, feeling a little more sober after lunch.

"You have a lot of feelings about her," Mitch observed.

"What do you mean by that?"

"It means that you practically hyperventilated all through the meeting."

"I was not!"

"Trish, I've known you for a long time now," Mitch said gently, "and I've never seen you react to a woman quite like you did to Judy. You gave off more heat than a radiator."

"It was the wine," Trish offered her best defense and then conceded, "How did you know?"

"The tip-off was that very sexy smile that made a dozen encores during lunch."

"She's a nice looking, intelligent woman."

"And so are you, so don't let any personal feelings get in the way right now. We're embarking on a dangerous game, and you need all of your wits about you. Afterward, you can explore any and every possibility you choose to dream up."

"You're not putting her in danger, are you?"

The plan suddenly belonged to Mitch alone.

"*We* are trying to protect her from the danger she's already in. Put your feelings on the back burner until I can devise a good plan."

"Why didn't you go after Lisa months ago?"

"Because I was embarrassed," Mitch confessed.

"You get embarrassed when you belch in public. You get angry when you get bilked."

"I loved her, Trish. I spent the first week after she was gone in a daze, waiting for her to come back. I realize now that it was the drugs, and I was in shock, and disbelief, and mourning."

"That's amazing. A sniveling con artist takes your money and you spend the next several months in abject poverty and you took no action?"

"I assumed a good lawyer would have charged me about half the money anyway, and I guess I figured that Lisa had already spent the other half. So, what would have been gained? Besides, I would have given her the money if she had just asked. Handed it over to her with a smile, in fact. My pain was never about the money. It was about breach of trust."

"Honey, you can't afford that attitude anymore. Not with millions to lose."

"Isn't it ironic? I mean, if Lisa had stuck with me, if it had been true love on her part, she'd be rich beyond even her wildest dreams, and believe me, she could come up with some wild ideas. And here I'd be, happily fulfilling all of them." Mitch's voice cracked just enough to shed light on the one truth she still knew.

"If she loved you, truly, the money would have been the least important issue, just like it is with you right now."

"And that's what I need to look for in a woman."

"First, you need to get over Lisa."

"I think I'm over Lisa."

"You're not even close to being over Lisa. You're about two-hundred twenty-two miles away from being over Lisa."

Mitch didn't say anything in her own defense.

"My God, you're still truly smitten with her, aren't you?"

"Maybe in a different way."

"How different?"

"It's like that mule that kicks you in the head when you're not looking. You still feed the dear animal, but you keep a closer eye out on its feet. You stay out of kicking range until you can teach the animal not to kick."

"Can you teach a mule not to kick?"

"We're about to find out, aren't we!"

With that bit of homespun wisdom, they paid the check and went back to the condo. Trish paced back and forth, too nervous to think about real estate. Mitch mumbled something about "true love" and proceeded to pack a suitcase.

"Where are you going?"

"Back to Denver. You stay here and keep an eye out on things. I'll do the same back home."

"That sounds reasonable, I think."

"I thought you'd think so. Call me if you need me. I'll be at the Lucky U if I'm not home."

Mitch was in the corporate limo and heading back to the city by the time Judy discovered Lisa, at their condo, busily rearranging the liquor cabinet.

"Hello there!" Lisa chirped.

"What are you up to?"

"Well, don't you sound like the prosecuting attorney. Okay, I confess, I'm guilty. I'm taking inventory of our stock, for goodness sake. Remember, the holiday season is hard on the liquor supply. We need to have refreshments on hand for entertaining and the inventory is a little low."

"I guess that sounds reasonable."

"And that's just me, good old sensible Lisa."

"Uh huh."

"Geez, Baby, your body may be here but the rest of you is about a jillion miles away. Anything wrong?"

"It isn't like you to complain about my body being here," Judy bantered back, trying to shake off the effects of the lunch meeting.

"You know I never have any complaints about that, Baby."

"I know."

"Why don't you go and soak in the hot tub for a while. You look tired after your day. Nothing's so bad that you can't soak it away."

Judy nodded agreement and drew Lisa into her arms. Slowly, she guided her hands over Lisa's body, wanting it to betray her, to show her in some tactile way that she was dishonest. What would the sign feel like? Would she recognize it with her passion on fire? All she could feel right now was the soft, compliant flesh that had drawn her to Lisa not so many weeks ago. Judy put the lunch meeting as far back in her mind as she dared.

"So go and soak already!" Lisa pulled back, not ready to succumb to Judy. Judy enjoyed the chase. Lisa was always ready to run, just a little.

"You'll be here?"

"Where else would I go? I have everything I ever wanted right here, right now. Go and ease your mind. I'll be here to ease your body."

"Keep me company. Now? Please?"

Lisa shrugged out of her clothes on the spot. It was like she custom ordered them that way from some store, like Shruggable Clothes.

"See you in the tub."

Lisa was immersed and pouring wine before Judy could disrobe. They drank and chatted, Lisa ever curious about Judy's comings and goings.

"So where were you today?"

"You're being nosy."

"I am not! So where were you?"

"It's the holiday season," Judy said, as if that were enough of an explanation.

"So."

"Maybe I was shopping."

"You didn't bring anything home."

"I'm here."

"Okay, fine. Be stubborn."

"I'm not being stubborn."

"You didn't go shopping."

"I went window shopping."

"Buy any good windows?"

"You want me to buy you a window?"

"Oh, you went shopping for *me*! Well, why didn't you say so in the first place."

"I thought I did. I have a good idea. Let's get dressed-"

"Do we have to?"

"And go to dinner."

"It's three in the afternoon."

"Let's stop by the bank first."

"Why?"

"To get money to go shopping."

"Oh, Honey, let's not do that."

"Why not?"

"You're too tired."

"Well, we can get money and go shopping first thing tomorrow?"

"That's a better idea. I'll even fix you dinner. Then, you won't even have to get dressed. When we get done in the tub, we can go put on our pajamas and have dinner by the fireplace."

Lisa moved closer to Judy, ready to add an incentive to her plan. It wasn't necessary.

"That sounds like a great idea."

"Okay, you soak for a while longer and I'll go cook."

Lisa was out of her grasp and control in a flash. She walked through the house and got a robe on before she started dinner. It would be quick. Some salmon, rice and broccoli. Ready in twenty minutes. She took Judy's robe

41

to her, and traded it for her wine glass. She was busy refreshing Judy's wine when Judy came through the house.

"Here you go," Lisa held out the glass.

"Red wine with fish?"

"I told you that the stock was low."

"Okay, no problem."

Judy took the glass into the bedroom with her and studied it for a minute. Red wine could disguise drugs better than white wine, at least it did in all the crime novels. She poured it down the sink, but was careful not to rinse the glass. Then, taking the glass with her to bed, she made herself comfortable, waited a moment, and then tipped the glass over. It made an audible clink on her night table. She pretended to be asleep as Lisa came into the room. Lisa soundlessly picked up the glass, and Judy couldn't tell what else was going on for a moment. Sensing that Lisa was leaving the room, Judy strained her senses to pick up any clues. The only thing she heard, or thought she heard was a mumbled, "horny bitch."

Judy settled in to think. It was too early for bed and she hadn't eaten dinner. It didn't seem to matter. Lunch was sitting like a rock in her stomach. She was running phrases through her head. What else sounded like horny bitch? What else could Lisa have said? She made up about fifteen excuses for Lisa's behavior and then drifted into a restless sleep. She didn't hear Lisa leave the condo.

Chapter 8

Mitch sat back in her now-favorite booth at the Lucky U to enjoy the quietude before happy hour. Two or three other semi-regular patrons were gathered around the TV set, watching the early news. Trish was still in Aspen, but Mitch had come back home to wait out the lull between the holidays with Marge. The days between Christmas and New Year's Eve were quiet. People who had travel plans were already gone. People who had family in town were spending time together. People who had nowhere else to go were spending time with Marge. Lucky them.

A young woman walked into the bar. A stranger in a black-leather jacket. This was, indeed, out of the ordinary. With practically everyone else gone, the woman approached Mitch. As she got closer, Mitch realized that she was, truly, out of the ordinary. A stunningly beautiful young woman, but with a presence about her that reeked of duty. Although giving the impression of shyness, she stopped at Mitch's table and introduced herself.
"Hello, my name is Mary."
"Hello, Mary." Mitch found her voice. "Have a seat."
"Thank you."
"I bet you already know my name, don't you."
"You're Mitch, the woman who won the lottery."
Mitch had become accustomed to having people, particularly women, coming up out of the blue and introducing themselves to her. She'd just never had one quite this good looking do so, and refer to her as the "woman" rather than the "lesbian" made her all the more intriguing. She was speechless. Almost.
"Would you care for a drink?"
"Orange juice would be nice, thank you."
"Marge, could we get an orange juice and another wine."
"I thought you were drinking beer?" Marge argued from the bar.
"I'm upgrading."
"Is that what you call it."

Mitch ignored the comment and focused her attention back on her new visitor. Angelic face, nice jacket.

"I can imagine you're tired of complete strangers coming up to you and telling you about your incredible good luck."

"I've had people approach me, that's true, but never one as beautiful as you."

Mary blushed such a deep shade of red that Mitch thought they would need to call 911 for a resuscitation. Biker babes don't normally blush. This had to be a disguise.

"And I wouldn't blame you if you told me to take a hike."

"I never tell young women to take hikes, unless of course we're in the mountains."

Mary stopped, breathed deeply and laughed, "I'm sorry, I'm a little nervous."

"Don't be nervous. What's your cause?"

"I work with abused children," Mary said, not afraid to come to the table with her story.

"That must be very demanding work," Mitch said seriously.

"It is. Anyway, I'm on the fund-raising committee and I guess I'm just used to being bold."

"Bold is okay, especially with such worthy work. Would ten thousand dollars be well used?"

"Ten thousand dollars would be very much appreciated."

"Okay, I'll talk to my financial advisor and set it up. What's your last name, Mary?"

"Oh, you don't make the check out to me."

"I understand that. I just need to tell my financial advisor the full name of anybody who approaches me for a donation. He's a stickler for those kind of details."

"It's Fairbanks," Mary whispered about the time that Marge rustled around the table, dropping off wine and juice.

"Sorry, I didn't catch your name."

"Fairbanks."

"As in Douglas Fairbanks Jr.?" Marge quizzed, always ready for a guessing game.

"Right."

Marge wandered away, leaving Mitch with the second best guess.

"As in Governor Rebecca Fairbanks's daughter?"

"Right again."

Mitch sat for a moment, reassessing the situation. Her mind went blank, and the only thing she could think of to say was, "Does your mother know you're here?"

Mary laughed, in spite of her nerves. It was a sound from heaven. Mitch prayed for redemption after sticking her foot in her mouth. It came.

"Not exactly."

"Your mother doesn't know that you're in a lesbian bar asking a semi-famous lesbian for money?"

"You consider yourself semi-famous?"

"You're the one who approached me."

"Good point."

"So you know I'm a lesbian and you're not going to hold it against me?"

"Not if you don't hold it against me, either."

It took a half second to sink in. Mitch couldn't stop her mouth, it seemed to be on a mission of its own.

"And I bet your mother doesn't know that, either."

"Heavens no! And she can't know either. Nobody can know. She'd be recalled. She'd be impeached."

"She'd get over it."

"You're not going to out me, are you?"

"Oh good grief, no. That's the last thing I would do. I'm not an outer."

Mary laughed again.

"What's so funny?"

"Sounds like a term you'd use to describe your belly button."

"Have you had my belly button under surveillance?" Mitch teased, winking at this nubile yet so innocent child. She blushed again. How did this child have any blood left in the rest of her body?

"My mother would have a stroke if she knew."

"She seems reasonable enough on TV," Mitch lied.

"You don't know the real Rebecca Fairbanks!"

"I'd like to meet her someday."

"I can arrange that. In fact, I'm on the organizing committee for the banquet for the fund-raising celebration. I could get you a seat on the dais. Maybe not right next to

45

my mother, but close," Mary began to run her words together like she was nervous.

"Sounds lovely."

"With your generous donation, I could see about making you the guest of honor?"

"Now you're teasing me. There's no way you could have me be the guest of honor, not with such a paltry donation."

"You're one of the larger private donors. Corporations are where the big bucks are, but you have been extremely generous. Besides, we like to warmly welcome our newer contributors."

"You're very good at what you do."

"Thank you."

"So you'll come to the banquet?"

"Sure, but maybe you better forget about the guest of honor stuff for now. While you're at it, maybe you should think about having your mom and me on opposite sides of the room, too."

"I thought you wanted to meet her?"

"I will, just not in front of throngs of people."

"She's too busy for private audiences."

"That's okay, so am I. Usually."

Mitch signaled Marge for another wine and juice.

"So, why haven't you come out to her?" Mitch tossed the question into the gap of silence.

"I'm waiting for the right time. Why?"

"Don't get me wrong. I think that coming out to one's parents is a personal decision. I was just curious about your reasons."

"When did you come out to your parents?"

"Me? I waited until it was safe."

"When did that happen?"

"After they died. It was a one-sided conversation."

"Sounds sad."

"I don't recommend it. You look ridiculous out there talking to a grave marker in a cemetery."

"Lots of people do that."

"It was five below zero at the time. I take that back, I didn't look silly. I looked insane."

46

Mary took a long sip of juice before steering the conversation back to the banquet.

"The banquet is next week. I hope that's not inconvenient?"

"Why would it be?" Mitch was still reliving graveyard moments. She sounded harsher than she intended.

"People tend to dress up for these events."

"Okay, maybe you'd let me borrow that jacket?"

"This is mine, all mine. But I thought you'd just like fair warning. I don't make it a point to go overboard in the dressing-up department myself, but some of the corporate contributors tend to dress to the nines."

"So I should go shopping is what you are telling me?"

"Well, my research indicates that before you won the lottery, you were, well, you weren't rich to begin with."

"You've been doing research on me?"

"My dad helped."

"Your dad helped?"

"Yes."

"Does your dad know that you're gay?"

"I haven't been on a date with a boy in nine years."

"But your mother is oblivious."

"So far."

"So good. Hey, I have a great idea. Let's go shopping! You and me."

"You mean, right now?"

"Is now a bad time?"

"I'm expected home for dinner by six."

"That gives us a couple of hours. We could make it quick. I don't have any fashion sense but I can tell you do."

Another blush.

"I'll help, but it will have to be quick."

"Gee, I hope the newspapers don't get wind of this. Lesbian and governor's daughter go out for quickie."

Their shopping spree was as spontaneous as any outing could be. What Mitch truly lacked in fashion sense, Mary made up for. She had Mitch decked out in stunning clothes within the hour. And she helped her find a jacket that matched hers. Now, they could be twins, with Mary, of course, being the much younger, much more beautiful twin. That was agreed upon from the start.

47

Mary dropped Mitch off at the Lucky U, promising not to be a stranger, and sped toward home after a hug and one more blush. Mitch enjoyed a whole three seconds of silence before Marge started in. "Trish called while you were gone. I told her you were out with a date. I'm not your secretary. Buy one of them new-fangled phones or a pager or something useful like that."

"Was there a message lost in that?"

"Sit down and wait."

"I am sitting. I am waiting."

"That was the message, sit and wait."

"Trish said that I should sit and wait."

"She's coming by."

"I thought she was in Aspen."

"How would I know?" Marge grumbled as she went back to the bar.

Two glasses of wine later, Trish arrived, and bolted for Mitch's booth.

"She called her a horny bitch!" Trish exclaimed in place of her usual "Hello."

"Who called who what?"

"Lisa called Judy a horny bitch!" Trish said, even louder.

"Hey, hey ladies," Marge came over. "You know I don't allow talk like that around here, damn it!"

"Sorry, Marge, I'm quoting someone else."

"Well, in that case, scoot over and tell me what happened," Marge said, crowding her way into the booth next to Trish. Trish and Mitch exchanged glances. What should they reveal? What should they keep to themselves?

"Marge, you remember Lisa?"

"Sure, she was the little snitch that took you for everything you had?"

Trish shot a glance at Mitch, who shrugged her shoulders. This would take some explaining, later.

"That's right," Trish picked up the story, "We found her."

"You found Lisa?"

"In Aspen," Mitch helped.

"With your money?"

"I doubt it. She's probably gone through my money by now."

"But she's found another mark," Trish tried to keep the momentum going.

"A mark?"

"Another victim."

"Oh yeah, another rich pigeon. Present company excepted, of course," Marge directed the comment to Mitch.

"Of course," Mitch nodded. "So, we made contact with this newest pigeon and we're going to try to keep her money safe."

"But it's a lot more serious than that," Trish insisted. "She's using drugs."

"The pigeon?"

"Yes and no. Judy, the pigeon, is being drugged by Lisa."

"And Lisa is probably already drawing money out of the bank. The holidays are a good time to do that. By the time the banks are closed for a day or two, the loss is practically irreversible."

"Do we know that for a fact?"

"Lisa was insistent that they don't go to the bank. She gave Judy another Mickey and called her a horny bitch."

"She's absolutely sure?"

"She thinks that's what she heard. What else would it be?" Marge started thinking about this, what would rhyme with horny bitch. Her thoughts wandered until Mitch pointed out a couple of impatient customers at the bar. She trundled off, mumbling under her breath, "witch, ditch, snitch."

"We have to come up with a plan, and fast!" Trish was beginning to sound fervent.

"I will, I will. Just calm down. Did you remind Judy to start rearranging her funds."

"Yes, I did," Trish nodded.

"So, I'm still coming up with a plan."

"You don't have any good ideas yet?"

"Sure, I do."

"Well, what is it!"

"If a small piece of cheese attracts a mouse, what would a huge piece of cheese do?"

"Attract a rat?"

49

"At the very least, keep the attention of the mouse."

"I don't know much about pest control. Could you just spell it out in layman's terms?"

"Lisa is greedy. The promise of a whole lot more money would make her stay put, at least long enough to try and steal it, too."

"Right. We figured that out already. So, how can someone make a whole lot of money, without raising suspicion?"

"Their rich Uncle Clyde could die."

"We don't know if Judy has a rich Uncle, who? Clyde?"

"She will if we make him up."

"A fictitious dead Uncle Clyde?"

"A fictitious dead *rich* Uncle Clyde."

"If somebody fictitious dies, do you still get to go shopping for something to wear to the funeral?"

"Absolutely!"

"Then count me in, Honey!"

"Count you in, hell. You're going to be the family lawyer. Trish, welcome to law school!"

Chapter 9

"This could work," Trish nodded her head. "This could really work!"

They had ordered another drink, and began to make notes on a cocktail napkin. Good thing the plan was modest, for now. The napkin was small.

"It's simple. Judy is going to inherit a small fortune and we have sole and complete control over the timetable. Estates can take six months to a year to sort out."

"We're not going to drag this out for a year."

"Of course not. But Lisa doesn't know that, now does she? Lisa won't have a clue about our plans. Think about it, for all we know or care, Uncle Clyde might have died way last year. And maybe it took them this long to locate Judy."

"So the funeral shopping is out?"

"I'll buy you something in black for your honeymoon with Judy if it will ease that burden."

"Shut up and think. We need more details, particularly if you're throwing me out on the front lines."

"Okay, we need a way to keep Lisa from interfering."

"I'll tell them that I can only discuss things with Judy."

"That won't be enough. Lisa will nose around on her own. She'd go to the courthouse to attempt to meddle into documents. She's not stupid."

"So, maybe Uncle Clyde lived and died somewhere else, like, in Texas. That would mean that the estate would be probated in Texas. She wouldn't go to Texas to meddle."

"That's pure genius!"

"But how are we going to explain your presence here in Denver?"

"Well, maybe I'm a halfway lawyer."

"Halfway lawyer?"

"Maybe I spend time in Colorado and Texas?"

"Don't you need to be licensed to practice in one state or the other?"

"Here's a thought. The story line will be that I'll be licensed in Texas, but I'll have a vacation home here in Colorado. Ten trillion other Texans do the same thing."

"So, you'll need fake ID and documents from Texas. I'll see what I can do about that. What law school do you want to have graduated from, fictitiously, of course."

"Harvard."

"Harvard?"

"Maybe Lisa won't have time to check that out, either."

"I'm hoping that Judy will be able to help us out with Lisa," Mitch said carefully.

"What do you mean?"

"She needs to keep her preoccupied."

"I was afraid of that."

"Maybe shopping or going out to nightclubs?"

"Speaking of going out, I heard from Marge that you were out on a date with a sweet young thing."

"I was out. Marge got that part right," Mitch did her level best to set the record straight.

"Not on a date?"

"I was shopping."

"A shopping date? Without me? What were you thinking?"

"I had another offer."

"Not a better offer?" Trish needed reassurance.

"Just another."

"Who were you with?"

"I had to buy something to go to a banquet," Mitch dodged the question.

"Who are you going with?"

"Myself."

"Let me see if I understand. You went on a shopping date with someone other than me, a sweet young thing according to Marge, so you could go to a banquet by yourself? What were you *really* doing?"

"I was *really* shopping. I'm *really* going to a banquet."

"Because?"

"I was asked."

"By whom?"

"I donated some money to a charitable cause and they are having a dinner and I'm going."

"What cause?"

"Abused children."

"That's a noble use of your money."

"I hope so."

"So who were you shopping with?"

"You're not letting me out of this, are you?"

"Just because you're a millionaire doesn't mean you automatically get a private life. Now, who did you go shopping with?"

"A nice young lady named Mary."

"Mary who?"

"Mary Fairbanks."

Trish read the paper. Daily. She made the connection. Quickly.

"Are you nuts!"

"Depends on how you define 'nuts'."

"You've lost your mind. You donated money to a Republican!"

"The daughter of a Republican."

"Those acorns don't fall far from those oak trees!"

"This is beginning to sound like my mice-and-cheese analogy."

"You know what I mean. You're donating money to the enemy."

"I'm donating money to abused kids."

"You're donating money to the daughter of the most right-wing nut case in the state of Colorado."

"I think my donation will be safe."

"You had better be right about this."

"Trust me, I think I know what I'm doing."

"Which brings me to one more thing, why did you tell Marge about Lisa when you wouldn't tell anybody else?"

"I had to tell someone. Besides, I knew she wouldn't feel sorry for me."

"And I would?"

"You're just an old softie."

It was ten in the morning. Mitch, needing a quiet place to further concoct her rich Uncle Clyde caper, had arrived early to the Lucky U. Marge had offered her juice and then went about her chores, which included the usual mopping of the floor. It was Marge's version of aerobics.

"Mop a floor once a day and save money on all those gym fees," she would say.

It was a little long for a mantra, but it suited Marge. She had finished and gone into her back office to rest before the crowd appeared for lunch. Needing something physical to do, Mitch wiped off the bar, got a few boxes of liquor out of the store room and was washing up a few more glasses when the back door swung open. Three people came in. Two of them were very big, very burly gentlemen in dark blue suits. The third person was a woman in a raincoat, sunglasses and scarf. Everything but her ankles were hidden from view.

"Sorry, we're not open yet," Mitch said in a warm, yet authoritative tone of voice.

"You're open for the lady," one of the men announced.

The "lady" placed her hand on his arm and he bent down. They talked. He didn't agree with what she was saying. Mitch could tell by the bovine way he swung his head to and fro. He hesitated a moment and then gave some sort of universal bodyguard signal to the other gentleman. They turned and walked out the door, leaving the "lady" on her own.

"Well, I guess I'm open for you, but I can't serve you a drink yet, unless you want some juice?"

The woman stood motionless, apparently at a loss as to her next move. She finally took off her sunglasses.

"Oh my goodness," Mitch smiled, "Good morning, Governor Fairbanks."

Marge came out of her office just at the right time to see the sight of one of the most powerful women in Colorado meeting face to face for the first time with one of the wealthiest women in Colorado.

"What the hell?" Marge said.

"Marge, I'd like you to meet Governor Fairbanks. You know, *Mary's* mom."

"It's so nice to meet you," Marge said.

The governor made no sound, no greeting toward Marge. She directed her remarks to Mitch.

"Is there somewhere we can discuss an important matter?" her tone was cold. She clipped off each word like her tongue was made of ice.

"You can use my office?" Marge volunteered.

"No, that's okay, Marge. The governor can sit in my usual booth."

Mitch was doing her best to stay cool and unaffected, but the sight of the governor's eyes had turned her into jelly from the feet up, and the numbness was about to invade her knees. She didn't know a good next move. If she walked to the governor, the bodyguards might make another sudden appearance. Instead, she gestured in the direction of the booth, and the governor came forward.

"Please, have a seat."

"Would you like a drink?" Marge asked.

"Maybe some wine?" Mitch suggested.

"I don't drink before noon!" her tone was straight out of Pilgrim's Progress.

"Do you drink after noon?"

"Yes, sometimes."

"Well, you know the old joke, it's always afternoon, somewhere. The pope's probably eating his dinner about now."

"I'm not here to discuss the pope."

"Oh good, well, now that we have that settled, I'll see about that wine."

Mitch stood up and walked over to the bar where Marge stood like a post.

"I've never had a governor in my bar before," she whispered like she was in church.

"Gosh, I can't imagine why. I thought all governors patronized the local lesbian bars. You got any of that good Chardonnay back there?"

"The ten dollar or twenty two dollar stuff?"

"The twenty two dollar will be fine."

"Here you go. Here's a couple of clean glasses. Wouldn't do to have the governor get dish water poisoned in my bar."

Mitch walked back over to the booth. Governor Fairbanks had removed her scarf, and unbuttoned her raincoat.

"Here we go," Mitch said, feeling her knees about to fly the white flag.

"I'll just have half a glass."

"Top or bottom?"

"Excuse me?" the icy tone was back.

"It's bar humor. You want the top or bottom half of your glass to be full."

"I'm sure someone finds that amusing," she now sounded like the Queen.

Mitch poured the wine and they drank.

"This is almost acceptable wine."

"Well, we common folk do our best. Of course, it's not like what you must have at the mansion."

"What I have at the mansion is of no concern to you."

"I thought the idea of a democratic government was to have leaders who would actually stay in touch with the people who elected them."

"I didn't come her to discuss government with you."

"Okay, so you're not here to discuss the pope or the government, and you find the wine barely acceptable. Just exactly why are you here?"

"I'm here to tell you that if you ever again get within three feet of my daughter, I will personally find you and break one or both of your arms."

"Well now, that would be something to see!" Mitch chuckled softly.

"You find that amusing?"

"I have you by at least twenty pounds. If you wanted my arms broken, you'd have to get those blue suits out in the parking lot to do it for you."

Governor Fairbanks sat quietly for a moment.

"It's no fun when somebody calls your bluff, is it?" Mitch said kindly.

"You stay away from Mary."

"Here, have some more wine."

"I don't want any more wine," she said, "But I want you to leave Mary alone."

Mitch refilled both of their glasses. This stuff was good, even if the governor didn't agree.

"Mary approached me, or have you not understood the chain of events?"

"I understand that my daughter is impetuous at times. Going into a lesbian bar to beg for money is her idea of raising money. She needs better judgment."

"Your daughter is a good kid. She followed up on a hunch. I think she has a bright future and she's just following her own star."

"She doesn't need to follow you."

"I agree. She needs to be her own person. And she will be. Trust me."

"You don't know anything about my daughter!"

"I know that she's a lot like you in some respects."

"What are you talking about?"

"She knows how to get money out of people to support a cause. Do you want to know how you and your daughter are different?"

"You don't know anything."

"Your daughter has found an honorable and good cause to support."

The governor had obviously heard enough, she stood to leave.

"You and your daughter have one more thing in common."

"And that is?"

"You both have the most beautiful eyes I've ever seen."

The Honorable Governor Rebecca Fairbanks blushed, an involuntary response to an unexpected compliment. She doused Mitch with the rest of the wine in her glass, which wasn't much, and exited before Marge could complain about the mess. Still thinking about the blush, Mitch said softly to herself, "Like mother, like daughter."

"I guess I'd better go and get the mop back out," Marge grumbled.

"Don't worry, Marge, I'll clean it up. Most of it is on me anyway."

Mitch got a rag from the bar and cleaned wine off herself and the booth.

"Imagine the nerve," Marge groused.

"Oh, I think it's kind of sweet in a way," Mitch said.

"You're not angry?"

"Oh heck no. Marge, what we have just seen here is a momma bear protecting her cub or cubbette, as the case may be."

"Cubbette? Sounds like one of the Mouseketeers?"

"She's just doing what she thinks is right."

"And you don't mind?"

"I think it's sexy."

"I think you've lost it."

"I think I have, too. Hey, Marge, if I ever call you and tell you that I'm in a cast, don't go out and buy tickets for opening night."

"That's it. That's the last time I serve you and the Governor Chardonnay before opening time!"

"I sincerely hope not."

While Mitch sat around, waiting for lunch hour to get underway, she called Mary.

"Oh hello, Mitch. How are you?"

"Oh, I'm fine, just a little damp."

"A little what?"

"Never mind. Could you do me a favor, Mary?"

"Sure, I'll try."

"You remember that banquet?"

"The one we went shopping for."

"Can I sit in the back of the room?"

"You don't want to sit up front?"

"The back of the room is better for me. And can we forget all about any special honors?"

"Sure, but why?"

"I just need to keep a low profile for a while."

"Have you been getting threats?"

"Oh no. Nothing like that. I just want to remain anonymous."

If Mitch had been seated any further back at the banquet, she could have helped with the valet parking. Mary had followed through, and Mitch was basking in the lowest of the low lights. Rebecca was up in front, accepting the praise from all of her supporters and sycophants. She would be too busy to do any damage, real or otherwise. Dinner was lovely, and Mitch looked up once or twice to find Rebecca looking in her general direction. It had to be coincidence. Mitch gave it the walk-around-the-room test. Rebecca tracked for a minute or two and then became distracted by other rich contributors. As long as they were playing games, Mitch thought up a good strategy and located the woman who had helped Mary arrange everything. It was never hard to spot these people, they were too busy with staff and volunteers to sit and eat. Besides, Mary had been in her company most of the evening as opposed to anyone else.

"Can I help you?"
"You're the one who's helping Mary?" Mitch asked.
"I'm taking care of the details."
"Could you do me a favor?"
"I'm kind of busy right now..."
"It won't take too long, I promise."
They spoke for a few minutes, Mitch explaining, the woman smiling and nodding.

The time for the recognition of contributors arrived with dessert. Names were called off, people stood to applause and soaked up the honor. Mary, as mistress of ceremonies, made everyone feel special. She was captivating. To wind up the evening, Mary had saved the announcement of Mitch's anonymous donation for last. When she announced it, there was mild applause as people scanned the room, trying to guess who the unnamed person was. Rebecca looked over in Mitch's direction again. Then, on cue, the woman who Mitch had talked to handed Mary a note.
"Oh my goodness," Mary said into the microphone. "There's been a mistake."
People in the room buzzed, wondering what was happening.
"Apparently, there was a miscommunication in regards to this final donation. Instead of ten thousand dollars, the donation is one-million dollars!"
People gasped and applauded, and stood to show their appreciation. Mitch stood also, applauded also, looked

around also. And then she saw Rebecca, watching her. Mitch smiled, waved, and left the room. Ah, revenge could be so sweet. It was the best million she had spent all week. Matter of fact, it was the only million she had spent all week.

Chapter 10

"Hello, I'm here to meet with, uh, a Ms. Burke," Trish had
her hand out and her eyes in her appointment book. She
had wanted to appear bookish, like any good family lawyer
would look. A soft, gentle hand took hers. She looked up.
Lisa was checking her out from behind sunglasses.
"Is that you?" Trish felt a warmth spread through her face.
How many years could she get in jail for this she wondered
to herself. Not even Rich Little did impersonations of
lawyers.
"No, I'm not."
Trish watched Lisa's lower lip. Petulant, but very firm.
"I'm Trish Carter, the attorney. I called ahead for an
appointment."
"Oh, it's you. You know, Judy, uh, Ms. Burke, cried when
you called. I didn't even know she had a death in the
family. I guess she didn't either until you called."
The lower lip worked fast, and then Lisa took off her dark
glasses. Trish couldn't help but stare. She had never
studied Lisa's beautiful eyes before. Never. No wonder
Judy was so caught up. And Mitch. Still.
"Won't you come in?"
"Thank you."
Trish stepped into the condo and looked around, just to
have something to do with her eyes. If she continued to
study Lisa, the plan would fly out of her brain and then
where would they be. Mitch had been so careful to run
Trish through rehearsal after rehearsal. "We can screw up
a lot of this plan, but this first meeting has got to go off like
clockwork or else we're sunk."
Trish scanned the room for support. Judy came out from
another room to answer the need, dressed in black.
Whatever was left of Trish's knees was hit hard again by
the sight. So much for support.
"Hello, you must be the attorney?" Judy held out her hand.
Trish gripped it like it was the last life boat on the Titanic.
Trite but true.
"Are you feeling okay?" Judy noticed the shakiness.
"I think it's the altitude."

"Come and sit down. Would you like a cup of tea, or perhaps something a bit stronger?"

"Got any scotch?"

"Gallons!" Lisa laughed, "What do you want with that?" she asked.

"A glass?" was the only thing Trish could think to say. Lisa giggled as if this was fodder for the late show. She hurriedly poured the drink and handed it to Trish. After one swallow, Trish was feeling a little more grounded. Judy was watching Lisa, and when Lisa became aware of the scrutiny, she burbled out, "You want a drink, too, Dear?"

"Maybe just a bottle of beer."

"Okay," Lisa chirped and went to the refrigerator. Judy assumed it would be much harder to doctor a bottled product when people were watching. However, they weren't watching Lisa. They were watching each other. Whatever magic had happened in O'Brien's Pub was resurfacing and they only had a few seconds to indulge before Lisa reappeared.

After a moment of stilted small talk, Lisa asked, "Shall I leave the two of you to talk alone?"

"That won't be necessary," Trish assured her. The scotch was helping.

"It won't?" Judy asked, truly puzzled.

"No, Lisa can hear what it is I have to tell you today. If that's okay with you, of course. Later, we might need a confidential meeting or two to sort out the details. This is just a preliminary meeting to pass along our condolences, to notify you of the nature of probate and to answer or promise to research any questions you may have."

When Trish had said the word "questions" she had been looking at Judy, but it was Lisa who jumped right in with what she considered the most important question, "So how much was Uncle Clod worth?"

"It was Clyde, Dear," Judy corrected her. "Uncle Clyde."

"Of course, well? How much exactly?"

Trish started to repeat the lines that she had gone over with Mitch just a day ago, "We don't have all the figures yet."

"Well, how long will that take?"

"We've been working with the family to sort everything out."

"Who in the family is working things out?"

"The personal representatives of the estate, as set forth under the terms and conditions of the will."

"Well, who are they?"

"Family members."

"And what are they doing?"

"They are determining assets, liabilities, taxes, that sort of paperwork."

"You don't do the paperwork?"

"Think about it in these terms. When you have an accountant do your taxes, you still need to furnish the information, correct?"

Lisa and Judy nodded. They both were starting to look like bobble-head dolls. Judy for show. Lisa for real.

"The personal representatives of the estate are assembling the paperwork, so that later on, we can sort through it. Right now, I need Judy's social security number."

"What for?" Lisa was a curious one.

"She will be an heir. We need that information to begin her paperwork."

"It isn't you who requires it, right?" Judy said by way of explanation.

"Right. It's Uncle Sam who wants it."

"Judy, why didn't you ever tell me about all your uncles? Clod, Sam, are there any others? And are they all rich?" Trish had to struggle to maintain her composure. This was either the best act in town, or Mitch had been swindled by the dumbest blond in history.

"As I mentioned earlier," Trish resumed after a couple of deep breaths, "You will be an heir. You will need to plan your personal finances around that fact."

"There will be that much to plan for?"

"I can't say now."

"I understand."

"Well, that about wraps things up. Did you have any other questions?"

"How difficult will it be to determine the date of death values of the assets?" Lisa tossed the question out like she was asking for more drink requests.

"That's never very difficult in a case like this," Trish bluffed.

"Why?"

"Because we know the date of death," Trish stated as if it was obvious.

"Of course," Lisa nodded.

"Could I trouble you for a drink of water before I go?"

"It's no trouble at all."

When Lisa went to the kitchen, Judy looked at Trish.

"What's a date of death value?"

"I have no idea. But I'll go and look it up tomorrow."

Lisa returned with a glass of water which Trish drained in front of them. Lisa also handed a glass of wine to Judy.

"You haven't touched your beer. Thought you might like this."

"Thanks."

All three looked at the glass like they expected it to put on a floor show. Trish decided, after a split second that she had had enough of her own performance and prepared to leave. Judy would be okay, probably better with Trish gone.

"I'll go now, but I'll be in touch."

"What about my social security number?"

"Do you know it by heart?"

"No," Judy confessed.

"I do," Lisa piped up, and then she recited it slowly so Trish could make a note in her appointment book.

"Thanks for the drink and the time."

Trish left after shaking hands with Lisa and Judy. It left her trembling as she walked to her BMW.

"You weren't very thirsty, Baby." Lisa said after Trish had been gone a moment and Judy still hadn't touched her wine.

"I guess not."

Lisa took the glass and drank the wine in one deep drink. It began to add a glow to her already youthful complexion.

She had taken up residence next to Judy on the couch and now began to touch Judy's ear with the tip of her finger. Why this always seemed to arouse Judy, Lisa didn't know. Right now, she didn't care. Even though Judy smiled at the attention, she was still withdrawn. Lisa put her arms around her.

"Honey, I'm so sorry about your Uncle Clem."

"Thanks." Judy replied, not bothering to correct her again.

"I love you."

"I know."

Lisa kissed the ear that she had fondled a moment ago. Judy closed her eyes and breathed, not wanting to fight the attention too hard. In fact, until the plan was farther down the road, she had to behave as normally as possible. Which had been, up until now, a love sick middle aged woman under the spell of a gorgeous, sexually creative, lithe and supple twenty-something year old. How hard could this be? Every time she closed her eyes, she saw Trish. Trish the fake lawyer. God, the woman looked absolutely fetching in her business suit. Anyone can look good in silk and satin. When a woman haunts you in her business suit, you've got it bad.

"Let's go shopping," Judy said.

"You're serious," Lisa commented, not knowing whether to feel rejected at Judy's apparent disinterest in her advances or thrilled at the prospect of spending more of Judy's money.

"I think shopping will be a very stimulating experience. Not nearly as stimulating as making love with you, but we can save that for tonight," Judy assured.

"I'll go and change," Lisa jumped up.

Judy closed her eyes and saw Trish. Again. Then Lisa. Then Trish.

"I hope you know what you're doing," she said softly to herself.

Chapter 11

"We need what?" Mitch asked Trish to repeat her request.
"The fake lawyer is going to need help from an
accountant," Trish explained.
"You need a fake accountant?" Mitch was still puzzled and
having this conversation over the phone at the Lucky U
wasn't helping. "This isn't one of those light bulb jokes is
it? Like, how many fake accountants does it take to screw
one in."
"I know the answer to that one," Marge said from across
the bar.
"It's not a quiz, Marge. I need an accountant or someone
that thinks like one."
"The answer is ten and forty. You know, like the tax form.
1040."
"How about just a fake bookkeeper?" Mitch was talking to
Trish, still long distance from Aspen.
"A fake bookkeeper? Not nearly as funny as my answer,"
Marge huffed.
"We need someone who looks bookish, low key, and can
add and subtract."
"How about one thousand and ninety nine," Marge offered.
"You know, like 1099?"
"How about another beer!"
Marge went off, still trying to guess punch lines to non-
existent jokes.
"This might not be as easy as it looks, Trish. Where am I
going to find someone who owes me a favor, and is smart
about money and willing to go along with a scam?"
"Hi Mitch."
Mitch looked up to see Mary Fairbanks standing at the
booth.
"Uh, Trish, let me get back to you. And don't worry."
Mitch ended her call and invited Mary to sit with her.
"I came by to thank you for the outrageous donation."
"I'm sorry I sprang it on you. Are you angry with me?"
Mitch thought the humble approach would work best.
"Absolutely not."
"I was worried that it made you look-"

66

"Foolish?"

"Uninformed."

"It's the best thing that could happen to the Center. As for my mother, she's still in shock."

"Good shock or bad shock."

"You never know with my mother."

Visions of Rebecca's visit to the bar came floating back to Mitch.

"You know, your mother doesn't want you to spend time with me."

"What were you talking about a minute ago, on the phone. Something about a fake bookkeeper and a scam? I don't need to worry about the donation, do I?"

"Oh no. This is something completely different."

"Well, can I help?"

"Can you help what?"

"I know a little about finances. But, why on earth would you need a fake bookkeeper."

Mitch looked at Mary. Then, she closed her eyes. Rebecca was back in front of her, with two burly bodyguards. Then, Mary, and Trish and Lisa and Judy. It was like a mental parade.

"Are you okay?"

"I'm fine. I'm just trying to make a decision."

"Can I have a beer while you decide?"

"Better make it a double."

When Trish came back to Denver, Mitch immediately put her to work. Not with the business of scams. That would wait. Besides, Trish needed a diversion. She had Judy on her mind and it wasn't exactly helping her to think clearly.

"Let's go house hunting!"

"I thought that's what we were doing in Aspen."

"I can't afford Aspen. I just gave a million dollars to Mary."

"I'm not going to scold you about your spending habits, but why did you do that?"

"Because I could. Can we look at houses today?"

"Sure."

It did the trick. Mitch kept Trish busy most of the day looking at listings just west of Denver.

"Why do you want to stay so close to Denver?"

"I think I can stay occupied living closer to Denver. My hobbies are in Denver."

"Your hobbies? Aspen is the hobby capital of Colorado!"

"Not if it's politics."

Trish let the remark pass. As long as it was Mitch's money, she wasn't going to argue. They wandered through several houses, one in particular caught Mitch's attention. It was a huge home, sleeping room for about eight people, beautiful oak kitchen, a backyard fit to grow anything from trees to a truck garden. The major selling point for Mitch was a custom built elevator. Trish, ever interested in health, made Mitch climb the stairs and then, as Trish scouted out the bathrooms, Mitch stretched out on the bed. Hopefully, the current millionaire occupants wouldn't mind. It was either that or pass out from the ostentatiousness.

"What are you doing?"

"I'm checking the ceiling."

"Come look at the closets, they're walk-in."

"No thanks. I try to avoid closets."

"You can't stay in bed forever."

"It's tempting."

"There's room for your furniture and your exercise equipment."

"That, and about a million other things."

"It's a nice, big place. You could entertain."

"I do that at the Lucky U."

"What is it, Mitch?"

"What's what?"

"Something's on your mind. If you don't like the place, we can look at other houses."

"I like it, I just don't think it's either practical or moral for one person to live in a house big enough for a family of fifteen."

"You have a unique sense of morality. So, let's go look at something smaller. You don't need to buy this place if you don't like it."

"Oh, I'm going to buy it. Don't worry about that."

"You are?"

"Sure, I'm just not going to live in it. Let's go find a small place, now."

Mitch was off the bed and downstairs before Trish could catch up. They drove around for another day, looking here and there until Mitch found a cozy place. It had five small rooms, an acre of land, and a dirt driveway. The land made it relatively expensive, but not in a showy way. Trish and Mitch went back to the office to begin the paperwork, and stopped for dinner at a fast food restaurant. Mitch was buying.

"Mind if I say something," Trish ventured, halfway through her salad.

"Are you going to suggest I get some therapy?"

"No, I'm just wondering what you're going to do with the other house?"

"The one I'm not going to live in?"

"Yeah."

"There has to be a big family out there somewhere who needs a huge house with an elevator."

"What do you have in mind?"

"Isn't there some family who is down on their luck, maybe someone is in a wheelchair, maybe a child. Maybe some unexpected health catastrophe."

"I'm sure there is."

"I'm sure there is, too. Maybe Mary can help me with this. Did I tell you, she's going to be in on our little scam?"

"You've got to be kidding! She's the daughter of the governor."

"So, we need the best, don't we?"

"We need the best. I'm concerned about Judy."

"I know, it shows. You're a woman in love."

"Don't tell me I glow, I don't want to hear it."

"Okay. Can I tell you that everything is going to turn out okay?"

"I hope so."

"Honey, Judy's a smart woman. She'll stay out of trouble until we get things organized."

Chapter 12

"Honey," Judy called through the condo. "I'm going to the bookstore. Want to come along?"

Lisa poked her head through the den door. Judy was sitting thoughtfully at her desk staring at a blank computer monitor.

"Bookstore you said?"

"The trip could double as a coffee break, or even lunch if you're hungry?"

"Sounds like a splendid idea. Are you looking for any book in particular, besides, of course, *yours*?"

The addendum to the question brought a smile to Judy's face. She had made a habit, over the months, to check on the availability and stock of the three books that she had penned. Years of teaching and research and a burning interest in American history had led to publication of three books about war. Not exactly a pleasant subject but still worthy of literary notice. After years of sacrifice on her teacher's salary, the rewards of publication had secured the condo in Aspen. University students toted her tomes to class and studied about the sacrifices made to buy the American dream. She lived the dream. Unfortunately, it also made her feel at times a bit egg-headed. Understanding war inside and out didn't attract many invitations to dinner parties. No one wanted to hear war stories over lobster mousse, except if you were the soldier and had scars to prove it.

"Actually I am looking for a different book."

"Which one?" Lisa assumed it was a specific title.

"I'm looking for a book on how to kill someone."

The comment brought only the slightest reaction from Lisa, "Sounds like one of your war books to me."

"I've decided to branch out. Enough war for one lifetime. I'm going to try my hand at writing a murder mystery so I need a reference book about poisons."

"Have you seen my shoes?" Lisa called from the bedroom.

"Check under the bed!" Judy shouted suggestions back.

"I'll be ready in a few," Lisa reappeared with her cross trainers in her hand.

"Maybe you'll find a book of interest as well?" Judy framed her question carefully.

"I hope they have hazelnut coffee today," was Lisa's only concern.

Together they ventured into the crisp day and drove to the bookstore. On the outside, it appeared as a modest storefront. Inside, the extensive renovation had created the perfect blend of retail bookstore and European café. During all seasons, the place was packed.

"Coffee first? Please?" Lisa asked.

"Sure, poison can wait."

They maneuvered to a cramped table for two and ordered two macadamian flavored mochas. Hazelnut took a backseat to Hawaii.

"Why poison?" Lisa quizzed after spooning three sugars and almost a fourth cup of cream into her coffee.

Judy muttered to herself, "About time," and answered back, "Why not?"

"Is the killer male or female?"

"Well, I don't know yet..." Judy drew out the answer.

"Does it make a difference?"

"Of course, silly. Don't you know that poison's a female thing!"

"Says who?"

"Agatha Christie, I think. And so does "Arsenic and Old Lace". Women are the poisoners."

"Are you sure?"

"It's practically a kitchen industry. Men don't cook up murder. They use guns and stuff. If I was writing a murder mystery, I'd just throw the intended victim under a semi-truck when they were least expecting."

"I just can't see myself writing about gore and violence."

"You've written three books about war, for goodness sake!"

"But not for entertainment. Murder mysteries are a hot industry now and poison is a big part of the intrigue. Order us some lunch while I browse."

71

Over turkey and ham sandwiches, Judy murmured about oleander, foxglove, digitalis, belladonna, and nightshade. "Oh wait, here's your favorite…" Judy sought out Lisa's eyes.

"My favorite?"

"Yeah. Arsenic! It's in ant poison, paint, wallpaper. What a hoot!"

"So, all you have to do is have one character convince the other character to chew on wallpaper."

"Actors do that all the time to scenery. Speaking of which…weren't you in summer stock one year?"

"Ancient history." Lisa muttered.

"Five years ago, right."

"I guess."

Judy sensed Lisa drift away, an ocean of evasiveness threatening to separate them. Reaching out, she took hold of Lisa's hand and brought it to her lips, teasing her at first with a kiss and then the barest touch with the tip of her tongue. Lisa inhaled sharply, trembling by instinct.

"We're in a public place, for heaven's sake!" Lisa tried to protest. Judy wouldn't let go, holding her hand steady, keeping Lisa's attention.

"I don't see anybody but you making a fuss," Judy scanned the room, seeking out gawkers. "But I am right, aren't I?"

"Yeah, nobody's looking."

"I meant about you being an actress."

"I was Juliet for three weeks. Romeo was a macho pig. Open mouth slobbering was his idea of a kiss."

"And didn't you both kill yourselves? Wasn't there poison in the story somewhere?"

"For a teacher, you don't know much about Shakespeare, do you?"

"I studied Twelfth Night in high school."

"Shakespeare on lesbians."

"That's right. The parent group had a fit. Tried to censor opening night. So, what was it like, acting I mean?"

"Why the sudden interest?"

"You know why, don't act so innocent!"

The instinctual shivers made an encore performance and
Lisa cast a clouded expression toward Judy. Judy let Lisa
dangle just for another second or two before giving slack.
"I just don't know much about you. We haven't been
together all that long. I'm kind of embarrassed to say so,
but in balance, we've spent less time talking than, well, you
get my drift."
"Oh, I get it! So now, you want to convince me that you're
attracted to me for more than my fabulous body."
"You were so easy to fall in love with. But I want to get to
know you better. I'm interested in more than just sex. Is
this coming out right?"
Judy took Lisa's hand again, the one she had let slip away a
moment ago, and ran her index finger gently from wrist to
elbow and back. She had already rehearsed the speech a
dozen times, but she wanted it to appear spontaneous. Lisa
wasn't the only actress at the coffeehouse.

"I'm almost forty-two years old."
"Is this a reminder to go birthday shopping?" Lisa asked
coyly.
Judy's eyes crinkled up into a warm smile.
"And you're just barely twenty-two."
"Okay, and my mom's got a parrot that's ten. What's the
point?"
"A ten year old parrot?"
"She had a cat once that lived seventeen years."
"You see, that's what I'm talking about," Judy improvised.
"I don't know that much about you. I want to know about
your mom's menagerie, and your year in summer stock and
all the other things that are important to you."
"Let me see if I understand," Lisa said, "You want to hear
about my mother's parrot more than you want to have sex
with me? That's strange."
"I don't mean that it has to be one or the other. I just want
to know all about you. Everything that's important to you."
"I'll begin to tell you all about myself, little by little, in the
same excruciatingly slow but sweet way you make love to
me..."
It was Judy's turn to inhale deeply.

". . . but it may be more of a letdown than anything else.
I'm boring."

"Time will tell. In the meanwhile, I need you to do
something else."

"Take me home and I'll grant your every wish."

"And after that," Judy laughed, "I want you to make a list
of all the things that I can buy you to spoil you way past
rotten after I get my inheritance."

"I don't want you to do that. You keep hold on that money
for your old age, which isn't, contrary to your mood,
today."

"But I want to treat you right."

"Every day you share with me is a gift. Take me home and
make love to me."

They paid the check and, arm in arm, braced themselves for
the cold frontier. Their good-natured argument about
spending money continued as they began to cross the street.
This small distraction was only one factor in the mishap
that ensued. Lisa saw it first, and began to react with a
surprising strength for her size. As the Porsche twirled out
of control in their direction, Lisa used the seconds available
to push Judy out of danger. She nearly cleared the danger
herself. Nearly. The car slid into her, knocking her off
balance. Her momentum was rudely stopped by a parked
car, and the collision snapped her forearm and lower leg
into awkward positions, making it seem like she had one
too many elbows and knees. Judy pushed away from the
place where Lisa had shoved her and began to scream for
help. She was at Lisa's side without remembering how she
got there and held her head off the icy pavement. Lisa was
breathing. Good sign. Not bleeding, at least not anything
that Judy could see, but there was always danger of internal
damage. Lisa's eyelids fluttered and then Judy was pulled
away by paramedics. Someone guided Judy to the
ambulance and checked her vital signs.

"Is she a friend of yours?" someone in medical uniform
asked.

"Huh?" Judy said, still fighting the effects of adrenaline.

74

"The woman who was injured, is she a friend of yours?"
"Oh, yes."
"Okay, we'll transport her to Mountain View Hospital.
You can ride with us in front."
"Can I drive?"
"We have to drive the ambulance, Ma'am."
"I meant, can I drive my own car and meet you there!"
Judy was growing impatient with the man to whom she felt
intellectually superior.
"You can drive if you feel up to it."
"I'm okay to drive. I'll be there."
"They'll take information at the hospital."
"I understand."

Judy also understood that Lisa was badly hurt and only
years of professional restraint had kept Judy from
screeching to all in range of her voice that Lisa was more
important than paperwork. She watched and waited until
Lisa was secured and loaded into the ambulance before
realizing that the police were also waiting to talk to her.
"I'm going to the hospital. You can take my statement
there."
"Of course, do you need a ride?"
"No."
Two reasons compelled Judy to drive her own car. The
first reason was generic. Leaving it on the street was never
a good idea. The other reason was more specific. She
wanted a private moment on her phone. As she warmed the
engine, she dialed three different numbers until she reached
a live person. Marge answered the phone and wagged her
finger at Mitch. Phone calls at the Lucky U were becoming
so common for Mitch that she fished a quarter out of her
pocket to help assuage Marge's monthly phone bill. They
traded commodities.

"Yeah, Hi Judy."
With those words, Trish's eyes jumped to Mitch.
"What's that? A broken arm and leg!"
"What's going on?" Trish demanded to know.

75

"I'm trying to hear!" Mitch hissed. Then into the receiver, "No, go on, I can hear *you* fine. Uh huh, okay, where?"
Every syllable agitated Trish more. "What did Lisa do to Judy!"
Mitch ignored the question and began scribbling information on her standard stationary, the cocktail napkin. "Do you need anything?"
"I'm going up there," Trish announced.
"Do you need us to come there?" Mitch asked Judy. "Okay, bye."
Mitch abruptly ended the conversation without giving Trish a chance to talk to Judy, which irritated her no end.
"I'm going up there!"
"She doesn't want us up there, at least not right now."
"She's got what? A broken arm and leg! How's she going to defend herself against Lisa?"
"Trish, it isn't Judy who's got the broken bones, it's Lisa."
"What!" Trish couldn't believe what she was hearing.
"Apparently, Lisa was injured while trying to save Judy's life. She pushed her out of the way of a car and ended up with a couple of broken bones."
"I still think we should go up there."
"Why? Our plan is working. Lisa is protecting Judy instead of drugging her and now, Judy is in charge of everything. Driving, drugs, money. Lisa's dependent on the kindness of Judy."
Trish thought it over for a moment. "That's what has me worried."

Judy listened intently to the doctor's orders. Lisa was being released into her care in a few minutes and there was much to remember. Pain medication, elevation and ice were at the top of a long list of instructions. Keeping Lisa overnight for observation had been vetoed early in the process, with Lisa objecting loudest of all.
"It's only a couple of broken bones," she begged with Judy after the pain killers had taken effect.
"You were screaming in pain an hour ago."
"I'm better now. Really I am. Please take me home. I don't want to stay here. People die in hospitals and-"

"Okay, okay! Enough already geez."

"Take me home."

"If the doctor says you can go home, I'll take you home."

Hence the long list of "must dos", ending with the usual, "And bring her right back in if she runs a fever or loses consciousness."

"Thank you, doctor. I'm sure we'll be fine."

"Make an appointment for two days from now."

Affirmations complete, hospital personnel wheeled Lisa to Judy's waiting car and loaded her gingerly into the backseat. Judy fought the urge to panic at the thought of extracting Lisa all by herself. Everyone was smiling, biggest and brightest of all was Lisa. Oh, the miracle of pharmaceuticals!

When they arrived back at the condo, Lisa was giggly. Maybe it was her first encounter with pain medications. They hopped, hobbled, wiggled, and finally navigated the way to the bedroom.

"Thank goodness we have a big bathroom. How do people who live in tiny apartments ever go to the bathroom with a cast on their leg?" Lisa mused out loud while Judy gathered extra pillows for her arm and leg.

"I can tell you're in pain."

"It's okay," Lisa grimaced, "once I get my leg elevated, it should feel better."

"I'll get you one of the pain pills."

"I don't need pain pills. I need you to come over here and snuggle up to me and hold me."

"You're serious."

"One-hundred percent."

Judy had barely, and carefully gathered Lisa into her embrace when Lisa's tears began to flow. They started reluctantly, but quickly grew to sobs. Five minutes of soothing made conversation possible.

"I don't know why I'm crying," Lisa snuffled.

"Are you in pain?"

"A little, but that's not it."

"You've been through a trauma. You're allowed to cry after what you've been through."

"I feel like an idiot."

"No you don't. Remember, I'm an expert, and I'm feeling you right now and not one part of you feels idiotic."

"Have you been dipping into my pain pills?"

"No. Why?"

"You're rambling on and on."

"I can easily do that without pain pills."

"Oh yeah, I remember, you used to be a history teacher. Rambling on and on was an occupational necessity."

"I owe you my life," Judy abruptly changed the subject.

"What are you talking about?"

"You saved my life today."

"I did no such thing."

"You pushed me out of the way."

"So? I'm not dead. The only thing I saved you from was a thump or two."

"A broken arm and leg!"

"I just landed wrong," Lisa reassured and then grimaced.

"Can I help? What do you need? Another pain pill?"

"Are you going to be like this the whole time I'm laid up?"

"You think I'm being a mother hen."

"I think that I'm not the only one in this bed who's been through a trauma. I just want you to settle in a little. I'm going to be stuck in this bed for a while, in no shape to pursue our usual interests, and fussing isn't what I need."

"What do you need?"

"A diversion."

"How about a TV set?"

"No thanks. Have you seen the crap that passes for entertainment these days?"

"I have an idea. You may hate it."

"Try me," Lisa challenged.

"Well, this whole adventure today started with thinking about writing a book. Maybe we could work on it together?"

"You and me. Write a book. A mystery."

"Sure. Why not!"

"I don't think I'm that clever," Lisa demurred.

"Oh come now. Don't sell yourself short. I'm sure you have some great ideas and besides that, you'll be taking your pain medication. Who knows what will pour out of your brain then?"

"I think snoring will come out of that."

"Maybe. But could you just think about it?"

"I've never written before…"

"Well, we could always go back to the TV idea."

"Okay, I'll try writing. Anything but the TV! Where do we start?"

"I did get that book about poisons."

"What are we going to call it?"

"You mean the title? It's a little soon for that, don't you think?"

"Why?"

"I think we need to know what the book's about before we slap a title on it."

"We could do it the other way around. I've heard of authors that do that. How about, 'The Transvestite Who Played Hockey on Tuesday'? Now, there's a title."

Judy carefully extracted her arm from under Lisa's head and sat up.

"Where are you going?"

"To check your pain medication for possible hallucinogenic agents, and then I'm going to start dinner. What sounds good?"

"Lobster and steak and cherries jubilee."

"Macaroni and cheese instead?"

"Sure. And after you check the pills, can I have another?"

"I'll see."

"And can I have some paper and a pen?"

"Getting a head start?"

"Just need to pass the time."

After delivering paper, pens and one pill to Lisa, Judy left her to rest. She busied herself in the kitchen, and the mundaneness of the tasks helped her to calm herself and reflect on the events of the day. How hard it had been for Lisa to wrestle Judy out of danger and how easy it would have been to do the opposite. What had she said at the coffeehouse, something about throwing the intended victim under a truck? Okay, so a Porsche was a long way from a truck, but still… Floating through her thoughts were too many blurry details, the push, the fall, the snap crunch of bones. Judy stood closer to the stove to ward off a muscle-cramping chill.

An hour later, a slow oven had baked dinner to a maize brown and both Judy and Lisa awoke from naps. They ate in bed, not an uncommon ritual.

"What did you write so far?"

Lisa held up a page filled with question marks of every size, artistically drawn with no discernible pattern.

"Do that in oil or acrylic and you could have a new art career."

"I don't think I'll paint in bed, though. Too many other things to do."

Lisa was smiling again. Although it was a welcome sight to Judy, it would still be a long six weeks.

"So, who are we going to write about? That's another important decision."

"I suppose we should write about people," Lisa replied.

"I meant, are we going to write about gay or straight characters?"

"I hadn't thought much about it."

"Well, many people assume that if you write a story about lesbians, then you must be one. If we write about straight people, our readers will naturally assume that we're straight."

"Following that logic, everyone must think that Agatha Christie was a murderer, and Jessica Fletcher killed all those people in Cabot Cove."

"I thought you didn't watch TV?"

"For goodness sake, Judy, you'd have to hail from Mars not to know about Mrs. Fletcher!"

"Then there's the problem of commercial success."

"Money?"

"Right. If we write about gay people, the book might not be picked up by a mainstream publisher. Might not be picked up at all. So we have our first dilemma. We can write about straight people, take the money and run…"

"Or we can write about gay people. Did you stop to think that maybe gay people don't want to read a book where gay people kill each other?"

"For starting out innocently, this book thing has become complicated. I think we've met enough straight people to be able to write about them."

"And the love scenes?"

"There's going to be love scenes?" Judy asked, looking a little askance at Lisa. "Mrs. Fletcher never had sex and she was on TV for years."

"It's still something to think about. We need to keep our options open. Maybe we could go and get one of those books with Fabio on the cover."

"In the meantime, let's just settle for a couple of notebooks, some pens,-"

"And a plot." Lisa finished the thought.

"And a plot. So tell me, Lisa, why do people kill each other?"

"Lots of reasons, I guess. And sometimes for no reason."

"There's passion, jealousy, power," Judy began to count on her fingers, "And of course the biggest reason of all…"

"Ratings?"

"Money!"

If silence could be pregnant, the lull would have delivered twins by now.

"So," Judy forged ahead, "Let's begin there." She picked up the paper that Lisa had been scribbling questions marks on and wrote, "Murder for Money".

"That's the title?" Lisa sounded disappointed.

"Let's call it a working title. Of course, we can still work in all that other stuff: lust, sex, politics. This just gives us a jumping off point."

"How much money?"

"Will we make?"

"No. How much money would people kill for?"

"Gee, I don't know. You read in the newspaper every day about robbers killing for fifty dollars."

"That's rage and stupidity, not greed."

81

"You think we need more money in the plot?"

"At least hundreds of thousands. Maybe millions."

"Which means that one of our characters needs to be rich."

"Of course! Who on earth wants to read about poor people. Imagine that story line: get up, go to work, go home, go to sleep, get up, go to work, yak, yak, yak."

In spite of the gist of the conversation, Judy found herself chuckling.

"What's so funny?"

"Rich people can be just as boring as poor people. Get up, go spend money, go home, go to sleep, get up, etc."

"It kept Dallas on the air for years."

"More TV references?"

"People talked about it at the water cooler. Besides, it's *how* they spent the money that was interesting."

"Maybe our character needs millions then?"

"Millions and millions!"

Chapter 13

Mitch and Trish were still quibbling.

"How are we going to set up a sting if Lisa's on crutches?" Trish was agitated.

"I don't see any complications," Mitch tried to use reasoning to sooth Trish.

"Well I do! How is she going to take the money and run if she can't even walk?"

"The time frame is going to be about the same as I had figured at the beginning. It was going to take a few weeks to make this whole inheritance scam believable. Now, we have a six week window to work within."

"Six weeks! That's a long time."

"I'll keep you busy."

"How?"

"Well, first, you have to come and help me move into my new house. That was in the contract, wasn't it? You sell me a house, you help me move in?"

"What about the other house. Have you found a family for it, yet?"

"I haven't had a chance to talk to Mary."

"I think I can help you out. Don't bother her."

"You don't like her, do you?"

"She's okay, for a governor's daughter. I just don't see why you're getting her involved in the scam."

"She practically begged to be in on it," Mitch stretched the truth.

"I hope her mother doesn't find out."

"Mary keeps a lot of secrets from her mother."

"You don't mean, the "L" word, do you?"

Mitch looked up at Trish, hoping to avoid discussing Mary's personal life with her.

"The "L" word?"

"Yeah, you know, LIBERAL!"

"Nothing gets past you, does it, Trish," Mitch breathed a surreptitious sigh of relief.

Once the plans were made, it only took about four hours to move Mitch into her new, rustic surroundings. The house had a few quirks here and there, but it beat the heck out of a two room apartment. Moving the family anonymously was another story. Trish called in a few favors from a couple of her real estate buddies. They took care of the notification, the paperwork and the moving. It truly wasn't hard to find a needy family. They were relocated in one week. Mitch was impressed.

She was complimenting Trish while they were hanging out at the Lucky U before opening time.

"It didn't take you long to find someone in need."

"We have a nation full of needy people. You could probably give away one house a day for the rest of your life and not even come close to making an impact on the homeless."

"That's damn depressing."

"I know, but at least one family is thrilled and one other note of interest…maybe I'd better not elaborate."

"There's more to this story? What else is going on?"

"I'll show you. Let's go."

Winter's generous blessing of snow had reduced the daytime traffic to a scattered brave few. Trish's Christmas gift to herself, a monstrous four-wheel drive SUV, plowed through the snow-packed streets like a tank. Her BMW was fine for summer, but to successfully drive around in the heavy snow, you needed an SUV. Getting to the house was easy. Sitting outside without attracting attention was the challenge.

"Someone's going to call the police on us, you just watch."

"This isn't going to take long."

"What am I looking for?"

"You don't see anything out of the ordinary? Look around."

Mitch exhaled slowly. She hated guessing games. The house looked the same, more or less.

"Had I known there would be a test, I would have studied."

"It's not your house that's interesting. Look on each side."

Mitch shifted forward in her seat to get a clear look. Then she looked at Trish and got out of the car.

"Where are you going?"

"I just getting some fresh air."

"Need help?"

"No, I've been breathing on my own for quite some time," Mitch said as she walked closer to the house. What seemed to be fresh new For Sale signs decorated the homes on both sides of hers. She started toward the front door.

"What are you doing?" Trish called from the car.

"Asking directions to Mildred Schoenberger's house."

"I've never heard of Mildred Schoenberger."

"Me neither."

Mitch sauntered up to the house, at least as much as anyone could saunter in a foot of snow, and rang the bell. In a moment, just as the prickly mixture of cold air and cold feet were making Mitch question her judgment, the door swung open soundlessly. Hesitant smiles were exchanged.

"Can I help you?" the woman inquired.

"Yes, ma'am, I'm lost. I think I'm lost anyway. I'm looking for the Schoenberger's house. Is this it?"

"No, I'm afraid not."

"Do you know if they live on this street?"

"I wouldn't know," the woman explained pleasantly, "We're new to the neighborhood ourselves."

"Well, isn't that nice. I guess Mildred, that's my friend Mrs. Schoenberger, gave me wrong directions," Mitch put on her best helpless expression. "She said Mockingbird Lane."

"This is Meadowlark Trail Drive."

"There's my mistake right there, Meadowlark, Mockingbird, I just got my birds mixed up. I'm so sorry to bother you. Congratulations on your new home."

"Thank you. Have we met before? You look familiar."

"I've been around the block a couple of times. You probably just saw me out the window. Have a nice day," Mitch called over her shoulder as she trudged back to the car. Trish had left the motor running and they drove three blocks in silence. Trish pulled over near a park, with deserted swing sets that looked like giraffe skeletons in the snow.

"You haven't said a word. Are you okay?"

"Not really."

"So talk to me. You seem upset."

"Let's take a walk."

"It's ten degrees."

"The fresh air will feel good."

Three hundred paces later, they arrived at the playground. Mitch sat on a bench.

"Are you upset with me?" Trish asked.

"Heaven's no. Come here and sit with me."

Trish complied, and Mitch put her arm around her shoulder.

"I'm so proud of you I could kiss you. Do you think Judy would mind if I did?"

"I just did what you asked."

"And you did a great job. Better than great. Super-great. Tell me more about the family."

"Okay, there's the mom, who you've already met. There's a dad and three kids and grandma, and one of the kids is in a wheelchair. They had been living in a trailer, the dad had to change jobs, and their medical insurance had gaps for a while. What else do you want to know?"

"Is the house going to be big enough? Do they need anything else?"

"I heard from my friends that they are a little short on furniture."

"So maybe they can get a gift certificate from Harry's House of Furniture?"

"I'll see that it's done."

"When did the houses on each side go up for sale?" Mitch finally got to the point that had been bothering her.

"About ten minutes after your family moved in."

"My African-American family."

"The house across the street is listing next week."

"I thought we got past all this in the 60s?"

"Some did. Some didn't. There will always be those who use their money to buy exclusivity. White neighborhoods, white schools, white churches. What part of that surprises you?"

"You didn't tell me if you thought Judy would mind if I gave you a big kiss."

"We better stick to hugs. I'm a one-woman woman."

"That's what I love most about you."

"Are we about done out here? I'm freezing."

"How much are the homes selling for on each side?"

"A lot. Right now, anyway. Why?"

"Watch the price for me, would you? When they turn into bargains, if they do, let me know."

"You're thinking about playing Monopoly on Meadowlark Trail Drive?"

"The thought had crossed my mind."

As if on cue, Trish felt a vibration just below her waist. It was her pager.

"I don't like it when it beeps," she said. "It goes squawk, squawk, squawk"

"If anyone ever asks, I'll be sure to tell them that you prefer vibrators."

"Enough out of you! Let's go back to the car. I have to make a call."

Trish took the lead, but Mitch drifted through the snow. By the time she got to the car, Trish was handing the phone to her.

"It's Dan."

"Dan?"

"Dan Rojas, your financial planner. I've already talked to him. It's your turn."

Mitch listened more than she talked. An "uh huh" here and there punctuated the conversation. She disconnected the call and looked at Trish.

"Good news, don't you think," Trish said.

"Good news," Mitch agreed.

"It's not every day that a portion of your portfolio doubles in value. Didn't I tell you that Dan was good!"

"Dan is good."

"You did have part of your money in that investment, didn't you?"

"Well, no," Mitch said.

"You didn't have your money in it?"

"I didn't have part of it in it, I had all of it in it."

"You mean to tell me that you just doubled your entire fortune? You had all of your money in that investment?"

"It seemed safe."

"Let's celebrate. Lunch is on you!"

They drove to the country club where Trish was a member and ordered appetizers of steamed clams and deep fried zucchini.

"Do you think it would be a good idea for me to invest some of my money in real estate?" Mitch asked as she waited for the food to cool off a bit.

"Not if you're going to give away every house that you buy."

"Well, can I rent them or make them available at lower finance costs?"

"You're talking about buying the properties and then holding the notes on them. Sure, you could do that. You won't double your money, but it would be a safe investment."

"So I could buy the bookends."

"The bookends?"

"The houses on each side of the first one, and then, what did you call it, hold the notes?"

"Right."

Trish continued to talk about real estate through most of the rest of their feast, which included every sort of culinary sin they could think of. Shrimp salad, pecan crusted veal, wild rice with cashews, apple pie with extra sharp cheddar cheese, coffee and brandy. The total bill was well over two hundred dollars.

"Wow! My total grocery bill for a whole month doesn't add up to this! Can you believe ten dollars for apple pie with cheese!"

"The cheese is probably imported."

"From the moon!"

"It didn't look green," Trish cajoled.

"Did you look real close?"

"I certainly hope you don't double your fortune every day."

"What's that supposed to mean?"

"You're grumpy as a bear without honey today."

"You're right. I've no cause to be cranky. I have more money than I could ever want, I have terrific friends like you and I have apple pie with green cheese. Why would I be grumpy?"

"I asked first."

"I'm preoccupied. It looks like grumpy and it acts like grumpy, but it isn't."

"What's got you so preoccupied?"

"I'm not able to affect real, substantial change."

Trish mulled this over while she drank brandy that was older than her. Mitch was lucky to get out for under a thousand at this rate.

"What kind of change do you want to make happen?"

Mitch closed her eyes, and described a vision.

"It would be houses, with gardens, and puppies, and oak trees, and patios with umbrella tables. And no one would ever need to be homeless again. A home for every person."

"And a car in every garage," Trish added.

"And a chicken in every pot."

The waiter was standing there when Mitch opened her eyes.

"I'm sorry madam, but we don't serve chicken pot whatever."

He didn't sound very sorry at all. Mitch asked for the check, but Trish waved it away.

"Just put it on my account, William."

"Yes, ma'am."

"I thought I was buying?" Mitch said as William walked away.

"Next time. So your vision is to eradicate homelessness."

"America is a great nation. If that's what we chose to do, we could solve the homeless problem tomorrow."

"And then you would tackle racism. Is America great enough to get rid of racism?"

"I think that America is great enough and smart enough and tough enough to solve the problems of racism and sexism and homophobia and every other ism you can think of. I just think we're too caught up in the daily grind to concentrate on the issues. If everyone were personally affected by all of these 'isms', it would be easier to improve things. But too many people are too far removed or too well insulated to see what goes on."

"And it's going to take all of us. You could double your money every day and buy a house a day for a year and still not even make a dent in the problem."

"There's got to be a way to leverage the money."

"Why don't you leverage your charm and good looks along with your money? With all of your assets, I think you could make headway with our new governor."

"I don't think so. She probably has her own personal fortune. You can't run for state office anymore without having a ton of money."

"Well, you won't know until you try. Why don't you call her up and make an appointment to talk to her. I've never seen a politician hang up on a millionaire yet."

Trish was maddening when she made perfect sense.

"Keep an eye on those other two houses for me, will you?"

"Your wish is my command."

Chapter 14

"Governor's office, may I help you?"

The greeting sounded worn out, the voice out of breath and the tone not very helpful. Mitch's stomach was too busy giving birth to butterflies to be annoyed or put off.

"Is the Governor available?"

"I'm afraid she's in a meeting."

"Why are you afraid?"

"Excuse me?"

"You said you were afraid."

"I'm sorry. She's not available."

"Why are you sorry?"

"Pardon me?" the voice began to sound exasperated.

"Well, maybe I'm a nasty person with a huge complaint. You wouldn't be sorry if that were the case, now would you?"

"Are you calling to complain?"

"No. I'm calling to see if the Governor is free for dinner."

"Free for dinner?"

"Well, free is such a relative term nowadays. I guess I should have said available."

"I'm afraid not."

"There's that fear creeping into the conversation again. Just sneaks right up on you, doesn't it."

"May I take a message?"

"Just tell her that Mitch called."

"Mitch who?"

"She'll know."

With that, the phone went dead in Mitch's ear. She had time to brew a whole pot of coffee and help Marge wipe down the bar before the phone rang. Mitch gave a quarter to Marge and answered the phone.

"Hello."

"My secretary was two minutes away from calling the police!"

"Why? Is something wrong down at the capitol?"

"No, but she thinks you're some dangerous nut crank caller."

"She's probably right. I've been nothing but trouble so far."

"And are things going to change soon?"

"Gee, I hope not. I just wanted to take you to dinner."

"Dinner! Tonight?"

"That's when most people eat dinner."

"I'm afraid that's entirely out of the question."

"Why is everyone so afraid down there?"

"Afraid?"

"No wonder you want to call the police. With that much fear, maybe you need a good therapist instead."

"My schedule is full."

"I understand it's short notice. I didn't expect you to clear your entire schedule for me."

"What did you expect?"

"Less problems, more dinner."

"I'm booked days, weeks in advance. You've no idea how important I am."

"Are you trying to impress or dissuade me?"

"You're not going to take no for an answer, are you?"

"You haven't said no, yet."

The governor paused, Mitch held her breath.

"Dinner won't work, ever."

"Lunch then?"

"Today?"

"That sounds nice."

"I didn't say I could make it."

"Did I happen to mention that, now that I'm a millionaire many times over, I might have more time to get interested in politics. You know, support candidates. Did I forget to mention that I doubled my money yesterday in an investment..."

Mitch took advantage of the silence to drink half a cup of coffee. It settled the butterflies.

"My politics aren't for sale."

"Then prove it. Have lunch with me today and *don't* solicit a contribution."

"I'll have coffee with you. Be here at 9:30."

"I won't come there. Meet me at the Millster. It's close to your office."

"I'll need to arrange a driver."

"It's two blocks away. I'll pick you up."

"I'm supposed to be escorted by my security people."

"I'll take good care of you, I promise."

"I'll meet you there."

Again, the phone went dead in her ear. Apparently, nobody at the governor's office believed in saying goodbye. Mitch finished her chores and was on the way downtown by nine-fifteen. She arrived at the Millster and breezed in like she was crossing an imaginary finish line. Blocking her path, and guiding her roughly against a wall, was one of the two gentlemen who had accompanied the governor to the Lucky U the first time Mitch and the governor crossed paths. Mitch stood stock still, putting up no resistance. One turned her to face the wall while the other looked on. The governor was nowhere in sight. The frisking could have doubled as a yearly doctor's physical exam. In some countries, she would have been technically engaged to this guy in blue. Satisfied, perhaps, he turned her back around and escorted her abruptly to a table where the governor was sitting.

"Thank you, Charles," Rebecca said as Mitch sat down and the bodyguard moved slowly away.

"Good morning to you, too," was Mitch's opening volley.

"I'm afraid it's standard procedure."

"Oh sure, they did everything but a blood test and a pap smear. I suppose I'll have to make another appointment for that."

"I'm sorry if you're offended."

"Between being afraid and being sorry, you probably don't have much time for feeling anything else," Mitch said as she smoothed her collar and sleeves.

"Do you want some coffee?"

"Sure."

The governor crooked a finger at Charles. He was a reluctant waiter.

"Our guest wants something, Charles."

"What?" he more or less sneered at Mitch.

It was tempting to request that he dance the tango with a rose between his teeth. Mitch's outer child prevailed.

93

"Just the usual."

"The usual?"

"They know me here. Tell them I want the usual. Should I write it down for you?"

He stalked off, and pushed three people out of line to place the order.

"Charming fellow."

"I'm here." The governor tried to get down to business. "What do you want?"

"Besides the *usual*, I was hoping we could talk, privately?"

"We have nothing private to talk about."

"Actually, I was hoping you would go on a drive with me."

"A pleasure cruise around town? I don't have time for that."

"How much of a pleasure would it be? You'd be with me." Charles brought the order and sloshed it in front of Mitch.

"He better keep his day job, he's got no future as a waiter," Mitch whispered loudly enough for him to hear.

Mitch sipped her coffee once she mopped up the spillage. It was rich and strong and had enough cream and sugar to qualify as a top ten artery clogger.

"I don't suppose you'll leave me alone until I do whatever it is that you want me to do."

"Spoken like a true politician. Actually, I wanted to show you something. But you'll have to get rid of your men. They've had enough fun for one day playing friskies with me."

"That won't be easy."

"You are the most powerful woman in the state, aren't you?"

"That's right."

"So, send them home. I'll bring you back to the capitol, in plenty of time for lunch."

"Where are you parked?"

"My handy dandy super duper four wheel drive Subaru is parked out back in the alley just in case I need to make a run for it. I park out there because you never know when a fracas is going to break out right here in this coffee shop! They could run out of coffee and all holy heck could break loose. Coffee cups flying through the air, whip cream

94

everywhere. You know how caffeine addicts get when they don't get enough espresso."

Mitch stopped her narrative. Rebecca was staring.

"I should have let my secretary call the police after all. You're out of your mind."

"I may be out of my mind, but at least I don't have bodyguards trailing around after me pushing innocent citizens around. You know," Mitch began to sound a little exasperated, "I've been nothing but nice to you and Mary and all you do is treat me like I'm the official state nudnik. I'm just asking you to take one itty, bitty drive with me. That's all."

"Give me a minute."

Governor Fairbanks stood and approached her two companions. She talked, they listened. They didn't like what they heard. They shook their heads, and looked like a couple of car toys that you see in the back window of people's vehicles. Wag, wag, wag. Finally, they walked out, got in their official state car and drove off.

"There, that wasn't so hard," Mitch said quietly.

"You have until eleven o'clock. Then, they're calling the police."

"Then let's get started."

Mitch grabbed a plastic lid for her coffee cup and led the way to her car. The day was still cold at ten, but the car heated up quickly. She drove carefully through the icy streets, not wanting to cause a major crisis by getting into a fender bender.

"You've lived in Colorado all your life?" Rebecca asked. After ten minutes, the governor seemed to want to talk, and Mitch, mildly surprised and caught off guard only momentarily, answered back.

"Yes, I have."

"Where is your family now?"

"Dead."

"I'm sorry."

"Me, too. How about you? Any family besides Jeff and Mary?"

"I have some distant relatives. My parents are dead as well."

95

"They must be proud of you."

"Some more than others."

That remark opened the door for another ten minutes of silent contemplation. Mitch parked in the same spot where Trish had parked the other day. She looked at her giveaway house and smiled.

"Where are we?"

"This is my house."

"You made me go to all the trouble to rearrange my schedule so you could show me your house?"

"Just keep watching," Mitch said.

At precisely ten-thirty, the door opened. The mother and handicapped child appeared and mom cheerfully rolled the wheelchair to the van parked in the street. They loaded up and were on the way without even glancing around to see Mitch and the governor of Colorado looking on.

"I thought you said this was your house?"

"Well, it is and it isn't. I don't live here, but I bought the house. See the houses on either side? I'm thinking of buying those as well."

"To live in?"

"No, I live in a nice cozy five room shack a little bit east of here. Not much to look at, but it has some land. I think I'll put in a garden in the spring."

"What about the house across the street. It's up for sale, too?"

"I heard that was going to happen. I might buy it as well."

"And what are you going to do with all the houses?"

"I think I'll make them available at low cost to poor people with handicapped kids."

"Are you finished bragging about your good deeds? I need to get back to the office."

"I didn't bring you here to brag. I brought you here to hear how you're going to use your power and influence to find a way to solve the homeless problem."

"The homeless problem?"

"That's right."

"In the United States?"

"I think you could start small, right here in Colorado."

"I'm not convinced that we have a massive homeless problem in Colorado."

"Maybe it doesn't seem massive, unless, of course, you're the one without the home. Would you like me to drive you to the places where homeless people spend their days?"

"No thank you."

"It's no trouble."

"No thank you!"

Mitch studied the governor's face, watching her grow paler with each passing moment.

"I'll drive you back to your office."

"Thank you."

"I thought politicians had to have strong stomachs."

"I just don't feel well."

"Do you want to go to the hospital emergency room instead?"

"No, just take me to the office."

"Okay."

As Mitch carefully negotiated the streets, the governor nodded off to sleep. Mitch was glad that her new car was so comfortable. She would have to thank Trish for talking her into trading in her Yugo. From the shock absorbers to the cushioned bucket seats, it was like driving a recliner through a cloud. Fifteen minutes later, just under the eleven o'clock deadline, she pulled up to the capitol and eased to a stop. Reluctant to wake the governor, she turned off the engine and sat still. Noise from the traffic that Mitch had no control over roused her passenger.

"We there?" she muttered, trying to summon instant alertness from deep sleep.

"We're here."

"Thanks for the ride," she murmured and tried to muster up the strength to open the door.

"I could take you back to the mansion. You look like you could use some rest."

"I'll be fine."

Mitch was unconvinced. She got out of the car and walked around to help the governor out of the car. As she opened the door, the governor slumped over and nearly fell out. Mitch pushed her back into the seat and said, "That's it, I'm calling 911."

"No, don't do that."

"Sorry, you're not in charge anymore. You're in my jurisdiction once you were aiming for a quick trip to the sidewalk. It's 911 for you."

Mitch used her phone to dial the number with one hand while she held the governor to her body with the other arm. She calmly informed the dispatcher that she had an emergency, remembered to mention that the *governor* was involved and gave their location. A total of thirty-four seconds elapsed before the response team showed up. Seven vehicles responded, and over a dozen professionals crowded around the scene, unceremoniously pushing Mitch aside. It was a welcome pushing. She went over to one of the ambulances and leaned against the bumper. Someone came over and asked her a few questions, and then someone else came over and asked her the same questions. After the third go around, it began to feel like an interrogation. Only a female paramedic was interested in how Mitch was feeling, since she had by now, gone a little pale herself. Her answer was drowned out by the siren as they carted the governor off to the hospital. They checked Mitch's blood pressure, asked her to come to police headquarters to give a statement and impounded the Subaru. After an extended police interview, she was delivered back to the Lucky U by the police. She would have to wait for the car.

"I told you that all that money would bring you to no good," declared Marge as she delivered a beer to Mitch.

"I'm a hero, haven't you heard?"

"Then where's your car?"

"The car is being examined."

"They impound and examine a hero's car?"

"They're looking for toxic fumes or carbon monoxide leaks or something like that. You know, the usual."

"Do you want to start from the beginning, or would that confuse things farther?"

"Further."

"Further?"

"You said farther. It's further."

"Who died and left you in charge of the language?"

Mitch felt nausea creep up and took another drink of her beer. It helped, a little.

"I was out with the governor…"

"On a date!"

"No, not on a date! We were having coffee…"

"Coffee with the governor! At the mansion!"

"No, not at the mansion. We met at the Millster."

"A coffee date in public with the governor?"

Mitch ignored the interruption. "We were talking about homeless people."

"You were bragging to her about how you gave that house away, weren't you!"

"I mentioned it as an example."

"Are you going to do that often?"

"It's a good example," Mitch defended.

"I meant, are you going to give more houses away? I could use a new house."

"You have this place! Who could ask for anything more."

"Another waitress would be nice."

"Do I look like an employment agency?"

"You don't even look employable."

"Do you have any wine?"

"You mix beer and wine you'll get a headache."

"Too late. How about a couple of aspirin with my wine?"

"Let me see what I can find."

"Just make sure it's good."

"You drink the coffee at the Millster and complain about my wine cellar."

"It's not that bad, Gee, I wonder…"

"What?"

"I wonder if the police checked the coffee at the Millster?"

"Sure would take the burden off of the health department."

"I can't remember if we drank the same thing."

"Why would it matter?"

"I didn't finish the story. The governor passed out."

"At the Millster?"

"No, in the car, at the capitol."

"You met at the Millster and you drove her back to work?"

"You don't miss much, do you?"

"It doesn't take the concentration of Kreskin to see the gaps in this story."

"I drove her to the house and then back to the capitol and she got sleepy and dizzy. So I called an ambulance."

"Sounds like you did the right thing."

"I was questioned, poked, prodded and given the bum's rush."

"You're an embarrassment to the governor because you're a lesbian. Get used to it. Be glad that they aren't arresting you for attempted poisoning."

"Aren't you the cheery one today."

"Just hope that you didn't leave your fingerprints on the coffee cup. I'm telling you, people hang for poisoning!" Marge admonished as she went in search of the aspirin.

Chapter 15

"Are you sure we should use poison?" Lisa asked.

"It's bloodless. Do you want to write a gory story instead?" Judy shifted her body around to check Lisa's reaction. She seemed dissatisfied.

"I don't think I have a bloody story in me. But isn't poisoning a little unpredictable?" Lisa asked.

"I thought you'd think the opposite," Judy stated, "that poisoning might be overused."

"As a plot line or in dosage?"

"Either one," Judy answered.

"What I'm getting at is, doesn't it bother you, for instance, that arsenic is so varied in its manifestations?" Lisa clarified.

Judy lapsed into a nodding silence, leading Lisa to assume that she was pondering the effects of rat poison. What Judy was actually contemplating was how many more big words Lisa knew besides manifestations?

"Well, doesn't it?" Lisa asked.

"Um, uh, well, I guess." Judy replied, distracted to the point of losing her train of thought.

"You read the symptoms to me. Remember? It could look like anything from arthritis to influenza to a heart attack. And then there's that old worn out ploy of the murderer taking little doses of arsenic to build up an immunity so that a lethal dose wouldn't kill him but everyone else goes under. Give me a break! Even if it works, who would take that risk, besides a madman. And I don't want to write about a madman."

"Who else commits murder?" Judy pondered out loud.

"It could be a greedy person, or a single act of passion. Couldn't it?"

"Sounds like an everyday occurrence could set it off."

"You know what I mean," Lisa droned, "I don't want to write about a serial killer."

"I think I understand what you're getting at. You want to write a story about a murderer who is generally an okay person but who makes a terrible mistake and could one day be redeemed, or at least understood and forgiven."

"Yeah, something like, 'The Accidental Murderer', or 'A is for Accident' or, 'The Cat Who Had an Accident'."

After Lisa's third mock title, laughter weakened them both. After recovering from the spasms, Judy looked at Lisa with a gleam in her eye and said, "I know what you want. You want a murderer with integrity."

"I do?"

"Sure. Almost any reader will be sympathetic toward a person of integrity. It's those scheming, slimy characters they hope get the gallows."

"Okay, so we only have one big limitation so far in who is going to be our murderer."

"We do?" Judy asked.

"It can't be a politician!"

Chapter 16

Mary and Mitch exited the elevator with bodyguard in tow. Mary hated the escort and hurried to the door of her mother's hospital room. Named, all too appropriately, the Governor's Suite, it was the room used when visiting dignitaries and other important people became ill. It wasn't very often that its namesake was also its tenant.

Mary was prevented from going into the room by still another security guard. Mitch recognized him as the one from the Millster, the man of a thousand hands. First, Mary's identification was checked.
"Standard procedure," was his only words to her.
To help her out as she searched her purse, Mitch held the beautiful bouquet of roses that Mary had brought. She passed the test. Without even asking for anything from Mitch, she was rejected.

"What do you mean, she's not allowed in!?" Mary snapped, each word reverberating like a taut rubber band.
"She's not on my list," he growled back.
"Gee, that's funny," Mitch jibed, "You're on mine."
He sneered and took a step forward. Mitch held her ground and they were almost nose to nose. The roses were being mashed, and their thorns were helpless to protect them. Mary pushed him back and gave him his orders. "You go in there and inform my mother that I'm not coming in without her," Mary indicated Mitch.
After a reluctant shrug of the shoulders, he backed off and entered the room with his orders. Mary nervously began to search through her purse for something to fill the time. A mirror to check lipstick, a cough drop to ease her dry throat, a copy of War and Peace to read during the lull. As she was bringing her search for the elusive lipstick to a conclusion, the guard returned.
"You can both go in, but the governor doesn't accept bribes."
With that, he snatched the somewhat bedraggled bouquet from Mitch and unceremoniously dumped it in the trash.

Before Mary could react, Mitch gently guided her into the room. Her first thought was centered on the literally dozens of bribes that had found their way into her room. The place resembled a greenhouse, and in the middle of all the floral splendor reposed the leader of the state.

"Hello mother," Mary said.

"Hello Mary."

"How are you feeling?"

"Better, at least I was," she stated with a glance Mitch's way.

"I helped Mitch get past the guard because I thought you would want to thank her *personally* for coming to your rescue."

Rebecca turned her full attention to Mitch, and she seemed to be trying to form her thoughts into sentences. Mitch took the opportunity to be bold, as usual.

"I was just wondering," Mitch said as she perched on the side of Rebecca's bed, "are you sure you haven't been to a beauty spa instead of this hospital room. You look absolutely radiant."

"I've been right here all along," she tried to avoid eye contact, and distance herself ever so slightly from Mitch.

"You look wonderful. You have so much more color than when you were passing out in the car," Mitch spoke honestly and took Rebecca's hand into hers. A collective moment of silence ensued until Rebecca finally looked at Mitch. The cool detachment in her voice couldn't hide the rising color in her face and neck.

"I look like hell."

"Then hell's a glorious place with beautiful women. How are you feeling? Your pulse is a little rapid."

"Have you been reading my chart?"

"No, I've been doing my own examination."

Rebecca looked down at her hand. Mitch had taken her pulse as easily as any paramedic. She tried to free her hand from Mitch's gentle yet firm grasp without appearing to make a fuss. Finally, gradually, Mitch let her have her way and her hand.

"I'm tired. That's how I'm feeling."

"I understand. I'll tell you what. I'm going to go now, and let you and Mary visit. I'll come around again and visit when you feel a little better."

"You and Mary didn't come together to see me?" Rebecca blurted out the question.

"No, we just happened to meet in the lobby, mother!" Mary was back in the conversation.

"Oh, I see." Rebecca said, relieved.

"What a relief, huh!" Mitch laughed as she stood to leave.

"I can meet you downstairs for coffee?" Mary said hastily.

"You'll do no such thing. Stay here and visit with your mom," Mitch said with a wink which meant 'coffee shop in about ten minutes'.

The bickering ensued the minute Mitch left the room.

"Why are you going around with her?"

"We ran into each other in the lobby."

"I don't want you to be seen in public with her."

"Why are you so rude to her?"

"I'm tired."

"You weren't even going to see her. You didn't even thank her. Obviously you've had other well-wishers that you weren't too tired to see."

"I didn't want the news to get hold of the story of a lesbian bringing flowers to the governor."

"I was bringing you the flowers. She was just nice enough to be holding them for me."

"That's not what the guard told me."

"Where ever did you find that guy. I didn't know you could hire a gorilla in a suit. Is he housebroken?"

"He's good at his job."

"He sure showed those flowers a thing or two. I'll bet every rose in this hospital is shaking in their vases."

"What has gotten into you lately, young lady?!"

"This isn't lately, mother. You've been far too busy running for public office to realize that I'm not twelve years old anymore."

"So act like a grown up!"

"That's exactly what I intend to do. I'll be seen in public with anyone I damn well choose, but you need to think about two things."

"What's that?"

"It's not my bed she's sitting on, and it's not my hand she's holding."

Mary left the room and Rebecca lamented to no one, "Oh God, now what."

Mitch had found the coffee shop small and yet welcoming. She bought two coffees and was waiting at a table for two in the corner. Mary steamed in, and threw her purse down, nearly tipping over the drinks. Mitch had seen her coming and took precautions for typhoon Mary.

"I see the visit went well," Mitch joked, knowing Mary was mature enough to handle it.

"She's so maddening sometimes!"

"You want something to eat? I got you some coffee, but I'll spring for a meal as well."

"I wouldn't do that. My mother will think we're out on a date!"

"What happened up there?"

"She thinks I need to stay far away from you. And she's petrified to think that the press might get wind of your visit and the flowers."

"Those were your flowers."

"You know that, and I know that, but if somebody waves money in front of the bodyguard, they'll be your flowers on the news in two hours."

"You can't be serious."

"Someone would pay big money to link the governor to a lesbian."

"You know, I don't think this is about me and the flowers as much as it is about you."

"At the risk of sounding narcissistic, why?"

"I think a bigger risk would be if the press and your mother's political supporters found out that the governor has a gay daughter."

"Well, you can count on one thing for sure, she'd blame you for recruiting me."

"I could deal with that, but what else would happen, seriously?"

Mary wrinkled her brow, the effect added five years to her looks.

"There is a possible recall to consider."

"She wouldn't be impeached?"

"Only if she did something wrong."

"Wouldn't a recall need the same test?"

"Even if those two things didn't happen, she sure wouldn't get reelected."

"Four years of being governor would be enough for any normal citizen, don't you think?"

"She's not normal. Once you get politics in your blood, it's like a disease. You eat, sleep, dream, think, walk, talk, politics. It permeates your entire existence."

"And everything and everyone else takes a back seat. I bet you discussed that today as well."

"We touched on it," Mary smiled.

"And you blew in here like tropical storm Fairbanks."

Mary nodded, glad to be able to lose her cool with someone who could understand why, but her forehead remained on guard.

"What else is on your mind?" Mitch asked.

"Just something that happened while you were visiting. I can't remember the last time my mother blushed."

"She blushed?" Mitch tried to pretend temporary amnesia. It wasn't working.

"You didn't notice!"

"I guess I wasn't paying attention."

"I guess you were too busy gazing into her eyes."

"What's that supposed to mean?"

"What exactly are your intentions with my mother?"

"How exact do you want me to be?"

"Do you care about her, or do you do things just to unnerve her?"

"That's quite a question."

"Can you answer it?"

"I like your mother, despite her political leanings and I would like very much to nudge her into rethinking a few of her beliefs. But I don't go after married women, if that's your concern."

"She's not going to be married much longer."

Mitch was truly shocked by the utterance.

"What are you talking about?!"

"My dad's filing for divorce."

"Why!"

"He can't take it anymore, I guess. He doesn't like the person she's turned into. He married a sensible moderate."

"So that's why she's in here. Must have been quite the shock."

"That's not why she's here. She's just anemic. She fainted. She doesn't know about the divorce, yet."

"When is he going to tell her?"

"Later today. He thought he would break the news to her while she's in here, just in case she has a reaction."

"I hope he knows what he's doing."

"I hope so, too. It's going to get ugly."

"Are you going to be okay? Can I do anything to help you?" Mitch offered.

"Help me dig a bomb shelter?" Mary joked and then rubbed her face tiredly.

"I'll go get my shovel."

"Why don't you hold my hand like you did with my mother?" Mary asked suddenly.

"You remember a minute ago, when you asked about my intentions toward your mother?"

"Yes."

"She asked me the same thing about you not too long ago."

"What are you talking about?"

"Your mother told me that if I ever came within three feet of you, she'd break my arm."

"She did not?"

"She did too! She was scared to death of my influence over you."

"Did this just happen? Just now? Upstairs?"

"Oh, no. A while back, she came by the Lucky U one day, incognito, with Fido and Gruff by her side."

"Fido and Gruff?"

"Her bodyguards."

"Oh God, I'm so sorry."

"I'm not. We had quite a nice conversation. I even managed to talk her into having a glass of wine. Two, in fact. She was actually nothing more than a concerned mom. It was kind of cute and touching in a way, especially when she threw her wine down the front of me."

"You're telling me that my mom came to the Lucky U in disguise, promised to break your arm and threw a glass of wine on you and you still came to see her in the hospital?"

"Call me irrepressible!"

"Can I just think of you as a friend instead?"

"An improvement! Let's go before I need surgery to extract my body from this chair."

Mitch headed home to relax and take stock of the day's events. She wasn't on the news, that was good. She stretched out on her couch and watched TV late into the night. All of her new possessions, and her new run down house, while very nice to own, still didn't bring half the joy of meddling in the affairs of the governor, so to speak.

"So she blushed again!" Mitch said to no one.

The next morning dawned clear and bright. Cold as hell, but at least you could see the sun. Mitch ventured bravely to the hospital, as if invisible strings were pulling her there. She couldn't fight the urge to go, and found it pointless to resist. Gruff was standing guard today. Fido must have been soaking his paws. Once again, the list was checked. Once again, Mitch wasn't on it.

"Just go in there and tell her I'm here and if she doesn't see me, I'll start sending roses to her until the press can't help but notice."

He disappeared with the message and even before Mitch could look around for an empty chair, he was back.

"You got five minutes."

"I'll use it wisely."

Mitch tentatively peered around the curtains, feeling suddenly intrusive.

"I don't like threats," was today's greeting.

Mitch looked at her for a moment and then stated the obvious, "You've been crying."

"What do you want?" she snapped.

"I want to know why you've been crying. Maybe I can help?"

"You! Help? I don't see how!"

"I'm a good listener. Go ahead, try me," Mitch said as she took her now usual seat on the side of the bed. It was all she could do to keep from taking this distraught woman into her arms to ease her pain.

"You're not going to hold my hand again, are you!" she recoiled.

"Only if you want me to."

"Why would I want that?" she asked sharply.

"Why do you blush?"

"Why do you ask so many damn stupid questions!" she blurted out and then began to cry again.

Mitch retrieved the nearest tissue box and handed several to Rebecca. She said, through her tears, "What's the matter, haven't you ever seen a governor cry before."

The question so caught Mitch off guard that she couldn't think of a decent reply. Finally, she explained, "Before I met you, I'd never seen a governor do anything, I mean, in person."

"Well, you must feel so complete now. Your enemy is vanquished before your eyes."

"You're not my enemy," Mitch argued back, reaching out to hold her hand again.

"Don't start with the hand holding."

"Yes, Ma'am," Mitch heard but did not obey. Her hands took their own course, and were holding Rebecca's hands. The Governor didn't seem to mind.

"What's going on?" Mitch coaxed gently.

"You're going to read about it in the newspapers anyway. My husband is asking for a divorce."

"Oh gosh, that's too bad," Mitch did her best to act surprised. The Oscar would go to someone else.

"You already knew."

Mitch shifted uncomfortably and then stood and walked over to the window. The view was depressing, overlooking

110

nothing but other buildings, apartments for medical students.

"Mary told you, didn't she."

"Only yesterday."

"Sounds like we found out about the same time."

"It's not very good timing on his part, is it," Mitch observed.

"At least it's not in the middle of an election."

"Be thankful for small favors, I always say."

"If this is your idea of being helpful, it's coming up way short."

"Sorry, I guess for one brief moment, I thought you'd be more interested in saving your marriage than your governorship."

"Not that it's any of your business, but my marriage has been over for quite some time."

"Were you ever in love with him?" Mitch wondered out loud.

"You ask a lot of nosy questions!"

"I figure when you're tired of me and my questions, your bodyguard out there will be more than happy to bounce me down a couple of flights of stairs."

"Why exactly are you here?" Rebecca asked, losing patience.

"I was worried about you. I was drawn to this place. I was pulled toward you by forces I can't comprehend."

"You came here to lobby me."

"About what?" Mitch asked, truly stumped.

"Let's see, what would it be today. Medical care for the poor, more money for medical research, a boost to the hate crimes bill?"

"That would all be great. Which one are you going to do first?"

"None of it."

"I think you'll do what's right in your heart."

"I'm a tough-minded conservative Republican."

Mitch came back over to the bed and sat back down. Rebecca stood her ground, so to speak.

"If that's supposed to scare me, I have to go now and buy a pair of boots so I can shake in them."

111

"I'm not trying to scare you."

"Then what are you doing, besides practicing your blushing, again."

"I'm not blushing!"

"Rebecca, you are such a beautiful shade of crimson that the roses are jealous."

"Stop teasing me."

"I'll stop when you stop."

"I'll have you thrown out."

"Okay."

Before pausing to consider the repercussions, Mitch leaned forward and kissed Rebecca. She kept things soft and gentle, giving Rebecca plenty of room to back away. She didn't. When Mitch pulled back, she expected just about anything, a good slapping, a call to the guards, disgust. What she saw was a composed, calm governor.

"Are you quite finished?" Rebecca asked, with no discernible tone in her voice.

"I'm sorry. I lost my head."

"You have a very unique lobbying technique."

"If you think my lobby is unique, you should see the rest of the building sometime."

"I've seen quite enough of you today. You'll need to leave now. I have a contingent of supporters coming in a few minutes. It probably wouldn't be good to have all of you here at once."

"You're right. I'd never want to put you on the spot. Thank you for your time."

"Goodbye."

Mitch walked out of the room on knees that were sending signals of betrayal. The waiting area was buzzing with activity, at least thirty people were packed into the hallway. Mitch could almost taste the excitement in the air. Meeting the governor was a pilgrimage for this group, and they divided their time between congratulating each other and fixing their hair. Every person had a bible, and Mitch walked out of the way as inconspicuously as possible. She ran into Mary by the elevator and grabbed her by the arm.

"We need to talk," Mitch said.

"What's wrong? Can't it wait?"

"No, trust me, it can't. Let's go down to the coffee shop."

"You've been in with my mother. What happened?"

"I'll tell you when you're sitting down."

They ordered their coffee and found a table in the back of the room.

"Okay. I'm sitting. What happened?"

"I went to see your mom, and she figured out that I already knew about the divorce."

"She knows we talked."

"I tried to act surprised. There's just something about your mother that totally disarms me. I hope it isn't awkward for you."

"How can it get much more awkward between my mother and me."

"I'm getting to that. And then, of course, we exchanged words. You know how it goes with your mom and me."

"You two don't see much eye to eye. I'll go up and see what I can do."

"There's more. She's got other visitors anyway. About thirty people with bibles and perfect hair."

"I know the group you're talking about. They're here to lobby her to veto the hate crimes bill. I think she's going to cave in on that one."

"I guess we can only hope for the best."

"Is that it?"

"Not quite."

"Well, what else happened?"

"I kissed your mom."

"Like, a friendly hello?"

"Well, it wasn't hello."

"A friendly goodbye?"

"Well, I did leave soon after…"

"What are you saying?"

"I'm still speaking English, aren't I!"

Mitch hadn't noticed that she had raised her voice until a table full of people turned to look.

"Did she kiss you back?"

"Gee, I'm not sure. Things happened so fast. One split second I was kissing her and the next, I wasn't. But she

113

was nice and polite about it. It was just that, after all, a nice, polite kiss. Nothing intense, for her, I'm sure, at least."

"You don't need to go on. I get the point."

"I know you're upset, and I know you have a right to be. Do you want me to go back upstairs with you?"

"No, you've done enough for one day."

"You know where to find me if you need me."

A stopwatch could've verified that Mary reached her mother's room in record time. Thankfully, the governor was alone, having dispatched her visitors. It saved Mary the trouble of throwing them out herself.

"What's new, mother?" Mary asked with an edge in her voice.

"It's been a busy morning," she replied, somewhat upbeat.

"So I've heard."

"From who? Oh wait, don't tell me, you ran into that dreadful Mitch woman again. Why on earth did you tell her about the divorce!"

"She's a friend. I confide in her. She confides in me. Need I say more!"

"And that gives you a right to tell her about our family business."

"She's a good listener. Maybe you'd care to tell me what else she's good at?"

"Obviously talking too much."

"You two were kissing?"

"She kissed me. She did it, I didn't."

"And that's all?"

"I was polite."

Mary watched her mother for a moment and then quite unexpectedly, began to laugh.

"What's so funny!?"

"I don't believe this."

"What don't you believe?"

"First you're holding hands and then you're blushing and now you're kissing. All within the space of uh, let's see," Mary looked at her watch to make her point, "twenty-four hours and daddy isn't even out of the picture yet!"

114

"It isn't like that at all. She's a very forward woman. She took my hand, she had the advantage. I wasn't about to struggle and make a fuss. I'm trying to be very modern about all of this."

"Why didn't you call the bodyguard in here to protect you?"

"Because it wasn't necessary. I had the situation well under control."

"Yeah, you were polite, I heard."

"I can't help it if the woman is attracted to me. Some women are just that way."

"Some women are just that way?"

"That's right."

"Well, you know what mom?"

"What?"

"I'm that way, too."

Rebecca didn't say anything for a moment, and then, like any true politician, summed up the discussion. "This has been quite the day. My husband wants a divorce, I get kissed by a lesbian, my daughter comes out of the closet herself, and it isn't even noon yet. What else could possibly happen today?"

Not known to her, her question was being answered by a hissing and clicking sound in the building across the street.

Now that Mitch was a woman of leisure, the passage of time was all relative. In spite of the fact that Trish was still counting the days, minutes and seconds until Lisa's casts came off, things were calm. The legislature was in session, Mary was out of the closet, if only to her mother, and Mitch spent most days being helpful around the Lucky U. She finally cajoled Marge into letting her do the floor mopping chores. It was a fight to the finish, but Marge surrendered in three days. So just about every morning, Mitch was swabbing the deck of the Lucky U while Marge rested in her back office. The stocking of the bar was Mitch's new hobby as well, and she learned quickly how unnecessary her weight machine had been. She built up plenty of muscle wrestling cases of liquor to the bar, and kept good count for the inventory. In return, Marge let her have one

115

day off a week. It was on this day that the call came in about 6 a.m. Mitch grumbled, and answered the phone in a stupor. If it was anybody but God, they were in trouble.

"Mitch, it's Mary."

Okay, God and Mary.

"What's up?"

"There's a situation down here."

"What's a *situation*?"

"A problem."

"And where is here?"

"Here at the mansion."

"Okay, there's a problem at the mansion. I'm with you so far."

"You should know about this."

"So tell me."

"Not over the phone."

"Come to the U."

"You'd better come down here instead."

"I don't think that's such a good idea," Mitch was up and looking at herself in the mirror. If it had a voice, it would have laughed at the sight. "Your mom has seen about enough of me for one lifetime."

"This concerns her, too."

"Let me see if I'm understanding this. There's a problem down there and it concerns both me and your mother?"

"That's right."

"Okay, I'll be there. It's going to take a while. I need to shower and shave."

"Hurry."

"One more thing, do I need any password to get past Fido and Gruff?"

"I'll be here when you get here."

Mitch took extra time in spite of the urgency in Mary's pleas. After all, you can't go to the mansion looking like hell. She showered and shaved as promised, and then dressed in one of the suits that Mary had picked out for her. She looked like the proverbial million bucks. Rush hour traffic was a nightmare, and she was running about thirty minutes later than if she had gone down in her jammies. True to her word, Mary was waiting at the gate.

"Good morning, Mary."

"Your opinion will change when you hear this news."

"Is breakfast ready?"

"You can eat at a time like this?"

"I'm starving. Does your mother know that I'm here?"

"No. Not yet. Not exactly."

They walked through the mansion's lower rooms. It was a spectacular home, with furniture and artifacts dating through the history of Colorado.

"Where is she?"

"In her office."

"I thought her office was at the capitol?"

"She works all the time. She has an office in the capitol and an office here in the mansion. If she had a summer home on the moon, she's have an office there as well."

Mitch heard Mary's inner child loud and clear, but made no remark. They didn't seem to be on the best of terms after the hospital visit.

"Do you want something to eat?"

"Maybe I better see your mom first. I'm still confused, does she know I'm here? Does she know why I'm here, because I still don't."

"She knows I called you and asked you to come down. She knows why you're here and I know why you're here."

"So the only person who doesn't know why I'm here...is me."

"That's right."

"So, why am I here?"

"I'd better let my mom tell you."

"What kind of a mood is she in?"

"She's angry at you, angry at me for calling you, and she still thinks she can handle this all by herself."

"And whatever it is that she thinks she can handle is what I don't know about yet?"

"That's right. I think you understand the situation. Let's go."

With that faint call to battle, Mary led Mitch down a corridor. She knocked on a door and then went in without any pause. Rebecca was sitting behind a massive oak desk.

It was meant to intimidate. It was working. Mitch had promised herself that when this moment came, if it ever did, she wouldn't be in awe of the surroundings. She would stand firm and aloof, just like any common, ordinary citizen had the right to do in front of elected officials. However, the sheer splendor and magnificent decor made her gape in silent wonder. Without looking up from her work, Rebecca said, "I told you not to bring her here."

"She deserves to know what's going on. Maybe she can help."

"I asked Mary to leave you out of this."

Still no eye contact, which was okay since Mitch hadn't quite gotten her mouth shut.

"I don't see how that's possible, Mother!"

"It would have been possible if you hadn't interfered."

Mitch felt like she was at a verbal tennis match, and chose to sit in one of the leather wing back chairs nearest Rebecca's desk to wait out the point.

"I didn't tell you that you could sit down."

"I didn't ask."

"You don't ask before you do a lot of things, do you."

"I take my chances. Most of the time, things turn out well. Sometimes better."

"Leave us alone, Mary," Rebecca ordered curtly.

"But, Mother!"

"Leave us alone!"

Mary stood her ground for a moment, and then stormed out, slamming the door. The echo reverberated down the hall. Silence descended on the room as Rebecca rearranged the papers on her desk. Many CEOs and other powerbrokers used this tactic to unnerve people. Mitch closed her eyes and basked, instead, in the quietude. In fact, she may have nodded off, so early had been the call.

"Have you eaten?"

"No, I'm starved," Mitch answered without opening her eyes.

Rebecca punched a button on her phone and negotiated breakfast with her kitchen staff.

"You want a cup of strong coffee while you wait?"

"Sounds great."

Rebecca poured something in a cup that looked like it was made about midnight and handed it to her.

"I get up early to work. You want fresh coffee, you'll get here before five next time."

"I'll set my alarm clock back the minute I get home."

"You think this is funny."

"I don't know what 'this' is yet. No one has told me anything."

"You mean for once Mary didn't tell you something?"

"She thought you should tell me."

"I'll do better than tell you. I'll show you."

Mitch watched, her eyes following Rebecca, as she came around the desk with an envelope in hand. She gave it to Mitch without comment.

"What's this?"

"Let's just say that it isn't a belated Christmas card."

Mitch took her time opening the envelope. She wanted to appear unaffected, and avoid a paper cut as well. She pulled out the contents and in spite of her casual manner, said out loud, "Well, how about that! They even got my best side!"

"Yeah, how about that," Rebecca echoed.

In her hand, Mitch held a perfectly focused color snapshot of her kissing the governor.

"And you don't look so bad yourself, Rebecca." Mitch complimented.

"This is a *big* problem!"

"It was a little kiss."

"I'm being blackmailed."

"For how much? I'll foot the bill."

"That's what I like most about you, you're so politically naive."

"That's the sweetest thing you've ever said to me. I should have kissed you sooner."

"I'm vetoing the hate crimes bill."

As Mitch had enjoyed the relatively quiet couple of weeks, choosing to keep only a cursory watch on the legislative session, she and everyone else on the planet was aware of the hate crimes bill. It had been quite the argument. Those wishing to add the language 'sexual orientation' to the list

119

of protected classes were deemed the minions of Satan and promoters of homosexual behavior. Those wishing to stop the addition were called homophobes and right wing fascists. Just the usual bantering back and forth in a state set against itself. So, with much fanfare, the added language had narrowly passed the legislature, and the bill was coming toward the governor's desk like a runaway train. She could veto it, and there wouldn't be the votes to override, or she could sign it, and derail her future as a promising Republican politician.

"I had assumed all along that you were going to veto the bill."

"I wasn't going to. You look surprised."

"I'm stunned. I fully expected you to veto every scrap of gay friendly legislation that crossed your desk, particularly after meeting me."

"I felt that, although I thought the legislation was unnecessary, that it wouldn't be damaging to my career to sign the bill. Then, things began to change."

"What changed?"

"That photograph changed things. Now, not only am I going to be painted as gay friendly, but I will be targeted to be gay as well."

"Worse things could happen, although probably not to a Republican."

"And then Mary and I talked. She came out to me."

"She what?" Mitch again tried to act surprised. In a way, she was, to realize that Mary had mustered up the nerve.

"But you knew that already, too, didn't you."

"That she was gay or that she came out?"

"Don't get cute with me."

"I'd never think of it."

"So, all in all, it's been one very interesting couple of weeks."

"You're vetoing the bill," Mitch had followed the thread of the conversation that far.

Rebecca didn't answer.

"What if I could figure a way out of this?" Mitch offered.

"You, the most politically naive person in the state, find a way out of this."

"I bet I can."

"How?"

"What are you willing to bet?"

"What are you willing to lose?"

"Okay, here's the terms: I win, we have that dinner that you can't seem to find time to have with me. I lose, I stay out of your life forever."

Mitch assumed that these terms would be great news. She expected at least a gleam in Rebecca's eyes. When that didn't happen, she didn't know what to think.

"What's your plan?"

"Can we talk about it over breakfast?"

The members of the press corps buzzed louder than usual this morning. Press conferences had been few and far between lately due to the schedule, the health emergency and the relative newness of the office. No one complained, although they received a scant two hours notice. If the fact that the press conference was being held at the mansion instead of the capitol had any appreciable effect on the press, they didn't show it. In fact, they seemed happy to be served coffee and cookies while they waited. Several were still setting up their cameras and opening notebooks when Rebecca took the lectern at noon.

"I have two announcements today. Number one, I am going to sign the hate crimes bill into law."

Not unexpectedly, the members of the audience began to chatter, and Rebecca calmly smiled at them, waiting for the buzzing to die down. Hands shot up in the air, people wanted to quiz her on this decision.

"I'll answer questions after the second announcement."

Everyone quieted down and soon things were eerily silent.

"My second announcement is that there was an attempt to blackmail me into vetoing the hate crimes bill."

Again, the buzzing started, growing louder until it was slightly less than a roar. Flash bulbs popped and questions, shouted to the front of the room, dropped in the void. Rebecca stood her ground and waited. Glacially, the room returned to a manageable noise level. Mitch was so proud of Rebecca. She was handling this like the true professional that she was.

"I'd like to now introduce someone to you, who will discuss this blackmail with you. Ladies and gentlemen, Mitch Tanner."

As Mitch walked up to the lectern, the room was once again lit up with flashing cameras. The photographers wanted the best shots possible and waited until Mitch held her head up. Mitch caught on quickly, glancing around the room in a slow panoramic motion so that all could get a picture.

"Has everyone had a chance to get the picture they need?" A voice in the back yelled "No!" Mitch stood still another few seconds while the last of the flashes went off.

"In a way, that's what this news conference is all about," Mitch began her talk, shaking on the inside but calm on the outside.

"Those in public office are routinely followed around and photographed, not nearly enough during their campaign, it seems, and probably too much after their election."

The remark garnered a few smiles.

"Right now, in our country, we seem to be having a tug-of-war with ourselves concerning our press. We talk about good press and bad press and the liberal press, and what gets lost in all of our fighting about the issue is that those among us who have seen firsthand what it's like to have no freedom of the press understand how precious freedom of the press is. You get to ask tough questions, play the answers however you want to on TV, and use well-crafted legislation to gain access to all sorts of documents that were once hidden from public view. In return, I think that the public, for all its complaining wants only one thing in return. They want a sense of fair play.

A few days ago, I visited our governor at the hospital. As I was getting ready to leave, I gave the governor an innocent kiss. A genuine expression of affection that was photographed by an industrious individual. This person then decided to attempt to use this photograph as political leverage. I'm here today to tell you that this incident does not rise to this level of importance. I must confess that I'm just a kisser. It's just in my nature. I'll kiss anyone in the press corps right now to prove my point and allow anyone to take a picture of the event. Then, we can all make the ten o'clock news."

Someone shouted from the middle of the group, "We'd rather see the picture!"

"Actually, we've made copies for all of you. The staff will hand them out at the end of the press conference, but I have this copy to show you."

Mitch held up the photo that Rebecca had showed her so early this morning. They all craned to see it, and Mitch slowly displayed it to everyone in the room.

"Why did you kiss the governor," the question part of the conference began with a bang.

"It was a get-well kiss."

"On the lips?"

"Well, where would you kiss her?" Mitch asked back.

"On the forehead, maybe," someone else replied.

"The next time the governor is in the hospital, I'll kiss her on the forehead and invite all of you to take a picture."

"Did she kiss you back?"

"No."

"Why didn't you kiss her back, Governor Fairbanks?" Rebecca took control of the lectern again and began to speak to the questions.

"I chose not to."

"Did the blackmail attempt make you rethink the hate crime legislation?"

Finally, Mitch breathed a sigh of relief. They were on the topic that mattered most.

"It made me all the more determined to sign it into law."

"What about your supporters who say that this bill promotes homosexuality?"

"I'll tell you my thoughts on that subject. I know for a fact that there is no study anywhere that proves that hate crime legislation promotes homosexuality. There has never been one documented case where, after any legislative body enacted hate crime legislation, that straight people began to turn into gay people just to take advantage of the law. Not one straight person ever turned gay and then hoped they would be killed so that their attacker could get an added punishment. However, the law may serve to dissuade those who may be violent against gay people. The hate crime legislation, in reality, asked me to make a decision. Am I more inclined to protect gay people or violent people? I choose to protect gay people. Violent people don't need any more protection. They need to be stopped."

More questions cascaded through the crowd. Some about hate crimes, some about schools, some about highways, and one press corps member wondering if they were always going to have cookies at the press conferences. The conference turned somewhat routine. Mitch quietly edged her way to the door and left virtually unnoticed. Mary caught up with her about twenty paces down the hall, after Mitch had sat down on one of the many antique chairs adorning the house.
"You did great back there!" she bubbled.
"Thanks," Mitch said weakly, holding her head in her hands.
"Are you okay?"
"I'm getting a headache. A bad one."
"You look ghastly."
"It's a migraine. This onset is precipitously fast. I get about five minutes warning."
"What can I do to help?"
"I need to lie down and take my medication."
"Where's your medication?"
"Glove compartment, car." It even hurt to talk.
Mitch tried to fish the car keys out of her pocket but Mary had to help with the task. Then Mary went away for about a year and returned with two security people. One of them picked Mitch up like she was rag doll. The other must have been opening doors or parting the Red Sea. The trip was painful, every step agony, and they arrived in what she thought she heard to be Charlie's room. It had to be the pain, distorting reality. No one here was named Charlie. She was placed fully clothed on a bed and then they disappeared. After a decade, Mary came into view, with pills and water.

"What do you take and how many?"

"Two white. One red."

"Okay, I'll lift your head."

"I'll sit up. It's easier to swallow."

Together, they managed to get the medication down.

"You can't go to sleep fully clothed," Mary admonished.

"You just watch me."

"Let me at least take your jacket off while you're still sitting up."

Mitch didn't fight back. Her strength was sapped by pain. Mary stripped her to her waist with gentle efficiency. Then, she carefully guided her head down to the pillows. Starting with shoes and working her way up, Mary removed the rest of her clothes. The medication kicked in and Mitch dropped off to sleep. She would lie still for five hours in deep slumber.

Mitch stirred carefully, wiggling first one foot and then the other. They were still numb, as were her hands and arms. But she smiled in spite of her weakness, the searing pain was gone. Her mind was clear. The world was still spinning on its axis. She tried to raise her head, but then relaxed back into the pillow. It wasn't quite time yet, but she continued to wiggle her fingers and toes, and took delight in the action. She was free of pain, and it was a joyful thing indeed.

Air stirred in the room and she turned her head slowly to see if the angels were peeking in the door. It was Rebecca. Close enough.

"How are you feeling?"

Mitch hadn't tried speech yet. It took a moment for her to get the process back under control.

"Better," she finally managed.

"Are you sure?" Rebecca sounded unconvinced.

"Come here, sit."

The moment's hesitation wasn't lost on Mitch, even in her weakened condition.

"Come on. I - won't - bite," Mitch was getting the humor track back on line.

"I'm not worried about you biting. I'm worried that your migraine will come back."

"I'm not."

Rebecca came over and sat on the bed next to Mitch.

"Where am I, anyway?"

"You're in bed."

"I know that," Mitch was returning to normal. It felt great. Everything was beginning to function again. "But who's Charlie?"

"Oh, I see. You're in Charlie's Room."

"I thought your husband's name was Jeff?"

"It is."

"So there's a Jeff and a Charlie? Good grief, woman! What haven't you told me!?"

"This room is nicknamed Charlie's Room because Charles Lindbergh once slept here."

"Is that a fact?"

"That's a fact."

"So I'm in a famous bed."

"You sound unimpressed."

"I'd rather be in your bed."

"Don't even start. We've just managed our way out of one crisis. Please don't start another."

"How did the rest of the press conference go?"

"It went well. Most of the press didn't even bother to pick up the pictures we had made up. I guess if it isn't an exclusive, it's useless."

"I'm framing my copy."

"Do I even want to ask why?"

"It's the first time I ever kissed a governor. It was very memorable."

"Do your headaches always come on this fast? You had Mary scared to death," Rebecca changed subjects, knowing that Mitch would follow along a topic she was interested in.

"She was great. I'll be sure to thank her."

"She's not here right now. She is working at the center."

"So it's just you and me."

"That's right."

"Then can I ask you for one more favor."

"That depends."

"You're probably going to hate this."

"I'm sure I will."

"I listened to your speech in the press conference. I was very impressed. You've done the research. You understand the concepts. It was all very intellectual."

"Thank you."

"So kiss me."

"Kiss you?"

"If what you say is true, that no amount of hate crime legislation or other protections for gay people will turn any straight person gay, then you have nothing to fear. There are no hidden cameras, no press peeking in through the door, it's just you and me and scientific inquiry. This may be your last chance to conduct hands-on research. I'm too weak to fight back, too emaciated to respond and I won't even look."

With that, Mitch closed her eyes, and waited. She assumed that one of three things would happen. She would either feel Rebecca stand up and leave, the event punctuated by the now famous slamming of doors exit. Or she would succumb to the medication and fall back asleep, still giddy with relief. Or, and this she figured was about a quadrillion billion to one shot, the governor would actually have the nerve to kiss her. It happened in a second. It was there and gone. Mitch opened her eyes when she thought it was safe. Rebecca was watching her, carefully, with no discernible expression.

"And now, you know for sure," Mitch said, her eyes now brimming with benevolence.

"Dinner's in a few minutes," Rebecca said, in a voice as strange as Mitch's had been a few moments ago.

"I'm not staying for dinner."

"That was our bet. I owe you a dinner."

"Some other time. Some other place. Besides, we can't be sure that I've won the bet, yet. There could still be fallout and damage."

Mitch sat up, slowly easing her unwilling body to move. The sheets barely covered her, and they both realized at the same time that Mitch was naked. "Can I have my clothes back?"

"I'm not sure where Mary put them. Let me go and see what I can find."

"Thanks."

Rebecca left quickly, not even checking the nearest closet. Mitch stood up and checked for herself. Everything was still there, hanging up in perfect condition. She dressed after using the bathroom facilities and left the room. She didn't know the way out of the maze and Rebecca caught up to her in the hallway just outside the bedroom.

"I see you found your clothes."

"I thought I should dress before driving home."

"I don't think you should be driving in this condition. Please let one of my people take you home."

"I'm fine. I can get home with no problem."

"Are you sure?"

"I'm sure. Tell Mary that I appreciated her quick action. And thank you for being such a gracious hostess. You know, I only pass out in the best of homes," Mitch teased, well on the way to recovery as she went out the door.

"Drive safely," Rebecca said.

"One more thing," Mitch called from the sidewalk, "You're my hero, Governor Fairbanks!"

Chapter 17

"Who was on the phone?" Lisa called from the bedroom.
"Just the lawyer about the estate," Judy yelled back, using
volume to scrub emotion from her voice.
"What?"
Judy realized that most of her answer ended up in the oven.
"Just a second!" she hollered.
In the past couple of weeks, Judy had learned a great deal
about meal preparation for invalids. It had proven
cumbersome to go out with Lisa. Their visits to the
doctor's office had been a nightmare of planning and
execution. Going out to dinner was too much work right
now. One cast would have been manageable, two were a
gawky predicament. Judy had been thankful for Martha
Stewart and Betty Crocker to see her through these times.
She gathered together a main dish, a single rose and a
strong cup of tea to take to the bedroom.

"Another gourmet dinner? How do you do it and stay so
sexy?" Lisa said, obviously getting used to the attention
and loving every minute of it.
"Enough flattery already. Let's eat before it gets cold."
"Who was on the phone, Sweetie?"
"I'm Sweetie today?"
"I always call you Sweetie.'
"You never call me Sweetie."
"Today, I'm starting. Who was on the phone?"
"You forgot the Sweetie."
"Sweetie."
"The lawyer was on the phone."
"Is it good news? Is your money ready?"
"I'm not sure."
"You'd know if your money was ready. She'd be bringing
it."
"I think she just needs some more information. She's
coming back up tomorrow."
"I suppose she expects a meal."

"It'll give me a chance to try out my culinary skills on someone new," Judy bantered, noting Lisa's declining good humor.

"She just better not get used to it. You're *my* gourmet."

"I thought I was 'Sweetie'?"

"You're my everything," Lisa said with emotion in her voice. "Don't you know that by now?"

"We haven't been together even a year. How can you know such irrefutable truths?"

"Some things you just know. I know, for instance, that you're a lot smarter than me."

"What are you talking about?" Judy asked, as she felt her stomach begin to tighten.

"Everyone knows that."

"That doesn't make any sense."

"Of course it does. We walk into anywhere, a coffee shop, a bookstore, a restaurant; and everybody knows right away that you're the smart one. It's like ostosis or something."

"I think you mean osmosis?"

"That's exactly what I'm talking about. Osmosis, ostosis, only you would know the difference."

"I don't think there is such a word as ostosis."

"See, you're proving my point. There's no point in arguing with you. You're so smart that you can debate both sides of any issue and win, twice."

"I didn't think this was so much of an issue. I don't think it's a matter of intelligence. I think it's just more a matter of knowledge."

"You think I'm stupid."

"No, I don't think you're stupid. I never said you were stupid."

"Whenever we go anywhere, people look at you like you're a genius and they look at me like I'd be a good lay."

"Well, if it's any consolation, I'd trade places with you in a minute. I'd give anything if a whole roomful of people thought I was great in bed."

"For what it's worth, this roomful does."

"And for what it's worth to you, I know that you're a whole lot smarter than people give you credit for!"

Judy paused a moment and then looked deeply into Lisa's eyes.

"A whole lot smarter."

The following morning, the day when Trish was coming for a visit, it was snowing a typical Aspen, Colorado snowstorm.

"If it snows more than an inch an hour, she's out the door and at the nearest motel in six minutes," Lisa declared, moodily, to an empty room. Lisa's entire mood had become foreboding ever since she rolled over in bed that morning to find a note pinned to Judy's pillow.

It read, "Gone shopping, be back soon."

Lisa easily made her way from the bed to the bathroom to the kitchen. She saved her helpless act for a more appropriate time. She was sure to be back in bed when Judy returned, which happened right after Lisa had drowsed back to sleep.

"Are you awake already, Hon?"

"You've been shopping?"

Judy took the extra time to come to the side of the bed and kiss Lisa good morning.

"We're having company, remember?"

"She truly expects dinner?"

"It never hurts to be nice to lawyers."

"What are you going to cook?"

"I thought a turkey dinner would be nice."

"A turkey dinner! You are kidding? That's hours of work."

"It takes about an hour to start and then five or six hours to lay around in bed while it cooks."

"You've never made me a turkey dinner," Lisa groused, not willing to give in.

"I did so. What do you call that feast we had on Thanksgiving?"

"That's different!"

"How is that different?" Judy found this too amusing to be angry.

131

"Well, everybody cooks turkey on Thanksgiving!"

"So it doesn't count."

"You've just never cooked one out of the blue, for me anyway."

"So I'll cook another one next week, just for you."

"That's too soon."

"Next month?"

"With pumpkin pie?"

"You want pumpkin pie, you got pumpkin pie."

"And whipped cream?"

"And whipped cream."

"For the pie?"

"For whatever your heart desires."

Judy used her leverage to gently restrain Lisa. She kissed her forehead, around her eyes, and nuzzled her neck before Lisa worked her good arm out of the tender grasp of Judy. Instead of pulling Judy into an embrace, she pushed her back.

"You better go and get that turkey cooking. Otherwise, we'll be eating peanut butter sandwiches."

"Okay, just let thoughts of whipped cream keep you company."

Judy brushed Lisa's forehead with one more kiss and then went out to begin her meal.

The one thing you have to remember about turkeys is that you're bigger than they are. Judy had selected a sizable bird, twenty-two pounds naked. Simmering her own special blend of vegetables, nuts and herbs took about a half hour. Maybe it was longer, time seemed to slip by while she was cooking. It was certainly becoming one of her top ten things to do that brought enjoyment. Sex with Lisa had dominated the top spot for weeks until her chance encounter with Mitch and Trish, and while it had slipped considerably in the ratings, it was still enjoyable. She thought for a moment about the episode where she thought she had heard Lisa call her a horny bitch. Maybe it had been a dream after all. Since saving Judy from the collision, Lisa had been nothing but slavishly compliant, wanting more, not less, in the bedroom. Maybe wanting wasn't the right word. What was? Inviting, available, creative? Certainly, with two casts involved, creativity was very necessary. And while Lisa was on pain medication, Judy was the designated dispenser. If Lisa had been drugging Judy, where was she hiding the other stash?

Judy had only been cursorily nosy, and hadn't found any damning evidence. Maybe it was hidden in the kitchen? Pulling up a step stool she rummaged around the top shelf of her all-purpose spice cabinet.

"Looking for the secret ingredient?"
The interruption made Judy jump, and she had to steady herself before turning around.
"I can never find the sage," she explained. "What are you doing out of bed?"
"I came out here to apologize and beg for mercy."
"What are you talking about?"
"You don't have to cook a turkey for me next week. Or next month. Or even next year."
Judy got down off the step stool.
"Come here," she pulled Lisa close, in spite of the crutches. "I'm being a big bother!"
"No, you're not. What's on your mind?"
"I'm jealous of this lawyer lady."
"You don't need to be," Judy said, wishing it was the truth.
"But I am."
"At least I know it's jealousy. I thought for a minute that you just hated lawyers in general. You act like you were bitten by one."
"I think she's being pushy, barging in on us, expecting dinner. When was the last time you heard of a lawyer who made house calls, anyway. There's something that's just not right about this."
"My gut feeling about this, Lisa, is," Judy spoke slowly, stalling until a good explanation popped into her head, "is that she works for Texans."
"That's your best answer?"

"Who knows what her instructions are? Maybe it's all spelled out somewhere in the will. Maybe everything had to be handled a certain way?"

"She could use registered mail and save a bundle. And since part of that bundle will soon be yours, she could stand some advice on how to be a little more economical."

"Be ours."

"Beours?"

"Be – ours. The bundle will soon be ours."

"Isn't that sage?"

"I like to think I'm wise in these matters."

"No, I mean, isn't that a tin of sage on the counter?"

"Yes."

"But, when I came in, you were looking up there for it."

"I...was...looking for the old tin of sage."

"The old one?"

"I thought we had a little left that I could use up. Give the lawyer the old sage and save the good stuff for you."

"Now, that's a sign of true love," Lisa smiled and laughed. "Saving the good sage for me."

"Now, if you don't let me go and get back to my cooking, it won't even be peanut butter sandwiches for you!"

"Can I stay and watch?"

"Would that make you happy?"

"Very much."

"Then let me pull up a stool for you over there at the counter. How about a cup of coffee?"

"Love some."

Judy didn't blame Lisa for wanting to be out here. The bedroom could get boring very quickly all by yourself. As Judy cooked, Lisa brought up the subject of the book they were trying to write. So far, they were stymied in their creative process.

"We still haven't decided who we're going to kill," Lisa nearly whined.

"Let's kill a bully."

"Why?"

"Why not?" Judy countered, still wrestling the turkey.

"That's too easy."

"Let's kill a rich bully."

134

"How many bullies do you know that are rich?"

"Aren't most rich people bullies anyway?"

"How would I know?"

Judy was getting a slight headache.

"Well, let's suspend the discussion about the victim for a moment and talk about the process," Judy offered as she hoisted the turkey into the oven.

"You mean, the murder itself!"

"The murder itself," Judy nodded, glad that the hardest part of the dinner was on its way.

"You don't want gore."

"And you don't like poison."

"I don't mind poison, I just don't know what hasn't been used to death, no pun intended."

"So, we can't decide on a victim, and we can't decide on a method. What's left?"

"Motive," Lisa said, darkly.

Judy was too busy peeling potatoes to study the expression on Lisa's face.

"Revenge, for years of nastiness," Judy offered.

"That would mean we need to write about old people killing each other."

"A power struggle."

"Over what?"

"A corporation?"

"Too boring."

"I'm all out of ideas. What do you think people would kill for?"

"The only thing that matters, money."

"We already talked about this once, didn't we?" Judy said as she put the potatoes in a big pot of cold water. They would keep until it was time to boil them.

"I believe so. It was the one thing we could agree on. We wanted the killee to be very rich."

"The killee?"

"The murder victim. So we have this rich old coot and a bunch of people who want to kill him for his money. Hey, wait a minute. You don't suppose that's what happened to your Uncle Cleve, do you?"

"I don't think so, Hon."

135

"What if it was?"

"Then there's only one thing that I would ask of you?"

"What's that?"

"Give me an alibi for the night of the murder!" Judy said, as seriously as she could.

"How do you know the murder was at night?!"

"Are you sure you don't want to go back to bed?"

"Are you done cooking for now?"

"I will be in about ten minutes."

"I'll meet you there," Lisa agreed as she slid down off the stool and headed toward the bedroom.

Judy shook her head and mumbled to herself, "The Murder that Happened to the Person Who Never Was."

They spent the better part of the day in bed. It was less physical and more companionable than of recent days, but it was still enjoyable. Lisa was busy writing down ideas, notes to herself more than anything. Judy was silently going over good topics of conversation for dinner. She dropped off to sleep. Cooking was such hard work, but keeping one step ahead of Lisa, even on crutches, was proving even more daunting.

Sounds of tire-crunched snow put Lisa on alert. She roused Judy from her slumber.

"She's here!"

Trish, decked out in her best fake lawyer blue business suit disguise, arrived at Judy and Lisa's condo in the midst of a fluffy snowstorm. By now, three inches of snow had fallen, nowhere near a record pace but enough to make Lisa nervous about possible overnight accommodations.

Judy handled door duty while Lisa gathered herself together. The aroma of turkey had filled the condo, and it was a warm, welcoming smell. She could hear the murmuring of greetings.

"...something smells wonderful..."

"...let me take you coat..."

Further niceties were exchanged as Lisa made her appearance.

136

"Come in and make yourself at home," Lisa chimed in, sounding like a 50's sitcom mom.

"Hello, Lisa. Don't you look good!"

"Do I?" Lisa always knew how to coyly ask for more compliments.

"You look great, for what you've been through," Trish clarified.

"So do you," Lisa shot back.

Trish cocked her head a little to one side, not daring to ask for further explanation. This didn't hinder Lisa.

"This snowstorm must be awful to drive in."

"It's always a challenge. I just go slowly."

They walked together into the living room, Trish still holding tightly to her briefcase. She sat down on the couch and Lisa took up residence right next to her.

"So, you've had quite the accident. Judy told me all about it," Trish spoke first.

"Now I know what it's like to get totally plastered," Lisa smiled, enjoying being center stage in her element.

"Remind me to sign your cast before I leave."

"Honey, you can write a whole chapter."

"Would you care for a drink?" Judy asked.

"Oh, no thanks, I'll just hurry through this paperwork so the two of you can get to your dinner."

"Oh, but you're staying for dinner!" insisted Lisa.

"I am?" Trish looked from Lisa to Judy.

"Oh absolutely," nodded Lisa again, "so let Judy get you some scotch and you just relax until after dinner."

"Are you sure?" Trish directed the question to Judy.

"What Lisa says goes."

"Well, in that case, I'll have a cup of coffee."

"Cream or sugar?"

"A little of both."

"And how about some bourbon mixed in?" Lisa was getting creative in her own unique way.

"Oh, no. Can't do that. I'm driving."

"You were driving last time?" Lisa pointed out in her best wide-eyed innocent expression.

"I have a longer drive today."

"All the way to Texas?" Lisa asked, lips parted coyly. It was a sign. Trish read it like a book.

"Texas?"

"That's where the ranch is, right?"

"That's right. The estate is being settled in Texas."

"So you came all the way up here from Texas again?"

"Well, actually, yes and no."

"Well, which is it? Yes or no?"

Judy was watching Trish for some sort of clue to help her out.

"My law practice is in Texas. But I also have a home here in Colorado. So there comes a time when I sort of get thrown work in Colorado because everyone knows I have a little place up here."

"So you combine business with pleasure?" Lisa asked pointedly.

"Whenever I can get away with it."

"So are you going home or back to Texas after tonight?"

"I'm going to Denver. I rent office space there as well."

"Are you sure this is legal?"

"I wouldn't be doing this if it weren't legal," Trish lied like an expert. She had definitely been around Mitch too long. "And I'm glad that since my last visit, you've been thinking about things. I was hoping you had more questions, like for instance, the date of death values that you were wondering about. The personal representatives have been going through those, one by one. It's interesting that although some of the stocks are being liquidated, the stock brokers still go through the process of opening up new accounts just to run the money through their books. It's an awful temptation to just leave the money where it is, but that can't happen in this estate. So, you need to make phone calls, and provide tax payer identification numbers and all sorts of odds and ends. Then you need to take the liquidated assets and put them in an account that you've opened with the estate's tax payer identification number, which must be procured at the beginning of the process, because if you use someone else's tax payer identification number, well, that screws up the entire process, so then everything must be perfect for the accountant's tax returns.

Understanding which assets have interest and which assets have dividends is a whole other kettle of fish. But it all needs to be accounted for, and any slip up would delay the process even further. It's quite tedious and boring, but someone's got to do it."

Trish stopped to take a breath. She had obviously been doing a little bit of homework. It paid off. Lisa was ready to talk about the weather now. The snow had tapered off and Judy went to set the table, trusting Trish to banter about the weather as easily as she had about estate probates.

"You sure are smart," Lisa breathed the remark to Trish when Judy was out of earshot.

Trish looked back and smiled, "I sure am."

They walked arm in arm to dinner, and Trish shut down all talk of business as they ate. She wanted to hear all about Aspen, as if she had never been there before, and Lisa talked like a travel agent on commission from the city. The meal was perfect, but Trish ate out of habit. Every time she looked at Judy, she lost her appetite. It was either true love, or the flu. She knew which it was, and she forced herself to eat. Only after coffee and pie in the living room did Lisa get to ask more nosy questions.

"The paperwork you brought today must be very important!"

"It is," Trish agreed, pulling one single sheet of paper out of her briefcase.

The effect was humorous.

"That's it!" Lisa said, trying to get a good look at the document.

Trish had practiced this for days, and now put on her most serious pretend-lawyer expression.

"You know, when you're the personal representative of an estate, you must sign your name dozens of times, maybe a hundred or more by the time you're done. Being a personal representative is a thankless task. But for you lucky heirs, you don't need to do all that much. You remember a while back when I came up here to get your social security number?"

Judy nodded, quite caught up in the act.

"Well, what has to happen is that you need to sign this piece of paper which generally states that you understand that your name and social security number are going to be provided to the IRS, and that they are on notice, if you will, that you are going to inherit money. It's a serious step, that's why I like to do it in person."

"It doesn't seem like a big deal to me."

"Well, of course it doesn't. You're a fine, upstanding, law-abiding citizen."

"So I just sign the paper?"

"That's right."

As Judy signed her name, Lisa was still puzzled.

"Why do you have to do this in person again?"

"I don't have to do this in person, but if Judy wasn't in good standing with the IRS, it's something I would need to know. People tend to confess their sins to me in person more willingly than over the phone."

"I see."

"If you had done something wrong, would you confess to me over the phone?" Trish locked eyes with Lisa.

"I wouldn't know. I've never done anything wrong."

"Obviously, neither has Judy. So, I'm done here. There will still be some time before the estate is settled. I hope you both know that."

"How much will there be?" Lisa couldn't resist asking.

"Weeks."

"No, how much money will there be?"

"I don't know yet," Trish replied, the most honest answer she'd given all day.

"It's still a secret, even from Judy?"

"It's still a mystery to me. And even if I knew, I still wouldn't be at liberty to say."

"But it must be a lot, it's taking so much time."

"I've seen estates worth $100,000 take a year or more to settle. It isn't the money involved, it's the assets that take time to sort out."

"We trust you," Judy cut in, wanting the questions to be gone.

"Do me a favor, Judy, walk me to my car."

It wasn't a question, it was an instruction from a counterfeit lawyer.

"Be back in a minute, Hon," Judy reassured Lisa as she gathered coats together and walked out behind Trish. Once out of earshot, Trish asked, "Is there a spot where we can be unobserved, just for a minute?"

"Over here," Judy pulled her into a space between the garage and the yard. "Why?"

"Because," Trish said as she pulled her close, to neither frighten nor leave in doubt her next intention. Then, she kissed her gently, not knowing what to expect. Would there be a hardness that had haunted her thoughts on the drive up? A pulling back? Judy answered with surprising openness. Trish shivered, though not from cold, but instead an instant warmth that spread through her body.

"I thought I'd catch you off guard. I guess I was wrong." Trish said.

"Kiss me again, now that I'm ready."

Trish, willing and more than eager to comply was called up short by a voice in the distance.

"Judy, Judy, are you still out there? Is everything okay?"

"Everything is fine, Sweetie."

"I'll go now," Trish said, "but I'll be back."

"Don't come back. She already suspects something."

"You're not safe."

"She's the one in the cast, remember? Go now, and don't come back until this is over."

Judy walked away from Trish, not even trusting herself to look back. Lisa was still at the door, peering out.

"Thanks for holding the door, Hon. Let's go in before you freeze."

"I thought you might have slipped on the ice."

"I'm fine. She just had a couple more things to make clear to me."

"About the estate?"

"Uh, well, let's just say that she gave me an inkling of what's to come."

"And is it good?"

"Good doesn't even begin to describe it."

"Tell me about it in bed."

"Okay, but do we have something for a headache?"

"You don't feel well?" Lisa asked, concerned.

"My head is pounding and my knees are weak."

"Sounds like the flu."

"I think I'm just tired."

"And well you should be," Lisa was more than agreeable. "You cooked all day for some upstart hotshot overpaid toady lawyer who seems to specialize in running up an expense account!"

Judy ignored the diatribe as she sorted through the medicine cabinet. "Someday I should really clean this out," she muttered to herself. There was stuff in here dating back to who knows when. She opened three different bottles of aspirin, only to discover little pink pills that weren't chewable cherry.

"Hide in plain sight," she softly chastised herself.

"Your ibuprofen is on your bed table, Sweetie."

"I know," Judy said quickly, "I'm just getting my toothpaste."

Lisa peeked around the corner in time to catch Judy dutifully brushing her teeth.

"I'll pull down the covers and fluff your pillows. Here's your headache medication."

"Uh huh," Judy nodded, still gummed up with toothpaste. She took the pills with her free hand, finished up her nighttime routine, which took all of three more minutes, and allowed Lisa a light kiss on the forehead before turning out the light.

"You're flushed. Did you take your temperature?"

"No, but feel my forehead and give me your expert opinion."

"You feel fine."

"Maybe it's just an oven burn."

"An oven burn?" Lisa didn't know if she heard right.

"Cooking can make you overly warm."

"You're babbling. I think you're delirious. Get a good night's sleep."

"You too, Sweetie."

"Maybe that's what killed Uncle Clive?"

"Cooking a turkey?"

"No, food poisoning."
"Good night!"

Judy slept in. Unusual, but then again, she had taken two more doses of ibuprofen in the night to ease her tension headache. By the time she wandered out to the kitchen, to a half-empty pot of coffee, Lisa hobbled in from the balcony, freezing blasts of frigid air escorting her.
"What are you doing! You're going to freeze to death!"
"I'm fine."
"You don't even have your robe on."
"So, take me in your arms and warm me up, like only you know how to do."
Judy complied willingly, anything to assuage her pangs of guilt from yesterday's kiss with Trish.
"What were you doing out there?"
"Shoveling snow."
"Why?"
"Because there's going to be a big snowstorm. I heard it on the weather this morning. maybe a foot or more!"
"And you thought you'd get a head start?"
"Are you making fun of me?" Lisa pushed away with unexpected strength for one good arm.
"No," Judy reassured calmly, "You've just never let the snow on the balcony get to you like this."
"I wanted to be useful."
"Let's sit and talk over coffee."
"Uh oh, the *couch treatment*!"
It was their procedure for clearing the air, sitting together on the couch. Coffee before noon, wine after. They were damn close to wine.
"What's up?" Judy probed, not unkindly.
"What did you and Miss Smart Aleck Lawyer talk about last night, after you were out of earshot?"
"I already told you most of it. She talked to me about the time necessary to complete the settlement."
"And?"
"She also advised me of a couple of things I should do, in preparation for possible tax liability."
"And?"

143

"And she said that she and I would need to meet once or twice more and that you shouldn't be there for those meetings. It has to do with the privacy of the estate. Since you're not a legal heir, the law restricts your presence during the final decisive meetings."

Judy was making this up as she went along, but it all made sense to her. Lawyers couldn't control what you said after the estate was settled, but certainly they could control who heard information from them.

"The other heirs don't want the family business to be made too public." Lisa surmised it better than Judy ever could.

"That's right." Judy agreed, relieved.

"And she had to take you to a private corner outside just to tell you that?"

"She left it to me to cushion the news."

"How many more secret meetings are there going to be?"

"They're going to try and keep it under a hundred."

"That's not funny!"

"You're having a problem with this, aren't you?"

A period of silence stretched to hell and back.

"She's a nice woman," Lisa admitted.

"And...?"

"She's a very intelligent woman."

"Okay."

"And you're a very unique woman."

"You've lost me completely," Judy said, hoping that Lisa would see it as a figurative rather than literal statement.

"You're one of the few women who doesn't act like you're smarter than everyone else just because you have a higher degree."

"So you think Trish is snobbish?"

"She doesn't miss the chance to impress us with her knowledge."

"She's a smart lawyer. Would you rather have a smart lawyer or a stupid lawyer on your side?"

"You don't act that way."

"I'm probably not as smart as she is."

"Oh, give me a break. You're ten times smarter than she is! You just don't have the need to lord it over people."

"Are you done buttering me up or will we need to buy a cow to supply you with more cream?"

"How many more secret meetings will there be?"

"I'm not in charge, but I suspect that there should only be about two more meetings. Three at the most."

"Far less than a hundred."

"I'm sorry. I didn't think you were so upset about this. I know it's hard to be on the outside of a process, especially when your life is truly involved as well. I promise that I will tell things to you as I find them out myself. To tell you the truth, I get a little frustrated from time to time myself."

Lisa nodded and put her head on Judy's shoulder.

"Look at the snow. Isn't it beautiful?"

"Why were you out there shoveling anyway?" Judy still hadn't gotten the answer she was looking for.

"I guess I was restless."

"You still seem a little on edge. Do you want me to take you for a drive? You haven't been out of the house except for doctor's appointments."

"I would like to go for a drive!" Lisa agreed enthusiastically.

"Where do you want to go?"

"Texas!"

"Excuse me!" Judy nearly inhaled her coffee, and coughed it up before it went clear down her windpipe.

"Isn't that where the ranch is? Somewhere in Texas?"

"I don't know the exact address..." Judy stalled.

"I bet Trish the know-it-all lawyer does."

"You're serious about this!"

"I've never been to Texas. I bet it's nice this time of year."

"You're in two casts."

"I'm due to get lighter casts next appointment. Let's plan to drive. We can go slowly, stop in Amarillo overnight, and then it's only a hop, skip and jump to Dallas. I remember the TV show. All those buildings and cows and oil wells. We haven't had time away with each other since we met and then we can nose around and find out who killed Uncle Clove and if it was one of the other heirs, you'll get more money because they probably couldn't inherit money if they were murderers. . ."

145

Perhaps only oxygen deprivation would have silenced Lisa had Judy not interrupted.

"Hold on there, darling. We need to do some serious planning. To begin with, we probably need permission or at least an invitation to go there. I don't want to languish in a Texas jail for trespassing."

"So go call Trish and get the wheels turning."

"You're absolutely, positively serious about this?"

"Yes."

"You wouldn't rather go to Hawaii, or the Bahamas?"

"Now how would we ever find out who killed Uncle Clod in Hawaii?"

"I hadn't thought of that."

"I know a great steakhouse in Amarillo. Do you think we need new luggage? I wonder what they're wearing in Texas nowadays? Can we rent a van and camp out under the stars?"

"No. Jeans. Can you do that in a cast?"

"What?"

"No, we don't need new luggage, they wear jeans in Texas, and I'm not sure you can get there and back in a van with your casts."

"Let me worry about that. You call Trish and set things up."

Judy located the forged letterhead and took at least three deep breaths before dialing. A voice answered, giving only the barest generic greeting.

"Trish Carter's office."

"Hello Trish? It's Judy."

It had been Mitch's idea to get a phone number just for this purpose. Everyone thought it was overkill. It was sure paying dividends now.

"Hello Judy. How can I help?"

"Hello, Trish. Lisa and I were sitting here and came up with an interesting idea."

"She's sitting next to you right now?"

"Uh huh."

"So, she's not listening in on the other line?"

"She's right here, she says 'Hi,' too."

"I'm still thinking about last night."

"I'm glad you enjoyed the dinner."

"Dessert was great, too," Trish breathed quietly.

"My question is, Lisa wants to go to Texas."

A seven-second pause hung in the air. Judy nodded like Trish was still talking.

"I know that wasn't a real question. Let me try again. Lisa and I thought it would be fun to take a drive to the ranch before all the estate was settled or probated or executed, and wondered if it would be possible to do that?"

"You have got to be kidding. You're kidding, right. Please tell me you're making this up just to scare the hell out of me!"

"Lisa says Texas is nice this time of year."

"There's nowhere to go!"

"I understand that it might be hard to arrange things. Isn't there someone you could talk to?"

"Oh yeah, you bet. There's someone who's going to hear all about this."

"You need a time frame?" Judy asked the question for a good reason. "Just a minute."

Judy turned to Lisa. "Sweetie, could you go in the bedroom and get my calendar? She needs a time frame. Can you manage that? When you get to the bedroom, just pick up the extension, okay."

"Okay."

Lisa hopped up like she was a kid again and made her way toward the bedroom. Judy took the scant few seconds to convey one more message to Trish.

"She also thinks Uncle Clyde was murdered!"

"There's no Uncle Clyde to murder! How the hell did she get that idea?"

"It's all my fault. I'll explain it later, but as long as you're telling Mitch the bad news, she might want to know that as well!"

Lisa picked up the phone.

"Hello Trish! Isn't it such an exciting idea! Us going to Texas to meet Judy's relatives!"

"Sounds like an idea worth pursuing."

"Hon, tell me when your doctor's appointment is?" Judy interrupted sweetly.

"Two days from now. I could have told you that out on the couch, you silly thing!"

"Sorry, I just wanted to make double sure. Then, it would still take a while to make other arrangements. We aren't even talking about going down for about a week, maybe two."

"The sooner the better!" Lisa gushed.

"I'll see what I can do," Trish said to the both of them. "Bye, now."

"Bye, y'all!" Lisa answered.

Judy hung up as well. Lisa was back out in a flash.

"Sounds like she needs to make a couple of calls," Lisa said, and added, "and then, it's Texas, here we come!"

"I hope Texas is ready for us," Judy said, weakly.

Chapter 18

Good thing Marge installed heavy-duty hinges on the door
of the Lucky U. It flew open like it was tornado season,
and hurricane Trish made a path straight for Mitch's booth.
She made landfall to find Mitch seated, not alone as usual,
but surrounded by three remarkably lovely ladies. It looked
like backstage at the Miss America Pageant. One was ash
blond, as natural as granola. The second was brunette,
deep deep brown. The third, the redhead, was telling the
punch line to a joke.

"And then the fourth one said...."

"Could you three ladies excuse Mitch and me for a few
minutes. We have important business to discuss!"

Mitch could see that Trish was clearly agitated and
expected dust to start swirling any minute. Good thing she
had mopped.

"Who's she? Your old girlfriend," drawled the red head.
She put way too much emphasis on the word *old* to suit
Trish.

"Ladies," Mitch intoned with as much authority as she
could muster. "Why don't the three of you go grab a table
and we'll have dinner in a few minutes. They acquiesced,
although the brunette whispered something to Mitch before
they departed.

"What in the hell do you think you're doing?" Trish
scolded as she sat down.

"Having fun, at least until you showed up."

"I didn't think getting underage bimbos drunk was your
idea of a good time?"

"They told me that they are triplets," Mitch smiled and
waved at the brunette. She waggled four fingers back.
"Do you think they're teasing me?"

"Oh yes, indeed, I do believe they are teasing you, and it
has nothing to do with being *triplets*!"

"You sure came back cranky from Aspen."

"That's not the half of it. That's not even the beginning.
Didn't you get my message?"

"My phone started ringing and the triplets are playing keep-
away with it. They thought it was annoying."

"Oh great. Now, a set of fake triplets has my phone number."

"And your complaint. . . ?"

"Look, we've got big problems with Judy and Lisa. *Big* problems."

"Hi, everybody," Mary chirped and sat down next to Mitch where the redhead had been.

"Gee, the seat's still warm," she remarked.

"I don't doubt it," Trish muttered, suddenly reticent.

"Hey Mary, how about an orange juice or a beer?"

"Sounds great. You look all recovered from your episode."

"I feel better. Thanks for coming to my rescue."

"Thanks for coming to my mother's rescue. Things appear to be calming down."

"That's great to hear."

Marge appeared to take Mary's order. After some deliberation, she decided on beer.

"What about your other table of girlfriends?" Marge asked. "You still buying?"

"Anything they want."

"Whatever.'

"So your mom is doing okay?" Mitch asked.

"She's cranky as hell."

"Uneasy lies the crown."

"She's better around you. I wish you could spend more time with her."

"She'll have to get in line behind table number one over there," Trish observed.

Mary glanced shyly over at the triplets and asked Mitch, "Why are those three women staring at me?"

"They think you're pretty."

"Nice save," muttered Trish.

"So, back to your big, earth shattering news, Trish. What's going on?"

"The problem is that Lisa has talked Judy into going down to visit the homestead. You know, the one that doesn't exist!"

"It exists in our imagination."

"We're going to need something a whole lot more concrete."

"Can't Judy talk her out of it?" Mary asked.

"It's hard to talk Lisa out of anything," Mitch spoke from experience, "Not that I ever tried. It was more fun not to." Trish gave Mitch a withering stare before continuing, "Apparently, Lisa's got the suitcases packed. They want to rent a vehicle, a van or something. Lisa gets new, lighter-weight casts in a day or two. Judy can't come up with any more good excuses as to why she can't just drop in and say howdy to all the long lost imaginary relatives!"

Marge hovered over to the table, a tray full of drinks.

"Mary, do you know anybody in Texas?" Mitch asked.

"Not a soul. How about you, Trish?"

"Don't look at me! I'm Colorado, two generations."

Marge continued to hover, until Mitch looked up.

"Is this another one of your riddles?" asked Marge.

"Is what a riddle?"

"Whether or not you have someone in Texas? Do I win something?"

"You're from Texas, Marge?" Mitch asked.

"No."

"No?"

"Not exactly."

"But...?"

"But my sister is, sort of."

"Have a seat, Marge, and tell us about it."

"Okay, but why are your girlfriends staring at me?"

"It's because you're pretty," Mary assured her.

"So your sister is from Texas?" Mitch concentrated on Marge.

"No."

"But...?"

"Her husband is."

"Do they live there?"

"Well, of course they do. What kind of fool question is that!"

"Just the generic fool kind, I guess."

"Are you sure they think I'm pretty?" Marge gestured toward the other table.

"Honey," Mitch assured her, "the closer we get to Texas, the prettier you're gonna get."

151

"Well then, I'm gonna be damn gorgeous by the time we get done with this story."

"Do they own a house, or a farm?"

"Oh hell no!"

"Do they own anything?" Trish was sounding desperate.

"Of course they do! They own one a them big ole ranches. You know, like in the opening of Dallas. You remember, Patrick Duffy, Larry Hagman, Barbara Bel Geddes. Now, there was one pretty woman...." Marge's narrative dwindled away.

"Oh yeah," Mary picked up the story. "Remember that whole deal about who shot J. R.? Wasn't it Cathy Lee Crosby?"

"It was Mary Crosby, I think?" Mitch furrowed her brow.

"I don't care if it was Bing Crosby," Trish stated irritably. "We need to get going on this plan! Are you on good terms with your sister?"

"Oh the best," Marge assured her. "I make it a point to stay on squeaky clean speaking terms with all my rich relations."

"So could we figure out a way to sort of borrow this ranch for a day or two?"

"Maybe even just a barn on the north forty?"

"I'll go and make a call. Usually, they plan a trip to Europe this time of year."

Marge stood up stiffly and disappeared into her back office.

"How many more rich relations do you think she has?" Mitch wondered out loud.

"I wonder how long she had a crush on Barbara Bel Geddes?" Mary added.

"So," Mitch came back to the moment, "How is Judy holding up under the strain?"

"She looked okay," Trish answered.

"And Lisa?"

"The blue casts go well with her eyes."

"What about Judy's eyes? Were they clear?"

"They were fine."

"She didn't look or act doped up?"

"She looked great."

"Great?"

152

"A little tired, but she cooked a complete turkey dinner for me, from scratch."

"A complete turkey dinner!" Mary repeated.

"Yeah, why?"

"It must be love," Mary explained. "My mom never cooked my dad a turkey dinner, and they were married for years!"

"Here comes Marge," Trish was on edge.

"What's the news?" Mitch asked.

"Got good news and bad news."

"Bad news first," Trish jumped in.

"You gotta wait a couple days."

"I have to wait a couple days for bad news?"

"No, you have to wait a couple days for the ranch."

"What's the good news?" Mary piped up, getting more and more enthused by the minute.

"You've got a month."

"We have access to this huge ranch for a month!"

"And the staff," Marge added.

"The staff?"

"Y'all can't run a ranch without some help!"

"How many staff?" Trish was curious.

"I dunno right offhand. Y'all want me to call her back?"

"No," reassured Mitch. "I'm sure we'll get that worked out in a day or two."

"I wonder if they can look sad?" Mary mulled out loud. Everyone looked at her.

"Well, there's been a death in the family, so to speak."

"She's right. We need a plan in place within two or three days. Trish, why don't you call Judy and tell her we need at least a week."

"What if that's not fast enough for Lisa?"

"Tell Judy to take her clothes shopping in Denver for a week. That should keep her busy."

"I'll suggest it."

"Meanwhile, let's figure out who's going and what part they'll be playing."

"Marge should go," Mary took charge of the plan. "After all, it is her family's ranch."

"Have you ever met Lisa, Marge?" Mitch asked.

153

"Sure have, but she never took no notice of me. She was too busy pulling the wool over your eyes at the time to study up on me."

"Thanks for reminding me. I lie awake nights worrying that I'll forget about that."

"Just trying to make a point."

"Marge, you can be the grieving widow. Can you do that?"

"Who's gonna run the bar while I'm gone?"

"Me," Mitch announced.

"You don't know the first thing about running a bar. You couldn't tell the difference between a sloe screw and a Mickey Finn."

"Besides, Mitch, we need you down there to help orchestrate this show," Mary insisted.

"I have a good idea," Trish announced.

"You usually do," Mitch said.

"Close the bar for a couple of weeks and get it ready for some cleaning and remodeling. You'd help pay for that to thank Marge for the use of the family ranch, wouldn't you, Mitch?"

"The place could use some new booths," Mary suggested, ever helpful.

"And the floor tile is shot," Trish was liking Mary more and more since they seemed to agree on most things.

"I've always wanted some of those Tiffany style swag lamps over the tables and the bar," Marge stared wistfully at the ceiling."

"I suppose you want gold plated toilet seats as well!" Mitch muttered, not at all surprised that they all jumped on the bandwagon so willingly.

"That would be a nice touch," Trish giggled.

"Shut up!" Mitch said, not unkindly.

"Maybe just new toilet seats," Mary offered a compromise.

"Why don't you make up a list of ideas and call a couple of contractors and get an estimate or two for me to study in my spare time, all two minutes of it," Mitch instructed Marge.

"Okay," she squeaked, about to burst out in tears of utter joy. "Gotta go, I have customers besides you, you know!"

With that, she retired to her back office, leaving the triplets
without a drop to drink.

"Tell you what," Mitch pointed to Trish. "You go call Judy
and tell her she's got to stall for a few days. Okay?"

"There's one more thing I forgot to mention. It might be
important."

"What is it?"

"Lisa thinks that Uncle Clyde was murdered."

"Why on earth would she think that?"

"I don't know. I hope to find out more."

"Try to do that."

"Should we let the grieving widow in on that little plot
twist?"

"I will," Mary piped up.

"Mary, while you're back in Marge's office telling her
about the alleged murder, get something to write on. A
legal pad, a notebook, anything that will give us enough
room to work out the details. And a bunch of pens, if she
has them."

"Sure thing. But while Trish's calling Judy and I'm getting
paper and pens, what are you going to do?"

"I'm going to refresh the drinks of those three lovely ladies.
It's the least I can do."

"As long as they don't order a Mickey screw, you'll be
fine," Mary patted her hand.

Within the hour, all seven of them were bent over the plan
being drawn up and annotated by Mary, the logistics
expert. The three lovelies all had names (of course) and
Mitch had now recruited Hilary (the blond), Monique (the
redhead), and Cloe (the brunette) into the scheme.

Judy's rich Uncle Clyde had a ranch. On the ranch he had a
staff. With a widow here and a murder suspect there, here
an heir, there an heir, everywhere an heir. Uncle Clyde had
one big ranch. Mitch had to bite her tongue to keep from
singing a chorus of e–i, e-i, o.

"Do you have any black dresses, Marge?" Mary was
making a list.

"And a veil?" Trish was checking it twice.

"I'm a pretend widow, not a funeral director!" Marge huffed.

"I look great in black," offered Monique.

"I bet you do," Mitch said, agreeably.

Trish had nearly fainted dead away when she returned from her phone conversation with Judy to find three new people in the plan. Now, she began to see the necessity. It wouldn't look believable to show up at rich Uncle Clyde's ranch with a total of three in the cast of characters. There had to be more heirs, more suspects, more complications, and most important, more distractions to keep Lisa occupied. The possibilities were promising.

"Lisa always did have a thing for brunettes," Trish was voicing her support of Cloe.

"She has a thing for big bank accounts," Mitch grounded the conversation.

"She'll be in seventh heaven for a week."

"Which will give you and Judy a chance to connect."

"Ladies, pay attention!" Mary rapped her pencil on the table like a gavel.

"We are," Mitch assured her. "You're drawing the ranch house. Looks like half of the sun."

They all looked at the page like Mitch had deciphered hieroglyphics.

"It does look weird," Monique stated, "It's like one of those spiky hairdos that punk rockers wear."

"Seven spikes, seven hallways, six interior rooms, all leading to one major entrance way," Mary talked as she drew from Marge's verbal description.

"He won his grubstake playing craps. Seven was lucky," Marge divulged family history.

The layout, starting from the left and going clockwise, was music room, den, dining room, kitchen, ball room, library. Down each hallway were two bedrooms, each with a bathroom and walk-in closets.

"Fourteen bedrooms, eight people. It should work out," Mary did the math.

"But there are nine of us," Hilary looked around, "Seven here, two from Aspen."

"Obviously, I'm not sleeping in the big house," Mitch explained.

"Where are you going to be?"

"In the bunkhouse, with the other cowpokes."

"Where does the staff sleep?"

"There are separate servants' quarters scattered around the property, for those who choose to live there," Marge talked on, "others have their own homes and families."

"Who's going to prepare the staff?"

"All of us should plan to go down in a couple of days, and by then, Mary will have a more organized plan in place. We could even get everyone a copy to study if we get our act in gear," Mitch said.

"But what are we going to call it?" Trish asked.

"Call it?"

"Don't we need a code name for the plan?"

"Okay," Mitch thought for a moment. "I got it, we'll call it 'Operation Waysouth Fork.'"

Mary had pored over the plan for so long that Mitch thought she had changed her mind about participating. Two days had passed and they were doing a final check of all the details, ready to copy the script for the staff and crew.

"Marge is the grieving widow," Mary spoke, coming out of her reverie.

"Check," Mitch answered back.

"Judy is the daughter of the deceased's long lost brother."

"Check."

"Himself now dead, also."

"Long lost dead brother, check."

"Hilary is the family doctor."

"Check." Mitch had thought carefully about this choice. Now that Lisa was on a self-styled murder mystery weekend, they would need someone to convince her that the death had been from natural causes. Hilary was the best candidate. She had an undergraduate degree in chemistry.

"Monique and Cloe are the other greedy heirs."

"What about you?" Mitch asked Mary. "I thought you were going to be a greedy heir as well?"

"No, I changed the plan. I'm going to be the upstairs maid."

"Why do you want to do that?"

"It makes more sense. I can keep an eye on Lisa and still logically leave the premises to report to you."

"I don't want you working too hard."

"Oh, I won't. I'll just dress in whatever the rest of the staff wears and do light cleaning and snooping."

"God forbid your mother should find out about this," Mitch warned.

"No problem, I told her that I'm going camping with my dad."

"He knows about the plan?"

"Thinks it's a hoot!"

"We leave in a couple of days. Are we ready?"

"Almost ready, more than willing and very able!"

Chapter 19

"Honey, Sweetie, Dearest!" Judy called out. "Where are you?"

"I'm in bed, you know, where I've been since my accident."

"You did get some time out in the kitchen for good behavior."

"Yeah, what a reward."

"You sound like you're in the dumps."

"I'm depressed, I'm cranky, I'm restless."

"Four more symptoms like those and you'll be like the seven dwarfs on depressants."

"You get stuck with the cooking, the cleaning, the laundry, the snow shoveling, and you're so cheerful. I'm like the burden from the black lagoon!"

Lisa topped off her tirade by taking one of Judy's pillows, putting it over her face, pretending to hide from the entire world. Judy took the opportunity to slip off her shoes and lie down beside Lisa, resting on her remaining pillow until Lisa resurfaced.

"You're still here?" Lisa peeked over.

"Still here," Judy replied.

"You want your pillow back?"

"Only if you're finished hiding under it."

"It doesn't work so well for that," Lisa handed it over. "Now, when I really want to hide, I either cover my head with the blankets or I curl up inside the closet."

"Happens to a lot of us."

"Well, are you going to tell me," Lisa inquired.

"Tell you what?"

"Who was on the phone?"

"I was just getting to that. You remember that trip to Texas that you have your heart set on?"

"How could I forget? It was just yesterday."

"You better take stock of your wardrobe and luggage. We're going in a week."

"Oh my God. Omigod, you're kidding. We can go?"

"Yes, ma'am."

"What's the catch?" Lisa probed, suddenly suspicious.

159

"Trish, your favorite know-it-all lawyer is going to be there as well. Also, I guess some other family members or something, too. It sounds complicated."

"You'll be meeting relatives you never knew you had. That might be nerve wracking for you, Baby."

"I'll get through it somehow. It isn't like we were all that close anyway."

"Close enough for probate."

"So, what do you want to do first? Buy some new clothes, rent a camper, make reservations?"

"Can we get one of those huge recreational vehicles? You know, with a refrigerator and a stove and a sink and a microwave oven so we can pop little bags of popcorn for a midnight snack?"

"We won't need all that once we get to the ranch. Apparently, there will be plenty of room for everyone there. But if that's what you want, that's what we'll do. I'll make some phone calls tomorrow."

"I think it would be a grand adventure!"

"You still need to plan your wardrobe."

"I don't want to buy anything new. Not with all my casts still on."

"Why not?"

"Well, we would have to cut them to fit and I won't stand for that. It's a waste of good money."

"We're going to the mall tomorrow!"

"No, we're not! If you insist on shopping, we'll do it in Denver, at the Army surplus store."

"Okay, I can compromise. Denver, yes, Army surplus, no. If we're going to be amongst my rich relatives, we had better dress the part."

"I'm wearing jeans and T-shirts, except when we're alone together."

"Are you absolutely sure you want to do the RV thing? You don't want fancy hotels and room service?"

"All I want is you and me and the big Texas sky."

Judy had made arrangements like she had been a travel agent in a past life. Not that people needed travel agents that many years ago. Most people used to just get in a car and drive somewhere. New York to Florida. Texas to Colorado. Colorado to California. And before that, they loaded up the covered wagon and forged a path through the prairie and over the mountains. So, getting in a car and driving from Aspen to Denver to shop and then pick up an RV wasn't really all that intense. Unless you were taking Lisa with you. The woman could talk nonstop. Honestly. Non. Stop. Like she had been vaccinated with a phonograph needle. At least at home, Judy could get away for a while. Here, she was a captive audience, if not totally captivated. At first, Lisa didn't seem to notice. She commented on trees and other cars and highway signs. Everything that you would've expected out of an eight-year old on their first-ever road trip. After about the nineteenth "uh huh" from Judy, even Lisa realized that it had been a one-sided conversation.

"Are you okay?" she asked.

"Yes, I'm fine. Why?" Judy replied with a question of her own.

"Well, you're just not saying much."

"I'm driving," Judy realized that her previous question might have been a mistake. First rule of thumb, never ask why. Especially of Lisa.

"So you can't talk and drive at the same time?" Lisa was beginning to sound miffed.

"I do try and concentrate on the road as much as possible."

"It's an interstate highway. It's not like you're driving the Grand Prix in Monaco."

Judy resisted the urge to snap. It would have been easy enough for her to come up with a clever reply, one that would sound like an admonishment. But they had many more miles left to travel and it wouldn't be fun to be on non-speaking terms for the remainder of the trip, no matter how much more Lisa could prattle on.

"Are you hungry?" Judy asked kindly.

"A little, I guess."

"Me too. Let's stop someplace nice and have something to eat."

The next town was about ten miles down the road. Lisa got out one of the travel books that she had bought at the bookstore at home to prepare for the journey.

"Define 'someplace nice' for me."

"Someplace where we can sit down to eat and hear each other talk."

Judy was a fan of quiet restaurants. In her earlier life, she had enjoyed the hub bub of jazzy places. But lately, she had grown more to appreciate places that didn't need to blare annoying music to cover the sounds of the kitchen noise. She blamed this phenomenon mostly on restaurants that were too small to have the kitchen far enough away from patrons, and, also, the all-too-popular notion of having a stage kitchen so you could watch your meal being prepared like it was a floor show. So, she was quietly congratulating herself on being able to convey this concept to Lisa in the succinct way she had when Lisa moped, "I suppose that means Playland Pizza is out of the question."

"That place with a hundred screaming kids?" Judy asked like she knew the answer.

"The pizza is pretty good."

"You've actually been there?" Judy had to laugh.

"I haven't been an adult all my life."

Lisa hadn't been an adult for the majority of her life, but pointing that fact out to her might not be the most productive topic of conversation. So she went back to pizza.

"Is there a place to get pizza that's a little more subdued?"

"I'm not sure that pizza and subdued go together."

"I imagine not," Judy stated quietly. They had five miles to figure this out.

"I'm really not in the mood for pizza anyway," Lisa said suddenly.

"Are you sure?"

"It might bloat me, and I don't want that to happen when we're going clothes shopping. I might buy something too big and then it won't fit right later."

Lisa hadn't bloated from anything she had eaten in all the time Judy had known her. But right now, it was as good an excuse as any to pick someplace else. Lisa continued to study the book and then without giving Judy any more information than directions, guided her to what was an extremely posh place for such a small burg. Judy looked over at Lisa. Lisa shrugged her shoulders. "It looked quiet in the book."

Indeed, it was quiet. And gorgeous. And huge. A place you wouldn't mind holding a wedding reception at for, oh say, a thousand of your closest friends and relatives. To many people, Colorado had the image of being a one-horse town. Hence, it wasn't known for its top-star destination resorts, with room rates and meal costs to match. So as they pulled up to the valet at the Bristlecone, Judy looked over and said, "Is it too late to go back to Playland Pizza?" Lisa only laughed as she got out of the car. One of those laughs that conveyed the clear message that Judy had had her chance and blew it.
The valet attendant was waiting patiently for Judy to exit her vehicle. For all her worldliness, Judy didn't know whether to tip before or after in this case, so she clung tightly to her purse as she handed over the keys. Nobody rolled their eyes, so she imagined the tipping came later.

They walked into a foyer that you could land an airplane in and looked around for a clue as to where the closest dining room might be that served lunch. Someone who looked like a concierge approached them and offered assistance. They learned that although you could luncheon in a small café poolside, that there was also an authentic English pub on the premises but it was a block away. The concierge offered to have them driven there, most likely since Lisa was on crutches. Judy and Lisa chose to hoof it instead. Judy tipped immediately this time, since she felt that they wouldn't be using the concierge service again. They covered the journey in about five minutes. The grounds of the resort were magnificent and Lisa was commenting on how wonderful everything was every slow step of the way. Soon, she was going to need a thesaurus to convey her descriptions.

The Mottled Horse Pub was nestled in a grove of trees surrounded by a modest parking lot. Before they got close to the door, it was opened for them by the hostess and since the concierge had called ahead, obviously on speed dial, they were immediately shown to a booth. Their waiter was right behind the hostess. Drink orders were placed, menus were presented, napkins were placed in laps and only then were they left alone to converse.

"This is a lot fancier than the description in the travel book," Lisa said innocently.

"Uh huh," was Judy's only response.

Lisa immediately picked up on the tone of disbelief in Judy's voice.

"I can go back to the car and get the book so you can read it for yourself," Lisa sounded a little bit hurt with her reply.

"You don't need to do that. I believe you," Judy used as soothing a tone as she could muster. It was like talking to that eight-year-old again.

"Seriously. How could you put all of this wonderfulness into a one-page description in a book," Lisa wasn't willing to let go of her defense.

"No one could," Judy murmured agreement as she looked at the menu. How on earth could a sandwich cost twenty-five dollars?

"It just looked like a nice place."

"The Bristlecone is a five-star resort."

"What's a five-star resort? Is that, like, the company that owns it?" Lisa queried.

Judy looked around for that drink. Surely, red wine couldn't be taking this long to pour.

"Are you feeling okay?" Lisa asked.

"I'm a little tired."

"Of course you are. You're stuck with all the driving. I wish I could help."

"You are helping. You're my navigator," Judy tried to make her sound important.

"Well, I navigated you all the way to here, didn't I!" Lisa smiled brightly.

When Lisa smiled, it took a little of the sting out of the overpriced food. It wasn't like Judy was hurting for money, but at these prices, they could fill up a small shopping cart at the grocery store and eat for a week. Besides, there weren't a hundred screaming kids. It was almost a hushed silence. The wine and root beer finally arrived. Lisa wanted to clink glasses and propose a toast to their adventure.

"I hope that Texas is nice this time of year!" was all she came up with. It wasn't exactly Shakespeare, but Judy finally got a good, long sip of wine. It was worth the wait. They both studied the menu for a moment. Judy would be content with a turkey sandwich, but Lisa had exotic tastes and wanted something with lobster. And there was nothing like living in a land locked state to drive up the price of seafood. When they placed their order, Judy added another glass of wine to the list.

"You should've bought a carafe," Lisa said as the waiter left.

"I'm driving, remember!"

"Oh, you'll be fine. After your sandwich and maybe some dessert. Did you see the dessert menu? What's that stuff called? Cream Broolay?"

"Close enough," Judy took another long draw of wine and drained her glass. This was going to be a long trip.

A blessed moment of silence crept up on them before Lisa started talking again.

"So what kind of clothes are you going to buy for the trip?"

"Haven't we already talked about this?" Judy asked.

"You said something about jeans when we first talked about it. But not everyone in Texas wears jeans, do they?"

"I really don't know. I've never been there."

"But you did say jeans?"

"I was thinking about cowboys."

"Why would you be doing that?"

"I honestly don't know," Judy began to feel closed up again, like she had felt in the car. It wasn't the physical proximity to Lisa anymore as much as the emotional and intellectual distance between them. Judy knew that she only had herself to blame for her predicament. She knew from the onset of their relationship that Lisa wasn't exactly Mensa material, but at the first, her small talk didn't seem to be quite so shallow.

"I like the cowboy motif, personally," Lisa interjected into Judy's reverie.

"You do look good in jeans," Judy wanted above all else to remain agreeable and pleasant.

"But I like it better if it's on somebody else," Lisa finished her thought.

Judy had a sinking sensation that would've rivaled the Titanic. One of those feelings where she knew that she would be the one in the jeans and flannels and a ten-gallon hat if Lisa went wild in the mall.

"Well, I think we all need to dress to fit in down there, don't you?"

"You'll be the cutest cowgirl at the ranch."

Judy smiled and nodded and the only thing that kept her from a meltdown was the idea that everyone down at the ranch was in on the scam.

Their lunch arrived as did another glass of wine for Judy. Lisa was right, she should have gotten a bottle. Midway through the meal, when Lisa came up for air, she said, "This is such a nice place. Too bad we can't stay here overnight and get a massage or something."

By the tone in her voice, Judy knew that if she didn't at least try to get lodging for the night, Lisa would sulk the rest of the trip.

"Let's check at the desk after lunch. Maybe there's room at the inn?"

"But I wanted to stay here," Lisa sighed.

"That's what I meant."

"Well, then why did you talk about an inn?"

"It's just an expression," Judy strained to keep her voice level.

"Oh. Okay!" Lisa was all smiles again.

It took so little to make Lisa happy. Only a three-hundred-dollar-a-night hotel room. And a massage. And a bottle of champagne. And another outrageously expensive meal.

The next morning, she was happy and lively and had shed

the sulkiness of the previous day. They drove the rest of
the way to Denver and the first stop was one of the high-
class malls in the city. It had many trendy and posh shops,
but wouldn't you know it, there was a store especially
suited to cowboy attire. Home on the Range was open for
business. Judy could never quite figure out how some sales
clerks could tell just by looking whether or not you had
money to spend. She had both dressed up and dressed
down to go on shopping forays in the past and they still
knew. The minute they walked in the door, they were
given world-class customer service. The layout of the store
was explained to them and then they were left to their own
devices for a few minutes to make some selections. Lisa
did most of the selecting while Judy located the dressing
room. She settled in to wait the outcome of the first wave
of shopping. Lisa handed her a pair of jeans and left her
alone to undress and dress. It was taking longer than
normal. Judy could do this pretty quickly when she set her
mind to it.

"Come out of that dressing room before I come in after
you!" admonished Lisa.
"Hang on, I'm zipping up!" Judy answered.
"What's the problem?"
"These are tight! What size did you send in?"
"Six."
"A six! I haven't worn a six since I was in high school."
"Come on out and let's take a look."
Judy walked stiffly out from behind the curtain, trying to
not hurt herself.
"Those look great!" Lisa announced.
"I can't sit down and breathing is touch and go."
"But you look so good."
"Put your eyes back in your head and bring me a ten."
"An eight, maybe."
"It's a long drive to Texas."
Lisa hailed the salesclerk, surrendered the size six, and
requested an eight and nine, both in relaxed-fit style. Judy
modeled the eight, managed to sit and breathe and even
cross her legs, but she bought both sizes just in case. Next,

she found several earth tone flannel shirts that would blend right into the terrain and finished her shopping spree with three cotton shirts, two white, and one blue.

Outfitting Lisa would prove to be much more exotic. For all her pretend reluctance the prior day, she was now in retail heaven. Her new casts were lighter, and a little less bulky. There would still need to be alterations, but she preferred leather and silk to flannel. Boots were still on the list for both of them, and they traveled across Denver to find the best. Exhausted, they drove to the hotel they had called from the road to make room reservations for the night and stashed their purchases in a closet.

"Room service or lobby restaurant?" Judy narrowed the choices to two.
"I'd like to eat and have sex at the same time."
"Don't some restaurants frown on that?"
"Just the fancy ones!"
"You order while I shower, then," Judy said.
"Got yourself a deal," Lisa agreed.

Judy took five extra minutes in the shower. Not that she had a stopwatch going at the time, she just knew how long she usually took and then drew out the process. Pulsating hot water pounded some of the fatigue out of her shoulders and she slipped her robe on without even taking time to dry. Never knowing quite what to expect from her young lover, she walked out of the bathroom with just a pinch of heightened awareness. The extra time had done Lisa in and she was sound asleep, naked right down to her socks. Judy slipped the socks off without disturbing her sleep. She must have been exhausted. Then, she waited around for room service. It was prompt, they were quiet, Judy doubled the tip and they were out in a flash. Judy pondered for a moment. Should she try and rouse Lisa, or should she let her sleep.
Leaning down, she nuzzled Lisa's cheek.
"Dinner's here, Hon."
". . . um. . . sleepy...."

"You better eat something to keep up your strength."
Judy's soothing voice lulled her back to sleep. Famished,
Judy helped herself to dinner and finished off way more
than her fair share. Good thing Lisa had slept after all. She
settled in to watch TV and fell asleep in fifteen minutes.

"Hey, wake up sleepyhead! I'm hungry!"
Judy jumped awake. It was morning already. Ten hours of
sleep had evaporated in a moment.
"Of course you're hungry. You slept through dinner."
"Why didn't you wake me up?" Lisa demanded, petulantly.
"I tried to, twice!" Judy informed her, a little on the snappy
side herself upon hearing Lisa's tone.
"You did?" Lisa wasn't convinced.
"I took off your socks, and even kissed you. You talked
and everything." Judy said, still not backing down from the
rude awakening.
"I'm sorry. I must not have been all the way awake."
"Well, I was! I came out of the shower expecting dinner
and sex. Remember?"
"I remember now."
"And there you were, sound asleep!"
"I'm sorry," Lisa repeated, not quite used to this new side
of Judy. The one she hadn't seen. The cranky side.
"It's okay," Judy calmed down a little. "You did look
absolutely charming in just your socks, though."
"Did you cover me up? You must have. Thank you," Lisa
blurted on and on, not waiting for answers. "You take such
good care of me."
Judy looked into Lisa's big, innocent, sensual eyes and
silently cursed the day she ever met Trish and Mitch. After
one more day on the road, they would be face to face.
Whatever they had in mind, they had better be right.

Chapter 20

Mitch had a gift. One that she really couldn't give away. She was a good observer of people. If she really wanted to pursue a career as a writer, she would've had success if for no other reason that she saw and understood the human condition better than most. Oh, she gave the impression that she was usually wrapped up in herself and her activities, but all along, particularly when no one else was watching, Mitch was observing.

Much of this had occurred while they were in the planning stages of the trip to Texas. While everyone else was trying to get a grasp of the complexities of the scheme, and honing their Texas accents, y'all, Mitch had been keeping an eye on Mary and Hilary. When the other participants had grouped up for practice, Mary and Hilary inevitably worked with each other, almost to the exclusion of everyone else. So much so that it didn't even take Mitch's powers of observation to pick up on this. If Marge poked Mitch in the ribs one more time, the bruises would never go away.

So when the time came to get everyone seated on the flight, Mitch took pains to sit next to Mary, if for no other reason than to try and keep her focused on the impending intrigue. It was what Mitch didn't know that became the focus of the flight. Mary did great until the airplane actually lifted off the runway. Then, she began to hyperventilate.
"Are you okay?" Mitch asked.
"I'm not very good at flying."
"Neither is anybody else. That's why we take airplanes."
A very nervous, very weak laugh emerged from Mary.
"Maybe I'll be okay in a minute?"
"Is this what happens every time you fly?"
"What *every* time?"
"This is your first time on an airplane?" Mitch asked for confirmation.
"Yes."
"Oh my, I've got an airplane virgin on my hands!"

"Would you shut up! Everyone will hear you."

"Everyone who? We booked up the first class section."

"You know who I mean!"

"Oh, you mean Doctor Hilary," Mitch nodded sagely.

"And Marge!" Mary added.

"And Doctor Hilary," Mitch repeated.

"And Monique and Cloe."

"And Doctor Hilary."

"Would you please be quiet!"

"I could, but don't you feel better already?"

"Are we flying at a steady altitude yet?"

"Almost. You going to be okay? I could go and get Doctor Hilary?"

"Shut up!"

Mitch glanced around at the boarding party and felt a little like Lee Marvin leading the Dirty Dozen behind enemy lines. For a moment, she regretted getting them so deeply involved in the chicanery.

"Do you think she noticed?" Mary's whisper broke through her reverie.

"Huh? She what?"

"Do you think she noticed?" Mary was now hissing.

Mitch glanced over at Mary and then the meaning of the question dawned on her.

"You mean about you and your crush on Hilary?" Mitch mouthed.

Mary nodded twice, quickly.

"Honey, we all noticed. In fact, we have a pool going. Everybody put in ten bucks and a guess as to how long it was going to take before you and you-know-who are going to, uh, let's see, how should I put this…get together. Marge picked ten days, Cloe bet a week, Trish, well, you know Trish!"

"Oh God," Mary moaned and tried to sink clear through her first-class seat.

"Come on, it's not that bad," Mitch soothed. "Look on the bright side, Hilary knows you're interested and she's not running the other way."

"Did Hilary get in the pool?"

"What pool?" Mitch winked.

The flight attendant, who was handing out pillows, supplied Mary with ammunition. Mary used her pillow on Mitch. Twice.

"I surrender. I'm going to go and talk to Trish for a few minutes. Try to behave yourself while I'm gone."

"I'm going to sit here and look out the window. Once you get up here, it's not nearly so scary. It's beautiful, in fact."

"Gorgeous," Mitch agreed as she walked down the aisle. She dropped a visual clue to Hilary and then sat next to Trish.

"What are you doing here?"

"Getting out of love's way."

After gazing out the window for two minutes, Mary turned to see Hilary standing in the aisle. She silently congratulated herself for not jumping a foot.

"Mind if I keep you company for a while?"

"Please, have a seat."

"Thanks. It's a beautiful day for flying."

"Gorgeous," Mary agreed, not even thinking about the view out the window.

"Is this the first time you've ever flown?"

"Didn't you hear Mitch blurt out that I'm an airplane virgin?"

"Sorry, didn't hear a thing."

"Oh, okay."

"So, how is it, not being an airplane virgin anymore?"

When Hilary said it, it sounded a whole lot more sensual. Mary became aware, instantly and intensely, that she and "Doc" were flying hell-bent toward uncharted territory.

"I'm getting over the initial shakiness."

"Just like the real thing, huh!"

"Um...uh." was all that Mary could muster for a response.

"So, you've spent a lot of time organizing the plan."

"The plan, yes, the plan. Well, it didn't take long. I've planned other events before."

"What else have you done?"

"Fund raisers, dinner parties, campaign stops...."

"Campaign work! That sounds exciting. So, whose campaign have you worked on?"

172

If Mary had had a can of paint and a brush, she's be in a corner by now. Not knowing one truly convincing lie, she told one half of the truth.

"My mother's."

"What a thrill to have a politician in the family. Who's your mother?"

The other half of the truth didn't seem willing to come without a fight.

"Rebecca Fairbanks."

"Governor Fairbanks?"

"Yes."

"Governor of Colorado Fairbanks."

"Right."

"That's certainly...interesting," Hilary stated in monotone.

"Some days are more interesting than others."

"I'd better go back to my seat before lunch arrives. Promised to keep Cloe company," she explained quickly as she stood up and walked away.

"Thanks for stopping by," Mary said to Hilary's back.

Mitch reappeared mid-lunch and tried three times to draw Mary into frivolous conversation. When that failed, she tried the direct approach.

"What happened with Hilary?"

"I told her who I was and it freaked her out."

"I see."

"I didn't want to lie."

"I admire that."

"And people, women especially, will need to know right up front who they're dealing with. It's going to be a struggle. Nobody should be fooled into thinking that I'll take them home to meet mom and they'll be welcomed with open arms. It just isn't going to happen."

"Most gay people don't expect the welcome mat treatment to begin with any time they meet the extended family. Hilary knows that. She's just overwhelmed by your celebrity status. Not just any gay woman gets the chance to flirt with the governor's gorgeous lesbian daughter."

"She didn't flirt long after she found out."

"Trust me, she'll be back."

"How do you know?"

"She loves you."

"Wake me up when we get there."

The rest of the flight was uneventful. Those who didn't nap studied their scripts or chatted quietly. Hilary kept to herself, deep in thought. They landed, picked up three rental vehicles, stowed all of the luggage and headed out to the ranch. Mary drove a full size van, Marge insisted on having a pickup truck and Hilary was given command of the luxury car.

"Well, somebody had to look rich, so we decided on the doctor," Mary explained the strategy to the group.

"How big is this place, anyway?" Mitch asked as she kept Marge company in the truck.

"You drive about thirty minutes once you're on the property before you get to the big house."

It sounded like a prison. It looked, however, like the promised land once they arrived. Eight staff members were waiting on the front drive after Marge had phoned in from the airport. They jumped into service the moment the vehicles stopped. Flowers and shrubs adorned the front entrance. It was a welcome change from the prairie.

"Does this stuff grow year round?" Mitch asked.

"Rich people can grow anything," Marge explained, as if to a child.

They wasted no time going into the dining hall where the staff had set out snacks and beverages. They served themselves, and then Mary took command at the head of the table. After thanking the staff for their help, she began to outline the basic events of the next few days.

"We don't know when our guests are arriving, but when they do, we need to be ready."

"What should we do?" asked the senior member of the staff, an efficient man named Luther.

"First of all, Marge is going to play the part of the grieving widow."

"And owner?"

"Yes."

"She looks enough like her sister, that should help matters," one of the housekeepers noted.

"The woman next to Marge," Mary pointed to Mitch, "stand up," Mary commanded, "you don't need to worry about her. She's going to hide out in the bunkhouse."

"The what?" Luther asked.

"Don't you have a bunkhouse?"

"We have a lot of structures on the property."

"Maybe a barn?" Mary asked with just a hint of a smile.

Mitch began to shift uneasily in her chair. The thought of living for two or three days in a barn wasn't exactly what she had expected. "Something with a bathroom would be nice," she interjected into the conversation.

Three of the staff nodded to each other and said, "Magnolia."

"Okay, Magnolia," Mary repeated, trusting the staff to know their own property.

"Next, we have the family doctor. Stand up, Hilary."

Hilary, who had been sitting next to Mitch, stood and nodded.

"Is she a real doctor?" Luther asked.

"No, but she's a quick study. Then, we have our fake family lawyer. Stand up Trish."

"So far, we have a fake widow, a fake doctor and a fake lawyer?" Luther confirmed.

"That right," Mary agreed.

Luther began to take notes. Or maybe, he was just calculating necessary bail money. As Mary explained why Monique and Cloe were there, making them sound a lot more important than window dressing, Mitch leaned over to Doc Hilary.

"She's doing a great job, isn't she."

Doc nodded.

"She's a nice kid."

Doc nodded, again.

"Don't let her family tree shake you up."

"I need everyone's attention!" Mary rapped on the table.

Mitch looked up, "I was just saying what a fine job you're doing!"

"Just pay attention. Now, I'm going to work undercover as a maid, to keep an eye on Lisa."

"Who's Lisa," quizzed Luther.

"Our guests will be Judy and Lisa. Lisa is a crook."

"A real crook or a fake crook?" Luther's pencil was poised.

"She's a real crook. She's the one in two casts. Judy is her roommate, her real roommate. We have two main objectives. The first is to convince Lisa that Judy will be very rich very soon."

"What's the other objective?"

"To convince Lisa that the dearly departed Uncle Clyde wasn't murdered."

"You need to convince Lisa, a real crook in two casts, that someone who never actually lived, let alone died, wasn't murdered," Luther nodded as he wrote. Without looking up, he asked, "How long will they be staying?"

Trish answered this query, "I told them that the invitation was extended for two days."

"Knowing Lisa," Mitch explained further, "she'll realize that she's landed in the lap of luxury, and will want to stay much longer."

"I can assure you, Madam, that this staff is prepared for anything. We will learn, understand and execute the plan with no slip-ups."

"I have unwavering faith in you and your staff. How can we be helpful to you?"

"Be prompt for meals. Breakfast at seven, luncheon at one, formal dinner at seven," Luther instructed, and then turned to Mary, "If you're going to pose as staff, you need to be outfitted. Mrs. Raymond will see to that."

"Anything else?" Mary asked.

"You and I will meet each morning, after breakfast, for a briefing."

"And then, I will also meet with Mitch and the others as necessary."

Luther and Mary stood in unison. Mitch had a good feeling about this. They were being led into battle by truly competent generals. Mary went to wardrobe. Marge, Monique and Cloe went to pick out bedrooms. Mitch, Trish and Doc Hilary followed one of the staff in the van to the Magnolia site. It resembled a miniature Tara.

"I must've missed this one on 'Bunkhouses of the Rich and Famous,'" Trish whistled as she stepped in.

The tour was brief and perfunctory. Three bedrooms, two baths, modern kitchen, fully stocked bar, a den with TV, stereo and plush sectional furniture. It was heaven in Texas.

The staff member, Michael, unloaded what little luggage Mitch brought, stocked the kitchen with supplies, and then left in his jeep. Trish and Hilary stayed behind to help Mitch settle in, which amounted to opening a beer and sprawling on the couch.

"I'm beginning to like Texas," Trish announced.

"You ever wonder why Marge didn't tell us about her rich relatives before?"

"I guess I'm usually not surprised when people don't talk about family."

"That's a double negative," Trish said out of habit.

"You're a fake lawyer, not a fake English teacher!" Mitch scolded playfully.

"Speaking of fake, what did Uncle Clyde die of, besides murder?" Trish directed the question to Doc Hilary.

"A heart attack."

"A heart attack!" Trish laughed. "Gee, Hilary, everybody dies of a heart attack."

"Everybody?" Mitch asked, now wondering if the fake lawyer and the fake doctor were going to someday enter into fake litigation.

"Sure. Haven't you ever read a death certificate? Heart failure due to heart disease, heart failure due to cancer, heart failure due to parachute malfunction. Well, maybe that last one is listed as accidental?"

"Do you, like, go somewhere and read death certificates?" Mitch asked, wondering about the macabre nature of their discussion.

"I'm just pointing out that Lisa is going to be tough to convince."

"Why does she think it was murder, anyway?"

Trish shrugged her shoulders. "Judy says it was her fault. I still haven't found out why."

"I'm going to say, in case anybody asks, that Uncle Clyde had atherosclerosis and hypertension," Hilary explained.

"What's that?" Mitch asked.

"That's a type of heart disease where the arteries clog up with fatty plaques, coupled with high blood pressure."

"What was your prescription?"

"Antiplatelets and diuretics."

"Which, in layman's terms, are aspirin and water pills," Trish elucidated.

"Exactly."

"Does Marge have this down pat?"

"She seems to have a knack for this. Knew the terms, the medications. We talked for a few minutes on the flight. She's ready for the show to begin."

"You managed to talk to a lot of people on the flight down," Trish put a fine point on it.

"Hey, I'm a doctor. I've got to get used to making rounds!" Doc Hilary bantered back.

"Did you find the equipment you needed?"

"Mary was very resourceful. She finagled a sphygmomanometer and a stethoscope."

"Between you and Mary," Trish assured, "you'll be experts at playing doctor before too long."

If the thought had already crossed Doc Hilary's mind, she was too polite to confess.

"You two need another beer?" Mitch filled the now gaping silence.

"We need to get back and unpack," Trish answered for both of them.

"Well, if you get bored, call me at 555-2424," Mitch read the number off the phone that was next to the couch.

They were up and gone, leaving Mitch suddenly alone. It was mighty quiet out here in the wilderness. What to do first? Unpack? Go for a walk? Mitch decided to open another beer and stretch out on the couch while she mulled other possibilities. Take a long nap? Take a short nap? She was just getting a good start on the second choice when the phone rang.

"What?" she answered from a jangling awareness. "You can't possibly be bored already."

"They're here. Our guests have arrived early!" Trish was talking fast.

"Was everyone ready?"

"Yeah, I guess."

"Good. The sooner we get started, the sooner we'll be done."

"There's one glitch to talk about."

"What's that?"

"Luther doesn't quite know what to do with Mary, at night."

"Don't let Doc Hilary hear that."

"I'm serious. There's a shortage of servant's quarters. They were planning on doing some repair work while the family is in Europe."

"Okay, she can sleep here with me."

"Look for her at dinner time. Technically, she's dismissed at four o'clock for the day, along with the other bedroom staff. Anything else would look suspicious."

"No problem. How does Judy look?"

"She looks tired. It's been a long trip. Lisa looks great."

"She always did. Cross your fingers."

"Already crossed. Gotta go. Bye."

Any concerns Mitch might have had about being bored soon evaporated. She rummaged around the kitchen. The handy staff person had unpacked several boxes of supplies while Mitch had been touring the house, and now she realized how well prepared this group had been. There was a freezer full of precooked entrees, a refrigerator crammed full of fresh vegetables and a pantry room filled with canned goods of every description. Dinner for twelve would have been a snap. Hopefully, dinner back at the big house would go as smoothly.

Indeed, the show had begun. Judy and Lisa had arrived tired after a whirlwind trip through Colorado and Texas. They had feasted, traveled and made love leisurely and still nearly caught Trish and the group on their heels. Marge, as usual, came through like a champ, embracing Judy like the prodigal daughter, crying real tears on her shoulder. Trish lingered in the background, avoiding eye contact with both Judy and Lisa. Nevertheless, she felt her color rise. This automatic response had to either go away, an unlikely event, or be used to an advantage. Trish occupied her mind on the latter as the rest of the family toured the mansion.

Cloe and Monique played the heirs apparent role to the hilt, keeping a distant and yet curious stance toward Judy. Mary, meanwhile, tried to fade into the wallpaper in her maid's uniform as Judy and Lisa were shown to their room. Certain people can fade well. Unfortunately, Mary wasn't one of them. Her stunning good looks, while draped in the unflattering wardrobe of house servant, drew a second and third glance from Lisa. Having little more to do than finish up with a feather duster, Mary was halfway out the door when Lisa called her back.

"Are you our servant girl?"

"Yes, Ma'am," Mary deferred to Lisa.

"Unpack my suitcase!"

Judy interjected herself into the conversation, "I can do that for you."

"I want her to do it! She's paid to do that, aren't you?" Lisa challenged Mary to argue.

"Oh, yes, Ma'am. I'm here to do anything you ask."

"Unpack my suitcase and press everything that is wrinkled."

"Yes, Ma'am."

"I'll want to bathe in ten minutes. Have my bath water drawn. Don't skimp on the hot water."

"Yes, Ma'am."

"I'll want to rest after my bath. Turn down the bed after you prepare my bath."

"Yes, Ma'am."

Lisa hobbled down the hallway, just to snoop apparently. Giving orders must be only so much fun. Judy looked at Mary and said quietly, "I'm sorry she's so rude. I'll talk to her."

"It's okay," Mary whispered back. "I'm part of the conspiracy and I'm here to keep an eye out. I don't know the first thing about being a maid."

"You're not a real maid?"

"No, but I can hang clothes."

"I'll do the bath. It's a specialty of mine. Leave the bed to me, too."

"Okay. There is another real maid who will take care of everything. We've already coordinated the effort."

"Is anybody else here real?"

"The rest of the staff is real, but they've all been fully briefed."

"It's like an episode of Mission Impossible."

"Except without Tom Cruise."

"Right...."

They heard the thump, thump of Lisa and sprang to action.

"Is my bath ready yet?" she asked petulantly.

"Follow me, Sweetie," Judy started toward the bathroom.

"What about her?" she motioned toward Mary.

"Come on, I'll explain."

Mary directed her sweetest innocent smile toward Lisa, who thumped away. The second the bathroom door was closed, Olga, the real maid, came in and started the unpacking process. She tut tutted dutifully and took all of Lisa's wardrobe away to be freshened. Mary, meanwhile, nosed through the various personal articles that Lisa had packed. There was no obvious stash of drugs. She heard laughter from the bathroom, rolled her eyes, and left.

"Like I said," Judy continued as she tested the bath water, "Nobody, and I do mean, nobody is going to help you with your bath but me!"

"Well, I was only going to let her run the water," Lisa murmured as she ran her fingers back and forth along Judy's shoulders.

"But only I know how you like it."

"That's for sure," Lisa surrendered.

"Now, are you going to take off your clothes, or do I need to do that for you as well?"

"I didn't see a beauty shop the last ten miles, did you?" Lisa chatted as she undressed, slowly.

"I'll wash your hair. Just let it dry. We're on vacation, not contestants in the Miss America Pageant."

"I wouldn't qualify for the Miss Cowpoke Contest."

"What are you worried about, Sweetie?"

"Haven't you noticed? This place is like something out of the movies. Your relatives are sooooo rich. And those granddaughters? They know where the closest beauty parlor is, I guarantee."

"They're just family," Judy shrugged.

"I just want to make a good impression."

Judy looked at Lisa, stripped to the waist. "If they could see you now, they'd be impressed."

Lisa blushed, a rare occurrence. "You're going to pay for that," she promised.

"Oh, I sincerely hope so," Judy sighed. "Now, if you don't hurry, this water's going to be cold."

Bathing with one cast could be a chore, bathing with two took the planning and logistics of an invasion on the moon. Judy took her time, helping with balance until Lisa was situated comfortably in the bubble bath. She followed through on her promise, washing Lisa's hair, scrubbing her back, keeping her company.

"I don't know what I would do without you. Have I told you that?"

"Only about a dozen times a day."

"I mean it, you know I do."

"I know," Judy nodded and then studied Lisa for a moment.

"What?" Lisa asked, sensing a change of mood.

"I sometimes think that it's my life that was so wonderfully changed by you."

"Tell me more."

"You were my first," Judy revealed.

"Your first what? Blond?"

"You were my first woman."

"You're kidding, right?"

"You were my first woman."

"But not your first, first," Lisa made it complicated in her unique way.

"First, first?"

"First ever?"

"Oh, I see what you mean. No, you weren't my first ever. I had been married. Twice."

"I had no idea I was your first woman. I would've never guessed."

182

"I was that good?"
"You were great, and believe me, I've been with a real virgin before and that was unmistakable."
"You've been with a real virgin?"
"A real virgin, virgin."
"How very interesting."

Mary arrived at Magnolia fifteen minutes early.
"Come on in, dinner's almost ready," Mitch called from the kitchen.
"Smells great."
"Oh, please! It's tuna casserole."
"I like tuna casserole."
"They serve tuna casserole at the governor's mansion?"
"Why can't anyone forget, even for ten damn minutes, that I'm the daughter of the governor!"
Mitch had to take a second look. She had never seen Mary quite this angry before, except at her mother. Honestly, it was a welcome sight.
"What are you smiling about?"
"Sorry," Mitch apologized. "I'm just happy to see you get ticked off more than once a year about something."
"It's something important."
"That's even better."
Mary relaxed, knowing that Mitch was on her side.
"So, how are things with Doc Hilary?"
"Still quiet."
"Not any worse?"
"Not any better."
"What else is going on with Operation Waysouthfork?"
"Judy is great. What a nice lady. Lisa is a witch. How did you ever get mixed up with her?"
"Oh, I was young and stupid," Mitch said wistfully.
"Wasn't it just last year?"
"What's your point?"
"She must be very charming, if you're not wearing a maid's uniform."
"She could be a charmer."
"She sure casts a spell on Judy. Judy follows her around like a puppy."

183

"I think it's part of the act."

"Yeah, well the *act* is going to send Trish right through the roof. It's only been half a day and the tension is already brewing."

"Do I need to find a way to talk to Trish, to settle her down."

"Tomorrow afternoon might be a good idea. I think Trish is planning a meeting with Judy to touch base."

"Tell her to check in with me."

"Is dinner ready, I'm starved!"

When Mary decided to eat, she didn't let much get in the way. She finished off one helping and started on a second.

"I made dessert."

"What did you make?"

"It started out as Flaming Baked Alaska. But it ended up as pudding."

Mary didn't catch the humor until she looked at Mitch's crinkled up eyes.

"Thank goodness, because I'm so burned out on flaming desserts."

"Oh, boo," Mitch gracefully acknowledged the pun.

"What flavor?"

"Chocolate."

"My second favorite."

"What's your first?"

"Butterscotch, of course."

"At least it isn't vanilla."

"Why would it be vanilla?"

"Never mind. I'm so tired, I'm babbling."

"You go put your feet up, I'll clean the kitchen."

"That's a deal."

Mitch heard the rattle of dishes for about five minutes before she dozed off. Mary covered her with a blanket, locked the door, and left the pudding for breakfast.

Breakfast at the big house was a production. The dinner the night before had been even more celebratory. Marge had toasted Judy, fawned over Lisa and kept a lively dinner table repartee going from soup to dessert. The undercurrent of tension between Judy and Trish was lost in the confusion. Only the sharpest ears heard Trish tell Judy that they needed to have a meeting the following day, after breakfast, to discuss estate issues. Those ears belonged to Lisa.

Now, between omelets and lox, Lisa remained sulky. She had been pouting since the night before, and her long-suffering stance had put a damper on Judy's morning. They were late for breakfast, and were now alone at the table. The staff wasn't particularly enamored with Lisa, and this temper fit wasn't helping.

"You're sure you're okay?" Judy asked, again.
"I'm fine," Lisa clipped the answer.
"I know you aren't happy that I'm having a business meeting alone with Trish, but it's convenient for us. Besides, you're the one who wanted to come down here."
"She has more than business on her mind."
"What are you talking about?"
"She has her sights set on you."
"That's just her Texas charm."
"I'm going back to the room and rest. I'm getting a headache."
"I wouldn't be surprised with all the needless worry you're putting yourself through. I'll help you."
"No! You stay here. You have business. I'll be fine."
Lisa hobbled out of the room, holding her head high to complete the effect.
"Too bad we don't have any Oscars to hand out," Trish said, coming out from hiding in the hallway.
"You're being way too careless around her."
"Remember back at O'Brien's Pub? You said back then that she didn't have the brains for this."
"This isn't brains. This is jealousy."
"Come into the study, we have work to do."
Judy followed Trish into the secluded room, but when Trish even came within arm's reach, Judy backed away.
"What's wrong?" Trish asked, afraid of the answer.
"What isn't wrong, Trish?"

185

"What do you mean?" Trish needed to stem the trembling tide that was taking over her legs.

"So far, Lisa hasn't lived up to the stories you've told me about her."

"She drugged you."

"That's just a guess on your part."

"She called you a horny bitch."

"That could have been a dream."

"You're losing your nerve."

"No. But I am willing to give Lisa the benefit of the doubt."

"That's one of the things I love about you."

"Trish, I don't go easily from one relationship to the next. I feel that, rightly or wrongly, I've become involved with Lisa. She depends on me, she saved my life. She hasn't done one wrong or bad thing that we can prove."

"Yet."

"Even a pretend lawyer knows that you're innocent until proven guilty."

"Do you want to go through the paperwork with me?"

"No, I'll go and study it in front of Lisa. The sooner I get back to her, the better it will be for all of us."

"You have just one more thing to explain."

"What's that?" Judy asked, impatiently.

"Why does Lisa think that someone murdered Uncle Clyde?"

"I got too clever for myself. I decided to involve Lisa in the writing of a mystery book, in order to get the subject of poison out in the open. Now, it's her favorite topic."

"It's also her favorite choice. Keep on guard. And keep the Sherlock Holmes of Aspen out of trouble until you get home. She's already been talking to Doc."

"I'll try."

"The kiss in Aspen, it was special. It meant something to me. I just wanted you to know that," Trish clarified.

"I know," was the only goodbye Judy could voice.

Without any more delays, she went to check up on Lisa. Propped up in bed, with freshly changed linen, fluffed pillows, and a box of chocolates, Lisa appeared completely over her headache. Mary, meanwhile, looked like she was coming down with one, provided solely by the demands of Lisa.

"You're back? So soon?" Lisa chirped, perky beyond good measure.

"I'm back so soon," Judy confirmed and then turned to Mary, "Mary? It is Mary, isn't it?"

"Yes Ma'am."

"Please leave us alone. And close the door on the way out."

"Yes. Ma'am," Mary scooted out, delighted with the reprieve.

"I thought your meeting would take longer," Lisa was over being chirpy and working on aloof.

"It doesn't take long to find out you're going to be rich." Judy carried the folder over to the bed and sat down. She tossed the file to her side of the bed and looked deeply into Lisa's clear eyes.

"What? What are you looking at?"

"I'm looking at your pupils."

"Why?"

"Because I'm concerned about you. How's your headache? Do I need to get the doctor?"

"It's better. Don't fuss over me."

"You took something for it?"

"Just these," Lisa held up the box of chocolates. "The universal cure all."

"Here, have one," Lisa picked out the exact one she knew was Judy's favorite.

"No, thanks," Judy said, pulling away only slightly. She couldn't shake Trish's warnings about being cautious.

"Okay, suit yourself," Lisa said as she popped the chocolate into her own mouth.

Acute guilt washed over Judy. How dare she suspect this sprite.

"Is it too late to change my mind?" she asked Lisa.

"Too late?" Lisa was puzzled.

Judy placed her hands on both sides of Lisa's face and pulled her into a kiss. She tasted chocolate, Lisa, and aching desire all at once. When Lisa decided to share, she could be more than generous.

187

"You certainly came out of your meeting in a good mood," Lisa probed.

"All I thought about was you, sitting up here in bed, needing love and attention and apparently, chocolate."

"Tell me about the meeting."

"No."

"No?" Lisa echoed.

"You can read about it yourself. Here's the file," Judy reached over and picked up the paperwork she had casually tossed aside a moment ago.

"Do I have the choice of reading this file or making love to you?"

"It's up to you."

Lisa tried her hand at tossing paperwork aside. "I can read boring paperwork any old day."

Mary had to ask three staff members before one knew the whereabouts of Trish and directed her to the study.

"You don't look so good," Mary said by way of a greeting.

"This just hasn't been my morning."

"How can I help?"

"You can find out if there's another bunkhouse where I can hang out tonight."

"You can come over to Magnolia. We have three rooms there."

"I don't want to bother you and Mitch. There has to be some old, deserted place where I can just go and be a hermit. I need to get out of here. I'm causing suspicion and it's just driving Judy closer to Lisa."

"You can't hide how you feel about her, can you?"

"Not any better than you can hide how you feel about Doc."

"It isn't easy."

"Speaking of Doc, how is she handling Lisa's questions about Uncle Clyde?"

"So far, so good. As long as Lisa doesn't launch a full scale investigation, I think we're okay."

"She buys the heart attack scenario?"

"If she doesn't, she isn't telling Doc."

Mary went to find Marge and Luther. They were talking over family history in the kitchen. Mary explained the situation, leaving out all the angst, to Luther. He had an immediate solution. Mary delivered the news to Trish, still camped out in the study.

"Come on, I'll help you pack."

"Where am I going?"

"Rattlesnake Ridge."

"Sounds lovely," Trish sounded sarcastic.

"Would you come on already. I'm due back to fluff and dust."

Trish muttered profanities under her breath as she shadowed Mary out of the room.

The staff loaned a jeep to Trish and, over her objections, Mary insisted on following her there. It was only a fifteen minute drive, but the area was beautiful. Someone had painstakingly created a quaint, bucolic vacation cottage surrounded by trees and two ponds.

"This is beautiful," Mary exclaimed. "Let's get you unpacked."

"I can take care of that myself. You go back and fluff pillows."

"Okay, but watch out for snakes."

"You too, especially the two-legged variety."

"Luther is making arrangements for provisions to be brought over."

"What kind of wine do you serve with rattlesnake?"

"I'll ask Mitch when I go over there for dinner," Mary said over her shoulder as she hurried off.

When the knock on the door happened fifteen minutes early for Mary's usual arrival, Mitch didn't think too much about it, until she opened the door.

"Doc Hilary! Come in."

"Do you mind that I dropped by?"

"Heavens no! It gets lonely out here in the north forty. Come in, stay for dinner."

"I'm sorry. Were you about to eat?"

189

"You should eat before you get any more transparent," Mitch smiled.

"It is that obvious?"

"Mary will be here in a few minutes. Have a beer while you wait and fill me in on what's happening at the house."

"I just need to talk to Mary. I've been a jerk."

"Why do you think that?" Mitch asked, realizing that she wasn't going to get any Lisa updates anytime soon.

"I prejudged her."

"Because she's the daughter of the most right-wing governor on the planet?"

"She's like a cross between a celebrity and a puzzle. I don't know what to say or do."

"She's going to be here in a few minutes. You need to have something prepared to say."

"What would you say?"

"I'd tell her the truth. It will serve you well."

"And I suppose you know what the truth is?"

"Tell her that you love her."

"How do you know?"

"I pay attention. She loves you, too. Rely on that. She just needs a little time."

The front door swung open and Mary was halfway into the room before she saw Hilary.

"Oh, hi," she said, trying to be nonchalant.

"Hi yourself," Hilary answered.

"Just in time for dinner," Mitch announced. No one was listening to her, simply because she no longer existed in their private universe.

"Anybody hungry?"

More quiet looks, but not at Mitch.

"I'm going to take a walk. Perhaps to Kansas. I'll be back," Mitch left the cabin unnoticed.

"I needed a break from the big house," Hilary explained, afraid to take a step forward.

"I need a break once a day myself," Mary agreed.

"I came to apologize for being a jerk."

"You haven't been a jerk."

"I've been a jerk."

When Hilary said jerk, it immediately made you want to join the club.

"You had an absolutely normal reaction to me."

"You're just saying that to make me feel better."

"Is it working?" Mary found her voice to be teasing. It wasn't planned.

"It's working!" Hilary laughed, feeling the uncomfortable tension in the room evaporate, and at the same time realizing that the vacuum was quickly filled with another type of tension. Much stronger, much, much better.

"What else do you need to hear from me?" Mary offered to elucidate further.

Hilary took a couple of steps toward Mary and was pulled into a hug.

"I need to hear everything."

"That's going to take a while."

"I love you," Hilary went first.

"We've only known each other less than a week. How can you know how you feel?"

"Feelings don't run on a time clock."

"I don't know how I feel."

"You feel great, trust me."

"Let's sit and talk."

"Okay."

Hilary followed Mary over to the couch, where they sat together, but not too close.

"I guess I'm just an old-fashioned girl," Mary explained.

"It's a charming trait," Hilary reassured her as she held her hand.

"I was reared in a conservative family."

"Does your mom know you're a lesbian?"

"She and I don't discuss it much."

"What about your dad?"

"He's great, but they're separated."

"I remember reading about that."

"You have me at a disadvantage, you know that."

"What do you mean?"

"You can hear about my life on the news. Tell me about you."

"What do you want to know?"

"Everything."

"My mom and dad live in California, I moved to Colorado to go to school, and I'm good in bed."

On cue, Mary blushed.

"You said everything!" Hilary defended her truthfulness.

"I know. I'm rethinking that request. I know you're a chemistry whiz."

"I'd like to go to medical school, but I don't have the funds."

"But you have the aptitude and the grades?"

"And I'm good in bed. Did I mention that?"

"I think you touched on that, briefly," Mary reddened further, turning the famous Fairbanks's shade of crimson.

"Oh my goodness," Hilary blurted, "You're a virgin, and not just the airplane kind."

"That's right," Mary nodded.

"Well, you remember how much fun it was flying once you got over the initial concerns?"

"I remember."

"It's the same with sex, only about a thousand times better."

"A thousand times better?"

"Oh, yeah."

"I'm shy, I guess you can tell."

"I'll make you a deal. I won't do anything until you ask. That way, you can set the pace. Would that make you more comfortable?"

"You'd do that for me?"

"How old are you?"

"I'm twenty-two."

"You're old enough to ask for what you want. Now, you need to figure out what it is that you do want. Not what your mom wants or what your dad wants or even what I want. Just you."

"I'll think about it."

"I'd better go. Can't be gone too long. Someone will get suspicious. And one more thing...."

"I know, you're great in bed," Mary recited.

"Well, actually, I was going to ask you to say goodbye to Mitch for me."

They walked to the door. Mary stirred up her courage.
"Can I have a hug?"
"My pleasure," Hilary said, but kept the hugging brief.
"And a kiss?" Mary pushed her luck.
Hilary kissed her ever so lightly on the forehead and then
departed before Mary could ask for more. Not that she
would have. Yeah, right.

A scant three minutes passed before Mitch showed up.
"I'm back."
"You were never gone, were you."
"What do you mean?"
"Kansas called and said you never got there."
"How did things go with Doc?"
"We talked things over. She's a real brave lady, wanting to
get mixed up with the governor's daughter."
"This is good news!"
"I'm just not sure I'm ready."
"Love takes time, in some cases."
"She knows I'm a virgin."
"How did that happen?"
"I told her, after she guessed."
"And?"
"She makes it sound so tempting, you know, not being
one."
"Is there anybody else in your life?"
"You know the answer to that!"
"Then I suggest you allow Hilary to call on you."
"My mother's going to have a fit!"
"You just let me handle your mother, figuratively speaking,
of course. Invite Hilary to dinner tomorrow night. I'll
defrost something special."
"Okay. Now, for the bad news."
"What's up?"
"Trish has moved to Rattlesnake Ridge."
Mary told the story over dinner.
"Tell you what," Mitch planned out loud, "You have a
dinner guest tomorrow, so I'll go up and spend the night
with Trish. Get her settled back down."

"Between keeping Trish settled down and Lisa out of the detective business, this has been one busy undertaking."

"What's the plan for tomorrow's distraction?"

"I heard it was a trip to the beauty parlor."

"Who's going?"

"Lisa, Judy and the two remaining suspects."

"Cloe and Monique?"

"Right."

"I hope everybody studied their script," Mitch moaned audibly.

Chapter 21

You would've thought it was a trip to Antarctica, all the planning that took place. Of course, they had to leave early. The big city was a long ways away from Waysouthfork. Added to the early start time was the complication of makeup and hairdo time. This struck Judy particularly funny, and she laughed as she asked, "Lisa, why do your hair when you're just going to pay somebody to do it again?"

"Well, Sweetie," Lisa explained, "for the same reason you clean your house before the maid gets there!"

"And that reason is?"

"You don't want anyone to think you're a slob!"

"But you're going way beyond that with your hair."

"Well of course. Look, when you walk into a beauty parlor looking like a slob, they don't need to do very much to make you look better, right?"

"Right."

"So if you go in looking like a million bucks, they have their work cut out, and you get your money's worth!"

"I never thought of it that way."

As Judy escorted Lisa down the hallway, they were joined by Monique and Cloe, each looking as stunningly beautiful as Lisa, in their own redhead and brunette way. Judy couldn't fight the feeling of deja vu, that she had seen this before. Three lovely women and one rather ordinary looking escort. Oh yeah, it was all coming back to her. This was just like Charlie's Angels. And she was Bosley.

They took the most expensive rental car and headed toward the big city. Cloe sat upfront to keep Judy company, while Monique shared the back with Lisa and her casts. The interrogation began almost immediately.

"It must have been a shock when Uncle Clyde died," Lisa directed her opening statement to Monique.

"It was. We all thought he would live to be a hundred."

"He must have been well known around here. How many people came to the funeral?"

"There wasn't a funeral. He was scattered."

"I see," Lisa said quietly. "Where?"

"Where what?"

"Where was he scattered?"

Monique had to think about this one. "All over, I guess. That's why they call it scattered?"

"Apparently so," Lisa knew when it was useless to continue. If Monique was a murderer, she would be behind bars already. And Lisa could hear it now, "You mean there was poison in that there little itsy bitsy bottle!"

To Cloe, Lisa said, "So, have you lived here all of your life?"

"Most of it," Cloe bluffed.

"And you haven't found a cowboy yet to settle down with and, you know, raise some little cowpokes?"

Somehow, it all sounded pornographic to a class act like Cloe, but she tried to answer like a nun.

"Cowpoking isn't exactly my idea of fun."

"What exactly is your idea of fun?"

"Spending money is my idea of fun and Uncle Clyde, God rest his hay-raising heart knew how to show us a good time."

It all began to sound a bit on the incestuous side to Lisa, so she stopped talking about heirs and money for the duration of the afternoon. Deep down she hoped that Judy wouldn't take after the other heirs, wanting to spend all the money on herself. Or poking cows. Ick.

Hilary arrived at five o'clock sharp. Mary took one very long, very deep breath as she went to the door.

"Hi."

"Hello."

"Come on in, dinner's about ready."

"Smells good."

"Mitch defrosted."

"Where is she?"

"She went up to spend the night with Trish at Rattlesnake Ridge."

"That's a nice thing for her to do."

"So, are you hungry?"

"Starved. I missed lunch. Boy, if you aren't at the table when the staff thinks you should be, you're out of luck."

"Well, that doesn't happen here."

Mary was as efficient in serving dinner as everything else she undertook. They chatted easily about how events were progressing. Other than the fact that Lisa was still looking for murder or murderers unknown, the plan was going like clockwork.

"How's that maid routine working out?" Hilary asked, aware of the amount of work and stress it involved.

"I can riffle through drawers with the best of them," Mary assured her.

"I bet you can," she teased back with a smile.

"You stop that, or I'm going to make you do the dishes."

"I'll help. You start washing. I'll catch up."

Mary took the entire load, all twelve items, to the counter and ran a sink full of warm, soapy water. As she began to wash, Hilary came up behind her and nestled close to her, gently placing her hands on Mary's arms.

"What are you doing?" Mary asked, fully aware, but wanting to hear.

"I'm helping you do the dishes," Hilary answered, running her fingertips along the inside of Mary's arms.

"That tickles!" Mary wriggled.

"Doesn't tickle me a bit."

Hilary moved her hands down further, joining Mary's in the water. She took over the washing while Mary held on.

"You're holding your breath," Hilary whispered.

"I'm nervous."

"You don't need to be. It's only dishes."

Mary rinsed her hands and turned in the embrace to face Hilary.

"I'd like to talk about something."

"Serious?" Hilary acknowledged.

"You said yesterday that you'd wait until I asked before you did anything."

"I remember," Hilary said, pulling away a little.

Mary pulled her back, closer than before.

"I don't want our relationship to be that way."

"What do you want?"

197

"I don't want to ignore your needs."

"You've told me twice what you don't want. Tell me now what you want."

"I want to make love with you."

"Just so there's no doubt, I love you."

"I love you, too."

Trish had conversed amiably enough through dinner to the point where Mitch wasn't too concerned about her overall attitude. Mitch had arrived with goodies in tow, including pudding and tuna casserole leftovers. Rattlesnake Ridge wasn't kept up like Magnolia, but Luther and staff had shuttled supplies out to Trish. So now, the smorgasbord included pate, bread, lobster Newberg, fruit salad and three bottles of screw top wine. Trish had the good taste not to inquire which one went well with snake. Together, they had managed to overeat and were enjoying a crackling fire with a dessert wine.

"Things sure are working out a little differently than I expected," Trish finally admitted.

"How so?" Mitch prodded the conversation along.

"I thought that by now, Lisa would have shown more of her true colors to Judy. I had hoped to at least be able to offer comfort. I can't even get near the house without causing more trouble."

"Things are going to work out."

"What if they don't?"

"What's got you most worried?"

"What if Lisa and Judy go back to Aspen and you hand over the cash to Judy and slowly but surely, Lisa just spends it?"

"All the while keeping her hooks into Judy?"

"Lisa could do it and Judy would let it happen. She's committed to the relationship."

"And that's one of the nice qualities about Judy."

"I know. But it isn't fair."

"So what we need is a plan to make Lisa show her true colors."

"Have you got one?" Trish asked.

"Not yet, but let me work on it."

Trish exhaled, an impatient sound.

"Do me a favor," Mitch said.

"What?"

"Let me give you a hug."

"You don't have to ask to do that."

"I know, but I wouldn't blame you if you were angry with me."

"Why would I be angry with you?"

"If I'd never won the lottery," Mitch said as she put her arms around Trish, "we wouldn't be here in this mess."

"If you hadn't won, I would have never met Judy."

"But if I wasn't intent on revenge, we wouldn't be knee deep in Operation Waysouthfork."

"You're hell bent on taking the blame for this, aren't you?"

"I'll figure out a way to get you and Judy together. I promise. You'll be in her arms just as surely as you're in mine right now."

"Start figuring things out, and fast."

Mitch nodded and then asked, "Did you say you're spending the night out here?"

"I have to. Mary and Doc are at my place."

"They're together!"

"With any luck."

"Mary and Doc! Wow!"

"They do make a cute couple."

"The governor is going to be very unhappy with you."

"No, she won't."

"How can you be so sure?"

"Because people evolve," was Mitch's mysterious explanation.

Hilary was fifty pages into a book that she found on the shelf when Mary came out of the bedroom. It was still dark, a little after four a.m.

"I woke up and you weren't there."

"Come over here and sit by me," Hilary invited, gesturing to a place on the couch, very near and cozy. Mary accepted the invitation readily.

199

"Couldn't you sleep?" Mary asked.

"I slept like a baby. That happens sometimes. I was so relaxed, I dropped right off. Feels like I got about eight hours of sleep packed into four. How about you?"

"I slept great." Mary nodded.

"Are you okay, after last night?" Hilary asked, just to make sure.

"Was I okay?" Mary answered with a question.

Hilary smiled sweetly.

"I was just sitting here wondering how could it be that a virgin would be so good in bed?" Hilary pulled Mary closer.

"You're teasing me."

"I'm not teasing you, although that is fun to do."

"You were sitting here reading a book?"

"My eyes may have been reading, but my mind, heart and soul were with you."

"So, I was okay?"

"You were great. I'm surprised you're even asking."

"I'm new at this."

"Not for long. Do you want to make love again?"

"You don't think Mitch will come back and – you know."

"It's four in the morning. If she's in the habit of prowling around people's houses that early, she deserves to be embarrassed."

"Okay, well, let's go," Mary said, trying to move out of Hilary's grasp and control.

"Where?"

"To the bedroom?"

"I'm staying right here."

"You mean, on the couch!"

"Beats the heck out of the back seat of a Buick."

"You're serious," Mary just wanted to make sure she was hearing this right.

"Absolutely."

Mary relaxed into a long, languorous kiss from Hilary, thoughts of a Buick slipping into her subconscious memory.

"Mary and Hilary!" Trish had said, three times during her extremely early breakfast with Mitch.

"Hilary and Mary," Mitch had confirmed, sleepily.

"If you and I are here, and Mary and Doc are at your place, who's left running Operation Waysouthfork?"

"How much is there left to worry about? Lisa and Judy will be going over paperwork. Marge, Cloe and Monique will continue the pleasant diversions. Mary and Hilary are probably back there by now. Hopefully, there's nothing to worry about."

"Except for the fact that Lisa is going to try to sleuth her way into more money by trying to prove that Cloe or Monique or maybe both are guilty of murder."

"She's still looking for the killer or killers that never were?"

"I think so, in very subtle ways. That's one of the reasons I'm going back today. I'm the only logical person to know whether or not murderers can inherit money."

"What's the other reason?"

"To show that I'm not affected by Judy."

"Do me a favor and check in with Mary when you get there. Just to see how she is."

"Okay."

"Oh, gee," Mary fretted, "We're going to be late!"

"But it was worth it, wasn't it." Hilary proclaimed.

"Absolutely!"

Hilary pulled Mary into one more embrace.

"We've got to go," Mary said breathlessly.

"You're very conscientious. It's like you're actually on staff."

"I just feel responsible for Judy's well-being."

"Have you found anything out of the ordinary so far?"

"No, but it's important to keep up the watch."

"What about tonight?"

"I'll figure something out."

They left separately, Mary going first. Hilary locked up and trailed behind. Traveling at top speed, Mary made it to the big house just under the wire, arriving five minutes to seven. Trish was already there, talking quietly to Marge. They were nodding. Then, observed by Mary from the hallway, Marge discussed something with Luther. Everyone nodded. Things seemed to be agreeable all around this morning. It was a relief to Mary, who then went upstairs to work. She ran into her counterpart, who was cleaning the bathroom.

"Good morning, Olga."

"Good morning, Ma'am."

"You don't need to call me ma'am," Mary reminded her.

"Yes, Ma'am."

Mary winced, "It there anything new?"

"They sure love bubble baths!"

Mary surveyed the usual places again. Bed stands, drawers, medicine cabinet. No drugs, no pills, no nothing. Breakfast would be over soon, time to fluff pillows.

"Hey everybody," Marge announced at the breakfast table, "Y'all can't come to Texas without going on a horseback ride. We've got an outing planned for the rough and ready! Be at the stables in an hour. We plan to ride a ways, stop and have a cookout in one of the historic line camp houses and then have you back in plenty of time for a nap before dinner."

"Everybody have fun," Trish said so that Lisa would hear perfectly. "I'm afraid I'm going to have to stay behind and do some paperwork."

"Are you sure?" Cloe asked.

"I'm sure."

The groups scattered to get ready, Judy followed Lisa back to their room.

"You better get ready for the cookout!" Lisa admonished.

"I'm not going."

"Why not?"

"Because you can't go with your arm and leg still all banged up."

"Look, Sweetie, just because I can't go doesn't mean you shouldn't go. I want you to go!"

"Are you sure? I could stay behind and rub your feet?"

"Go on the big roundup. I'll be fine. Just don't come back too saddle sore," Lisa winked.

Judy changed into her most comfortable loose jeans, sweatshirt and fleece jacket. It would be a chilly morning, even though it would be a relatively short ride. It was a cookout, not a cattle drive to Montana.

"Quick kiss, right here," Lisa pointed to her lips. "Have fun."

Lisa shuffled over to the window to observe the brave spirits depart for the barn. It looked about as much fun as having an ingrown toenail dug out.

"Hey there."

The familiar voice caught Lisa off guard. She turned and said, "I thought you had paperwork, lawyer lady?"

Trish was leaning on the doorway, looking absolutely fetching in a black silk outfit. Apparently she had changed for the day, as well. Lisa studied her for a second or two longer than necessary, but Trish didn't flinch. Hobbling back to the bed, she struggled to arrange herself.

"Let me give you a hand there," Trish offered.

"That's not necessary," Lisa rejected the offer in a voice that suggested otherwise.

"It's no trouble." Trish listened to the voice, not the words, as she came in and closed the door behind her. She gently but efficiently helped Lisa get settled, putting pillows where Lisa pointed with her good arm. Lisa left plenty of room to sit, and Trish made herself comfortable as well.

"It doesn't look like you're doing paperwork," Lisa wouldn't let her off the hook.

"Well, there's paperwork and then there's paperwork. I thought maybe you had had a chance to look over the paperwork I gave to Judy. She mentioned that the two of you were going to study it together. Judy doesn't seem to have any questions, so I thought I would drop by and see if you had any questions that you were too shy to bring to me."

"I'm not a shy person."

"So you don't have questions?"

"Wouldn't it be easier to invite me to the meetings?"

"Easier yes, ethical, no."

"But suddenly it's ethical to just drop in and see if I have questions."

"I'm just being neighborly. Besides, since Judy has made it clear that she's sharing information with you, I can clarify certain items. I'm more than happy to help."

"I don't have any questions, yet."

"That's good. I knew that you were a woman of intelligence. Some people read through a legal document and end up understanding less than before they started. I knew you'd be different. Well, if anything comes to mind, I'll be in the study, doing my homework."

Trish wandered out, leaving the door ajar. Halfway down the hallway, she ran into Mary, literally. Mary was carrying a full load of sheets and towels. Luckily the minor collision didn't cause a catastrophe.

"You okay?" Trish asked.

"I'm fine. Why did you stay behind?"

"It allays suspicion. If I can convince Lisa that I'm not interested in Judy, maybe things will calm down around here."

"You talked to Mitch?"

"We spent the night together. Remember! Somebody needed to be alone with somebody else at Magnolia. By the way, how are you? Mitch wanted me to ask."

"Everybody knows, don't they?"

"I don't think Lisa knows yet."

"I'm beginning to know how my mother feels. There's no such thing as a private life."

"Your life is private. You just have friends who care about you."

"Do you think Cloe and Monique are jealous because Hilary is spending time with me?" Mary asked out of the blue.

"Why should they, they're bi."

"Bye?"

"Bisexual. Why do you think they were the first out the door this morning for the big ride."

"I don't know?"

"Haven't you seen those exceptionally handsome guys who take care of the livestock?"

"I haven't seen anything but sheets and pillows and I don't need a smart remark out of you right this minute!"

"You mean like 'this undercover work is tiring' kind of remark."

"Here," Mary loaded Trish up with towels. "Go put these in everybody else's rooms except her royal highness, Queen Lisa of Aspen. I've got to get in there before she has a fit."

"Okay, then I'll be in the study, pretending to work."

"What are you going to do?"

"I'm going to wait for the royal mouse to get curious about the royal cheese."

The rest of the morning passed without incident. Lisa napped, tired from trying to keep up with Judy the day before. Texas seemed to have an effect on her. Maybe it was the lower altitude, or the climate, or the prospect of getting rich. After studying the folder, Lisa summoned Mary.

"Yes, Ma'am?"

"I want to go and have lunch with Trish. Help me get ready."

"I believe Ms. Trish is taking lunch in the study."

"Get my silk blouse and slacks. Now!"

"Yes, Ma'am."

Mary went to the closet and pulled out three outfits, one after the other, until she guessed correctly. As Lisa struggled into her clothes, Mary set out her makeup case.

"Brush my hair, not too hard!"

Mary complied while Lisa applied light makeup.

"You look nice," Mary offered sweetly.

"No one asked you," Lisa snapped back, her eyes flashing. "Go and tell the kitchen that I will be taking my lunch in the study as well."

"Yes, Ma'am."

Someone would have to send one great big thank-you gift to this staff. They would have arranged to send Lisa's lunch to the moon if she had asked. Frankly, that's where Mary would have preferred Lisa be right about now.

Trish heard Lisa approach and snapped the file shut that she had been studying. It was identical to the one she had given to Judy, but she didn't want to be caught refreshing her memory.

"Hello," Lisa smiled from the doorway, poised to look just a little bit helpless.

"Hello. Looks like you're getting a bit of exercise."

"I have to keep in shape."

"When are those casts coming off, anyway?"

"Invite me in and I'll give you an entire medical report."

"Come right on in and make yourself at home."

Lisa did so with no trouble.

"Have you eaten yet?" Trish asked, "If not, will you join me for lunch?"

"No and yes. In fact, even though it was forward of me, I told the staff I'd be taking my lunch in the study, with you."

"Well, that's settled. Of course you'll join me in a drink. Scotch or bourbon?"

"It's a little early for me," Lisa sounded unconvincing.

"Oh, nonsense. This is Texas. It's never too early for a drink."

"If you insist. Scotch, straight up."

Trish poured two and after toasting the good life, settled in a leather armchair opposite Lisa.

"So, what can I tell you?" Trish offered.

"Excuse me?" Lisa countered with coy.

"You did come here with questions about the estate, didn't you?"

"I did have one or two."

"Fire away."

"It's not spelled out in black and white just how much Judy will inherit."

"That's right," Trish nodded, just a shade shy of coy herself.

"Why not?"

"Have you ever seen a TV show or read a mystery book where they have a big scene referred to as the 'reading of the will'?"

"I don't watch much TV, but Judy and I are going to write a book."

"Is that so?" Trish tried to sound honesty surprised.

"We've been trying to figure out how to kill off the intended victim."

"Any good ideas?"

"We're not inherently evil, so we haven't come up with anything yet. Maybe we'll kill off our fictional victim the same way somebody killed off Uncle Clyde."

Trish pulled out all the stops with dramatic flair. "Uncle Clyde? You think somebody killed him?"

"Why not? People do it all the time to get their allowance early."

"But if you get caught, you don't get anything."

"But only if you get caught. If I can prove one of the other heirs killed Uncle Clyde, Judy will stand to inherit more money."

"Actually, it may not work that way. I've seen cases where the money intended for someone was placed in a trust fund. And even if it were to be redistributed to the heirs, it would still be a much smaller portion. It would probably cost more time and money to do that than to take the original amount."

"I guess you have a good point. Was there an autopsy?"

"He died of heart failure," Trish answered, avoiding a simple yes or no.

"And his ashes were scattered so there's no hope of investigating for foul play."

"His ashes were scattered. At the time, there was no reason to do an investigation."

"You were going to tell me about the 'reading of the will' scenes."

"Okay, but if you use it in your book, I want professional credit."

"You don't want remuneration."

"I have enough money," Trish replied honestly. It was easier to talk when you were telling the truth.

"So, about the will?"

"I guess scenes are written like that for dramatic purposes, but the real process of probating and executing an estate is usually filled with a bunch of mind-numbing details."

"Really?" Lisa smiled warmly, having polished off her too-early scotch. Trish got up and saw to the refills. Lisa didn't object.

"This will was written in an unusual way."

"In what respect?" Lisa was listening closely.

"In the majority of estates that I've executed, the husband and wife have their wills prepared so that if one dies, the other inherits everything. It's called a reciprocal will. Only when the surviving spouse dies, do things begin to get complex."

"Complex, how?"

"Well, let's assume that mom and pop own a house and a car. When both die, and for convenience sake let's say they had two kids, who inherits what? Does one get the house and the other the car? Depending on the house...."

"Or the car!"

"Or the car, how do you make things equitable?"

"You have an estate sale."

"That's right, and then you split the proceeds."

"But that's not the case in this estate. The wife is still alive."

"That's correct, but this estate was written so that there would be things to settle upon the death of Uncle Clyde. Of course, Marge will still keep the homestead, but there are other provisions."

"That's where Judy comes in?"

"Right."

"She thinks she's going to be rich."

"She does, does she?" Trish said, careful not to show too much interest.

"But she already has a lot of money," Lisa tossed in.

"You sure can't tell by the way she dresses, that's for sure," Trish said with an intended and thoroughly-practiced snippy tone.

"She has casual tastes," Lisa defended.

"Closer to Goodwill, if you ask me. But you didn't, did you?" Trish conjured up in her mind a likeness of Judy and transposed it on Lisa's face and then smiled. If Lisa was won over by the radiance, she didn't give any clue.
Lunch arrived, and the spell was broken. The food looked sumptuous and the staff set things up and then practically bowed out backwards. It was either a sign of utmost respect or they had a rule against turning their backs on Lisa. Lisa voraciously ate her food. Trish picked at her serving after pouring Lisa a glass of wine. At this rate, they would need Doc Hilary to perform liver transplants.

"So, Judy thinks she's going to be rich?" Trish picked up the thread that she wanted to follow.
"But neither one of us could tell by the paperwork."
"That must mean that I did my job well," Trish grinned.
"I did see a percentage number in the paperwork. How does that work?"
"Judy will receive that percentage in the settlement."
"It was one-half of one percent. That doesn't sound like much."
"Sure doesn't, does it."
"Is it much?"
"It would be if we were talking about Coca Cola or Microsoft."
"But we're not."
"I can't divulge the financial information at this time," Trish retreated, enjoying this game more than she thought she would.
"And you couldn't tell me anyway, even if you knew."
"That's right."
"But you did make an educated guess for Judy, didn't you."
"Yes, I did."
"She seemed happy."
"Sounds like she's easily satisfied." Trish made it sound like a disease you'd get from inbreeding.
"You're a lot different on your home turf," Lisa looked at Trish in the way that Trish hoped she would.
"Good or bad?"
"I like the difference."

"Speaking of bad, you've been a bad girl," Trish started another thread.

"Who me?"

"You haven't told me about your arm and leg."

"Oh, that. I'm healing. I'm young and hardy. I heal fast."

"Do you do everything fast," Trish kept her voice inflection innocent, but her eyes twinkled with mischief.

"When it's good to be fast, I'm fast."

"And otherwise?"

"I've been known to take my sweet time."

"You sure took your time getting to know me. I was beginning to worry."

"Worry?"

"That I was losing my touch."

"That's a terrible thing to lose – your touch," Lisa said as she stifled a yawn.

"I'd better get you in bed," Trish said and then added, "I wouldn't want anyone to think I'm neglecting your health. They'll hold me personally responsible if you miss your nap."

"I am a little tired," Lisa agreed.

They walked amiably down the hallway to Lisa's bedroom and paused awkwardly at the door. It was like a first-date moment, to kiss or not to kiss. Trish wasn't giving any clues or invitations. Lisa didn't require either. She pulled Trish to her, kissing slowly and deeply. And then she was gone, door shut, like it was okay to kiss someone like you had known them in three previous lives and then leave them to marvel. Trish sighed, unsure what she had accomplished. She turned to walk down the hallway, and for a second time, ran right into Mary.

"Have you lost your mind!" Mary hissed.

"She kissed me," Trish explained after they were out of earshot.

"You stood still for it."

"It wasn't as easy as it looked."

"I hope you know what you're doing."

"I'm trying to convince Lisa that I'm not interested in Judy."

"Looks like you're being very convincing."

"I can't help it. It's my Texas charm."

"You're from Colorado."

"Details."

As two blessed hours of calm descended on Operation Waysouthfork, everyone took advantage of the time. Lisa slept. Mary soaked her feet. Trish took a long walk and ended up at Magnolia. She broke in, helped herself to a beer to wash away the taste of Lisa and scotch. It took that beer plus the one she carried to the couch, where she settled, feeling somewhat awash. Mitch wandered in about ten minutes later, having stretched her legs as well. She wandered over to the couch where Trish was now looking a little green around the gills.

"Hey Sweetie. You okay?"

"I'm just peachy."

"You want another beer?"

"I've had three scotches, half a carafe of wine and one and a half beers and I'm still conscious."

"I'm surprised you're not in the bathroom."

"Can I stick around here for a while?"

"Of course you can. You're always welcome. You're not going to start throwing up, are you?"

"In between all my drinking, I've eaten like I'm on one of those cruises, you know, a meal an hour. I won't need a plane ticket, I could roll back to Denver."

"Does that mean I don't need to cook dinner?"

"Hell no! Can you whip up a soufflé?"

"How about a meatloaf?"

"Got yourself a deal."

Mitch left Trish to absorb the alcohol coursing through her bloodstream and busied herself in the kitchen. Mary and Hilary showed up at five on the dot and were setting the table when they heard another car pull up. A door slammed and Judy stormed in.

"Where's Trish!"

"I'm right here, you don't need to yell."

Judy walked over to her, wanting to deliver this message face-to-face.

"*You* stay away from *my* woman!"

Everyone in the room froze, looking from Trish to Judy and back. Only Mitch could think of a suitable comment.

"We've all been in Texas way too long."

Judy turned her anger toward Mitch, having found Trish a speechless foil.

"This is no laughing matter."

"So tell me what happened."

"She," Judy pointed to Trish, "is hitting on Lisa!"

"No, she's not," Mary interjected.

"Nobody asked you!" Judy replied, happy to finally find someone who would fight.

"I was there. I saw what happened," Mary stepped forward, getting in Judy face.

"You saw what happened?" Judy stood her ground but couldn't stem her curiosity.

"Trish was being real polite to Lisa while the rest of you took off on your little jaunt. She invited her to have lunch and kept her company. Trish was helping Lisa get back to her room, what with the crutches and all, and Lisa took hold of Trish and gave her the old double tonsillectomy treatment!"

"The what?"

"You know! The oral history. The fastest tongue in the west."

"Okay, okay, I get the point," Judy held up her hands and stepped away. "She told me a different version of the story."

Trish took over from Mary. "I was maybe a little too friendly, but she initiated the kiss."

"Could you do me a favor and turn down the charm a little. You made your point."

"At least she's not worried about you and me anymore. If I were you, I'd get back to the mansion before she wonders where you are."

"I don't need your advice. Just warn me before you do any more improvising."

Judy scanned the group, and then left as quickly as she had come.

"You know, with all of us over here, the big house probably seems empty," Mitch noted, glancing at Mary.

"I don't care, I'm staying here," Trish reiterated.

"Hilary, why don't you and I go back?" Mary said, nodding in a knowing way.

"You're off duty, aren't you?"

"Leave that to me."

"Who's staying for meatloaf?"

"There's leftover soufflé in the kitchen at the mansion," Mary told Hilary.

"I'm right behind you!"

They left holding hands.

Mitch glanced over at Trish, "It's just you and me and meatloaf."

"Got any ketchup?"

They ate quietly, comfortable in each other's company. Over dessert, Mitch asked, "So what happened between you and Lisa?"

"I got to thinking about something that Judy had said to me."

"And that was?"

"That we only have your word that Lisa drugged you and took your money."

"That's true."

"So, I figured I'd allay Lisa's fears about Judy and me, do a little testing of her character."

"And the results?"

"Well, she flunked the character test, but lord can that girl kiss. I'm beginning to understand what you and Judy saw in Lisa."

"Anybody can kiss."

"I haven't been kissed like that since college. Junior year."

"Undergrad?"

"Oh, it was *undergrad* alright," Trish giggled. "What about your old college days?"

"I frittered away my time studying."

"Are you going back someday, to finish?"

"It's on my list of things to do."

"You've never talked much about your life prior to Lisa."

"There's not much to tell."

"What about other girlfriends?"

"What other girlfriends."

"Lisa was your one and only?"

"You said it yourself, the girl can kiss. She spoiled me for anybody else."

"I think it's a case of once burned twice shy."

"Either way, I sleep alone."

"You know, a lot of people think we gay people sleep around all the time."

"That's their fantasy, not mine."

"What is your fantasy?"

"My fantasy? My ideal relationship would be to grow with someone. I would want to find someone intelligent enough to learn from them and still be able to teach them as well. Maybe that sounds too didactic, but I need more than someone who can kiss well."

"You want a companion?"

"I want a partner. An equal."

Lisa hid her concern well when Judy returned. After Lisa had embellished the story, Judy had taken off, apparently ready for a fight. Now, back with the truth, she was strangely quiet. Lisa couldn't stand the silence.

"You talked to her?"

"She apologized for being flirtatious. I accepted on your behalf. I told her to stay away from you."

"That's all?"

Judy nodded. It was easier to lie if you didn't have to use your voice.

"She certainly thinks a lot of herself. She was gawdawful snide about you."

"Can we just drop this."

"Sure, but she was so snippy about your wardrobe."

"My wardrobe?"

"Said you looked like a reject from the second-hand store, or something like that."

"I don't care."

"Well, I know you don't care, but Honey, where I come from, those are fighting words."

"Is that all?" Judy asked, wondering if Lisa was the long lost daughter of Calvin Klein.

"She made a comment that you were easily satisfied. I took that as a personal affront!"

"Why?"

"Well, you're satisfied with *me*, aren't you? I guess that means I'm not much!"

"Tell me exactly what she said," Judy asked, even though she was leery about this entire conversation.

"We were talking about the estate, and she said you were easy to satisfy. How would *she* know?"

"She was talking about money, not sex."

"Well, I took umbrage on your behalf anyway."

"Did she tell you how much I'm going to inherit?"

"Of course not. She said she made a guess for you. But she didn't think it was a lot of money? Why do you think that you're going to be rich?"

"Does anybody around here look poor to you?"

"One-half of one-percent doesn't sound like a helluva lot."

"It's more than I started with. Don't look that proverbial gift horse in the mouth."

"I think I'll take a walk," Lisa announced, out of the blue.

"I'll go with you."

"No, you stay here and rest up. You've had a long day."

Two minutes ago, Judy would have welcomed a break from Lisa. Now, she was suspicious. Why, she didn't know. Trish was with Mitch. Mary was with Hilary. What trouble could Lisa get into?

"Okay, you take a walk, but there's one thing I think you should know," Judy stated seriously, for effect.

"What's that?" Lisa took the bait.

"I'm not saddle sore."

"That's nice," Lisa answered distractedly as she left their room.

"I never knew leftover soufflé could taste so good," Mary said, sitting next to Hilary in the kitchen. It was a comfortable place to be, and the kitchen was homey as well. Escaping the ravages of stainless steel redecoration, the family had remodeled the room in oak and walnut. Sure, there was a bit of metal and steel here and there, but it was surrounded in the warmth of wood, and it had a distinctive glow.

"It's the company, definitely the company," Hilary reassured her.
"You can make everything taste better?" Mary cocked an eyebrow toward her.
"I do my best."
"Remind me to feed your ego at least once a day," Mary teased back.
"I won't have to remind you after the first week. It'll come naturally by then," Hilary winked back.
"I think this doctor act has rubbed off on you."
"Speaking of which, I have a dilemma," Hilary confided, suddenly serious.
"There's a problem?"
"As I was practicing taking blood pressures, I found out that one of our party has high blood pressure."
"Who is it?"
"I guess I'm not bound by any doctor-patient confidentiality rules, since I'm not a doctor. It's Marge."
"I believe it. She is a little older, and probably a little out of shape."
"It wasn't anything critical. If it had been, I would have taken her to the hospital. But her numbers are higher than the normal range. She should have it checked out when we get home."
"Do you think she'll be reluctant to have a physical?"
"I don't know. I think Mitch would be a positive influence. Should I tell her?"
"Tell Marge to get a check-up. Then tell Mitch later on that you suggested very strongly to Marge that she get a check-up. Mitch has a way with Marge. I'm thinking she will have a healthy influence on her."
"You're so clever about these things," Hilary complimented as she took hold of Mary's hand. They indulged in a kiss as Lisa came into view.
"Well, what do we have here?" Lisa sneered.
Hilary and Mary parted quickly, startled by her presence. They didn't know how long she had been listening.

"Hello, Lisa," Hilary said, nonchalantly.

"How long have the two of you been misbehaving?" Lisa gloated.

"Not long enough," Hilary retorted, angry at Lisa's haughty attitude.

"Well, maybe things are different in Texas, but where I come from, you'd never catch a doctor lowering his or her standards to consort with a common house servant."

Mary felt Hilary tense up, and squeezed her hand until they made eye-contact. Her eyes sent a message of silent caution. Don't blow it now.

"And you came all the way down here to tell me that?" Hilary answered, calming down a little herself.

"No, actually, I came down here to get a snack. Seems you two have beaten me to the punch."

"I'll fix something for you," Mary volunteered, slipping so easily into service mode that Lisa backed down.

"No, that's alright. I've lost my appetite after watching the two of you."

She thumped out of the kitchen as quickly as she had appeared.

"What do you suppose she was up to?" Mary asked.

"She was probably looking for this," Hilary extracted a container of rat poison from a locked cabinet under the sink that she just happened to have a key to.

"What is that stuff?"

"An arsenic-based poison. When I heard that Lisa was suspicious about Uncle Clyde's death, I knew she would be looking for possible poisons. So I did a check of the kitchen and surrounding areas and rounded up all the poisons I could locate. They've been locked up in here for two days. Rat poison, drain cleaner, stuff like that."

"You are so smart!"

"I know. But there is something I need your expert help with."

"What's that?

"Come on, I'll show you."

By now, between the two of them, they knew all the back hallways that connected the mansion. They entered

Hilary's room unnoticed and Hilary took Mary over to the bed.

"There's something wrong with my bed," Hilary said seriously.

"Your bed looks fine," Mary stated, equally seriously.

"No, there's something definitely wrong with it. You're not in it!"

"You are so ornery!" Mary declared, sounding more Texan every minute.

"That's real close to what I am!" Hilary agreed enthusiastically.

Mary laughed. A day ago, she had been nervous. Now, she was relaxed, comfortable, and scared to death to go home. She chided herself. She was over twenty, able to make decisions. Whatever would happen to her mother's political career would be blamed on her, but in actuality, it could just as easily be blamed on ignorance and prejudice. A right-wing governor who has a gay daughter. Stranger things have happened. Lost in thought, Mary was brought back to the present moment by Hilary.

"You're thinking about your mom."

"How do you know?"

"I can feel you tensing up."

"You're right. I'm sorry."

"You don't need to be sorry."

"I'm ruining the moment."

"No, you're not. I have a good idea."

"Let's hear it."

"First, let's fix this bed by getting you into it."

"And then?"

"Then, let's talk about what we're going to do when we get home."

In three minutes, they were snuggled together, sharing a smuggled bottle of champagne. Rat poison wasn't the only inventory Hilary had secured.

"I knew you'd understand my trepidation," Mary began.

"Remember, you had a dose of that on the flight down."

"I sure did. You scared the bejeesus out of me. There I was, about to steal a kiss from the prettiest woman this side of New York, and I find out she's the daughter of the governor. It threw me for a loop."

"So what changed your mind?"

"Mitch did. She understands people. She told me about you. About how intelligent you were and how good you were with people and your basic kindness."

"I'll have to remember to thank her."

"I'll remind you when we go home."

"What else about going home did you want to talk about?"

"I know we won't be welcome at the mansion, that's a given. I'll have to live somewhere else."

"With me. You'll live with me," Hilary assured her.

"That's a big step."

"Are you ready?"

"Are you?"

"Yes," Hilary affirmed.

"Where do you live?"

"Gaytown."

Mary nodded sagely. There actually was an area in Denver referred to as "Gaytown". It was an older part of the city, once run down, but now being refurbished by young couples, gay and straight alike, who were gentrifying the neighborhood.

"I've always wanted to live in Gaytown," Mary said.

"Here's your chance."

"That's not too far from my work."

"What do you do?"

"I work with a foundation that helps abused kids. I do the fund raising and help out at the Center. The salary is modest."

"That's an amazing career."

"I'll help with the rent and the groceries."

"Honey, don't fret about that. Tell me what has you worried."

"My mother's going to hate you."

"I can live with that. Keep going."

"And she's going to hate me."

With that statement, Mary began to cry. She had held this fear in for over ten years. It had been extracted by Hilary in less than ten days. As she wept, she relaxed deeply into

Hilary's arms and soaked up the unconditional love. After a few moments, she added, "But my dad, he'll be fine."

"Your mom is going to be okay, too," Hilary reassured, "We'll just give her some time to get used to the idea."

"About thirty years should do it."

"More like thirty days."

"That would be a miracle."

"I believe in miracles. You're in my arms, aren't you?"

"That's your idea of a miracle?"

"While everyone else is waiting for the second coming of Christ, I got to witness the first coming of Mary."

"And the second...."

"And the third!"

"The third?"

"Remember, the couch?"

"Oh yeah, the couch. Sure beat the back seat of a Buick."

"Sure did. Do you feel better now?"

"One-hundred percent."

"That's a big improvement."

"You're easy to talk to.'

"That's how relationships are supposed to work. I want all of you, your body, your mind, your heart and soul, to be comfortable with me."

"For the first time in my life, I am."

"Me, too."

Breakfast was funereal. The bloom was definitely off the yellow rose of Texas for Lisa. She hadn't gotten any closer to finding out about the actual inheritance, and had been thwarted at every turn to solve the murder mystery of Uncle Clyde. Judy was distant, Trish acted like a complete stranger, Hilary was standoffish, and Mary was as still as a hundred foot deep pond.

"Let's go home, now, right now, today," she implored to Judy after they had returned to their bedroom for Lisa's after-breakfast nap.

"Today?" Judy wanted to hear this again.

"Get that maid in here to start the packing."

"You're sure about this? I'll tell you what. Let me arrange to take you on a jeep ride around the ranch. You've spent way too much time alone, all cooped up here in this room and that's all my fault. I should have stayed home yesterday and kept you company."

"Nothing is your fault. I just don't want to wear out our welcome."

"You're sure?" Judy asked again, knowing that Lisa had worn out her welcome before they had even arrived.

"I want to get back to where it's just you and me."

"I understand. You're homesick. Okay, I'll let our hostess know and then I'll start packing."

"Find that lazy maid. She can do it."

"I need to get used to working hard again. There's no one at home to help me out."

"You're angry."

"No, I'm not angry," Judy said truthfully, "Just let me take care of things my way. I'm ready to go home, too."

Judy went down the hallway, and no surprise, found Mary making the bed in Hilary's room."

"Let everyone know that we're leaving today."

"What's wrong?"

"Too much Texas, I guess."

"I'll go start the packing."

"I'm going to do that," Judy said, "Why don't you do me a big favor and go make some camper reservations."

"That's a good idea."

The dismantling of the sting took less time than a football game. Between Mary and Judy, they had Judy and Lisa packed up in an hour. The sad tearful goodbye scene staged by Marge was good enough for Broadway. Almost everyone stood on the driveway to wave goodbye and then, the minute the camper was out of sight, they scattered to pack.

"What if they forgot something?" Marge asked.

Mitch, who had been called to the mansion when the coast was clear, had a good answer.

221

"Mary, why don't you and Doc Hilary stick around for a few days. If they return, or ask to find a lost article, you'll know where it is, right Mary?"

"I did enough snooping to know where things might be."

"And Doc Hilary will add credibility."

"Is that what they're calling it nowadays," Trish arched an eyebrow. "Credibility?"

"Don't tease the newlyweds," Mitch playfully admonished.

"Your airline reservations are set," Mary went on, ignoring with newly found ease the teasing.

"Marge, would your relatives mind if Mary and Hilary took up residence for a while?"

"Magnolia is always open," she affirmed.

"Rattlesnake Ridge is more romantic," Trish tossed out casually.

"Whatever," Mitch said, "Just let the staff get the mansion back to order. They deserve that much after all the help they've been."

Chapter 22

The convoy headed for the airport. The flight was on time. They were home in Denver by early afternoon. Mitch had barely put down her suitcase, still dusty from Texas when the phone rang.

"Where's my daughter!" the curt voice cut through the phone line.

Mitch recognized it instantly.

"Hi, Governor Fairbanks."

"Don't Governor Fairbanks me. Where's Mary?"

"Isn't she with her dad, on some camping trip?" Mitch stalled.

"No, he's in the hospital with appendicitis. Where's Mary? I'm getting tired of asking."

"Why do you think I know?"

"Her father said you would know."

"Mary is fine."

"Where is she?"

"She's quite a long ways away right now."

"You tell me, and you tell me now or so help me you'll regret the day you met me."

"That's beginning to happen already."

"I could have you arrested."

"But you won't. That wouldn't make sense, and I know you're a woman who makes sense."

"Just tell me where she is."

"Okay, I'll tell you, but not over the phone."

"Over the phone, now!"

"No."

There was a moment of silence. Mitch didn't know whether to pray or hang up.

"Come to the mansion."

"No."

"Okay, where?" Rebecca sounded exasperated and Mitch took pity, against her better judgment.

"I'll pick you up in about an hour."

"An hour?"

"I like to obey the speed limit."

"Be in the driveway in twenty minutes."

The phone went dead in her ear. Mitch sighed and called her favorite travel agent, again. The second time this month.

"Two tickets to Vegas? Let me check. There's nothing commercial. How about a charter?"

"A small plane?"

"Not terribly small, just a lot more money than two plane tickets."

"I'll take it."

The phone clicked in her ear again, she was on hold for a couple of minutes.

"Okay, you're all set. You'll need to go to the airport out south. Talk to Mike, he's getting ready for you as we speak. Anything else?"

"A nice suite somewhere out on the Las Vegas strip."

"Lots to choose."

"Just make it classy."

"First date?"

"I think I'm way beyond that."

"Okay, call me when you get to Vegas and I'll tell you where you're staying."

"You're a genius."

"I'm charging you double for the short notice."

"Charge me triple. You're worth it."

Twenty-five minutes later, Mitch had pulled up in front of the mansion. Rebecca came out and sat gingerly in the passenger's seat.

"So, where is she?"

"Just sit back and relax."

Mitch guided her car into traffic and noticed three unmarked cars pull into traffic discreetly behind her. Lord knows how many more were out there, ready to swoop.

"You look nice tonight, Rebecca."

Nothing. No response from the governor.

"Is that a new dress?"

A glare. At least it was something.

"Every time we go out together, you look so beautiful."

"Would you just shut up and drive. And we are not going out, you understand. We aren't going out! We have never gone out!"

"Well, you still look nice."

It didn't matter that Mitch ran a red light or two. No one stopped her. Heck, this was better than a police escort. Going on a joyride with the governor had its perks. They were at the airport in time to meet Mike, and buckle in. Rebecca opened up her mouth a couple of times to complain, but thought better of it. Now came an intelligent question.

"We need to fly to get to where Mary is?"

"That would be the truth."

Since technically it was truthful that they would have needed to fly to go to Texas, Mitch found it easy to lie. The fact that this lying stuff was getting easier bothered her just a little.

"This is a very small plane."

"Think of it this way, Amelia Earhart crossed the Atlantic in something this size."

"She also was killed flying around the world."

"You're the one who called me. Do you want to go or not?"

"Okay, well, then let's just go, and get this over with." This had been the best plan ever to get rid of the bodyguards. Mitch silently congratulated herself. They settled in for the relatively short flight. Mitch slept, needing rest after the big Texas adventure. This irritated Rebecca and she relished the chance to prod Mitch rudely awake when they were landing.

"Are we there already?"

"You snored most of the way."

"Oh good, that means I got good sleep."

They disembarked at McCarren Airport and Mitch called to find out about the hotel room. Another miracle, they would be in the Luxor. Nice place, funny shape.

A hotel limousine picked them up and they were checked in and settled in their suite in twenty minutes.

"Okay, take me to Mary."

"Oh, Mary isn't here."

"You said we were flying to where Mary was!"

"No I didn't. You said you would need to fly to get to where Mary was and I agreed."

"You're in a lot of trouble."

"I know. But I'm still the only one who knows where Mary is, and when you calm down, I'll explain things to you."

"I'm calm."

"Are you sure?"

"Yes, I'm sure," she said through clenched teeth.

"Okay, then the first thing I need to ask is that you make a choice between two things."

"What two things?"

"Choice number one, you need to hand over the wiretap equipment that you are wearing, or choice number two, take off your clothes and prove that you aren't wired."

"You can go to hell."

"I probably will in good time, but the faster you comply, the sooner you'll know what I know."

Rebecca sat for a moment, and then stood up, turned around with her back to Mitch and began to disentangle herself from her wiretap. She handed it over and sat back down. It was still warm and Mitch held it for a minute while she thought of a good method of disposal for the device. She carried it over to the ice bucket and submerged it in ice water. Not that it mattered. They were probably well out of range by now, but it felt good to destroy government property in front of a government official, and still be able to get away with it.

"How did you know?"

"You kept talking into your chest."

"Now what?"

"I'll tell you the whole story, but I would greatly appreciate your word that you won't make my life a living hell because of it."

"Is Mary okay?"

"Mary is fine, and please trust me that you and Mary don't want the FBI or the CIA or the police department to be in on this story. You don't need the publicity and Mary deserves some shred of privacy."

"Mary has lost her virginity, hasn't she!"

"Well, yes and no, I guess?"

"Well, is it yes or no?"

"I guess it's closer to yes."

"And you arranged for this and got her father to cover for her."

"That's not exactly how things started out."

"Well, how did things start out."

"It's a long story, can we discuss it over dinner?"

"You can eat at a time like this!"

"I found out that I can eat through almost anything. Tell you what, I'll make reservations at the nicest restaurant in the hotel and over dinner, I'll tell you the complete truth, from appetizers to dessert."

"This had better be good."

"You won't believe your ears."

Rebecca had been patient, Mitch had to agree. They were enjoying deep fried mushrooms and gazpacho soup as Mitch warmed up to the story.

"I once knew a girl named Lisa."

"Is this story going to be about your sex life."

"If this story was going to be about just my sex life, it would qualify as one of the top ten shortest stories of all time! Now, are you going to hush up and let me tell it?"

"I'm hushed."

"Now, where was I?"

"You once knew a girl named Lisa...."

"Who swindled me out of my modest family fortune."

"Probably the only modest thing about you."

"It's the wine, isn't it?" Mitch pointed to the empty glass. A waiter in a tuxedo appeared and refilled the glass.

"I think it's a combination of everything."

"If you stop and think about it, you're probably relaxed because deep in your heart you know I wouldn't let any harm come to Mary."

Rebecca had been relaxing almost from the moment Mitch had escorted her downstairs to the restaurant. The two glasses of wine that had gone down like water eased her prickliness even further.

"You once knew a girl named Lisa…" Rebecca reiterated *again*.

"So, what little income I made, I scrounged along, working nine to five, scraping money together to go to college, eating a lot of oatmeal."

"I bet your heart valves are as clean as a whistle."

"And then, as luck would have it, I win the lottery, the same night you get elected to public office."

"That reminds me, I'm supposed to check in."

"Do it later. They know you're with me, don't they?"

"That's what's got them worried."

Mitch laughed easily.

"So, I win the lottery and you win the election and Mary shows up on my doorstep and we become friends."

"So where is she?"

"I'm getting to that." Their dinners arrived and Mitch ate a couple bites of the best steak this side of the Mississippi River before continuing.

"Then, one day, on a trip to Aspen, I see Lisa."

"The swindler."

"One and the same, and she's with another lady, so I talked to the lady she was with and told her about my experiences with Lisa."

"The swindler."

"And so some friends of mine come up with a scheme to protect this lady, and to catch Lisa in the act."

"What act?"

"We deduced that Lisa had already planned to steal this lady's money, so we set up a sting and made Lisa think that this other lady was going to inherit a lot of money within a month or two."

"What has all this got to do with Mary?"

"Well, Mary and I had become friends after the banquet, and she dropped by the Lucky U one day to see me and she sort of caught us in the middle, well, actually closer to the beginning of coming up with this scheme."

"You are incapable of telling a short story, aren't you?"

"She wanted to be in on it. I guess having a mother for governor wasn't excitement enough for her."

"So you pulled her into this scheme."

"She pushed her way in, took over the planning, and did a great job. She could be real nefarious if she was so inclined."

"So Mary is in Aspen?"

"Oh heck no! Why would she be in Aspen?"

"Just a silly guess, so where is she?"

"So, things were going along just fine, and the plan was in place and then Lisa…"

"The swindler."

"Began to get suspicious."

"I can't imagine why."

"And she was in two casts to boot. Still is, in fact."

"You mean like plaster?"

"Yeah, apparently she threw herself between Judy and a car. Broke an arm and a leg. Snap, snap."

"Who's Judy?"

"The nice lady in Aspen."

"Where Mary isn't"

"Right, so we had to come up with something that would convince Lisa that Judy was going to be rich. That's when Marge spoke up."

"Marge?"

"The nice lady who owns the Lucky U. Remember, you met her when you came there and threatened to break my arm."

"It's all coming back."

"Turns out, her family owns a great big ranch in Texas. So we all went down to Texas and put on a show for Lisa so that she would think Judy was going to be rich."

"And Mary's still in Texas?"

"Right now, but she should be home in a day or two."

"What is she doing?"

"How descriptive do you want me to get?"

"She's sleeping with Lisa?"

"Oh heavens no! I wouldn't let that happen!"

"Judy?"

"No. Judy and Trish are an item waiting to happen."

"Marge?"

"Marge is sixty if she's a day."

"Okay, who is Mary sleeping with?"

"A nice woman."

"Nicer than you?"

"Lots and lots nicer than me. Lots nicer."

Rebecca finished her dinner in silence. Mitch hurried to catch up. The steak was juicy and tender, and didn't taste any worse for having gone cold during the story.

"So, it won't do me any good to go flying off to Texas."

"I don't think that's such a good idea. Even if you knew where to go, and you don't, and went in with the FBI and the CIA, what good would it do?"

"I was worried."

"We never meant to worry you. Trust me, Mary is in good hands."

"She's afraid to come home, isn't she?"

Mitch heard the break in Rebecca's voice that she tried so hard to hide.

"Tell you what," Mitch offered, "Let's go back upstairs and I'll call and see how she is. Would that make you feel better?"

"It would relieve my mind."

They went back to the suite, and sat down together next to the phone.

"Before I call, I just want you to know that I've told you more than I had a right to. I fully expect Mary to be angry with me, and she may take that anger out on you."

"Why does Mary tell you things anyway!" Rebecca groused.

"She feels safe with me."

"I'm her mother!!"

"That's true."

"She used to tell me things, before you showed up."

Mitch shook her head at the falsehood.

"What don't you agree with?" Rebecca challenged.

"Your daughter has known since junior high that she was gay and you're blaming me for her not telling you. Are you even listening to yourself?"

"She hasn't been gay since junior high."

"You're right. She's been gay since she was born. She only figured it out when she was twelve. And the sad thing is, she's had a long, lonely ten years to deal with it because you weren't there."

"I was too there."

"Not in a safe way. Not in an unconditional way. And not only weren't you there for her, but you literally surrounded yourself with people who weren't safe for her either."

"It wasn't like that."

"And then," Mitch continued, now on a roll, "When your political aspirations became the most important thing in your life, your gay daughter sublimated her entire existence to support you. To help you. I'm amazed she survived the ordeal with any self-esteem left intact. It's no wonder she tags along after me. She can be herself around me with no qualms. No reservations. No facade. Instead of planning her life with this new opportunity, she's worried sick about what it will do to you and your political career."

"Are you finished with the lecture?"

"I just have one more thing to say."

"What's that?"

"Mary wants *your* love and *your* support. I'll do everything in my power and sphere of influence to help both of you get to that point. But love and support do not translate into intolerance and destruction in any language. Most parents don't get a second chance with their gay child. You do. I hope you have the speech of your life ready."

Rebecca remained silent, but nodded.

Mitch dialed the phone, careful to conceal the numbers from Rebecca.

"Hello?" Mary answered, sleepily.

"Hey there."

"Hi Mitch. You get home okay?"

"Actually, I'm in Las Vegas, with your mother."

"You're in Las Vegas with my mother?"

"It's a long story."

"Let's hear it."

"Due to some complications, I'm afraid I had to tell her a few things."

"Oh, God."

"But she doesn't know exactly where you are."

"Okay, and what about my dad and the alibi?"

"That sort of fell through."

"Is he okay?"

"Do you want to talk to your mom? She's right here, listening to my half of the conversation."

"Is my dad okay?"

"He's okay. I wouldn't be in Vegas with your mom if he wasn't, would I?"

"Okay."

"So, you want to talk to your mom?" Mitch asked again.

"I want to go and wake up Hilary first. I think I'll need her support."

"That's a good idea. I'll hold the line."

It didn't take too long. Oh to be young and in love and willing to wake up for each other.

"Okay, we're ready."

"Okay, now, after I put your mom on the line, I'm going to go for a walk. I want to give your mom all the privacy she needs."

"Okay."

Mitch held on to the phone as she handed it to Rebecca. For a moment, they shared custody of the handset. Their eyes met and Mitch lightly kissed Rebecca's forehead.

"Good luck. I mean it."

Mitch walked out the door, went to the inclinators and arrived on the casino floor in scant moments. She passed by the gambling temptations and found herself in the coffee shop with a triple decaf mocha in front of her. She rubbed her eyes, swearing that she still had dust from Texas in them. She felt unwashed, cantankerous, and traitorous. Mary might never speak to her again, Rebecca might never speak to her again, and Judy might never speak to Trish again. This brilliant plan seemed to be spinning out of control and Mitch was running out of ideas.

"I checked the bar first."

Mitch looked up to see Rebecca.

"You're going to have to work on your pick up lines."

Undaunted, Rebecca sat down.

"You want something?"

"Let me taste whatever it is that you have."

"Sure."

Rebecca tasted the mocha and nodded affirmatively. "This isn't half bad."

The waitress bustled over to take their order. Mitch ordered another triple decaf mocha and one of everything on the dessert menu.

"One of each?" Rebecca quizzed.

"I've always wanted to do that."

"Seems to be your style," Rebecca made the remark like it was meant to be an uncomplimentary observation.

Mitch let it slide and a quiet moment passed between them. "I'm not going to ask," Mitch finally said.

"Mary is fine. She's fine. She sounds better than you look."

"That's not saying much. I look like hell."

"What would it take for you and me to have a nice, long, honest, non-defensive talk?"

Mitch studied Rebecca's face for a hint of where this was going. "Honestly?"

"Honestly."

"Well, I would need some sleep. I'm exhausted."

Seven desserts and a mocha arrived. Mitch picked up a fork and tasted chocolate cake from heaven."

"What else?" Rebecca must have been serious about wanting to talk. She was making a mental list of prerequisites.

"Neutral territory would be good. We could stay here a day. Relax, swim, get a massage, and talk. You know, a nice, hedonistic day."

"Mary's coming home in three days."

"Well, then let's give ourselves two days of talking."

"I did have appointments back home."

"Hey, you're the one who wanted to talk," Mitch reminded pointedly.

"I didn't think it would take two days."

"Maybe it won't. What is it that you want to talk about?"

"I want to talk about being gay."

Mitch had a bite of cheesecake poised on her fork. It escaped being devoured by falling back to the plate.

"That's going to definitely take a day or two. At least!"

"But we could at least get a start."

"Being gay is a lot like not being straight."

"That's a big help."

"But it's also alike, in some ways."

"I see."

"And your political supporters aren't helping at all to bridge the information gap."

"I'm still hoping we can keep this non-defensive."

"Well, it's going to take me a while to forget that you had the police listening in on us and following us around like we were criminals. I get defensive when people do that to me."

"You're right. I'm sorry. My security advisors were worried about a possible kidnapping."

"Your husband knew better."

"He was in surgery."

"Okay, you're forgiven. I forgive you for being concerned. I'm not one to hold a grudge for long."

Simple forgiveness was too much for Rebecca after such a long day. Her eyes welled up and she said, "I'll see you back in the room."

She deserted Mitch, no pun intended, and the waitress came over to inspect.

"Is there any way that I can get all of this to go?"

"What's your room number?"

"I'm in one of the suites. King Tut or something. Here's my pass card key."

The waitress took down the information and said, "I'll have it sent up to your room. Will there be anything else?"

"No, thank you."

Mitch left a hefty tip and returned to the suite. Rebecca was ensconced on the couch with a washcloth over her eyes.

"I'm going to take a bath. If someone comes to the door, it's room service."

"Room service?"

"They're bringing the seven desserts up. Nice people around here."

Thirty minutes later, Mitch emerged from the bathroom feeling almost back to normal. Eight hours of sleep would aid the cause. Rebecca had come out from behind her cold compress and was finishing off the brownie pie before the coffee flavored ice cream could melt.

"This is good. I saved the chocolate cake for you. When you had a bite downstairs, I thought your eyes were going to roll clear back in your head."

"Thank you. I think I'll take it to bed."

"So, we can talk tomorrow?"

"Sure, I'll get a good night's sleep and be ready to fill you in."

Mitch left Rebecca alone to debrief the day's events, check in with her office, and call Jeff. When Mitch's head hit the pillow, she was instantly asleep. She dreamed of riding the range. The sun nestled into the horizon. She felt at peace.

"Good morning!" Rebecca greeted.

"Huh, um, uh, what time is it? I thought you'd let me sleep in!" Mitch grumbled.

"I did. It's half past noon."

"Half past noon already? That can't be, I just went to sleep."

"I just woke up myself. That's the longest I've slept in since I was elected to office."

Mitch got out of bed groggily and subjected herself to another long, hot shower. It was beginning to do the trick. She came out dressed in a thick, hotel bathrobe. Something smelled wonderful.

"I ordered room service. Have a seat."

"Terrific."

Mitch looked at Rebecca with now wide-awake eyes. She was dressed in the same clothes as last night, but her hair was perfect and she glowed.

"Do you always look this good at…" Mitch checked her watch, "One fifteen in the afternoon?"

"I wouldn't know. I don't sit around in front of mirrors all day long, checking my looks."

"Do you pay somebody to do that for you?"

"Contrary to popular belief, we don't have money in the governor's budget for things like that."

"I bet you deal with that a lot."

"With what?"

"People who have preconceived notions about political lifestyles."

"Is this part of that long talk we're going to have?"

"Just a thought over breakfast."

Mitch didn't know how she could possibly be hungry again. She chose to eat first and talk later.

"You have a hearty appetite," Rebecca remarked.

"Do you like that in a woman?"

Rebecca was still trying to piece together a reply when Mitch asked, "Do we have any of those desserts left over from last night?"

"Dessert, for breakfast?"

"Sure, it's all part of this decadent gay lifestyle that I lead."

"You can't do this without being defensive, can you?"

"I'm trying to get things out so that they won't hide and hurt us later."

"Mitch, I want more than anything to have a conversation. But, don't come at me with everything at once. Go slowly, and I'll return the favor."

"Okay, that's fair. I just get hostile when people think that gay people should be taken out in the street and stoned to death."

"I'm not a bible literalist. I don't believe that way."

"Then stop taking political donations from people who do."

"I don't think I do, but I'll check into that."

"So, now that we know what you don't believe, what exactly is it that you do believe?"

"Right now?"

"This minute."

"I don't know what I believe anymore."

Mitch grinned, breaking the somber mood with an uplifting of spirit and soul.

"That's the best news I've heard all day. Let's celebrate!"

"How?" Rebecca asked, still erring on the side of caution.

"Let's go swimming. The hotel pool looks absolutely inviting"

"I didn't pack any other clothes, let alone a swim suit!"

"Well, then, let's go shopping!"

"I didn't bring a lot of money."

"It's my treat! Let me get dressed and then we can hit the shops over at Caesar's Palace."

"I'll pay you back."

"Consider it a gift. Remember, I'm rich."

"How rich are you, anyway?"

"I'm so rich, that I pay people to walk my dogs."

"What's the big deal about that?"

"I don't own any dogs."

Dressed in the same clothes they wore on the flight, they made good use of the hotel's limousine service for moneyed guests. Taking a leisurely pace, they shopped for, in no particular order of importance, athletic shoes, shorts, jeans, goofy T- shirts, swim suits, socks, underwear and something to wear to bed. Mitch playfully slapped Rebecca's hand lightly when she reached for a pair of pantyhose.

"No uncomfortable clothes allowed!" she chided.

The clerk must have thought they were eccentric, among other things, but kept her opinions to herself. They loaded up the limo with packages and returned to the hotel, ready for a swim. The weather was cool, and the pool was almost deserted. Mitch watched Rebecca swim like a seal for about ten minutes. She was warming to this vacation, with or without the sun's help.

"I didn't realize you were so athletic."

"I made swim team in college," she bragged, "I still swim every chance I get."

"I bet that's not as often as you'd like."

"Work keeps me busy. I'm a good governor. That takes time."

Mitch nodded.

"So, what are you good at?" Rebecca quizzed.

"I'm good at a lot of things."

"Don't be afraid to brag. I'm waiting for an answer."

"I'm good at listening to people."

"Okay, what else?"

"You only bragged about one thing."

237

"I bragged about two things, swimming, governing. Tell me a second thing."

"Okay," Mitch hesitated for only a moment, "I'm good at getting people to fall in love with me."

Her comment was greeted by silence. Going for complete loss of words, Mitch finished her thought, "I just haven't figured out why it isn't working with you, yet."

It worked better than expected. Rebecca didn't have a reply. Only out of mercy, did Mitch let Rebecca off the hook.

"I'm ready for dinner, how about you?"

"I could stand to eat. Swimming makes me hungry."

"Me, too. Race you to the towels."

They rode up the inclinator in silence, eyes everywhere but on each other. Changing into dinner clothes didn't take long. Wherever they were going to eat, it had to be casual.

"I heard about a little microbrewery at the other end of the strip. Let's go there," Mitch suggested.

"Sounds like fun," Rebecca talked as little as possible.

This time, they took a taxi, not wanting to bother the limo drivers. They would be busy escorting other guests to fancy shows. The brewery was packed, and they put their name on a list for dinner. A tiny table with two chairs finally opened up in the corner of the bar. They each ordered an amber malt for an appetizer.

"Goodness, this is strong," Rebecca commented after a taste.

"It's not for the faint of heart."

Half a glass later, Rebecca was beginning to appreciate the taste.

"I can see why Mary enjoys your company. You're easy to be with."

"I'm not trying to be."

"But you are anyway. It must be your nature."

"Yesterday and this morning, I was defensive and hostile."

"That's all gone away. So I know that that's not how you are. Which means that I must bring out that behavior in you. How close am I to the truth?"

"There's something else you need to know, if we're going to speak truthfully."

"And that is?"

"I love you."

"How do you know?"

"I just know. It's like being gay. You just know."

"And you don't want to be in love with me."

"I didn't say that. It might be easier to be in love with someone else. But I'm not."

"I have a feeling that it isn't your nature to do the easiest thing," Rebecca smiled.

"Why haven't you gone running out the door by now?"

"Why should I? I'm not afraid of you. Have you forgotten that we've already kissed."

"How could I forget. It was front page news."

"Do you think I'm ready to deal with Mary?"

Mitch welcomed the rapid change of topic, if not subject.

"What are you going to do when she gets back?"

"I want her and her friend to come over for dinner."

"Doc."

"I thought her name was Hilary?"

"It is, we just call her Doc because, well, just because. Where's Mary going to live?"

"With her, with Hilary or Doc. Whatever her name is."

"It's okay that she strikes out on her own, you know."

"I know," Rebecca admitted, with new tears in her eyes.

"It's just hard when a child wants to leave home."

Mitch looked around for some tissue and found extra cocktail napkins instead.

"Here you go."

After Rebecca daubed at her eyes, Mitch took hold of one of her hands.

"You're a good mom."

"I'm trying, honestly I am."

"You're doing fine."

There was an authentic jukebox in the corner. They spent their quarters on oldies from the sixties and ordered hamburgers, onion rings and more beer. It was good and greasy food and they ate like teenagers. For dessert, they split a chocolate milkshake.

"You're not old enough to remember the diner days, but I am," Rebecca reminisced.

"Oh, here we go, table number three is going to take a trip down memory lane," Mitch teased.

"Why were things so simple back then?"

"How were things simple?"

"People met, got married, had kids, lived in houses with picket fences..."

"Grew victory gardens?" Mitch prodded.

"Hey, I'm not that old!" Rebecca came to the bait, with a smile.

"You were up to picket fences."

"I want all that for Mary."

"So do I. The only thing she can't have right now is the marriage certificate in Colorado. You want to know my view on that subject?"

"I'm a captive audience."

"I think that gay people should have the right to get married, to each other, like wife and wife."

"Because?"

"Because we have the right to be just as miserable as straight people."

Rebecca seemed unusually pensive.

"It usually gets a laugh at the Lucky U."

"I'm sure it does."

"I guess, with your impending divorce, marriage humor is off the menu."

"Jeff was a great guy. Things don't always work out."

"I'm sorry I brought it up. I should have been more sensitive."

"Don't think another thing about it."

"So, what do you want to do now?"

"I've never been to Las Vegas. Is there more to do?"

"Honey, you haven't seen anything, yet. Have you ever gambled?"

"I'm in politics."

"I mean this kind of gamble. Cards, dice, roulette?"

"I don't know much."

"You want to learn?"

"How much is it going to cost?"

"I'll pay for the lesson."

They took a taxi back to the middle of the strip and walked from casino to casino, leisurely betting here and there until they found a fun loving group at a crap table. Mitch placed small bets on the come line and Rebecca mimicked her actions, keeping track of the winnings and losses like an accountant.

"I always bet on come," Mitch looked at Rebecca. "But then again, I'm just an irrepressible optimist."

Eventually, the dice came around to Rebecca, and she was going to pass the dice when Mitch urged her to roll. She nervously agreed and placed a modest bet, on the come line. Mitch followed suit, with a much larger bet.

"I'm betting on you to come," Mitch said.

After three rolls, the table began to hum. The tenth roll brought shouts of joy from a little old lady and the people around her. After twenty tosses, the table had attracted the attention of three pit bosses and people from surrounding tables. Mitch quietly continued to place larger bets and after thirty seven chances at lady luck, Rebecca finally crapped out. A tumultuous round of applause made Rebecca blush and she asked Mitch if they could leave.

"Sure, just let me cash out."

"How much did you win?"

"Looks like hundreds, maybe a thousand or two. I didn't stop to count it, I just kept betting. Lots of people made a bundle off you. You want the winnings?"

"No, I can't accept gifts like that."

"Well, then I'll just donate it to Mary's charity. Now what do you want to do?"

"Can we go back to the room?"

"Sure, are you tired?"

"It's been a long day."

Riding back to the hotel, they chatted about the lights, crowds and traffic. Even Mitch had to agree that the quiet room was a welcome relief. Mitch poured two brandies, and they settled into opposite chairs and put their feet up on the coffee table.

"What are we going to do tomorrow?" Rebecca asked.

"What do you want to do?"

"Go on a picnic."

"A picnic?"

"Maybe go for a drive."

"There's desert in every direction," Mitch stated the obvious.

"Hoover Dam?"

"It's always crowded. The traffic jam is terrible."

"You're not enthused about much of anything. Are you feeling okay?" Rebecca was a different person from yesterday.

"It's like you said, it's been a long day."

"We did okay today, didn't we?"

"We did great. We got a lot of things out into the open."

"You certainly did. At least I know how you feel about me. I'm assuming that's part of your moodiness tonight."

"I'm tired."

"No, it isn't just tired. I can tell. You can deny it, but you can't hide it."

"You seem tuned into my feelings."

"I know how you feel, about a lot of things, and I can't answer you in kind. I don't know how I feel. About you. About anything. Anymore."

"Do you hate me?" Mitch had to know.

"No, absolutely not."

"Do you love me?"

"I don't know how I feel."

"But you don't hate me?"

"Right."

"Well, that's better than it was a couple of days ago. From that standpoint, we're making progress."

"I didn't know you loved me. That came out of the blue."

"Tomorrow, let's rent a car, take a drive, and have a picnic," Mitch planned out loud. "I had my way today. I can compromise."

"You'd be a good politician."

"I'm a better dilettante."

"So whoever wakes up first tomorrow orders room service for breakfast and then we'll engage the help of the concierge to plan our outing."

"Good idea," Mitch agreed, not planning by any stretch of the imagination to be the first awake.

"Okay, well, then, goodnight," Rebecca said as she walked to her bedroom.

"Goodnight," Mitch echoed, relaxing into the chair. She never even made it to bed, falling fast asleep in the chair. Rebecca must have checked on her in the night, she was covered with a blanket when she woke up the next morning. Resembling a question-mark-shaped human, she extracted herself from the chair and shuffled to the bathroom. When she emerged, still a little bent over, Rebecca greeted cheerfully as ever, "Good morning. I see you're up."

"I'm up, just not quite upright yet."

"You slept the whole night in the chair?"

"When did you cover me up?"

"About two a.m."

"Thank you."

"You're welcome."

"Are we ready for our picnic?"

"You still want to go?"

"Of course! I'm not going to miss a chance to have the governor to myself for another whole day!"

"Maybe it's me who wants you all to myself for a whole day."

"Either way, I guess we're about to get our wishes."

The hotel staff had arranged a car and lunch, as if they did these sorts of things every day. Perhaps they did. Rebecca, being a typical leader, took the wheel and headed west to Red Rock Canyon. It was part of a national conservation area that offers a scenic drive, hiking trails and picnic areas. The more Mitch hiked, the better her back felt and she was nearly buoyant after a two-hour stroll through the unseasonable warm desert. Wisely, the staff had packed plenty of liquids, and they stopped at a picnic table to rest and eat. Mitch fixed Rebecca a plate of food as she propped her feet up on the picnic bench. Rebecca had carried the supplies in an elaborate backpack to ease the burden on Mitch. It took its toll.

"You look like you could use something to drink," Mitch said as she handed Rebecca a bottle of water. She took it

gratefully. Mitch opened one for herself, but instead
doused her head and shoulders with the liquid.
"You just showered with three dollars of water," Rebecca
remarked, still exhausted from the walk.
"These don't cost three dollars."
"They do by the time you get the room service bill!"
"It feels good. You should try it."
"I've never poured a bottle of water on my head."
"Really?"
"I had an inhibited childhood," Rebecca said as she ate
lunch.
"You're anal-retentive," Mitch nodded sagely.
For some reason, this made Rebecca stop eating.
"If that means you don't pour expensive bottled water on
your head, then that's what I am!"
"They must have had quite the time baptizing you," Mitch
mused, seeing a comic vision of the struggle over the holy
water.
"I'm sure I fussed."
"Here," Mitch said suddenly. "Do it now. Take this bottle
of expensive water and pour it over your head. Nobody's
here to stop you. Your constituents aren't here. Your
parents aren't here. The priest isn't here. I'll even close
my eyes if it will help."
"I don't want to."
"Okay, suit yourself, but aren't you hot?"
"It's a warm day."
"And a two hour hike with backpack full of overpriced
water. Imagine how good it would feel to have cool water
on your skin."
"If I do it, will you shut the hell up about it and let me eat
my lunch!"
"Not another peep."
Rebecca took the bottle of water from Mitch and without
further ceremony poured about half of it over her hair, like
she was in the shower. The rest she poured over Mitch,
explaining, "I was taught to share."
Nodding her head, as if to agree completely, Mitch took
another bottle and soaked Rebecca's shoulders, cooling her
off even more.

"I was taught to share, also," Mitch said quietly.

Rebecca shivered when the water worked its magic. She ran her fingers through her hair and shook it loose. Mitch couldn't look away, her eyes captivated by the sight. Rebecca finally noticed.

"What?"

"No one should be allowed to look as beautiful as you do, soaking wet."

"Oh please, I'm old enough to be your … older sister."

"My stunningly beautiful not-so-older sister."

"I wanted some time away from everything and everybody to talk to you."

"About what?"

"I wanted to tell you," Rebecca began awkwardly, "that I don't love you. That I never loved you and that I will never love you and that we should stop seeing each other and running into each other and going off to Las Vegas together."

"Uh, okay," Mitch said guardedly. "That's quite a speech."

"That's what I want to say…."

"You mean, that's what you want to mean," Mitch clarified.

"I want to mean it, yes."

"But you don't or can't mean it?"

"I can't even say it very well. How the hell could I mean it!"

"Why don't you tell me what you do mean?" Mitch invited gently.

"I'm just confused, I think."

"That works for me. I understand about people being confused. I was a little confused when I discovered my feelings for you."

"How long were you confused for?"

"Between one and two seconds, give or take a nanosecond."

"It must be nice to understand yourself so well."

"It's heaven on earth."

Rebecca finished eating and was about to stand up when she winced in pain.

"What's wrong?"

"My foot hurts."

"Let me take a look."

"I'm sure it's fine." Another wince.

"I'll take a look for you. It might be serious."

Rebecca shifted around in order to surrender her foot to Mitch, who took off her shoe and sock. There was a nasty red mark, right where the threads of the sock had rubbed raw the skin just below her toenails. She should have felt this pain way before now. Mitch took a lightweight towel from the backpack and doused it in water. She applied this to the sore spot in order to cool the area. It was the best first step. Meanwhile, she took Rebecca's other shoe and sock off to check for further damage. The foot was red, but not raw like the first. She proceeded to efficiently soak both feet in water-soaked cloths.

"That feels good," Rebecca conceded.

"Is there a makeshift first aid kit in the backpack?"

"Yes. Let me dig it out for you."

"Thanks."

There were ample supplies for sore toes: bandages, scissors, gauze, ointment. All were used by Mitch to make Rebecca good as one could be on the wilderness trail.

"Thank goodness it isn't two miles back to the car!" Mitch breathed a sigh of relief. They had been clever enough to walk in a circuitous path, and were only about two hundred yards literally from the car. A short distance if you were healthy. A tortuous distance if you were in pain.

"You know, this is interesting," Mitch said as she held both of Rebecca's feet in her lap while checking the inside of her shoes for stray pieces of loose fabric.

"Why?"

"Well, here I have you out in the middle of the Nevada desert, and I have your shoes and socks in my custody, and it seems almost like a great example of compassion. I mean, I could simply walk away with your shoes, and you would be stranded here. Of course, you would find a way to get out, even though it would damage your feet, but you trust me to do the right thing."

"Is this going to be another of your political meanderings. Something along the lines of how if we treated everyone like our feet, then the world would be a better place. One of those socialistic idealistic speeches?"

"Actually, I was thinking along more personal lines. Much more personal."

"I'm afraid to ask."

"You trust me with your feet. Why don't you trust me with the rest of you?"

"Good grief, I trust a shoe salesman with my feet. That doesn't mean I want to sleep with every man who ever sold me a pair of shoes!"

The remark stung Mitch in a way she could never have predicted.

"A shoe salesman?" when she said it, it sounded harsher.

"I was speaking in analogous terms."

"I don't care if you were speaking in tongues. A shoe salesman?"

"You're hurt by the remark?" Rebecca asked point blank, surprised by Mitch's sudden severity.

Mitch stood up and handed Rebecca's shoes to her, and then took the picnic basket. "I'll see you back at the car."

The ride back was quiet. Deathly quiet. Rebecca gave up any attempt at conversation. It was as if Mitch was never going to speak again. Even dinner was engulfed in a somber silence.

"I'm sorry if I've hurt your feelings," Rebecca tried one more time to bridge the gulf.

"I think we should go home tomorrow," Mitch answered.

"I guess that's best."

"Uh huh."

"I have a favor to ask."

"Just one?"

"You think I'd ask for multiple favors while you're in this kind of mood?" Rebecca asked rhetorically.

"What do you want?"

"I want you to come to dinner when Mary and Hilary are there."

"I don't know if that's such a good idea."

"I want you there."

"Wouldn't you rather have some time alone, as family?"

"Jeff can't be there. He's still recovering from surgery. I want you there."

"You wanted to throw me in jail a couple of days ago."

"I'm doing my best to make up for that. I'm asking for your help. How about if I appeal to your goodness. And kindness. Your benevolence and compassion. "

"Against my better judgment, I'll be there. But only for moral support."

"That's all I'm asking."

They packed, which took all of about fifteen minutes. A flight home was booked through the concierge. A wake-up call roused them at five a.m. and they were Denver bound by seven. Acting like strangers, they departed in separate vehicles at DIA. Mitch retrieved her car via taxi and Rebecca had an official car waiting at the curb. Dinner with Mary and Hilary would happen in thirty hours. Mitch hoped to sleep for about twenty nine of them.

Chapter 23

Judy held the door open for Lisa. Home sweet home looked better than ever. It had been a long haul for both of them. They had been homesick beyond belief and no obstacle would keep them from arriving in Aspen in record time. After turning the camper in at Denver, and spending one brief night in a motel, they were home at a decent hour. Of course the phone was ringing. Lisa picked up while Judy carried suitcases to the bedroom.

"Oh hi, Trish," Lisa said, checking to see where Judy had disappeared.

"How are you, Lisa?" Trish asked cautiously.

"You're the only thing about Texas that I miss."

"Remind me not to flirt with you as long as your girlfriend's in the same state."

"Are you going to hold that against me forever?"

"You're the one who left like a dust devil. I was just getting warmed up."

Judy had walked back into the living room. Lisa scrubbed the smile from her face.

"It's for you, Sweetie," Lisa handed the phone to Judy. "Hello?"

"It's Trish. Act serious."

"We got home just now," Judy said, unrehearsed and grasping for sensible dialogue.

"You still mad at me?"

"It was a long trip. I'm tired. Lisa is exhausted."

"You're still mad."

"No, I can talk for a minute."

"I love you."

"Uh huh."

"Lisa's right there still?"

"Uh huh." More affirmative.

"How long before she gets out of her casts? She wouldn't tell me."

"A while."

"One week?"

"Maybe more."

"Two weeks?"

"Sounds right," Judy answered, trying to remember her answers so she could make up credible dialogue for Lisa later.

"We'll have to get ready to set up the trap."

"That sounds like a good idea."

"I love you."

"I know that."

"I would never hurt you. I never meant to cause trouble. At least not quite that much."

"I understand. We can talk soon."

"Okay, bye."

"Bye."

"That sounded serious," Lisa noted curiously.

"Just more details."

"Are you getting more money?"

"How much did you want? I'll put in a request," Judy remarked, a tad more sarcastically than she intended.

"You don't need to jump on me. I'm just worried about you!"

"Worried how?"

"I think that Trish would screw you good if she got half a chance."

"Screw me good?" Judy fought back an involuntary giggle.

"I think she's trying to cut you out of part of your inheritance. The less you get, the more she can get in her own cut."

"She's not even an heir!"

"I know that, but she does work for the family, on a percentage too, I bet. So, the more money she saves them, the happier they'll be."

"I'm sure it's all going to be above board and legal."

"Oh, Judy, you're so trusting," Lisa sighed.

"I guess I am," Judy agreed as she made unflinching eye contact with Lisa. "I trust people until they prove they don't deserve it."

Lisa remained silent so Judy forged on. She knew what she had to ask. The wording was tricky, but the question had to be asked and answered. Mitch and company had made it all too clear in Texas. We need a dollar figure, and now!

250

"How much do you think I'll inherit, anyway."
Judy threw in the "anyway" to make it sound casual. If Lisa came back with 100 million, they were sunk.
"How would I know? Nobody was speaking to me by the end of the trip!" Lisa bandied back.
"No wild guesses?"
"Nope."
"How about hopeful estimates?"
"It's your family."
"But what do *you* hope it will be."
"A couple of million would be nice."
"A couple million?" Judy was now curious as to how Lisa came up with the figure.
"Well, sure," Lisa explained. "One half of one percent, calculated forward from two million would be four hundred million. It depends on how they figure the value of the ranch."
"You've given this serious thought."
"No one mentioned oil. So it's difficult to deduce if it's part of your settlement. I would guess it isn't. I think your share proceeds directly from assets not associated with oil or land reserves."
"Two million would be great."
"Two million would be adequate."
"Two million." Judy said quietly, trying to squelch the part of her that could hear her screaming this number hysterically to Trish over the phone at the next convenient call. Conveniently, Lisa went in to take a nap. Judy waited until she was sure that Lisa was indeed asleep and then dialed the phone.

"Two million!" Trish nearly dropped the phone.
"That's her low estimate," Judy whispered.
"She's not easily pleased."
"No comment,"
"Don't tell me anymore, I'm hanging up."
Trish followed through, not even waiting for a goodbye.
Mitch and Marge sat in silence. Trish looked at Mitch.
"Two million is a lot!"
"Two million isn't so much."

"It's a lot to put in a trap for a rat."

"I think we're getting off cheap. After seeing Waysouthfork, I'm pleased that she came in with a reasonable dollar figure."

"When she starts to make her getaway with the cash, you'd better have a full tank of gas."

"You let me worry about that. How soon do we need the money?"

"About two weeks. How are you going to handle that?"

"In a suitcase, I guess."

"I meant at the bank. Banks just don't hand out that much cash at the teller window. Lisa will need to make some sort of plan."

"I'm sure that the bank will hand over cash if given enough notice. It will only slow down the process."

"I'm still worried."

"What could possibly happen in two weeks?"

"Dinner with the governor?" Marge volunteered the answer.

"Thanks for reminding me, I'll be late if I don't go now."

"Aren't they sending an official car?"

"I'm driving myself. I don't like the idea of being chauffeured around in the state's vehicles."

"What time's dinner?"

"Six."

"It's only five now. You still have time to go home and change."

"I'm not changing."

"You're wearing that?"

Mitch looked at herself. She thought she looked okay. Slacks, blazer, goofy T-shirt.

"What's wrong with this?"

"It's dinner at the mansion!"

"It's a family thing."

Trish arched an eyebrow, "And how many family members are attending?"

"At least three, I hope. The soon-to-be-ex-husband couldn't make it."

"Probably why he's the soon-to-be-ex," Marge explained without being asked.

Mitch rolled her eyes and headed out the door. She was reluctant at best. Here she was, driving to a dinner where she would be with a governor, who had loathed her up until a week ago, the daughter of the governor, who was making a stand for independence, and a math/chemistry genius, who could outsmart anyone at the table. Did she have any expectation of the evening being remotely fun? She drove slowly, taking the scenic tour through the older neighborhood, admiring brave joggers fending for themselves in the cold weather. She arrived a scant few minutes before six. The security advisor ran a wand over her, making sure she wasn't packing a gun or service for four. He seemed like he was thinking about frisking her, but stopped short. Another staff member materialized from a hallway and escorted her to the parlor. Much to her relief, Mary and Hilary were already there. Rebecca, looking relieved, approached Mitch at the entranceway.

"I'm so glad you came."

"I try to come whenever I can."

The double entendre wasn't lost on Rebecca. She even had the decency to blush, just a little. Mitch never tired of it.

"Are you going to behave yourself tonight?" she whispered out of earshot of Mary and Hilary, who were straining to hear.

"Do you want me to?" Mitch breathed back.

"In front of the girls."

"No problem."

Rebecca allowed Mitch to enter the room now, and she gave Mary a big hug.

"Did you leave Texas in one piece?"

"We stayed out of jail."

"That's good news."

She hugged Hilary next.

"You okay, Doc?"

"Never better."

Dinner was announced promptly at six. Rebecca had been vacillating between the formal state dining room and the less formal family dining room. She had chosen the latter. It was a good and decent decision. Rather than trying to impress or overwhelm Hilary with the ostentatious setting, she chose to treat her like family.

"This is a nice room," Mitch remarked.

"We went on the grand tour before you arrived. Sorry you missed it," Hilary said.

"Well, maybe I'll get my very own tour someday."

"It's a beautiful mansion. Mary knows all of the history about the building."

"I've only seen 'Charlie's Room' myself," Mitch said offhand.

"You've spent the night here?"

"No, I had a headache for a couple of hours and Rebecca was kind enough to lend me a bed."

"Is that what was in the news, the famous kiss," Hilary asked, never afraid to broach.

Mitch had to stop and think. "The famous kiss happened earlier, at the hospital."

Apparently, Mitch emphasized the word "famous" too strongly.

"There was more than one kiss?"

Never argue with a genius, Mitch warned herself.

"There was just one kiss. And speaking of kisses, how are the two of you doing?" Rebecca interjected mostly to shift the subject from kisses to her daughter's welfare.

Mary laughed easily. "We're still unpacking."

"You like Hilary's place?"

"It's nice."

Mary and Hilary filled the remaining dinner conversation with stories about setting up housekeeping. They were glowing like a pair of lightning bugs at dusk. Dinner was exceptionally well done. Rebecca had informed the cook that everyone was health conscious, but famished, so they dined on chicken, steamed vegetables, garlic potatoes and homemade bread. Mary and Hilary had obviously been doing a lot of *unpacking*. They ate like they hadn't had a meal in three days. Coffee and dessert was served in the drawing room in front of the fireplace. They rewarded their good behavior with cheesecake. You could only be health conscious for so long. Rebecca ate a sliver, a carryover from swim-team days. Mitch ate slightly more. Company finished off the rest.

"This was great," Hilary complimented.

"Yeah," Mitch agreed, "Do you eat like this every day?"

"Why would you ask?" Rebecca asked guardedly.

"I thought if governors ate like this every day, I might run for the office myself."

"We don't!"

"Well, then, that helps me decide," Mitch winked at Rebecca.

"It would be easier to buy a deli than win the governor's race." Mary piped up.

"And probably cheaper, too," Hilary added.

"I have to save my money for the Aspen Sting," Mitch remarked without thinking.

"The Aspen Sting?" Rebecca repeated.

"I told you all about it in Vegas."

"I thought it was over?"

"Oh no," Mitch said, "We're just getting to the climax," Mitch said slowly, watching Rebecca like a hawk. For once, she didn't repeat word for word. Mitch made a mental note to use the word climax in more sentences.

"What's going on with Judy and Lisa?"

"Judy called in with a dollar figure. I'm transferring the funds soon. The casts come off in two weeks."

"So, the chase begins in two weeks and one day."

"Like I said, we're close to the climax."

Rebecca was agitated, "Are you putting Mary in further danger!"

"No, she's not," Mary answered for herself. "I haven't been in danger yet and I won't be."

"This sounds dangerous," Rebecca demurred.

"It's safer than sex with a condom," Mitch assured her.

"Like, you would know anything about that!" Rebecca retorted.

"Well, not firsthand," Mitch deflected the remark. "Look, Rebecca, I lived with Lisa, I took the worst she could dish out, I didn't have any help, and I came out okay. Broke and broken-hearted, but otherwise unscathed. One person is on the hot seat, and it isn't Mary."

"You're absolutely sure?"

"Absolutely. Just keep Mary's picture out of the paper for about two weeks."

"I'll change my looks, wear a hat and sunglasses."

"Just don't wear a maid's uniform and I think we'll be safe."

"A maid's uniform?" Rebecca asked, now thoroughly puzzled.

"It's a long story," Mary said.

"With a climax," Mitch added, impishly.

"I want a daily report about this," Rebecca notified Mary.

"I'll do that," Mitch volunteered. "Mary needs to stay out of sight."

"You'll report to me every day?"

"I just need to know one thing, do you want it written or oral?"

Rebecca looked at Mitch with an expression that Mitch had never seen before. She didn't know if she was in trouble, or about to break new ground.

"You decide."

The rest of the evening's conversation was taken up with familial chit chat. Yes, Rebecca knew that Mary and Hilary were happy. Yes, she understood that they wanted to live on their own. No, they didn't want to live in the mansion. Yes, they would come to dinner often. They were out the door and on their way home by eight.

Rebecca had seen them to the door, leaving Mitch behind in the drawing room to pour a brandy. She returned after a few minutes, and took the drink from Mitch.

"They make a cute couple," Mitch said.

"It's so obvious. They are so much in love."

"Come on over here and sit next to me."

"I'm fine. I'm not going to make a big scene. I don't need comforting."

"Well, maybe I do."

"And why do you need comforting?" Rebecca sounded more than a little skeptical.

"You still don't think I can be vulnerable? I do have a softer, more feminine side."

"Right or left?"

"Left, definitely left."

Rebecca walked over and sat on her right side.

"Wouldn't want anyone to think I'm getting friendly with the left."

Mitch smiled and put her arms around Rebecca, holding her gently. For formal furniture, this sofa was downright comfy.

"Did I do alright?" Rebecca sought the reassurance she denied needing a moment ago.

"You were perfect."

"Wow, you used a sentence without working in the word 'climax'".

"I'll have to work on my oral skills."

"You're not behaving yourself."

"The girls are gone."

"I want to know what you meant by something you said earlier this evening."

"Did it have the word climax in it?"

"No, but it did have the word kiss."

"Okay, what's your question?"

"You told Hilary that there was only one kiss."

"I remember."

"But there were two kisses."

"I choose to think that there were two half-kisses."

"What do you mean?"

"Well, when I kissed you at the hospital, you didn't kiss me back. When you kissed me upstairs in Charlie's Room, I didn't kiss you back. You'd think a math genius like Hilary could've figured that out. One-half kiss plus one-half kiss is one kiss."

"You didn't kiss me back upstairs that day?"

"I was too weak from the headache to respond."

"I guess I just thought that you had."

"If I had, you wouldn't have any question about it."

"There would be no doubt?"

"None."

Rebecca put down her brandy glass and turned her full attention to Mitch.

"If I kiss you now, will you kiss me back. So I'll know once and for all?"

"I'd consider it the highlight of the evening."

Mitch closed her eyes and felt Rebecca's lips. She was playful and gentle, sensual and soothing and there was no more doubt, for either of them. Sensations pulsed through Mitch and she shivered noticeably. Rebecca slowly moved away, and Mitch inhaled deeply. When she opened her eyes, she saw Rebecca watching for an honest response.

"I love you," was the only thing Mitch could come up with.

"What do lesbians do in bed?"

"Anything they can get away with?" Mitch replied, stalling for time, not knowing whether or not they were talking about Mary and Hilary, or just anybody. Anybody was an awfully inclusive group about now.

"I'm serious."

"I'm probably not the best person to ask about that."

"Why not!" Rebecca sounded genuinely surprised.

"I don't think I know everything."

"I don't want to know *everything*. I know you can tell me about the basics. I can't think of another person whom I want to have this discussion with. I trust you."

"Rebecca, you're asking me to describe things to you that I'd give my right arm to be doing with you. I'm at a severe disadvantage, here."

"I don't want to be afraid. Anymore."

The purpose of the conversation was becoming clearer. Mary and Hilary weren't even in the station let alone on the train of thought.

"Are you afraid right now?"

"No."

"Then there's no need to be afraid of later. It just gets better and better. There's nothing scary about lesbian sex."

"I wouldn't know what to do."

"You were married. Didn't you and Jeff have, uh, well, a fulfilling sex life?"

Rebecca looked away, at her hands, at the picture over the mantle, at the fire, at her hands. Mitch sensed an important revelation was about to take place.

"We had a standard sex life."

"Standard?"

"Well, maybe basic is a better word."

"Basic? Standard?" Mitch ruminated for a few seconds, then the light dawned. "Oh, I get it. You've never had oral sex!"

Rebecca nodded, still looking at her hands.

"Am I right?" Mitch needed more than a nod.

"Yes."

"It's okay. You don't have to be embarrassed about it. Do you want another brandy?"

"I'd better not."

"So you've never…"

"I couldn't bring myself to ask for it."

"Jeff never offered?"

"You need to understand. I am, was, still am a very conservative person."

"You told me you had an inhibited childhood."

"My parents didn't even talk about sex, let alone, talk about *that*."

"Oral sex."

"Yeah, that."

"You can say it in front of me."

"That's easy for you to say…."

"And I don't even mind if you blush. But maybe we can sort of build up to that slowly."

"Okay. Slowly is good."

"So, besides, you know, *that*, well there's always touching."

"Touching is important."

"Touching is extremely important. Very, very important."

"What about sex toys?"

"You got any good ones?" Mitch asked, now very curious.

"No!"

"Me neither."

"You don't own any sex toys?"

"I haven't needed any."

"I'm sorry I brought it up."

"I'm not! You're finally asking all the questions you never felt safe about before. Just because some of the answers surprise you, doesn't mean you should stop asking."

"So if, one day, you and I were to begin a courtship, you wouldn't ever spring anything on me. We could talk about everything first?"

"We can talk about anything, anytime, anywhere. You can ask me about sex until you lose your voice."

"I might just do that."

"Well, then, we will kiss when we can no longer speak."

"I don't want to wait that long."

Rebecca, being a natural leader, took Mitch's face in her hands and kissed her deeply. Mitch worked to keep up the pace Rebecca set. The governor was now hungry for more than simple knowledge.

"What's going on in here? Mother! Mitch!"

Mary was practically standing over them. They separated quickly.

"What are you doing?" Mary demanded again to know.

"We're kissing," Rebecca answered.

"I can see that. What were you thinking!" Mary chided.

"This is none of your business, Mary." Rebecca answered back defensively.

"It is when you're not even divorced from Daddy!"

"What are you doing back here anyway?" Rebecca asked, angry at the intrusion.

"I forgot my purse. It looks like I'm not the only forgetful person around here. You've forgotten you're still married!"

"You know what, Rebecca," Mitch said, standing up. "I'm going to go now and let you two talk things over."

Mitch let herself out the back door and extracted her car from the parking area. She noticed Hilary waiting in their car, but couldn't think of a thing to say. Mitch was angry at herself, at Mary, at Rebecca, at Jeff, and at the rest of the world for good measure. She drove around for a while, and found herself at home. It looked dark and empty.

Emphasis on the empty. Needing to be with people, even if it meant putting up with nosy questions, Mitch headed to the U. She walked in and sat down. Marge brought a beer over and then walked away without comment, a miracle for once. Even Trish, who had been talking to other patrons, noticed the pall from across the room. She extracted herself as politely as possible from the group and came over to investigate.

"What's wrong?"

"Nothing."

"I thought you were at the mansion, for dinner?"

"I was."

"Over so soon?"

"It's not soon. Even governors need their beauty sleep."

"Not this one. Would you look at her! God, she's good looking!"

The rest of the patrons turned to see as well. Everyone, it seems, hadn't seen the governor in a while.

Mitch looked up to see Rebecca standing next to her side of the booth. At least, she thought it was Rebecca. She was wearing a black leather jacket, a T-shirt and jeans. Mitch sighed. Trish bubbled.

"You must be Governor Fairbanks! Nice jacket!!"

"And you must be Trish. Mary has told me so many things about you."

"I hope you didn't believe them all."

Rebecca had the grace to laugh and banter with Trish for a moment or two while Mitch looked on. Mitch hadn't been aware up until now how in awe Trish was concerning the governor.

"Is it okay if I sit with you?" Trish noticed that Rebecca's question was directed toward Mitch and only Mitch

"You know what, Governor Fairbanks," Trish was on her feet. "You sit in my place. I have a few things to go and take care of."

Rebecca was still studying Mitch for agreement.

"Please join me," Mitch sounded like it was a garden party. All they needed was a garden. And a party.

"Thanks."

Both looked at each other, as if waiting for a clue where to restart the conversation.

"Nice jacket."

261

"I found it in one of the coat closets."

"I've never seen you in jeans?"

"I don't always wear business suits."

"I recognize the T-shirt, from Vegas."

"I know that things between us are awkward. They weren't an hour ago."

"An hour ago, I could forget you were married. Still."

"You know that's over. That's not an issue between us."

"It's an issue to Mary. She loves her dad."

"Mary is a big girl. She can work this out. She can see her dad. She can love her dad."

"She's angry at you for not coming out to her sooner."

"I know that. I'll work on that. But, Mitch, she's out of the house. She's got a life of her own, now. Don't use her for an excuse."

"And what about your governorship?"

"What about it?"

"They'll throw you out like rubbish. You'll never get elected in this town again."

"So, I'll find something else to do."

"Politics is a passion for you."

"I can still be political. Doesn't some group need a spokesperson?"

"I can think of about a dozen offhand. But, Honey, we're talking death threats here. Against you. Against Mary. It isn't easy being out."

"It is for you."

"I'm not a Republican."

"Look, an hour ago, you and I were sitting as close as two people can sit discussing the benefits of lesbian sex. Now, you won't even meet my eyes. I know this isn't easy, but don't walk out on me. Don't leave a conversation half finished. If you're afraid of something, tell me."

"I'm afraid of being so deeply in love with you that there's no turning back. Ever."

"You've been in love before."

"Not like this. You were some impossible dream and it's all coming true so fast. I don't quite know how to handle it."

"What can I do to help?"

"You can tell me how you feel about me. You've managed to avoid doing that so far."

"I feel about you – in a way that I've never felt about someone else before. That's why I've been so reluctant to talk about it. I never felt this way about Jeff. I didn't know what it was for a while."

"It didn't feel like love?"

"It felt like I had found someone who would stand up to me. I found someone who knew about something that I wanted to learn more about, because it meant that I would finally, know more about who I am. It felt like I wanted to fight with you because it was more fun than, well, not having fights with anyone else."

"You want a drink?"

"Sure."

"Marge is dying to come over here and talk to you. I'll flag her down."

"Please do."

Mitch only had to look in the general direction of the bar and Marge was over like a shot.

"Good evening, Governor Fairbanks."

"Good evening, Marge."

"You remembered my name!" Marge fluttered like a lovesick butterfly. A sixty-something-year-old lovesick butterfly.

"Can we get a drink here already?" Mitch asked.

"Oh, hold onta yer horses. I'm getting ready to write down your order."

"You need to write down the word *beer*?"

"I assumed the Governor, being a lady and all, would like a nice, fancy brand of wine. You know, one a them things with a cork instead of a screw top like you drink."

"Actually, I'll have what Mitch is having."

"Problem is, nobody around here can figure out what Mitch is having these days," Marge just couldn't help herself some days.

"How about what's on tap?"

"You gonna make the esteemed Governor drink that rotgut crap?"

"It's your bar. Surprise us."

263

When Marge fluttered away, Rebecca remarked, "Everyone here is so nice to me."

"That's because everyone here knows Mary. She's a sweet kid who has made a lot of friends in a short period of time. And they know you're her mom, so they're being on their best behavior."

"And if I wasn't her mom?"

"They'd probably all be hitting on you. You look absolutely ravishing in leather."

"I do, don't I"

"You're so agreeable tonight."

"Do they allow dancing here?"

"Honey, they'd allow anything you want. You're the governor."

"Let's dance. You can dance, can't you."

"Trish has been giving me lessons."

"Come on, then."

Rebecca and Mitch went to the dance floor. Two other couples were already up there, and the music was slow.

"Has Trish been teaching you to lead or follow?"

"She's been teaching me not to step on other people's toes."

"But only while you're dancing?"

Mitch had to laugh. This was too funny for words.

"Come into my arms," Rebecca said. "I'll teach you how to dance."

It was an invitation Mitch couldn't and didn't want to resist. Three songs later they were still dancing, much slower and closer than when they had started, and nowhere near the beat of the music.

"It's true love," Marge told Trish.

"How can you tell?"

"They're dancing slow through the fast songs."

"It's like they hear a different song."

"Straight from the heart."

Rebecca, holding Mitch as closely as she could, whispered, "Trish taught you well."

"Trish is a nice lady."

"Come back with me to the mansion."

264

"Tonight?"

"Tonight."

"This is kinda fast for me, Rebecca."

"You're the one who's been chasing me all around for the past two months."

"That was different."

"How?"

"I wasn't trying to get you to sleep with me, exactly."

"What were you trying to do, exactly?"

"I suppose I was trying to bother you."

"Well, you've succeeded. I'm bothered. I'm way past bothered."

"You're angry."

"No, I'm not angry. I've just decided what I want, and I didn't think you would be this hesitant."

"It's a big step."

"I agree," Rebecca nodded and pulled away from the embrace. "When you decide what you want, you know where to find me." With that, she walked out of the bar. Mitch went back to the booth. Trish couldn't stay out of it.

"What's going on?"

"She wants to sleep together."

"With you!"

"No, with the other forty nine governors."

"So if she wants to sleep with you, what in heaven's name are you doing here?"

"I'm thinking it over."

"You let that gorgeous, willing woman walk out of the bar while you're thinking about it?"

"What do you think I should do?"

"Three things come to mind."

"Three things come to mind? Only three? I would have expected nine or ten things to come into your mind."

"Okay, number one, go after her."

"She's going back to the governor's mansion."

"So, you know the way there! The two of you have practically worn out the highway between here and there."

"Number two?" Mitch prodded.

"Number two, get down on your knees and beg for her tender mercies."

265

"On my knees."

"It's a good vantage point. Number three...."

"I can figure out number three for myself. Thanks all the same!"

They sat in silence for a moment.

"If she loves you even half as much as you love her, you're one of the luckiest lesbians on the planet," Trish commented, trying to bring Mitch back to the moment.

Mitch emptied her drink and stood to leave. The expression on her face told Trish volumes.

"Call me when you come up for air," Trish said in the way of a goodbye.

Mitch drove slowly, again. It was still a twenty-minute drive at this hour of the night. She arrived at the mansion and knocked on the front door. One staff member was still on hand to send away the beggars and loiterers. This was the impression Mitch got when she was asked about her business.

"I'm here to see the governor."

"She's retired for the evening. Make an appointment."

"I did make an appointment. Tell the governor that Mitch is here. She will see me, I guarantee," Mitch bluffed her way.

"Very well. Come and wait in the parlor."

He took his time climbing the stairs. Mitch was beginning to worry. She had taken to her bed quickly. Maybe she was more upset than her cool exit suggested.

"Madam, there's a 'Mitch' to see you. She claims to have an appointment."

"Send her up."

"I have her waiting down in the parlor, Madam."

"I understand. Send her up here."

"But, Madam, you're in your robe and bedclothes."

"What would you suggest I do."

"Send her away?"

"Do I have to come down and get her, or will you show her up?"

"I'll escort her upstairs momentarily."

"Thank you," Rebecca said to his retreating back. She quickly fluffed her pillow and opened a book that was on her bedside table. Mitch was at her door in less than a minute, waiting for permission to enter.

"Are you going to come in? You didn't drive all the way down here to stand in the doorway, did you?"

Mitch walked in and closed the door behind her. The staff would have to guess from here on out.

"I came to beg for your tender mercies."

"You've either had too much time to think or you've been listening to advice."

"Trish told me that I was nuts to let you walk out of the bar."

"That Trish is one smart lady. What else did she tell you?"

"She told me to come down here, beg for your mercy, and, well, you know Trish."

"She has some great ideas, I'll bet."

Mitch came over and glanced at the book in Rebecca's hands. "That's a great book. Of course, I read it right side up."

Rebecca looked again at the book in her hands and then laughed, "I'll admit that I'm a little nervous."

"Are you sure this is what you want?" Mitch asked, sitting next to her on the bed.

"I know I don't want to spend one more day or night without you."

"This is a big step. You'll never be able to go back again. This burns every bridge, cuts every tie…"

"It seems to be a bigger step for you. You still seem reluctant."

"It isn't that I'm reluctant."

"What is it?"

"You're willing to give up all this for me," Mitch said as she stood up, gestured around the room with a sweep of her hand. "You're going to lose your job, your standing in society, your political support, this mansion…"

Rebecca just nodded.

"Your friends will stop talking to you, your enemies will gloat, the media will have a field day. Are you sure you're ready for all that?"

Rebecca nodded, "Yes, I am."

Mitch took off her jacket and came back over to the bed.

"And you'd do that to be with me?"

"Yes."

"I've just never had someone love me like this before. It's stunning."

Rebecca pulled Mitch closer and they kissed, softly, again. It was not at all unlike their first kiss of the evening, easy, gentle, exploring carefully. They took their time with all the preliminaries of lovemaking. They undressed slowly. This wasn't a toss-the-clothes-off affair. Mitch could have easily been instructive, but she chose to excite the curiosity of Rebecca by allowing her the opportunity of exploring new territory with very little narrative advice.

"You're not telling me what to do," Rebecca breathed into Mitch's ear after pulling her earlobe with her lips.

"I don't need to tell you what to do. You're doing things I've never thought of."

"Now you're stretching the truth."

"How long has it been since you've had sex?"

"Why do you want to know that?"

"Because whoever hasn't had sex in the longest time gets to come first. It's one of those unwritten lesbian rules."

"It is not! Is it?"

"I've been celibate for about a year," Mitch admitted, assuming she would win the contest. Rebecca had, after all, been living with Jeff up until a short while ago.

"Well?"

"It's been five years."

"Five years! Holy god."

"It seems longer."

"I can imagine. Mind if I look in your medicine cabinet for a minute?" Mitch asked, but not moving one inch away from Rebecca.

"You need something for a headache?"

"No, but I'm going to need a vitamin!"

"Would you just shut up and make love to me."

"It would be my pleasure."

Mitch complied with the request, taking a modest amount of time but not teasing to the point of frustration. When Mitch felt Rebecca relax after her orgasm, she helped assuage all the tension by cuddling with her and stroking her arms, legs, whatever felt in need of touching, until her breathing returned to normal. Five years was, indeed, a long time.

"You were remarkable."

"Five years is too long."

"Forty-five years is too long," Mitch did the gay math as well.

"I'll take more time, next time."

"More time? I don't think I can take more time."

"That was a long time for you?"

"Well, I wasn't exactly running a stopwatch, but it seemed like a gloriously long time."

"I'm glad to hear that."

"Are you teasing me?"

"No, I was just thinking how much fun we can have without worrying about the time."

"Tell me what you're talking about. You said you would talk to me about anything."

"You're right. I just know that I maybe hurried, maybe a little more than I should have. I guess I was worried about that first-time stuff."

"You thought I wouldn't achieve an orgasm."

"The thought crossed my mind. For a minute. When it seemed crystal clear that you would, I didn't waste any more time. There's an old lesbian adage that goes, 'It's better to come fast than not at all.' I wanted you to come, the fast part just sort of happened."

"Maybe I wanted to come fast."

"Nobody wants to come fast."

"I'll just have to be the one exception to the rule. Give me a couple of minutes to catch my breath," Rebecca sighed, "And then I'll test your adage on you."

"Oh, you can always take all the time you need with me."

If it was confusing as to what would take time, the answer arrived quickly. Three minutes later, Rebecca was sound asleep. Mitch smiled, inhaled deeply and surrendered to the night herself. It was always a good idea to sleep well the night before a test.

Chapter 24

It was close to noon. Mitch woke up to find a note on
Rebecca's pillow. Actually, it was more of an essay:

You,

I love you. I guess I fell asleep last night. I couldn't bring
myself to wake you up this morning. You looked so sweet.
Did I mention that I love you? I have a full schedule today.
I'll be home for dinner. Be here? I don't mean to sound
proprietary. Please be here? I know that, soon, all hell will
break loose with us. Not between us, just about us. The
public loves a scandal. Anyway, the staff knows you're
here. I've asked them not to disturb your sleep. They will
cook breakfast for you. Help yourself to the shower,
bathtub, toothpaste, and whatever else you need. If you
can't find something, ask the staff. They will see to your
every need. Well, maybe not every need. Save that for me.

Me

Mitch read through the note twice before getting dressed.
She was careful to put the love note in her pocket before
leaving via the back entrance. She went home to take care
of the many things she had been neglecting lately, like the
laundry, the housework, the exercise machine. She
engaged in domestic tranquility until it became boring, all
of about two hours. Dan, her financial advisor, had left a
message earlier in the week, so she called to arrange to
meet him for a drink, close to his downtown office. He was
more than happy to meet and share his good news. They
huddled together in a fashionable hotel lounge during the
lull between lunch and happy hour.

"Of course, I can gather up two million dollars, but I'd be
derelict in my professional conduct if I didn't ask why you
need the money."

"A good friend needs some help."

"Help doing what?"

"I'm investing in mousetraps."

"Your friend is trying to build a better mousetrap?"

"That's right."

"Is this going to be illegal?"

Gee, this guy was smart.

"I don't know. Tell me, if someone other than a police officer sets up a trap for someone to fall into, is that entrapment?"

"I'm a financial wizard, not a lawyer."

"That's true. When I called, you mentioned you had good news about my finances."

"Due to my genius, you're made bucket-loads of money on your investments. A couple of the businesses that I put just a part of your money into have suddenly boomed. So even though you asked that the majority of your money remain in the safer investments after the first doubling, the smaller investments have quadrupled in value."

"So two million isn't going to be a problem."

"None whatsoever. Just be sure you have a big enough briefcase when you pick it up."

"Too bad I just can't get two one million dollars bills and be done with it. Thanks, Dan."

They left before the happy hour crowd could get a noisy start. Mitch had wanted to stop by the Lucky U, but she knew that Marge was still collecting bids on the refurbishing of the place. So with a little time on her hands, she went to the mall. She picked out some good slacks in conservative colors, black, gray, blue. Then, she selected several oxford no-wrinkle shirts. She didn't want to spend any more time ironing than she already did. The real time was taken up choosing a wool jacket. The salesclerk was most accommodating and took time to remove all the price tags so Mitch could change quickly before dinner. She headed out toward the mansion, running late in traffic and arrived at six fifteen, a little out of breath, but dressed sharply. The staff still turned up their noses as they escorted her to the family dining room. Rebecca was halfway through dinner. She hadn't bothered to wait. This usually wasn't a good sign.

Mitch's escort was standing just behind her, hovering.

"You're late."

"I'm sorry. Traffic was bad."

"Will Madam be dining?" the staff person asked. Mitch didn't know who should answer.

"Are you hungry?" Rebecca directed the question to Mitch without even looking at her.

"Are you angry?" Mitch asked, not quite in the mood for the detached treatment.

"No, but I have to leave at six thirty."

"Where are you going?" Mitch struggled to keep the disappointment out of her voice.

"I have another meeting. I told you in my note that I had a full schedule."

"You said a lot in your note," Mitch spoke carefully in front of the still-hovering staff.

"Are *you* angry?" Rebecca asked.

Mitch felt that Rebecca hadn't paid adequate attention to her and her ego was threatening to get the best of her. "I didn't know that I was on a time clock."

The staff was waiting for a clarification about dinner. He ran out of patience and asked again, "Will Madam be dining?"

Mitch answered "no" at exactly the same time Rebecca answered "yes." Mitch repeated "no" and he left.

"Look," Rebecca came over to where Mitch was standing. "I'm sorry about the miscommunication. Most people around here know that a full schedule means just that, from six thirty in the morning until about ten at night, and that's on a quiet day." She reached out leisurely, taking Mitch by the hands and gradually pulled her closer.

"I'm sorry, too. I guess I'm just edgy," Mitch admitted.

"Sexual tension will do that to you," Rebecca smiled and kissed her. First on the lips, just once. Then, she traveled down to her neck and found a spot that made Mitch's voice catch.

"Right there," Mitch breathed quietly

"Here?" Rebecca brushed the spot again.

"Yes, there," Mitch said.

"I hope I don't forget where *there* is," Rebecca teased, looking into Mitch's eyes.

"If you forget, I'll remind you."

"I won't forget."

"I thought about you all day," Mitch confessed.

"Looks like you also spent some time shopping. You look absolutely dashing."

"I look like a Republican."

Mitch had chosen the most conservative of her new attire for dinner dress.

"You look like a very sexy Republican."

"I thought that was a contradiction in terms until I met you."

"Oh now, you're just trying to get on my good side," Rebecca teased and kissed again. Yes, *there*. She was a different person when her staff wasn't monitoring her.

The staff reappeared, and interrupted the moment.

"Your car is waiting."

"I'll be there in a minute."

"It is six twenty five now, Madam."

"I've been able to tell time since second grade. I'll be there when I get there."

He left again.

"Your staff hates me."

"I have a good idea."

"I'm in the mood for good idea."

"Why don't you make reservations at a nice hotel, one with room service all hours of the night. When I'm done with my meeting, I'll meet you there. It's Friday night. We can spend some of the weekend together."

"Is it Friday?"

"You've lost track of the days?"

"You have that effect on me. Hey wait, how will you know where to go?"

"Message me."

"In your meeting?"

"Sure. And see if you can round up something for dessert. Something chocolate."

"Something chocolate."

"Something chocolate," Rebecca repeated as she left for her meeting.

It took four stops, but Mitch finally gathered up enough Epicurean delights to suit her taste. She made on-the-spot reservations at the Brownstone Hotel, a modern yet welcoming new hotel in the downtown area and was in a three-room suite well ahead of schedule. She called Rebecca, left a short message and then tested room service with a wine order. What kind of wine *do* you have with chocolate? They made various suggestions, including champagne, so Mitch told them to bring several selections. They did so, promptly, had everything expertly chilled and ready, and left Mitch to her own devices as requested. She settled in to wait with a book. The meeting must have ended early, the knock on the door came a little before nine. Mitch opened the door and Rebecca came in, looking tired around the edges.

"You look like you've had a full day," Mitch greeted.

"It's been a long day."

"You're early."

"The governor came down with a headache."

"Can I get you something for that?"

"I don't have a headache, the governor has a headache."

"Oh, I get it. You lied to get out of your meeting."

"It was half a lie. I felt I was going to get a headache if I didn't get out of that meeting and into your arms. Come here."

Mitch obeyed, happy to be invited into such a loving place. Rebecca took hold of her lapels and kissed her. She showed no signs of wanting to let go any time soon.

"It's so nice to be here without your helicopter staff," Mitch uttered.

"They mean well," Rebecca explained. "Their first priority is to watch out for me. They take their work very seriously."

"They treat me like vermin."

"I'll talk to them about it. Later. Right now, I want to concentrate on chocolate and making love to you."

"In that order?"

"Leave that to me."

As Rebecca made herself comfortable on the bed, Mitch poured wine and gathered together the chocolate treats she had found. Chocolate ice cream, chocolate éclairs, chocolate cake, and chocolate cheesecake were there for the taking. Rebecca laughed and captured Mitch in an embrace.

"How long has it been since you're had sex?" she asked with a smile.

"About a year and a day."

"You've got me beat by a year!"

Rebecca undressed Mitch, ignoring the chocolate for only a moment. Then, she ran her finger along the frosting of the cake and placed a small amount of it on Mitch's left nipple.

"What are you doing?" Mitch laughed, somewhere between nervous and excited.

"I'm fixing myself a snack."

"Well, I sincerely hope you're hungry," Mitch tried to relax under the tenderness of Rebecca's tongue. Her mind relaxed. Everything else began to tense. The chocolate treatment was extended to her other nipple and then points below. As Rebecca indulged, so too did Mitch. She enjoyed the sensation, feeling helpless to stop, not wanting to. She surrendered to her cravings. Rebecca certainly knew how to savor an experience.

Mitch was still. Unmoving. Rebecca had watched her for a moment, after taking five minutes to freshen up in the bathroom. She wondered if she was asleep, or just in deep relaxation.

"You okay?" Rebecca asked, bending close to Mitch's face.

"I'm perfect," Mitch assured without even opening up her eyes.

"You're so quiet," Rebecca said, kissing her.

"You're totally forgiven for falling asleep last night. I'll never be able to look at a chocolate cake again without blushing. I had no idea you were into such creative experimentation."

"I think I'm past experimentation and very much looking forward to full scale research."

"I've never had better," Mitch's voice was still a little shaky.

"And the chocolate was good, too."

Mitch gathered Rebecca into an intimate embrace, molding their bodies so closely together that desire immediately stirred in Rebecca. She knew without talking what Mitch was doing, and she moved together with her, rocking gently in her arms. They didn't say anything. They didn't need to. Aching need was replaced by gradual soothing sensations.

Mitch was the guilty party this time, dropping off to sleep first. At least, she thought so. The last thing she remembered was hearing about the details of the meetings that Rebecca had attended all through the day. It was boring enough to send a caffeine addict off to dreamland. She awoke to, once again, find Rebecca missing. There was no note this time. Apparently she hadn't gone far. She heard the shower running and turned on the TV to occupy her mind while she waited. The news was on. There was a crowd of reporters in front of a hotel. Mitch groaned audibly. They were outside the Brownstone. What were the chances that they were here to cover a story other than the governor and her new lesbian lover. About a trillion to one. Mitch heard the shower go off and turned the TV off as well.

"Good morning," Rebecca appeared. "Your turn."

"My what?" Mitch said, still thinking about the news crews swarming below.

"Your turn in the bathroom."

"Oh, okay, but don't go anywhere till I come back out."

"You think I'm going to make a break for it?" Rebecca laughed.

"Just don't do anything until I come back out."

"Okay."

Mitch hurried through morning chores and came back out to find Rebecca back in bed, sans clothes.

"We need to talk," Mitch said.

"Kiss me first."

"Just one."

One turned into several, each more intimate than the last.

"We have to talk," Mitch reminded.

"What's wrong? You seem nervous? Was it the chocolate?"

"Rebecca, I think we're on the news this morning. The reporters are downstairs. You and I are probably the lead story."

"I know that."

"You know? How?"

"I got a message early this morning from my staff."

"And you're not worried?"

"I've had a lot of time to think."

"And what did you decide?"

"I'm just going to go about my official duties business as usual."

"They're going to hound you with questions."

"I'll have answers."

"What kind of answers?"

"You're beginning to sound like my staff."

"I'm sorry, but I need to know."

"I'm going to tell the truth," Rebecca turned to Mitch, "because I've lived with a lie too long."

"You won't be governor much longer."

"Well, it was good while it lasted, and I did my best. That's all I can give to my country. They can't have my personal life, and they can't have my soul."

"How can I make this easier for you?"

"I'd like some wine – for breakfast."

Mitch laughed.

"What's so funny?"

"Do you remember the first time we met?"

"How could I forget. I was so horrible."

"No you weren't!"

"I wasn't?"

"You were so sexy. I didn't feel my knees for about a week after you left."

"Stop teasing me."

"Oh no, I'm not teasing you. You showed up in that raincoat and scarf and sunglasses, and then you started to take things off. I was shaking."

"I was trying to intimidate you."

"And you talked real tough to protect your daughter. I was so impressed by that."

"What else?"

"I looked into your eyes and I never looked back."

"And I poured a drink on you."

"And I didn't even shrink."

Rebecca laughed.

"And I remember one more thing," Mitch said.

"What?"

"I remember thinking, when you first started to talk that your voice was so cold that I was sure your tongue was made out of ice. Boy, how wrong was I about that!"

"Isn't it nice to be wrong, once in a while."

"Especially about things like that."

"You wanted wine for breakfast."

"Forget about the wine," Rebecca said and then kissed Mitch lazily. It was a forewarning of just how much time she would take bringing Mitch to another orgasm. There was just no hurrying this woman! It is said that government moves slowly, languidly, methodically, deliberately, and that those in government understand and thrive on its pace. Apparently, Rebecca Fairbanks was a master of the pace.

The soft, buzzing hum of a pager interrupted the foreplay.

"Damn phone," they said in unison.

Rebecca kissed once more and then made the phone call. She talked for a minute and then hung up.

"What's wrong?"

"Apparently there's been some vandalism at the mansion. I have to go and check on it."

"I'm going with you."

"Are you sure you want to?"

"Sure I'm sure."

They dressed quickly, and met the police protection just outside their door.

"Have they been here all night?" Mitch whispered the question.

"Just since this morning, when the news people arrived." Mitch nodded and smiled at the bodyguards, hoping that the walls of the hotel had been sound proofed. No one smiled back. An official car was waiting at the back entrance of the hotel. Rebecca tried to convince Mitch to ride with her, but she insisted on taking her own car. Otherwise, it would just be a logistics nightmare to retrieve it later. The drive to the mansion took less than five minutes. The sight that met them took much longer to sink in. Vandalism was a mild term for what had occurred. Every window in the house that could be reached by a rock had been broken. Shards of glass made walking a dangerous venture. Furniture had been ripped apart, thrown outside, or overturned. Smoke from an attempted arson had damaged at least three rooms. Mitch studied the scene from a detached point of view. She closed her eyes and imagined a crowd of torch bearing villagers, much like those famous movie scenes outside the castle of Dr. Frankenstein. Burn and pillage, Pillage and burn. She looked up to the second story windows, which had also been broken out.

"Who can throw a rock that far?" she asked one of the police assigned to the case.

"Those windows weren't broken with rocks."

"How did they get broken?"

"They were shot out?"

"With a gun?"

"That's right."

"Well, it's a good thing the governor wasn't home at the time."

"Maybe if she was home, alone, this wouldn't have happened at all."

His tone and meaning were unmistakable. Mitch caught up with Rebecca, who had gone upstairs to survey the damage. All of her personal things were in complete disarray. Torn clothes, broken perfume bottles, and smashed photographs, were but a few of the messages left by the unwelcome callers.

"Well, I guess we're not going to make the cover of Home Beautiful anytime soon," Rebecca said coldly. Her anger was just under the surface, and she turned to look at Mitch. "Now what?"

"You've got a house?"

"A tiny, dinky five room rustic cabin."

"Sounds wonderful. I don't have much left to pack. Give me about ten minutes."

Rebecca consulted with the official authorities at the scene. Mitch may have thought she was seeing things, but they sure looked like ATF agents. They were driven to Mitch's place in a bullet-resistant vehicle. Another agent followed in Mitch's car so that it would be out of harm's way as well. Overhead, they could hear the helicopters hovering. Whether they were official or from the TV news stations was impossible to tell from the vantage point of the protected car. They pulled up in the driveway and waited until they could be safely brought inside the house.

Rebecca scoped out the rambling floor plan in fifteen seconds.

"This is rustic alright. I hope I don't have to use an outhouse."

"There's indoor plumbing, it's just sort of temperamental."

"How temperamental?"

"Let me draw you a nice warm bath. It will help your nerves."

"My nerves are fine. How are you doing?"

"I'm fine. I think we'll be safe here."

"I know we will be, it's all arranged. They are setting up protective barriers as we speak."

"They are doing what?"

"Look out the window. You'll see agents guarding us."

She was right. Dozens of people, men and women, were out on Mitch's acre setting up what could have passed for a fortress. It made her stomach clench. Her sanctuary from the world, however modest and unassuming it may have been, was now a sanctuary in literal and starker terms.

They hid out at Mitch's house for all of Saturday. Being a little low on the grocery supply, they settled for pizza brought in under armed guard. Somehow, they slept and when sleep eluded them, they talked about the future. It loomed out there, somewhere. Somewhere between love and hate. Somewhere between tolerance and intolerance. Somewhere between now and later.

Calls kept coming in to the now-tapped land line phone. The work of the republic went on under armed guard. If the calls gave any indication that they were placed by the perpetrators of the crime, Mitch was never included in the discussion. The fact that she was an outsider in her own home didn't seem to bother her. Whatever it took to keep Rebecca safe was all that mattered.

Rebecca talked to various people, including a panicked Mary. She gave everyone warm assurances and declined delivery of a bullet proof vest. Just the usual Saturday in the public eye. Sunday, Mitch went with Rebecca to church, once again under armed guard. It felt awkward, but they managed to survive the curious or hostile stares. By Sunday afternoon, the effort to recall was well underway, being organized by people who felt betrayed by Rebecca. They would stop at nothing short of total vilification to sway their minions.

Three days into the recall effort, Mitch made the news. Again. Just not in the way she had hoped. There had been, to that point, an ongoing barrage of criticism. Right-wing radio talk show had been a non-stop spewage of hatred. Anyone brave enough to support either the governor or Mitch had been shouted down. National news had camped out at the mansion, the capitol building, and all points in between. Mitch had had the brainstorm earlier in the week to convince Mary and Hilary to return to Waysouthfork, Texas. Two reasons made this logical. The first was to get them away from the long reach of the TV news. The second, more selfish, was to ensure that if Lisa happened to see a file photo of Mary during this frenzy of media attention, Lisa might get it in her head to call the Texas ranch to check on Mary the maid. Hey, Mitch rationalized,

doesn't everybody have a twin? Marge had closed the
Lucky U to begin the remodeling, using the time off to
keep a much-overdue appointment with her doctor. Trish
was busy keeping track of everyone and everything, which
proved a daunting task.

Rebecca, meanwhile, had attempted to keep up her
schedule, but after three days of constant harassment, even
she needed a break. Mitch had the idea of having a nice,
quiet dinner out, just to have one positive event to break up
the otherwise oppressive atmosphere. After clearing the
plan with everybody but NATO, they went out with armed
escorts to an upscale restaurant. The press and general
public were held at bay, so they had the restaurant mostly
to themselves.

Rebecca and Mitch talked through the meal like it was just
another day in heaven. Dinner had been fabulous, and they
were perusing the dessert menu, giggling about chocolate
when Mitch heard the sound. It was too distinctive to
mistake for anything else and she was up on her feet in a
flash. Two shots cracked the air like a whip snapping at
her ear. She had only time to push Rebecca out of the way
before the other shots found their mark. A split second
later, a cabal of agents were hovering. Mitch blacked out
to the sound of screams. They might have been hers. She
woke up to screaming. It must have been a siren, no one
screamed up and down a scale, unless it was bad opera.
Red light, blue light, white light. Time morphed into
another dimension. Someone bent over her and put a finger
on her throat. She lost consciousness. Again.

When Mitch came to, Rebecca was asleep in a chair. Mitch
croaked when she tried to talk and Rebecca jumped,
instantly awake. She had a bandage on her cheek.
"Don't try to talk."
"Huh?"
"How are you?"
"You just told me not to talk!"
"That's right. I'm sorry."

"Where am I?"

"In recovery."

"In the hospital."

"You're in Central Medical Center."

"What happened?"

"You tell me. You jumped up so fast out of your seat at the restaurant that everyone figured you for a psychic."

"I heard something."

"It was gun shots. There was some nut there dressed as a waiter who was out to kill gay people."

"Starting with you and me?"

"You saved my life. You're a hero."

"You're hurt," Mitch tried to lift her arm to touch Rebecca's cheek. Pain coursed through her body like an electric current, fast and scorching.

"Don't move."

"How bad is it?"

"You got shot in the thigh and the elbow."

"Oh, Damn! Not my elbow!"

"You're going to be okay."

"My elbow. I need that for making love to you."

"You use your elbow?"

"And you thought you were kinky."

A nurse appeared, injecting something into an IV tube. It instantly erased Mitch's pain, and she felt sleepy. But she must have resisted the effects of the drug, because she kept hearing Rebecca's soothing voice, "Don't fight it. Just go to sleep."

She slept fitfully, off and on again, hearing shots ringing in her ears and battling phantom waiters in her dreams. Every time she was about to land a punch, Rebecca caught her arm and stroked it lovingly until she dropped off again. Rebecca eased her to sleep again and again, until Mitch's mind allowed her to rest.

Morning dawned bright and clear. It brought Trish, flowers, the police, and a doctor. But no Rebecca. Trish explained to Mitch that she had ordered Rebecca to get some sleep. The hospital had opened up some private room for her. Yes, she was under guard. Flowers were pouring in from everywhere. The roses were from The Today Show. The police had a few questions, like how did you know that the noise you heard was a gun? Maybe because it was ear-splittingly loud! They rolled their eyes and left. Interrogating someone sky high on morphine must not have been their idea of a good time.

The doctor looked like he was about thirteen. Young, handsome, and how about that acne? He was very polite and obviously overqualified. Surely, they didn't let you into medical school unless you were a genius and toilet trained.

"Your thigh injury is looking good. There will be no permanent damage. Your elbow is another story. We repaired what was left. We'll just have to hope for the best after therapy."

"When can I leave the hospital?"

"In a day or two."

"How about later today?"

"Was it something we said?"

"I feel fine."

"Of course you do. You've had a snoot full of medication."

This kid was getting better and better. Mitch hadn't heard the saying snoot full since her parents had died.

"I want to go home."

"I'd feel better if you would stay one more day. You still have a risk of infection."

"Did the guy use rusty bullets or what?"

"Besides, you're an honored guest. We don't have an authentic hero in here every day."

"I'm not a hero."

"Don't pay any attention to her," Rebecca said as she entered the room.

"Good morning, Governor Fairbanks," the young doctor extended his hand.

"Good morning."

"Would you tell Marcus Welby M.D. here that I'm okay to go home!" Mitch said.

"I think she needs to stay at least a week, don't you?"
Rebecca nodded to the doctor.

"I think we'd better go day to day for a while."

"I agree," Rebecca nodded, catching Mitch's eye.

The doctor studied Mitch's chart for a moment, searching for something.

"What's wrong?" Mitch asked.

"I'm just checking to see which doctors have been here to see you. There's no Dr. Welby listed on the chart."

"Is there a Howser?" Mitch jibed.

"Howser, Howser, nope, no Howser."

Rebecca took pity on the youngster, "Thank you for your care."

He left, still shaking his head.

"You are so bad," Rebecca admonished with that smile that Mitch would never grow tired of seeing.

"I thought you were asleep?"

"I slept."

"All of three minutes?"

"I got in a couple of hours. You sure look better than last night."

"Where's Trish?" Mitch asked, remembering the kaleidoscope-like confusion of the early morning.

"I sent her home."

"You should go home too and get some real sleep."

"I'm not going anywhere. I'm staying right here with you."

"You have work to do. A desk full, I'm certain."

"Why bother? I'll be recalled soon anyway. When do you get to eat something?"

"I graduated from liquid to solid diet this morning."

"I'll have lunch brought in."

Mitch dozed on and off, every once in a while checking on Rebecca. She was pretending to be asleep too, but it was a terrible act. Every time Mitch so much as wiggled, Rebecca was alert and asking how to help. They were munching turkey sandwiches when the noon news started. Of course, Mitch was the lead story, but it was the second, related news item that caught their attention. A group of interested citizens had banded together to fight the recall effort. For a hastily formed group, they already had a name, a plan, and a press conference. The Citizens Speaking Out Against Hate urged all citizens to oppose the recall effort and they were shredding mock copies of recall petitions during their live press conference. By five o'clock, they were national news. By ten they were the lead story.

Rebecca kept vigil through the early evening, but Mitch begged her to go home to get some rest after the ten o'clock news.
"Go home. Rest. Sleep. Get ready for tomorrow."
"Are you sure?"
"I'm sure. I love you. Go home already."
"I love you, too."

Mitch slept well, the ghost gunshots faded. Morning arrived with still more flowers, a representative from the CSOAH group, and Rebecca. After about three minutes of deliberation, her release orders were drawn up and a nurse appeared with a wheelchair. They went out the front door amidst the press corps and drove to the house with their usual police escort. One of the several newly assigned bodyguards helped Mitch into the house and helped the visiting nurse to arrange her in her bed.

Rebecca appeared and dismissed everyone until further notice. They went away, trusting the governor to know what she was doing.
"I'm so glad to be home," Mitch breathed deeply, still tired from the ordeal.
"Me too. Are you in pain?"
"Only when I move, or breathe, or think."
"I'll get your medication."
"No, you won't. You'll stay right here where I can hold you. One of those other people can bring medication when I'm ready, which I'm not."
"Okay. What do you want?"
"I want you."
"Your elbow isn't ready for me."
"Oh, but when it is, you'd better be well rested."

"Are you hungry?" Rebecca asked, forging through her list of concerns.

"Yes."

"What do you want?"

"Something chocolate."

They ate a late breakfast together in bed and Mitch slept after her medication took effect. Rebecca slipped out and worked in the makeshift den until just before dinner. When she checked up on her patient, Mitch was standing up, testing her thigh for pain and weakness.

"You're supposed to be taking it easy."

"I am. I'm only doing fifteen minutes of calisthenics instead of twenty."

"You're going to rip out your stitches."

"I need to be able to get back and forth to the bathroom."

"You need to call one of us for help."

"How many of 'us' are there?"

"Me, the nurse, the bodyguard."

"This house isn't big enough for all of 'us.'"

"We don't have much say in the matter. I'm hoping we can all make the best of a crowded situation."

"Were you working?"

"I was going through some paperwork."

"That's a hopeful sign. It means you're going to stick around and fight it out."

"I'm taking care of business. It gives me something to do while you sleep the day away, you lazy thing."

"I feel a lot better."

"You look better."

"Come over here and give me an escort to the bathroom."

"It would be my pleasure."

Rebecca and Mitch had suddenly found themselves in such an intimate relationship that all necessities of life were approached as commonplace and ordinary. Nothing was embarrassing. Nothing awkward. Nothing too difficult to bear. Convalescing was so much more fun when you had someone to share it with. Soon, Mitch was back in bed, propped up on pillows, and holding Rebecca as close as casts and stitches allowed.

"Are we still the lead story on the news?" she asked.

"An earthquake has replaced us as top story, but the fight against the recall is still number two."

"If I had known that was going to happen, I would have gotten myself shot sooner."

"Don't even joke like that!" Rebecca snapped instinctively. Mitch scrutinized Rebecca. She realized how the events had taken their toll.

"Snuggle up closer," Mitch said softly.

"I don't want to hurt you."

"You won't hurt me. Come on." Mitch pulled her closer, cuddling intimately. Rebecca was as tight as a coil. Mitch began lazily kissing her forehead, her eyes, her cheeks. Rebecca began to cry. It had to happen sometime. Mitch waited out storm Rebecca.

"I'm going to be as good as new soon. It's going to take a lot more than a couple of gunshot wounds to keep me down."

"I feel so guilty," Rebecca tried to say more and started to sob again.

"You're beautiful when you cry."

"Shut up," she said, but not in anger.

"This isn't your fault."

"I know that. I feel so vulnerable that I'd prefer to feel guilt."

"We'll just take this in stride."

"God you're brave!"

"I'd take a bullet for you any old day of the week. Just don't ever leave me. That would kill me."

"I'm not leaving you."

"Well, then, who's going to get dinner for me?"

"You're hungry again?"

"I'm a recuperating girl!"

"Okay, but no chocolate."

"Chicken," Mitch teased.

As luck would have it, chicken it was. With stuffing and mashed potatoes and green beans and biscuits and gravy. They ate together in bed, with no interference from TV news or staff people. It was paradise.

After dinner, they relaxed together. Rebecca had canceled all evening meetings in light of the assassination attempt and they played gin for a dollar a point. Mitch was down about five hundred before she fell sound asleep mid hand. Rebecca knew she was losing on purpose, but played along until the snoring commenced.

Chapter 25

By morning, they were back to a normal schedule. Mitch didn't require invalid treatment, and wouldn't have stood still for it anyway. Rebecca returned to work full time, which allowed Mitch to sneak out the back door relatively unnoticed to get together with Trish. Trish picked her up at the house and spirited her off to a country club. It felt safe and secure, but then again, so had the restaurant. They sat in a corner booth with their backs to the wall and their eyes on the door. Trish ordered wine and then proceeded to get nosy.

"So, you and the governor?"

"Me and the governor."

"Sounds like a good title for a miniseries. Tell me more."

"She's nice."

"What else?"

"She's funny. She has a great sense of humor."

"What else?"

"What else do you want to know?" Mitch asked, knowing full well what Trish wanted to know. Mitch felt an obligation to put up at least a little resistance.

"Is she the one? I mean *the one!*"

"She's *the one*. She's so good to me, even though I'm all crippled up."

"Well, you took a couple of bullets for her. She should be very good to you."

"It goes way beyond that. She isn't doing this out of pity. It must be love, she's letting me lose at gin on purpose."

"Now, there's a sure sign! Losing at gin." Trish pretended to jot down the advice for future reference. "Anyway, everybody's worried sick about you."

"We've got the FBI on our side. What could possibly go wrong?"

"I'm keeping my eye on all the waiters."

"How close are we to the Aspen Sting?"

"Okay, Lisa's casts come off tomorrow."

"You'll help me transfer the money?"

"Sure. Are you able to go anywhere with all the bodyguards?"

"I'll give them the slip, just like today."

"What about the governor?"

"I expect she'll stay home and govern."

"Mary and Hilary can help out."

"I told them to stay in Texas. There's no use getting them in front of a camera. We're too close to the finish line to screw up now."

"Pick you up tomorrow?"

"Same place, same time."

Mitch got home a little later than she had planned. Rebecca was home, unexpectedly, and walking the floor.

"You're late," she started right in, no preliminaries, no opening acts.

"Trish says 'hi.'"

"I was worried, damn it! Why did you go out without protection?"

"I'm sorry. The service at the country club was slow and I don't want bodyguards following me around everywhere I go."

"Don't joke around about this. Too much has happened in the past few days. I don't like being this way, I don't want you to go somewhere alone where I don't know where you are."

"Well then, you're going to hate the next few days."

"Why?"

"Because I'm going to Aspen. It's time."

"You're not going through with that? Not in your condition!"

"I have to. Friends are depending on me."

"It's too dangerous."

"It can't be any more dangerous than going out to dinner with you!" Mitch snapped irritably. As soon as she said the words, she regretted them.

Rebecca held up her hands, didn't say another word and stomped the short distance to the spare room. It would have been a lot more dramatic if they had been at the mansion, with big doors to slam, but it still sent clear signals to Mitch. She gave herself a moment to breathe, to

291

prepare, to plan, and then she went over and knocked on the door.

"What!" came through the door.

"I want to come in."

"It's your damn house!" Each word was cut short, making for a very clear message.

Mitch opened the door and saw Rebecca standing at the window. She couldn't do much else, there was no furniture in this particular room. Without a word, Mitch came up behind Rebecca and placed her good hand on Rebecca's right shoulder blade. There was no recoil. That was a good sign.

"Is this our first fight?" Mitch said quietly, not able to think of another clever line.

"No, our first fight was over a shoe salesman."

"Oh yeah, that. Well, you know what they say, a relationship isn't a relationship until it sustains and survives a fight, or two."

"They can shove it!"

Mitch moved closer, and leaned her forehead on Rebecca's back. She slid her hand down and wrapped it cautiously around Rebecca's waist. It felt enervating to be so close and yet so far.

"I'm sorry I hurt you. I didn't mean it the way it came out."

"You're taking a foolish, stupid risk."

Mitch kissed the back of Rebecca's neck. It sent shivers through both of them.

"I'll be okay. Trish is going to protect me."

"Big, bad, ninety-eight pound Trish? That'll work out great if you're attacked by Calista Flockhart."

"Now, that's more like it. I told Trish you had a great sense of humor."

"What else did you tell Trish?"

"I didn't tell her anything about your bedside manner."

"I can't change your mind, about Aspen?"

"Rebecca, the way I see it, we have two basic choices. We can either live our lives in fear, or we can live our lives. I know that the past few days haven't exactly been the best introduction of what it's like to be gay in Colorado, but I

can't make the hate go away. I can only help make the fear
go away. Right now, my heart is so full of love for you that
there's no room left for fear."

"How long will you be gone?"

"I don't know. A couple of days? Why don't you come
with me?"

"I have work to do."

"Okay. I'd better go pack. I'll need a few things."

Mitch disentangled herself from Rebecca and walked to
their bedroom. Going slowly, using her one remaining
good arm, she rummaged through the closet until she found
her all-purpose duffel bag. She was clumsily trying to
work the zipper with one hand when Rebecca appeared.

"Let me do that. I'll help you pack."

"Thanks."

They folded clothes and tossed in spare socks and
underwear in silence. It took less than ten minutes.

"Would it help to talk more?" Mitch ventured into
conversation when the packing was complete.

"I don't know."

"You feel I'm deserting you in your hour of need?"

"I have the FBI to protect me."

"You think I'm choosing my friends' needs over yours?"

"What are you getting at?"

"The truth, I hope. I just want to know if there's anything
you aren't telling me, about how you feel."

"I'm concerned that you're caught up in revenge. That
worries me."

"I'm not. I made a promise to help a friend. Come with
me and watch and believe."

"I'll try to get up there in a day or two if things drag on."

"I'll call you every day."

"Three times a day."

"Three times a day," Mitch repeated and then pulled
Rebecca close.

"What are you doing?" she asked.

"I'm making love to you before I go."

"Not in your convalescing condition?"

"I have to follow the rules!" Mitch said innocently.

"Is this going to be another one of those unwritten lesbian rules again," Rebecca asked suspiciously, hearing the playfulness in Mitch's voice.

"You liked the last unwritten lesbian rule well enough."

"Okay, what's this rule."

"Actually, this is one of those well-worn hetero rules as well. Everybody knows you need to make up after a fight. Lots of my friends get into fights just so they can make up afterwards!"

"I might hurt you?"

"I could only hope."

Mitch kissed Rebecca in a way that was sensitive and yet unyielding. It took only a moment, but Rebecca responded in a way that even caught her off guard. A little. Her kiss was as fierce as her passion, and when Mitch only asked for more in the nonverbal language that lovers understand, she gave more. It was a fast, hard, no nonsense climax for Rebecca and she found herself still breathing deeply when Mitch held her gently by her side.

"You didn't have an orgasm?" Rebecca stated the obvious in the form of a question like she was preparing to appear on Jeopardy.

"It's the pain medication. Besides, I was having so much fun watching you have yours that I forgot."

"You were watching me?"

"Every minute."

"I hurt you, I mean, it hurt, didn't it?"

"A little. Not much."

"Does this hurt?" Rebecca asked as she place a knowing hand on Mitch's thigh.

"No, that doesn't hurt."

"How about this?" she probed again, finding softer places to touch and stroke.

Mitch stopped answering with her voice. She didn't have any other choice. Rebecca had learned so quickly what Mitch enjoyed that she didn't need any more clues. Pain medication notwithstanding, Mitch enjoyed every teasing sensation. Afterwards, as Mitch relaxed with her eyes shut, she remarked, "You were watching, weren't you?"

"Every minute."

"Passion is a strange thing, isn't it," Mitch said, feeling serene and peaceful.

"How so?"

"Hard one minute, soft the next, insistent and yet tender, needing and giving."

"And sometimes all in the same night," Rebecca mused.

Mitch looked at her watch, "Sometimes all within twenty-five minutes!"

"I didn't want to keep you up all night. You have an early morning start."

"You feel better about my trip?"

"Better. Not great, not overjoyed."

"Okay. I can live with better."

Mitch stopped philosophizing. That, and silence, was all it took to lull Rebecca to sleep.

Chapter 26

Trish was there before dawn and they drove an hour before stopping for breakfast. Dan had arranged to meet them for breakfast with the cash after he realized how complicated Mitch's life had become. They feasted on ham and eggs and then transferred an innocuous briefcase filled with packets of hundred dollar bills. Mitch handled it like a sack of potatoes. Trish helped Mitch get buckled up again and they drove hours before they arrived at the hotel. Being a stickler for rules, Mitch had insisted on renting a regular hotel room instead of using Trish's real estate condo. This was as far from real estate business as you could get. The next order of business, after checking in and unpacking, was notifying Judy of their arrival. Trish set up a time with Judy the following day to hand over the money.

"What are we going to do with it in the meantime?" Mitch asked.

"I guess we'll sleep with it between us," Trish kidded.

"I'll let you cuddle up to it," Mitch bantered back even though she was tired from the trip.

They both slept fitfully and Trish was up first, ready way too early for her nine o'clock meeting.

"Drive carefully," were Mitch's only words of wisdom.

Trish was back in less than an hour.

"That was quick!" Mitch stated.

"You should have seen Lisa's eyes," Trish acted the part. "It would have been impossible to catch them if they flew out of her head. Lisa fondled the money like a lover. She even licked two or three of the bundles!"

"She licked the money?"

"Yeah, she had a bundle in each hand," Trish demonstrated further, "And she would lick one and then the other. She even had the nerve to wink at me while she was doing it. When you get the money back, check for slobber."

"Uh, right."

"Are you okay, Mitch?"

"Terrific. When is Judy going to lock the money in the new safety deposit box?"

"That's what took most of the time. It's done. The bank's right down the block."

"And Lisa's signature is valid also?"

"She has full access to the new box. Judy told Lisa that they need to mull over investment strategies."

"I hope they don't take too long. This town isn't big enough for all of us."

"Your anxiousness wouldn't have anything to do with wanting to get back to the governor?"

"She wasn't exactly thrilled about this. If she shows up, don't be too surprised."

"You told her she could come up here?"

"It's her state! They allow her to go anywhere. Besides, I didn't tell her, I more or less begged her."

"You've really got it bad. I guess I never thought you'd get over Lisa."

"Lisa who?"

Trish chuckled.

"I've never had a good reason to get over Lisa, until now."

"Lisa who?" Trish echoed, and laughed again.

"Which reminds me, I should call Rebecca and check in."

"Do that. I'm going to take a shower. The sight of Lisa licking money made me break out in a cold sweat."

Trish went into the bathroom as Mitch dialed the direct line to Rebecca's office.

"The governor's in a meeting. Can I take a message?"

"This is Mitch. Does she want to talk to me?"

"Please hold the line."

Rebecca picked up in five seconds.

"Hi," Mitch said, sounding lonely to herself already.

"Hi."

"You're in a meeting?"

"That's right."

"Are you on the speaker phone or the handset?"

"Handset. Why?"

"I love you and I didn't feel like sharing that with everyone in the meeting."

"That's good judgment."

"And when you touch me, the world melts away."

"Okay," Rebecca drew out her response, unable to say much more in front of the participants in the meeting.

"And when you kiss me, I forget that I've ever been kissed before."

"I see."

"And I miss you terribly already."

"Are you okay?"

"As well as can be expected. I love you."

"I know. I feel the same."

"I miss you. I suppose I should let you get back to your meeting."

"Uh huh."

"Okay, but I'll call you later."

"Okay."

Mitch hung up the phone reluctantly. Trish was still in the shower so Mitch walked over to the window to watch the world go by. What she saw instead was Lisa crossing the street and heading straight for the hotel. Several thoughts flashed through Mitch's mind. Call Judy, lock the door, warn Trish. Ascertaining that there was no time for the first choice, Mitch locked the door and then, however embarrassing it might be, she had to tell Trish. She knocked on the bathroom door loudly to give fair warning and then, with eyes covered, she opened the shower door and yelled the warning, "Lisa is on the way to the hotel."

"What?"

"My eyes are shut. Lisa is in the hotel."

"Mitch, it's okay. You can open your eyes."

"No, no I can't do that. Lisa's coming."

"The hotel won't give her the room number."

"I guess not," Mitch agreed.

"The worst that could happen is that they will call the room."

As if on cue, the phone began ringing. Trish, wrapped in a towel, crossed the room to answer it.

"Hello?"

Mitch listened closely, now eyes wide open.

"I'm dripping wet, just got out of the shower."

A throaty giggle. A long pause.

"Sure, meet you downstairs in ten minutes. Lunch sound great."

She hung up the phone and went to get ready.

"So where's Judy?"

"Shopping, according to Lisa."

"So you and Lisa are having lunch?"

"Don't make it sound like adultery. Do me a favor and call me in about an hour. Give me a reason to get away from Lisa."

"Sure thing. Just don't bring her up to the room. I don't want to hide in the hall closet while you fend off her advances."

While Trish entertained Lisa, Mitch dialed Judy seven times. There was no answer, and no sign of her anywhere on the part of the main street that Mitch could see from her window seat on the hotel's third floor. She tried one more time to dial Judy, and she picked up on the third ring.

"It's Mitch."

"Hi."

"Lisa and Trish are having lunch, together."

"I noticed she was gone."

"Are you okay?"

"I'm fine, at least I'm okay."

"You want to get this over with as soon as possible?" Mitch asked the obvious question.

"Yes."

"Here's what you do….."

Mitch called Trish after fifty minutes. Her relief was palpable. Trish was back in the room in twelve minutes and Lisa left the hotel. Passing right by the bank, she apparently headed home.

"What happened?" Mitch asked.

"She offered to have my children."

"You're kidding, right?"

"No pun intended, I hope? No, she didn't want to set up housekeeping, but she did want to come upstairs and thank me personally for being such a good lawyer. Your call couldn't have come at a better time, I was running out of polite excuses."

"Do you think we need to switch rooms or hotels?"

299

"We have such a good view of the street that I hate to move."

"When do you think Lisa's going to make a break for it?"

"Soon, trust me. I'm going to take a shower and a nap."

"Okay, I'll hold down the fort."

The hot shower relaxed Mitch, even though she had to go through all the painstaking efforts to keep her cast and stitches dry. She slept the minute her head hit the pillow and didn't wake up until six p.m. She walked sleepily out of her bedroom only to find Trish entertaining company.

"Hi, sleepyhead," Rebecca greeted.

"Hi there yourself," Mitch smiled back. "You got out of your meeting, I see."

"Just to see you."

They embraced and showed no sign of leaving the clinch. Trish tried to extract herself, but Mitch stopped her.

"You don't need to leave, Trish."

"I think I'd better. She's already heard the shower story."

"I had my eyes shut, I swear!" Mitch looked at Rebecca with sweet and earned innocence.

"I believe you," she smiled back.

"Are you hungry?"

"Starving. How's room service?"

"It's my only choice. I'm so glad you're here."

"Let's order and eat in bed."

"My second favorite thing to do."

They ordered dinner for three since Trish wanted to stay out of sight as well, particularly after lunch. By the time dinner had arrived, the three women had entered into such an interesting conversion that Rebecca and Mitch kept Trish company through the meal. There was always time for dessert, later. Trish was too enthralled in telling Rebecca embarrassing stories about Mitch to stop her now. Rebecca, to her credit, not only listened but encouraged the story telling. Trish had been paying closer attention all these years than Mitch had realized. In a way, it was touching.

"Trish is a good friend," Rebecca said later in bed. They had made love, eaten dessert and talked all tangled up in each other's arms for about a half hour.

"Trish is a good friend," Mitch agreed, word for word.

"Making love to you is just like going to heaven," Rebecca pronounced.

"My goodness, that's quite a compliment. Thank you." Mitch stammered.

"Well, I didn't mean it quite like that."

"How exactly did you mean it?" Mitch asked with an arched eyebrow.

"Oh oh. Is this going to be like that shoe salesman thing? I'm going to say something inadvertently and tick you off, aren't I?"

"No, you won't. Don't worry. What were you trying to say?"

"You know that old story about going to heaven...."

"Does this involve a nun on a skateboard?"

"No! Haven't you ever heard the three surprises about heaven? The first surprise is that you're there at all. The second is that there are people there whom you didn't expect to see. The third is that the people you expected to be there aren't there."

"And that's like our lovemaking?"

"It's an analogy. You know, those things that get me in trouble."

"And you do it so well."

"Anyway," Rebecca continued, ignoring the interruption, "first, it's been an extraordinarily pleasant surprise to become your lover. Second, I feel things that I never expected to feel, and third, I don't feel some things that I thought I would feel."

"What don't you feel?"

"Oh, no, you don't! First things first."

"I was a surprise?" Mitch strained to remember the order of the story. Didn't great sex kill brain cells?

"Extraordinarily pleasant surprise. I know I don't have to go into great detail about all the new sensations and feelings that I've had with you. Suffice it to say that I know what true love finally feels like."

"And oral sex."

"That, too."

"So, what didn't you feel," Mitch had recalled the order, and could safely ask.

"I don't feel guilty. I don't feel masculine."

"I understand about the guilt thing and you've done nothing to feel guilty for or about."

"A lot of people, including my former self, would disagree."

"That's okay. Anybody can be wrong. I'm not sure I completely understand about the masculine thing, though?"

"I guess I'm stuck in my thinking. Gender based roles were so ingrained in my childhood that I expected to, I thought I would, I'm not saying this very well, am I?"

"You're doing beautifully so far. I know it's confusing. You've been taught from day one that a penis is required for proper sex. So how can we possibly have a love life without one, right?"

"It's even more than that. It's all tied up with traditional roles, assertive behavior, and passiveness. I thought I'd be getting more in touch with my masculine side, and all I did was feel more feminine. More tender. More loving."

"What would you consider to be masculine?"

"Asking for sex?"

"You did that."

"I guess I did."

"Several times, in fact. And don't ever be afraid to do that. Unless I'm sick or dead, I'll say yes. I'll never withhold sex to punish or control, so don't hesitate."

"Okay."

"What else is bothering you?"

"I don't want to be a traditional wife, and I don't feel like a husband."

"What do you feel like?"

"Besides the luckiest person on the planet? I feel like you accept me and welcome me as a partner, a confidant. You are the one safe, trusting soul who can sort through all the chaff of who I am and still not be too disappointed when you get to the wheat."

"Well, I'm no farmer, but I'll do my best. What else is on your mind? What are you having a hard time talking about?" Mitch asked, psychically.

"Besides oral sex?" Rebecca said, bravely.

"Don't look now but your lexicon is getting bigger!"

"That's what I want to talk about. That and other things. I want to take an active part in our sex life. I want to be able to set the pace, and know exactly what I'm doing and be in control once in a while."

"That's a great idea."

"You wouldn't mind?"

"Heck no! If the voters of Colorado trusted you to run the entire state, I think I can trust you to manage our sex life. You just tell me what you want, and when, and how, and where, and I'm here for you. The only thing I won't do is hurt you, at least not on purpose. Don't ask me to do the hot wax thing and I'll be just fine."

"Hot wax?"

"If hot wax turned me on, I'd work in a candle factory!"

"And so, you don't mind if I want to 'manage' things?"

"You think that's one of those masculine things that had you bothered?"

"I think so. Gee, I guess if I wanted to act masculine, I'd forget our anniversary."

"Oh, now, now, now, no male-bashing allowed."

"A lesbian that doesn't do male humor?" Rebecca looked at Mitch.

"I know too many great guys to indulge."

"Okay. No more male-bashing. But while we're on the subject of anniversaries, I wanted to ask you something."

"Sure."

"My staff and advisors want me to hold a press conference."

"And say what?"

"That's what we're fighting about. They want me to downplay our relationship. To deny if possible. To make up a plausible story. I won't go along."

"What are you going to do?"

"How would you feel if I announced our engagement?"

303

"Does that mean we'll still get to sleep together?" Mitch asked, smiling at the somber Rebecca. Since she had started on this particular subject, her countenance had taken on a deadly seriousness. Now, she smiled.

"Absolutely."

"Oh, good. I was worried there for a minute."

"There will still be major obstacles to overcome."

"How many times can they ransack the mansion?"

"I'm serious."

"I noticed."

"We'll be the most hated couple in Colorado."

"Wouldn't you rather be hated for who you are than loved for who you're not?"

"I couldn't do this without you."

"You won't have to. I'm right here."

Rebecca lowered herself to Mitch and kissed her face. It was a welcome nuzzle that Mitch stirred beneath. She couldn't stir very far.

"You know, my Dear," Rebecca smiled coyly, "I have you at a disadvantage."

"How so?" Mitch toyed back.

"I'm laying on your good arm and you can't do a thing with your other arm, so you're kind of helpless."

"Honey, I've *been* helpless since the day we met."

"Well, then, how are you going to open this?" Rebecca reached over and pulled a little velvet box from her bedside table.

"What's this?"

"You want me to open it for you?"

"Yes, please."

She opened the box to reveal a simple, yet expensive gold ring.

"It's beautiful. I've never owned anything gold before," Mitch was touched.

Rebecca slid the ring on Mitch's finger. It fit perfectly.

"How did you know what size to get?"

"I measured your finger one day while you were asleep."

"You measured my finger while I was asleep?" Mitch said, wondrously.

"Yes."

"What else have you been doing while I was asleep?" she asked with mock suspicion.

"That's for me to know."

"You are so clever, and so very thoughtful. I love it. I love you."

"You don't think this is too masculine, this ring-giving thing?"

"If this is your idea of masculine, you can be masculine any old day of the week."

"I'm glad you like it."

"When this is all over, I'll buy a ring for you."

"I can't stay in Aspen too long."

"I hadn't planned to shop up here. And don't worry, we won't be here much longer anyway."

"How do you know?"

"I just know. I'll wake you up at eight. The bank opens at nine. I want you to drive, and I need you to do exactly what I say. Without question. Just this once."

"Will it be illegal?"

"No, just difficult. Do you trust me?"

"With my life."

"It won't come to that."

"And then we can go home."

"Anything you say."

"You understand my needs."

"I'm trying to keep up. You've gone from right-wing conservative to terrific lesbian lover in a few short weeks."

"Terrific?"

"Way past terrific!"

"I'm a woman in love, inspired by a woman in love."

"Tell me about it."

"I'd rather show you."

Rebecca practiced her newly-found hobby of sexual assertiveness. Mitch had been honest, she took direction well. She could have worked in Hollywood, maybe as a cab driver. They slept soundly and as promised, Mitch roused everyone at eight. Trish was uncertain as to Mitch's instincts.

"How do you know something will happen this morning?"

"I just know."

Room service breakfast was light: juice, coffee, fruit and toast. They ate distractedly. At 8:50 a.m., the phone rang. It was Judy.

"You were right. She left the house a couple of minutes ago."

"Okay, you know what to do."

Mitch hung up the phone and announced, "Time to go." Without hesitation, they bundled up and went down the back stairs. Rebecca warmed up the SUV for five minutes, the time it took Judy to arrive via the back streets of the town. Judy got in the backseat next to Trish. Rebecca put the vehicle in gear and Mitch directed her to a parking area on the street where they could observe the bank unnoticed. At nine exactly, Lisa pulled up to the bank and went inside. She emerged ten minutes later with a valise, got in her car and headed down the street that led out of Aspen.

"Let her get at least a block ahead," Mitch instructed.

If Lisa checked to see if she was being tailed, she wouldn't perceive Rebecca as a threat. Mitch wore sunglasses and a hat. After all this time, there would be no instant spark of recognition. They followed Lisa at a discreet distance. After negotiating the town traffic, they merged onto the highway and traveled for about twenty minutes. Mitch had turned around a couple of times to check on Judy and when she finally nodded, Mitch told Rebecca to take the turn into the town of Basalt. Lisa kept going and was out of sight within a few seconds.

"What are we doing?" Trish asked, suddenly confused.

"We're turning around and going back to Aspen."

"But Lisa's getting away!"

"That's right, Lisa's getting away."

Rebecca looked over at Mitch, nodded agreement and followed directions as promised. The ride back was quiet. Judy watched nothing out the window, Trish watched Judy watch nothing. When they got closer to town, Rebecca asked for clarification.

"Hotel or Judy's?"

"Judy," Mitch rephrased, "You want to go home yet or do you want to hang out at the hotel for a while?"

"Home."

Trish gave directions. They pulled up and followed Judy as she opened the door. She invited them in, told them to make themselves at home and then retreated to her bedroom. Mitch set about making a pot of coffee as Trish began the interrogation.

"Why on earth did we just let Lisa get away?"

"It was the logical thing to do," Mitch stated matter-of-factly as they settled in the living room, waiting for the coffeemaker to finish.

"Logical thing? She's free with two million dollars."

"That's the point. She's free. Gone. Judy had to watch it to believe it. She told me when to turn back."

"And that's it?"

"Judy is now free of Lisa. Look, Trish, if we had tried to catch Lisa, there would have been excuses and alibis, police reports, criminal and civil charges, courtroom scenes and through it all would loom the specter of Lisa. Lisa the victim, Lisa the repentant, Lisa the fallen angel. Judy wouldn't be free of her. This way, Lisa's gone."

"With your two million!"

"It was two million well spent. Now, you and Judy can have a fresh start."

"You planned it this way all along."

"I did what made the most sense."

"I'll pay you back, I swear."

"Don't pay me back. I don't want to be paid back."

"Then how can I ever thank you?"

"You can go in and check on that lovely lady in the bedroom. She's going to need all the love and support you're willing to offer."

"Okay. What are you two going to do?"

"We're going home," Rebecca said, taking Mitch's hand in hers.

"I'll see you sometime, back at the Lucky U?"

"Whenever."

Chapter 27

The press conference was carried live by the national news.
For all the hoopla and anticipation, it seemed rather dull to
Mitch. Mary and Doc showed up to give moral support and
even Jeff was present. Mitch had taken the time
beforehand to talk to Mary, who was now well over the
shock of having her friend turn into her mother's new
suitor. Jeff was encouraging as well. He could hardly wait
to get on with divorce proceedings so that everyone could
make a new beginning. If he harbored any animosity, it
would have shown. He didn't.

Rebecca opened things up with a brief statement, outlining
the subjects that she hoped to discuss. As predicted, only
one subject held interest and Rebecca answered as honestly
as possible, holding a steadfast line of modest privacy.
Yes, they were sleeping together. Yes, they would still
need heightened security, for a while. No, she wasn't
resigning. No, she wasn't changing her political affiliation.
Yes, she would still go to her church.

The rest of the questions were mere reworded copies of the
first questions. Then, one reported shouted a question to
Mitch, who had stayed in the background.

"Did she kiss you back, Ms. Tanner?"

Rebecca turned to Mitch to see if she wanted any part of
this process. Mitch smiled and came forward, undaunted
by the seventy-two flashbulbs that went off like sparklers.

"Could you repeat the question, I'm not sure I understand?"

"In an earlier press conference, you stated that you kissed
the governor and that she didn't kiss you back."

"That's correct."

"Well, did she ever get around to kissing you back?"

Mitch laughed and answered, "Finally!"

"How's the arm?" came another inquiry.

"It's mangled. I won't lie to you and tell you that I'm
going to play the violin again. But we'll just have to wait
and see after therapy."

"How come you have a ring and the governor doesn't?"

"You people don't miss a thing, do you?" Mitch smiled. "I
have a ring because the governor wants to be engaged to

me. I just haven't had time to go shopping yet, so don't nag."

"Don't you think that your foray into adultery has done nothing but bring grief to the governor?"

As the questions became more serious, so too did Mitch. "We thought long and hard about each and every decision we made in our personal lives. I don't wish to comment on the governor's former relationship with her husband. I just think it's important for you to know that I would have never entered into this situation if the governor had intended to remain married. Does that answer your question?"

"Not quite," the man stood up to clarify the question, "Don't you feel that your immoral behavior has hurt the chances of the governor to be a good public servant?"

"This is a trick question, isn't it? Let me answer this way. First, I don't feel that my behavior or the behavior of the governor has been immoral. Maybe you feel that way. I don't. What is important to know is that Rebecca Fairbanks is as good a governor today as she was a month ago. The events that are causing the problems with her work are the attempted destruction of the mansion and the risks both she and I take every day when people may be lying in wait to hurt or kill us. That's what's getting in the way of the important work of the state. So if you truly want to have effective government, work on ridding the streets of dangerous, bigoted individuals who act above the law. Don't worry about everyone's personal lives. We'll answer to our God, you answer to yours."

Mitch hadn't realized how powerfully or emotionally she had spoken until everyone just sort of packed up their notebooks and left the room. Not even Rebecca cared to comment after the speech.

The following Saturday was quiet. Repairs on the mansion were steadily moving forward, but Mitch and Rebecca had gotten used to Mitch's tiny house by now. Phone calls of support and flowers still drifted in, but the crush had subsided. On Sunday, they ate an early breakfast and then went to church flanked by armed bodyguards. Afterward,

Mitch told Rebecca, "There's someone I want you to meet."

"There is? Who?"

"Come on."

They walked out to Mitch's Subaru and waved off the bodyguards. Mitch, still in her cast, had become an expert at navigation and directed Rebecca to a location that she recognized.

"Isn't this Hillcrest Cemetery?"

"That's right."

"The ground was covered with a light dusting of snow. Mitch got out of the car and took hold of Rebecca's hand. She led her slowly, wordlessly, to a small marker.

"This is all I have left of my parents."

Rebecca, standing now just behind and a little to the right of Mitch, hugged her from behind as they looked at the meager plot.

"I just wanted..." Mitch started to say as her voice broke.

"It's okay," Rebecca hugged her tighter. "Just take all the time you need."

"I come out here when extremely important events happen. Does that seem strange?"

"Not at all."

"I came out to my parents standing in this very spot. That's why it's so important for you and Mary to keep talking."

"I know. Did you tell them about Lisa?"

"No, I didn't want them to worry about me. I try not to worry them."

"Did you tell them about winning the lottery."

"Nope. It's like I said, I only come here to talk about important things."

"Okay."

"And I wanted them to know," Mitch turned to face Rebecca, "that you came into my life. That I found the woman of my dreams. That finding the gift of love is more important than winning money. Or losing money."

"You are something else." Rebecca said lovingly. "But you never did tell me how you knew that Lisa was going to make a break for it exactly when she did."

"Oh, that was easy. I got all the clues I needed from Lisa."

"You did? How?"

"Actually, everyone sort of helped out, acting as my eyes and ears, but I had to come up with a way that would convince Lisa to run. So I told Judy to tell Lisa that Judy was going to take the two million and buy land in Texas."

"And that did it?"

"Lisa hated Texas and hated even more the idea that Trish supposedly lived in Texas."

"Very clever."

"Pretty lucky, too."

"Your parents are proud of you."

"I know that a cemetery isn't usually considered the most romantic choice. In fact, most folks who think that way are either in jail or therapy. But this place, this spot, is somewhere where I feel at peace and comfortable. It's special to me."

"I can tell."

"So, would it be okay if I gave you this? Here?"

Mitch pulled a small box out of her pocket and handed it to Rebecca. It was a matching gold ring.

"It fits."

"I measured your finger in Aspen. Two can play that game."

"It's beautiful. I accept."

They hugged in the presence of family.

"Would you explain just one more thing to me?"

"I'll try. What's puzzling you?"

"Why is it that every time Mary and I talk about Hilary, and we call her 'Doc', there's this joke I must not be getting."

Mitch thought for a moment and then the coincidence dawned on her.

"It's because Hilary's last name is Martin."

"Why is that so funny?"

"Come on, I'll explain it to you on the way to the shoe store!"

"The shoe store?"

"Well, you trust me with the rest of you. So, trust me with your feet!"

Epilogue

The bar was dark. The women were beautiful. The men were rich. Lisa was settled into a booth, pulling hundred dollar bills out of her pocket, one after the other, to impress her luscious guests. A white piece of paper fluttered out. Curious, Lisa picked it up off the table and began reading. The print was so small that she had to squint to make out all the words. It said:

Dear Lisa,

I know you're having fun spending my money. I know you always did before, and there's no reason to believe you've changed. But please don't think that you got away unnoticed. Now, don't mistake this truth for hard feelings. I loved every minute I spent with you. I'm only sorry you had the shortsightedness to leave before I became even wealthier. But, you missed your chance, and now I'm with another, much more giving and special woman. I know, I'm rambling. The point is, I now have the resources and the conviction to keep an eye on you, to make sure you never swindle anyone ever again. Did that word *conviction* in the last sentence sort of jangle your nerves? Sorry about that. Not that I would ever legally pursue you. Only you can behave well enough to ensure your continued good fortune. Two million should last you until you're a beautiful, old woman. Don't waste my money or your time on cheap diversions. Do something productive with your life. Find someone or something to cherish more than money…

The note was unsigned. Lisa looked around the room, and then into the eyes of her puzzled guests.

"I'm sorry, but I have to go now."

"Where are you going? The party's just begun."

"I have something more important to do."

"What?"

"I don't know, yet. It's sort of a mystery. I have to find someone. Or something."

She paid the tab, and without even a backward glance, walked out of the bar.

www.ingramcontent.com/pod-product-compliance
Lightning Source LLC
Chambersburg PA
CBHW062117170626
46813CB00002B/485